Joe Hipp was born in Little Rock, Arkansas, but for nearly 50 years has called San Antonio, Texas, his home. He received a BA degree in journalism from Texas A&M University and a commission as a second lieutenant in the U.S. Air Force in 1954. He served a Texas Press Association internship at the San Antonio Express-News in 1953, and before going on active duty worked as a reporter for the Jackson County Democrat. During his Air Force career, he was stationed at Ramstein AB, in Germany and met Wilhelm and Anya, a couple living nearby. Since earning a master's degree in public administration at Auburn, and retiring in San Antonio, Hipp has written several articles and published three non-fiction books. A feature story he wrote for the Jackson County Democrat, turned into *A Robbery on the Iron Mountain Railroad*. While working on the Express-News, he wrote R.G. Jordan's *Cattle Clatter* column while Jordan was on vacation. That began his interest in South Texas ranching and resulted in his writing *The Oldest Ranch in Texas*. A story of his mother's teaching career, *Teacher, Teacher*, was a family project. Meeting Wilhelm and Anya, he listened to their stories and returned to Germany after retirement to get more details and received photos used in the novel.

Joe Hipp

All in a Lifetime

The Story of Anya, Wilhelm
and an Icon

Austin Macauley Publishers
LONDON • CAMBRIDGE • NEW YORK • SHARJAH

Copyright © Joe Hipp 2023

All rights reserved. No part of this publication may be reproduced, distributed, or transmitted in any form or by any means, including photocopying, recording, or other electronic or mechanical methods, without the prior written permission of the publisher, except in the case of brief quotations embodied in critical reviews and certain other non-commercial uses permitted by copyright law. For permission requests, write to the publisher.

Any person who commits any unauthorized act in relation to this publication may be liable to criminal prosecution and civil claims for damages.

This is a work of fiction. Names, characters, businesses, places, events, locales, and incidents are either the products of the author's imagination or used in a fictitious manner. Any resemblance to actual persons, living or dead, or actual events is purely coincidental.

Ordering Information
Quantity sales: Special discounts are available on quantity purchases by corporations, associations, and others. For details, contact the publisher at the address below.

Publisher's Cataloging-in-Publication data
Hipp, Joe
All in a Lifetime

ISBN 9781685627652 (Paperback)
ISBN 9781685627669 (Hardback)
ISBN 9781685627683 (ePub e-book)
ISBN 9781685627676 (Audiobook)

Library of Congress Control Number: 2023900485

www.austinmacauley.com/us

First Published 2023
Austin Macauley Publishers LLC
40 Wall Street, 33rd Floor, Suite 3302
New York, NY 10005
USA

mail-usa@austinmacauley.com
+1 (646) 5125767

Thanks to Carl and Gerda Miesner, dear friends from Germany and Arkansas, who translated many of the letters I received from Wilhelm and Anna written in German. And a special thanks to those who plowed through a computer printout of the manuscript, giving me their input: Al Bates, Bob Brubaker, Dee Grimshaw, Jim Gustine, John Seawell, and Earl Williams, friends, inmates, and confidantes at the Army Residence Community. Thanks also to Bob Flynn and Barbara Higdon for reminding me to include a list of characters, and that it is a "Russian" novel with all the connotations (good and bad) that brings up. My senior daughter, Denise ZitzEvancih, helped with the photos. To my old friend, Winston "Cape" Caperton—thanks for the diligent read and encouragement.

Table of Contents

Foreword   9

The People   10

Translation of a Bolshevik Document Found after the Revolution   12

Part One: Anna's Story   15

   Chapter 1: The Icon and the Frame Maker   17

   Chapter 2: The Departure   22

   Chapter 3: Enroute to China   37

   Chapter 4: The Trans-Siberian Express   50

   Chapter 5: Welcome to China   57

   Chapter 6: A New Life in Harbin   72

   Chapter 7: Shanghai   80

   Chapter 8: Reunions   92

   Chapter 9: Pre-War Shanghai   99

   Chapter 10: The War Years   106

   Chapter 11: Return to Germany   118

   Chapter 12: Post-War Germany   126

Part Two: Willi's Story   135

   Chapter 13: Wilhelm, Born a Saxon   137

   Chapter 14: Off to War   153

   Chapter 15: Basic Training   158

Chapter 16: Home for Christmas	*167*
Chapter 17: Taking French Leave	*181*
Chapter 18: Off to America	*189*
Chapter 19: What Is This Place?	*195*
Chapter 20: A Model Prisoner	*204*
Chapter 21: Repatriated	*216*
Chapter 22: Saxony, Home Again	*225*
Chapter 23: Escape to the West	*236*
Chapter 24: A New Start	*242*
Chapter 25: A Criminal Enterprise	*245*
Part Three: Their Story	**253**
Chapter 26: The Last of Life, the Best of Life	*255*
Chapter 27: The Secret of the icon	*264*
Epilogue	**275**

Foreword

It has taken over 40 years to piece together the story of Anya, Willi, and the icon, like trying to put together a Faberge egg shattered intentionally without a clue as to how it once looked. Anna (Anya) and Wilhelm (Willi) lived in a small German village when we met half a century ago. Their remarkable life stories are the heart of this novel. Real life has many detours and contradictions, each piece of their stories led to another story. An icon hung on the wall of the entry to their home and it was there that fact met fiction. Weaving related stories into this novel, preserving the memory of each individual and the times in which they lived, required some manipulation of facts. It is the story of a much-traveled icon and a treasure (not an ARC "Traveling Treasure"), including the lives it touched. And, it is a story of love found late in life.

A preface, foreword, or a prologue, in the lexicon of some who writes novels, only delays the emerging story. I find one useful in setting the stage for the unfolding story, allowing the author to add significant facts; for example: the term icon comes from the early Christian church in Greece. The Greek word "eikoon" (image) became icon, and the painting of religious images flourished in Greece before the "iconoclasm" (breaking of icons) under Byzantine Emperor Leo III. It was not until Empress Irene took power that the distinction between "worshiping images" and "veneration of images" was made, ending the "iconoclasm".

The People

(Principal characters by appearance in the novel.)

Dimitri Donesyvna – a skilled Russian woodworker, and lesser characters: Alexi, an iconographer; and Gustav II, a jeweler from the house of Faberge.

Anna Maria Donesyvna – wife of Dimitri.

Father Theodore – a Russian Orthodox priest.

Dunia Kulina – daughter of Dimitri and Anna Donesyvna, wife of Nikolai Kulina.

Anna (also Anya/Anyechka/Anushka) Kulina – daughter of Nikolai and Dunia.

Peter Kulina – Anna's brother, son of Nikolai and Dunia.

Sophia Yetchekov – daughter of Dimitri and Anna Maria, sister of Dunia Kulina, sometimes called Sofia or Sonya (the Russian diminutive of Sofia).

Ivan Yetchekov – professor at the University of Kazan and husband of Sophia.

Yuri Kochergna – Ukrainian farmer.

Elena Kochergna – youngest daughter of Yuri, later known as Helen Smith.

Valentin (Vali) Kulina – father of Nikolai and yardmaster of Samara rail station.

Homeric (Hom) Koopski – employee of railyard and family friend of Kulinas.

Nikolai Kulina – a railway conductor, husband of Dunia, father of Anna and Peter.

Lt. Emil Rozacky – Czechoslovakian Legionnaire.

The Voskovich Brothers – Mikhail (Misha), Nikolai (Nikki) and Sasha.

The Bouchers – Papa Frederick II, Gustav and Klaus.

Seichi Sakamoto – Texas Aggie and American missionary in Japan.

Nina Tokma (Wilson) – Russian railroad family, remarried to British sea captain Daughter Jenni (Jenny) Tokma marries Mark McMartin US Navy.

Dr. Kuentzler – Jewess doctor living in Shanghai during war.

Raya Rachlin – Dentist Jewess from Baltic States, living in Shanghai during WWII.

Karl Meissner – Saxon blacksmith, husband of Freda Stolle Meissner.

Wilhelm (Willi) Meissner – Story teller, machinist, soldier, son of Karl and Freda.

Klara Keitel – Paraplegic German widow, second wife of Wilhelm.

Translation of a Bolshevik Document Found after the Revolution

January 1917—Agents were assigned to recover items of value belonging to the Russian people, not the Czar. In the village of Palekh, a valuable icon painting and a silver and gold Risa were recovered; **however, jewels reported to be placed in the icon were not found.** A careful examination of the frame found only the initials of the maker, DD. The Czar's jeweler, iconographer, and frame maker did not survive interrogation. A case used for transporting valuable gems was found and a peasant's icon was also on the premises.

Agents were dispatched to follow family members of those involved. Only the widow of D. Donesyvna was observed removing the family icon and recovering his remains from the scene. Our committee in Palekh was in charge of the investigation and determined "a band of thieves committed a robbery and murdered five men."

Further investigation of the widow Donesyvna in Samara, including an intrusion into her home, found nothing of value. The Donesyvna family icon, a peasant's icon found at the scene, was given to a daughter, Dunia Kulina, and she was placed under observation. On the evening of 25 July 1918, it appeared the family was preparing to depart Samara; however, a storm broke during the night and our agents departed the scene. The next morning, the family had departed Samara before daybreak.

A reluctant droshky driver revealed he had taken the family to the train station during the storm, but Czechoslovakian guards prevented him from discovering where they were going. There were two rail departures that night, the Trans-Siberian Express going to Vladivostok by way of Omsk and a local freight also going to Omsk. The Kulinas were not on the Express, confirmed by officials. The freight train was commandeered by Czechoslovakian

Legionnaires and the Kulina's presence on that train was later confirmed by Comrade Kornodkin in Ufa after their departure.

Subsequent interrogation of Stationmaster V. Kulina revealed that the family had departed on the freight train with the soldiers, but carried nothing of value. Case closed. August 1918.

**Part One
Anna's Story**

Chapter 1
The Icon and the Frame Maker

Palekh, Russia
January 1917

During the last days of Czar Nicholas', a chain of circumstances brought the family Romanov in contact with the family Donesyvna, indirectly of course. Dimitri never met the Czar, but did meet Alexi, the Czar's iconographer and a jeweler from the House of Faberge in the village of Palekh, Oblast of Ivanovo, known for its rich contribution to the art of iconography. The term iconographer identifies one who assembles an artist's work into a final product, an icon.

The meeting occurred in a small workshop behind the iconographer's place of business on *Ulitsa Pushkina*, a short but important street in Palekh. In his cramped, poorly heated workshop Dimitri, an aging woodworker with bushy black hair, flecked with sawdust and wood chips, crafted a frame for the last icon commissioned by the Czar, with hidden channels in the frame. The Czar's frame appeared identical to one he made for the Donesyvna family icon, using expensive black walnut provided in Palekh; except in the frame for the Donesyvna icon there were no hidden compartments.

Applying finishing touches, Dimitri carved his initials (Cyrillic double D's) larger on the Czar's frame, hopefully to be noticed by the Czar himself. He had already discarded the original frame for the Donesyvna icon made on Tolstoy's estate. The paintings and risas easily distinguished the two icons, the frames looked the same. The Czar's icon had an artist's exquisite oil painting of Christ, with a silver and gold risa fashioned by another artist, and framed by yet another artist, Dimitri.

The Donesyvna icon was an inexpensive print of the "Virgin Mary and Christ Child" surrounded by an inexpensive tin risa nestled in the "look-a-like" frame. Brushing the dust and shavings from his best work clothes, Dimitri settled on a stool to await the arrival of a jeweler from St. Petersburg. Alexi, the ever-present iconographer, fed the wood stove in the workshop, attempting to keep the temperature comfortable for the task ahead. Darkness was descending on Palekh, and Alexi wanted the Czar's icon completed and on its' way to St. Petersburg by dawn the next day.

Gustav II, from the House of Faberge, was late. Not familiar with the village, he and his escorts had taken a left turn on *Ulitsa Gulikova* and traveled some distance before discovering their error. The escorts were two of the Czar's personal guards in mufti, civilian dress, the guards fooled no one and could be easily recognized by their military bearing, height and the manner in which they escorted Gustav.

Despite precautions, they had been secretly followed. Returning to *Ulitsa Zinov'yeva*, they took the next left turn on to *Ulitsa Pushkina* and reached the easily recognizable office of the Czar's iconographer, Alexi. Tethering their horses, the trio proceeded to the shack behind, following a well-beaten path in the snow. Gustav, a short, rotund man, with an imperialistic air, dressed warmly and wearing a fur hat made of Ermine, was carrying a velvet lined box made of embossed leather containing assorted jewels from the "Romanov Collection".

Design of the frame was known only to Dimitri, the iconographer, and the Jeweler. They intended to keep it that way. After introductions, and as the guards huddled by a fire outside the workshop, Dimitri watched Gustav II warm his hands and begin inserting jewels into channels he had drilled within the frame, and pack them tightly with cloth. Some jewels he recognized as diamonds, rubies and emeralds. Others he had never seen before. Smoke from the guard's fire drifted into the room as they made periodic checks.

Once Gustav's task was complete, Dimitri locked the corners of the Czar's frame in place, demonstrating how to unlock the otherwise seamless looking frame, then revealed how precisely the Donesyvna family icon frame and that of the Czar matched, *removing the painting and risa from each icon and placing each in the other frame.* On Dimitri's worktable, the two empty frames looked identical. No one would suspect such a common looking frame to contain a fortune in jewels. In the midst of doing this, they heard a commotion outside. Grabbing the nearest icon frame, Alexi snapped the Czar's icon inside, inserted slender blades of wood into kerfs in the frame locking it in place, ready to flee. Dimitri took the other frame and placed the Donesyvna family icon firmly inside as the workshop door burst open.

Burly Bolshevik thugs, who had followed the trio from St. Petersburg, rushed in, killing Gustav, Alexi and Dimitri. They took what was obviously the Czar's ornate icon from the arms of the deceased Alexi, the now empty jeweler's box from the body of Gustav, glanced at the Donesyvna icon in the grasp of a bloodied Dimitri and departed. They had followed their orders. But, before leaving, they ransacked the studio looking for anything else of value, unordered. The Czar's two guards lay dead outside the door, embers of their fire dying as well. It only took minutes.

Years earlier

Near Samara, Russia in the late-1800s, frequent visits of Leo (Lev) Tolstoy, a famous writer, could hardly go unnoticed. He purchased an estate east of the city producing kumis (mare's milk), allegedly a remedy for his stomach problems, and allowed him to pursue charitable work with peasants, establishing a school for children on the estate. Tolstoy sold part of the estate in 1888, to a widow from Simbirisk, Maria Alexandrovna Ulyanov. Her oldest son had been imprisoned in St. Petersburg and executed the previous year. Wanting to keep her remaining "activist" children from the same fate, she bought farmlands east of Samara with tree-lined lanes, and ponds for fishing and swimming, thinking it would appeal to the Ulyanov children. They spent only the idyllic summers on the estate and winters in the comfort of Samara.

Her remaining son, Vladimir Ilich (known later as Lenin), showed little interest in the 225-acre estate and was allowed to complete his study of law, some historians say at the University of Kazan, others say in St. Petersburg. Managing her estate, plus collecting debts owed by former serfs and resident peasants, was not how Maria Alexandrova wanted to spend her declining years. She gave up active management, hired an overseer and moved permanently to Samara.

The Donesyvnas (pronounced done-s-e-evnas) lived on the estate and, though Dimitri Donesyvna was not involved with "milking the mares," he had woodworking skills Tolstoy appreciated. In the caste-system of Czarist Russia, Dimitri was a peasant, bordering on being a Kulak after serfs were freed. He was married and had two daughters, Dunia and Sophia, both attending the school on Tolstoy's estate. Dunia, his oldest daughter, later studied nursing in Samara and married a young railroad worker, Nikolai Kulina. They had two children, a son and daughter. The daughter, Anna, was called Anya (the Russian diminutive of Anna) and, as Russian custom allows, variations of the name.

When the widow from Simbirsk purchased the estate, including servitude of the persons living there, Dimitri paid his debt to the estate and moved his family to Samara, establishing himself as a woodworker. He was welcomed by a tall (6'5"), red-bearded Russian Orthodox priest, Father Theodore, who had ministered to the families on Tolstoy's estate and was now on the staff of Samara's Alexander Nevski Cathedral. Dimitri was hired to repair and maintain the sanctuary. (There are several Alexander Nevski Cathedrals in Russia and elsewhere; to many Russians, he is their national hero!)

Dimitri's artistry with wood brought him recognition beyond Samara. In the winter of 1916, an iconographer in Palekh, Russia, asked him to make frames for expensive icons. Taking leave from Father Theodore, he took his wife, the Donesyvna family icon, and set up a temporary shop in Palekh.

Back to Palekh

The day following the intrusion, amidst the rubble and confusion, Dimitri's frail widow, Anna Maria Donesyvna, was allowed to remove his body and the blood spattered, nondescript, Donesyvna family icon. Returning to Samara by carriage and train, she made the 300 mile trip south in two days and had the icon cleaned and blessed by Father Theodore the following day. When family arrived, Dimitri was buried in a plot near the Alexander Nevski Cathedral. Czar Nicholas abdicated his throne in March 1917. Before dying of pneumonia later in 1917, Anna Maria's home in Samara was broken into and searched several times by thieves looking for an undisclosed treasure; once while she was there.

She had little of value, just a collection of frames for artworks with a double D carved in the frames, and the family icon which they examined, disassembling the picture and risa from the frame, even drilling a hole in the frame, and not bothering to put the icon back together. Calling on Father Theodore from Nevski Cathedral for help, she watched as he reassembled the icon, said a blessing, and departed. Knowing death was near, she gave the icon to her eldest daughter Dunia Kulina for safe keeping; it came with an admonition: "never part with the icon, it will bring good fortune."

Chapter 2
The Departure

Samara, Russia
25 July 1918

Since Anna Maria's passing, every day in her daughter Dunia's household begins the same, as each pass the family icon (including the children, Peter and Anya) they touch the image in respect, and make the sign of the cross before starting their daily routine. Anya Kulina, smallest and youngest member of the family, remembers the day, nothing routine about it. This day started the same but she was going to have a second birthday, an outing with Aunt Sophia (Sofia) Yetchekov, her mother's younger (and more sophisticated) sister.

A calendar change adopted by Bolsheviks in February (from Julian to Western) created a dilemma, which day to celebrate Anya's birthday? The Western calendar was thirteen days ahead of the Julian calendar; many families used both calendars to keep up with important dates. Anya was born in Samara, on 12 July 1912, under the Julian calendar then used in Russia. Using the new calendar, Anya's birthday became the 25th of July. Since Dunia Kulina thinks her daughter "…deserves the attention," she is allowed to celebrate both dates. "Just for this year," dilemma solved.

Sophia married a scholar from Samara, Ivan Yetchekov, now a professor of World History at the University of Kazan. Childless, she dotes on her niece and Anya enjoys the attention. Their outing included taking a *droshky* (one-horse carriage used for taxis) to the Volga River landing to meet Ivan. His return from Kazan by steamer is unexpected. Nibbling from a small packet of *khovrost* (deep-fried cookies) Aunt Sophia bought at a confectioner near Alexeyevskaya Square, Anya is quietly alert to the sounds and smells of the river front landing. Sophia appears aloof to events surrounding her, dressed in a tailored suit and wearing a broad-brimmed hat of French design; only her eyes reveal she is troubled. To an observer there is something incongruous about the sophisticated, attractive young woman, and the child standing with her. Six-year-old Anya's birthday dress is home-sewn of cotton material, yet freshly starched and ironed. Except for apparently liking each other, they appear not to belong together.

Samara is a sprawling industrial metropolis, no longer a sleepy town of spas and *Kumis* resorts. Resting in the crook of a "U" on the Volga, called the 'Bow of Samara', the city is protected from the river by a steep embankment, but it cannot protect the city from unrest sweeping the country. Anya has heard stories of the Ulyanovs from her mother and now this son of the Ulyanovs (Lenin) is causing trouble. Since Red Guards were ousted from Samara by Czech Legionnaires in June, unshaven, wild-eyed men, in soiled work clothes, roam the streets disrupting traffic, shouting obscenities at anyone well-dressed, calling for a revolution of the 'proletariat,' and making life miserable for everyone. Anya loudly asks Aunt Sophia, "What is a proletariat?" (She has a curiosity not bridled by propriety.) Sophia's soft reply, "A working man," is confusing; none appear to work. There is trouble in the river city and rumors the Czar has been killed.

Clouds darken the eastern sky as a summer storm bears down on the city. The western sky gradually turns deep red, then darkening purple; it's reflection on the smooth surface of the Volga River mesmerizing the onlookers. Most visitors stand atop the steep east bank to avoid the stench of rotting fish scraps from the fishermen's pier, and to have a better view of the river. There they contend with *droshky* drivers, loitering nearby, noisily arguing and cursing the effect of the war on their livelihood. Behind them are the *droshkys,* their horses restlessly stamping hooves on manure-littered avenues; no one cleans the streets.

Excited and alert, Anya spotted the river steamer rounding the upstream bend, "Aunt Sophie, he's here! He's here!" She points to the vessel as it drifts toward them; and, with Anya tugging on Sophia's hand, and holding her nose with the other hand, they descend to the landing.

Onboard the steamer, refugees grasp their possessions as the vessel turns against the strong current, tilting sharply to the port side. Most have gathered on deck to admire the beauty of the gorge. Among the refugees is Ukrainian farmer, Yuri Kochergna. Yuri, his wife and eight children huddle by the railing, their clothing mended and patched; nothing they wear is new.

Towering above other men on the boat, Yuri is a head taller with one exception, Ivan Yetchekov. A beard shadows Yuri's face as does the dusty peasant cap he wears. Holding five-year-old Elena in his arms, he watches his brood like an eagle guarding its nest. They are migrating to the eastern edge of Russia on a travel permit signed and stamped with a seal by an official in the Khabarovsk Bolshevik government. Tonight, they will stay with friends in Samara before continuing by Trans-Siberian Railroad to Khabarovsk.

Lines are tossed from the steamer and secured. Ivan waits before gathering his valise and a box of books, still pondering how to explain his departure from the university to an unsuspecting wife. Apolitical, he was bombarded with anarchist philosophy from other faculty members as the revolution progressed. His choice was to go along, or resign and find other employment. He resigned. Proceeding to the gangplank, he follows the Ukrainian farmer's family off the boat and gives a porter his books and valise. For a moment, Anya and Elena Kochergna's eyes meet as Anya pushes toward her uncle. *Their paths will cross again, and again.*

For the first time in weeks a beleaguered Ivan smiles and sweeps Anya into his arms. Taking a puzzled Sophia by the hand, they head toward the *droshkys* and a 20-minute trip to the Kulina's home.

* * *

Outside Samara's Railroad Station

Anya's paternal grandfather, Valentin "Vali" Kulina, is Yard Master of the railway junction at Samara, a job held for ten of his forty years with the railroad; he pauses to watch a crowd gathering in front of the station. Impressive in a dark suit and bowler hat, not his customary attire, Vali sucks on an empty pipe. Queues of people form at the station entrance, hoping for seats on an eastbound passenger train. Boats and barges heading south on the Volga have been packed with refugees fleeing to ports on the Caspian Sea. Some leave the river at Samara to travel the "Trans-Siberian" to Omsk, and far beyond Bolshevik territory.

Looking at the station clock Vali's eye twitches, more of a wink than a twitch except he does not control its occurrence. Cross-checking his pocket watch, he determines the station clock is slow. Since his wife's death he seldom wears the dark suit, choosing a work uniform for most occasions. Meeting daughter-in-law, Dunia, at an exclusive restaurant for lunch required him to dress appropriately. Taking her to Café Jean was part of his plan to persuade Anya's mother staying in Samara was unsafe. The Bolshevik Red Army is closing in and he plans to help his son's family depart, something he can arrange. Dunia was impressed by the opulence of the restaurant, and the practicality of Vali's plan. Finding an unused baggage car wasn't difficult; finding the right one and getting it added to a freight train leaving for Omsk, involved the complicity of his assistant. Vali is hopeful "little Anya" will soon be on her way to safety.

Quickly crossing the rail yard to the freight dock, Vali is greeted by an oddly-dressed Czech Legionnaire guarding the building. The Legionnaire's uniforms are a collection of clothing from the Imperial Army, uniforms captured from the central powers, and items scavenged on the battle fields. Saluting the Yard Master, the two men exchange greetings and Vali enters his office.

A brigade of Czech Legionnaires led by a young officer named Cecek, occupy barracks formerly used by Russia's 24th Army Corps. Czech Legionnaires control the Trans-Siberian Railway from Penza to Vladivostok and have been guarding the Samara terminal since June 8, after a skirmish with Red Guards left the city in their hands; "Russians fighting Russians with help from the Czechs," Vali muses. Driven from Poland by the German army, they fought Germans alongside Russians until the Bolshevik Revolution changed everything. It is an unusual arrangement that the controlling powers and the Railway Union have come to, allowing the Trans-Siberian Railway to operate the length of Russia for the benefit of all Russian people.

Cigarette smoke floats beneath the glare of a single overhead light bulb in the office. Homeric (Hom) Koopski, Vali's assistant, part-Greek and part-Georgian, tilts his green eye shade backward and wipes his perspiring brow, squinting at Vali through the cigarette smoke, a large man, nearly 300 pounds of solid muscle gradually turning to fat as he adjusts to an office job. A hand-rolled cigarette hangs from the corner of his mouth, "It is the curse of being confined in this office," Hom will tell anyone who notices his cigarette addiction.

"How is it with the Omsk run," Vali asks?

"Good, Comrade Kulina," his voice is gruff and deferential; addressing Vali as Comrade is noted. "All cars are loaded and marshaled, and the baggage car you wanted is last in the string. I've called the engine crew, saw them walking toward the yard a few minutes ago."

"You've done well! Make sure it's ready to roll when the track to Ufa clears. I saw a wagon from Zhigulevski's Brewery unloading beer kegs. Are they for the Legionnaires at Chelyabinsk and are they putting extra guards on the train?" Vali asks several questions to keep Hom from questioning the baggage car.

"The beer is for Chelyabinsk, not heard of any Czechs going," Hom replies, "just the usual gendarme on the engine. What are we transshipping tonight," referring to the added baggage car which could mean 'bootlegging' of supplies? Vali ignores the question because it is neither. "That Czech, Cecek, takes care of his people at Chelyabinsk. Our officers could learn a few things from him," Vali grumbles. "I'm leaving, Hom, Dunia is having a party for little Anya's new birthday and Nikolai is arriving from Penza." Hom grins, tobacco-stained teeth glistening in the overhead light. "When you see little Anya tell her 'many happy years' for me. Now go before you get your Sunday suit wet."

With a wave Vali steps outside, glances at the threatening sky and hurries to meet the express arriving from Penza. As the train steams into the station, a black-uniformed conductor holding a valise swings down from the first car, landing on the platform running toward Vali. "Hallo Papa! What brings you here, I expected you to be home enjoying cake and cream with Anya and Dunia?"

Nikolai Kulina is a second-generation railroad man, a mirror image of his father 30 years earlier wearing a well-groomed handle bar mustache as did Vali. Advancing from yard hand operating switch engines, to provodnik (attendant) on local trains before the war, he is now a head guard (conductor) on the Trans-Siberian Express. In January 1915, Nikolai and Dunia were sent to the Western front, south of Minsk, where Nikolai worked for the Red Cross and Dunia was a nurses' assistant. After two years tending wounded on the battle fields and in hospitals, they were discharged and returned to Samara where he was hired by Wagon-Lits, a French company manufacturing premium sleeper-cars for European railroads. Each Trans-Siberian train had at a minimum two conductors (sometimes more); one trained as a barber, the other an infirmary nurse, to accommodate passengers in Wagon-Lits coaches.

"We should both be there, my son. What caused the delay?"

"Skirmishes near Penza, we couldn't move until the tracks were secure, Wagon-Lits doesn't want to lose any more of their precious cars, and I don't want to be in one they lose! Besides, foreigners needed more time for shopping and I picked up another gift for Anyechka," (a pet name for Anya) he replies with a wink matching Vali's twitch.

"We've much to talk about and Anya is waiting. Could you sleep?"

"A little, not as many foreigners riding the express, they always need more attention. Papa, what really brings you here?"

"Wait until we're outside," Vali replies cautiously. "The station walls have ears!"

In the distance a fading reflection of the red sunset glows faintly on Samara's blue-domed Alexander Nevski Cathedral. A trolley sits in front of the station with several *droshkys* nearby. It takes thirty-eight minutes for the trolley to reach Alexandra Street, Vali has timed it, and the *droshky* can be there in ten or fifteen.

"Tonight we take the *droshky*," Vali grumbles, "only because we must hurry!" As a rule, Vali refuses to use *droshkys, karetas* or *troikas* when a trolley is available, the fare is cheaper and the trolley conductor does not expect a tip for doing his job. Vali gives instructions to the driver and off they go. "Now we talk! How long do you think it will be before the Reds are back in Samara?" Vali asks as he leans back in the *droshky's* cushioned seat. "Soon Papa, the only thing keeping them from arriving on the next train is the Czech Army!"

"Exactly what I think," Vali says, urgency in his voice, "I talked with Dunia at lunch today about you working on the CER (Chinese Eastern Railway)." Vali looks up to see if the driver is listening. The driver is racing through town, intent on getting the tip offered if he makes the trip in fourteen minutes or less. "I told her about a message from Dushki (Station Master at Omsk) asking for experienced head guards on the run through China. She agreed it is time to leave and I've a plan for you to leave with your family, tonight." Removing his bowler hat and tapping it sharply on Nikolai's knee, "Cecek is pulling all his troops back from Penza. Dushki says the White Army will pull back with them, and Dushki knows! When the Reds come back, Samara will not be a pleasant place."

Absorbing the information, Nikolai's first question is: "You took Dunia to lunch; where?"

"Café Jean!"

"Must have really impressed her, you've never taken me there," Nikolai pauses, his comment met with silence. "Back to our leaving, travel permits from the assembly take days; even if the new government allows us emigrate, nothing can be guaranteed on the Chinese Eastern. And, the Chinese are ready to throw out all foreigners. Have you considered that?"

"I can get you and your family out of Samara tonight! No permit, no tickets! About a job, all I can say is Dushki will help. He promises you will be taken care of as far as Manzhouli. (Extra crews are stationed at major terminals on the Trans-Siberian route.) Beyond there, Dushki has little influence."

The driver turns from Dvoryanskaya, a cobble stone street, onto Alexandra Street, an unimproved dirt lane and dust swirls around the carriage. Empress Alexandra Feodorovna would not be pleased having such a street named for her. Vali and Nikolai cover their noses with handkerchiefs and conversation ceases. Ahead at number 7, lamps have been lit, Peter and Anya called inside and the excitement of Uncle Ivan's return has been eclipsed by Dunia's news; she and Nikolai will be taking the children and leaving for China. Sharing some of Anya's cake, Ivan and Sophia continued to his family's home near Strukovski Garden.

Arriving in a cloud of dust, the *droshky* driver reins in his horse and turns to Vali with a toothless smile. Vali peers at his watch in the dim light, his eye twitches, "You made good time," Vali mutters as he digs into his money pouch. "Here's our fare and your tip. Go with God! You came with the very devil on our heels!" The driver pockets the coins and steps behind the *droshky* unfastening the rain cover. Hastily pulling it into place and glancing at the sky, he straightens the braces and secures the leather straps. "It will rain soon," he calls to Vali. "Want me back?"

"Give me a half hour and come back," Vali replies.

Brushing dust from their clothing, Vali and Nikolai stomp dust from their boots on wooden planks forming the walkway leading to the house. Inside, Anya and Peter wait impatiently for Nikolai to enter. When he does, Anya, small for her six years, unleashes a torrent of big questions after she hugs her father. "Papa, did you know we're going on a trip, where's China, what did you bring me for my birthday?"

"Slow down Anyechka, one thing at a time! Reach into my coat pocket, the inside pocket," he prompts. Anya tugs on her father to bend lower and then pulls a small gift-wrapped package from the deep pocket.

"Papa, may I open it now?" she asks, cocking her head to one side.

Nikolai winks, nods his head and sits beside Anya as she tears open the package. Inside is a shawl made of goat's wool, a specialty from the shops in Penza. Anya unfolds the shawl, feeling the softness of the material. Smelling it, as she has often seen her mother do upon receiving a gift, Anya brushes it against her cheek and places it over her blonde curls. Seeing her mother standing in the doorway, she asks, "Isn't it pretty, Mama?"

Despite a tiring day, Dunia takes the shawl, admires it and places it again over Anya's head, ties it under her chin and plants a kiss on top. "Very pretty Anya." She steps back as Nikolai rises from the bench; their lives had not been the same since the war, time apart, the bloodshed, leaving the children behind. Their romance had suffered, but for Dunia there was hope it could be rekindled. She has changed dresses and brushed her hair since Sophia and Ivan left. "It's time for Anya's party," she says folding her hands in front of her print apron. "Will you have a slice of her cake? Sophia made it! I've managed to keep some raspberries from Anya and Peter if you'd like a few with the cake."

"Exactly what I need and Papa will have some as well!" Nikolai follows Dunia into the kitchen, tugging at the bow of her apron string. "What is this talk of taking a trip? Are you and Papa up to something," he asks, stealing a kiss? "Did he tell you about taking me to lunch today?" Dunia responds, glancing coquettishly at Nikolai as she prepares cake for the men.

"Yes, to Café Jean! Were you impressed?"

"It was all I had been told, waiters in white jackets, the service and menu choices, such a treat. We talked about the Red Army coming back to Samara. Did he tell you what he learned from Dushki and the Czech officer?"

"We talked about it on the ride home, what do you think of the job in China now?" Nikolai wants to hear from Dunia she has changed her mind. "We must go while we can," she replies quickly, knowing her approval is all the encouragement he needs. "Papa Kulina has a plan and everyone is acting strange, talking crazy. A woman, I've never seen before, stopped me on the street today. She asked how many people live in our house. When I told her, she said, 'There's room for another family.' I think our house is being watched!"

"Sounds like more Bolsheviks are in town." Nikolai frowns at the thought of sharing their house with someone else. "The express train is running with a full load of refugees from the fighting. It will be here for a few hours and even if there is room for us, we don't have a travel permit or tickets. I'll ask Papa about his plan."

Vali explains his plan: "I've arranged for an empty baggage car to be added to the supply train going to Omsk. There's a stove and lantern in the car. Not much for comfort, however you won't be waiting for seats on the passenger train. We don't have much time. You'll need to be in the baggage car by eleven tonight, the track to Ufa opens shortly after and Hom has been told to get the train moving once the express leaves."

"You mean the plan really is for us to leave this evening?" Nikolai asks, in mock disbelief. "I just arrive from Penza and you want me to climb onboard a freight train and ride it to Omsk?" Vali picks up on the pretense in Nikolai's comment. "Who knows what tomorrow will bring, my son, can you be ready in an hour, Dunia?"

"Yes, Papa Kulina, I've set out all we can carry. I pray you can send our furniture once we get settled. Are you sure you'll be all right staying?"

"Absolutely, it'll take more than a band of Bolsheviks returning for me to leave Samara. I have my friends, and I'm too old to make difficult changes. Anyway, I'm not long for this world and I want to be buried with family."

"Enough Papa, you're not old, and certainly not ready to be buried," Nikolai frowns at the thought. "You and Dunia seem to have settled the matter of us leaving, so we'll depart tonight and you, Papa, will ship what we can't carry. Is that the plan?"

"Yes," Vali answers, "now finish packing. I'll be back in an hour with two *droshkys*." The *droshky* driver has returned and is waiting as Vali leaves the house. Vali gives him instructions and they depart with dust swirling behind the carriage. The storm breaks, flashes of lightening and heavy claps of thunder are followed by a steady downpour drumming on the tin roof of Number 7 Alexandra. Nikolai gathers the items Dunia has packed, including her mother's samovar and the Donesyvna icon, and moves them to a more protected area of the porch. Inside the samovar Dunia has hidden their family savings for the time being.

Across the dusty street and hidden in the shadows, there is movement. Someone is watching and seeking shelter.

* * *

The Kulinas are not the only ones hoping to leave Samara tonight. Farther down the Volga a *Bronevik* crosses the Alexander Bridge at Syzran, heading eastward toward Samara. *Broneviks* are a unique creation of the revolution, military fire power on the railroads of Russia. They are a menacing collection of heavily armored flat cars coupled to an armor-plated steam engine and several fortified boxcars,

Lieutenant Emil Rozacky is a trusted Czecho-Slovak Legionnaire on a secret mission. He stares through a gun port in the *Bronevik*'s troop car, watching brilliant flashes of red sky reflected in wind-blown ripples of the river. Near his feet is an ornate wooden chest with engraved brass corner plates and latch. The first leg of his journey across Russia is coming to an end. Red stubble of a new beard and smiling blue eyes, shields the toughness needed for the journey ahead. It has been a good plan to follow the passenger train to Samara, no skirmishes, and the trip has gone quickly. The Bronevik will stop at Samara and return to Penza. Rozacky wants to keep moving, tonight if possible.

In the warm, humid darkness of the car, Czecho-Slovak Legionnaires sprawl on the straw-covered floor, attempting to find a comfortable spot to nap as the Bronevik rumbles toward Samara. Some have bandaged wounds already showing signs of fresh bleeding. They are the remnants of Rozacky's platoon, decimated in battle near Penza finally on their way home, and a surprise meeting with little Anya!

* * *

Vali returns with the *droshkys* and the once dusty street has been churned to mud. He directs the carriages to park next to the wooden sidewalk for loading. Dunia brings out umbrellas and insists on carrying the samovar herself (she has secreted their savings inside). Vali wants Anya and Peter to ride with him in the first *droshky*, while Nikolai and Dunia follow in the other. Nikolai looks at Anya as she waits in the darkness of the porch, clutching Botto, her stuffed bear, and with her new shawl tied tightly in place. "Is that all right with you, Anyechka?" To Nikolai she looks remarkably calm for a six-year-old leaving the only home she has ever known. Her voice takes on a tone of importance as she responds, "Yes Papa!" Then after a moment's hesitation she asks, "Will you carry me to the wagon? I don't want to get my *valenkis* (felt lined boots) wet." Dunia has allowed Anya to wear her winter boots to keep from packing them. Holding an umbrella, Nikolai carries her to the first *droshky*. Inside, and behind the rain curtain, Anya scoots into the comfortable security of the leather seat. Rain and wind slacken as the Kulinas continue loading the *droshkys*.

The observers opposite 7 Alexandra have departed; darkness and rain obscure their departure to anyone else watching. Only the creaking, squeaking wheels of heavily laden *droshkys* being pulled through mud compete with the diminished sounds of the storm. Cuddled inside the first *droshky* Vali tells Anya and Peter about the trip they will be taking and the happiness awaiting them, hiding his own sadness; that is what grandpas do.

Arriving at the dimly lit freight platform the *droshkys* are challenged by a Czech Legionnaire standing under the overhang of the freight building. Vali pushes aside the rain curtain and steps down, identifying himself. Engaging the guard in an animated exchange, he turns and calls out, "We will walk from here." Nikolai helps Dunia out of the *droshky*, lifts the children onto the platform and begins unloading their packages.

Vali and Nikolai take a few of the heavier packages and set out for the baggage car, leaving Dunia and the children guarding the remaining packages. Vali locates the car, "Over here, Nikolai!" Sliding open the door to a converted box car, he checks inside then shoves his packages onto the floor. Nikolai lifts his bundle into the car and they return to Dunia and the children. Each carries something to the baggage car, Dunia the samovar under one arm, the icon under the other. Nikolai leaps into the car and strikes a match. He peers around in the flickering light, locates the lantern Vali has placed there and lights it. "Except for the smell, everything looks in order, let's climb aboard." Nikolai takes items handed to him and places them in a corner of the car. The fruit basket Dunia has packed goes just inside the door of the car, with other food containers. A cotton mattress rolled in a bundle and tied with twine, he tosses to a corner far removed from the door.

Vali lifts a bewildered Anya into the air and Nikolai gathers her in his arms, placing her beside the basket of fruit. After helping Peter into the car, Vali turns his head to listen. In the distance a train is approaching from the south on the parallel track. "Strange; we're not expecting any more traffic from that direction. Quick, Nikolai, give me a hand with Dunia." They make a step with their hands for Dunia to climb into the car then pass the remaining bundles into the waiting arms of Dunia and Peter. The train is approaching rapidly and has reached the yard, ignoring yard speeds. Through the rain and dim yard lights Vali makes out the unmistakable shape of a *Bronevik* bearing down on them, one of several running between Samara and Penza. "You go first, Nikolai, and give me a hand. I don't want to stand out here while that devilish contraption goes by."

The *Bronevik* is almost upon them when Vali is pulled inside. It rushes by with tree limbs (used for camouflage) slapping the side of the freight cars, throwing a sheet of rain into the open doorway of the baggage car. The engine steams by, trailed by several box cars. The *Bronevik* pulls into the passenger station spouting steam and braking to a squealing stop. "That was close, papa," Nikolai says taking a deep breath.

Vali wipes the rain from his face and watches the activity around the *Bronevik*. Stepping back from the door, he digs into his coin pouch and selects two coins. He rumples Peter's hair and hands him a gold five-ruble coin. "Here you are Peter, and here's one for you too, Anya. I intended to give it to you at your party, but it slipped my mind. You can see the Czar's face on one side and the Romanov crest on the other; probably the last coin to show the Czar, I'll bet on it! Now I say goodbye," a slight hoarseness has crept into his voice. "I wish we had more time, but the *Bronevik* means something unexpected is happening. Come little ones, give me a kiss and promise to remember your grandpa." They tearfully hug Vali's neck and kiss his cheek. "Thank you again for the present, Grandpa," Anya whispers, between sobs. "When will you see me again?" she asks hopefully. "Who knows, Anya?" Vali clears his throat. "I may come to China one of these years, we shall see each other again, I promise."

Vali steps toward the door and grips Nikolai's hand. "Good luck, my son. *Da svedahnya!*" They embrace and holding his bowler hat firmly on his head, Vali eases himself down to the rain-soaked ballast. He walks quickly, toward the station, looking back once in the dim light and drizzle toward the figures in the doorway of the baggage car.

Nikolai turns away and examines the car's interior. A pot-bellied stove sits at one end of the car, a little rusty, and vented through the ceiling. Next to it is an empty tinder box. A straw mattress lies on the floor to one side of the stove. The lantern hangs on a peg near the door and a chair lies on its side with a toilet can stuck between the chair legs. He removes the can and sets it behind the stove, then places the chair upright next to the open door of the car. At the opposite end from the stove is their cotton mattress, where he tossed it earlier.

Frowning at the sparse conditions, Nikolai tells Dunia, "With luck we will be in Omsk in four to five days and board a proper train." Settling into their new surroundings, Nikolai hears voices coming from the direction of the station. He steps over to the door and peers outside. A group of soldiers wearing bulky rain capes are walking toward the car, checking each car as they pass. "We have company," he whispers to Dunia and the children. "Quick, into the corner. Be quiet, they may pass on by." Nikolai douses the lantern and steps to one side of the door. Nearly a dozen soldiers are outside the car, speaking the Czech language as they tell one of their members to hurry and get in the car. A soldier climbs into the car and, after a few seconds fumbling around, strikes a match. As the match flares, he sees Nikolai standing by the door and drops the match in surprise.

"What's wrong in there?" a voice outside asks.

"Someone is already in here and he just scared the devil out of me," the soldier shouts to those outside. "Give me a minute. I'll light another match." As he strikes the match, Nikolai hands the lantern to the bewildered soldier. The soldier takes the lantern, lights it and looks around the car. He sees Dunia and the children huddled in a corner. "There's a family in here," he reports. An officer, taller than Nikolai, shoulders of his jacket soaked with rain, climbs into the car and nods to Nikolai. He asks, "Are you authorized to use this car?" Lt. Rozacky speaks Russian, with a Czech accent, emphasizing the first syllable of each word. "Yes! I am being transferred to a new job on the Chinese Eastern Railway and this car has been added to the train for our use," Nikolai explains.

"My men and I have priority use of this car. You and your family will need to find another to use," Rozacky replies quietly and firmly. His men begin tossing their packs into the car and one by one clamber inside, passing their rifles ahead of them. A canvas covered chest is heaved into the car and moved to one side. A few of the soldiers wear bandages from recent wounds and are helped into the car. "We would, but it seems the other cars are filled with supplies, as you no doubt have seen," Nikolai explains. There is a commotion outside; Vali arrives, followed by a Czech officer wearing a rain cape.

"Ah Nikolai, you have company for your trip! Allow me to introduce Captain Biehunko from our security forces." Vali steps aside as the captain catches up with him. Nikolai extends his hand to Biehunko, who almost pulls him out the door as he tries to jump into the car.

"Give me a hand, Kulina," Biehunko tells Vali. With Vali pushing and Nikolai pulling, Biehunko manages to get inside. He looks at Dunia and the children, still huddled in a corner of the car, and turns to speak quietly and directly to Rozacky. "I know your mission is important, Lieutenant, but I consider it a personal favor if you allow the Kulinas to share this car. I thought you would find room in the freight car with supplies for our detachment at Chelyabinsk. This car was set aside for Valentin Kulina, the gentleman outside, who is an important railway official and helping us to keep supplies moving to our outposts. These people are members of his family, moving to a new assignment in China."

Out ranked, Rozacky looks around the crowded car and shrugs, "If they can stand us, we can stand them," he replies. Vali grasps the gist of the conversation in Slavic and tells Biehunko, "I forgot to mention, my son and daughter-in-law were hospital helpers on the Western Front. They could help care for your wounded." Nikolai and Rozacky nod agreement and shake hands as Biehunko and Vali depart. Rozacky is big-boned and tall, perhaps two meters, he weighs about 90 kilos and in the middle of his square chin is a dimple. His blue eyes move constantly as he talks. "Kulina, you pick a corner of the car for your use, we'll use the rest, satisfactory?"

"We can make it work, Lieutenant." The Kulinas gather their packages in the forward corner furthest from the door and stove. As they get resettled, the affable Rozacky explains he and his men are going to Vladivostok to recuperate, which is not totally true. "My orders in Penza were to stay here until tomorrow, but with 'General' Cecek's permission, we will leave tonight. It is not good to start a big journey on a Friday; we have a superstition," Rozacky chuckles with a twinkle in his eyes, "do not start Friday what you can do Thursday."

"I agree," Nikolai responds, "better to leave tonight than wait for a passenger train with room for us, this way we can carry more. I was in Penza earlier today and the Red Army appeared very close to taking the city."

"You were fortunate. The city is being evacuated," Rozacky adds.

The sound of rain is louder. A sudden gust of wind whips the door, rattling the rollers. Sheets of rain pound the top of the car, spraying inside. Nikolai pulls the door shut and joins his family on the cotton mattress Dunia has covered with a quilt. Anya, holding Botto against her cheek, fights sleep and thinks about all the events happening on her birthday, but is soon fast asleep. Peter is restless and Dunia strokes his hair as he fights to stay awake.

The thunder and crash of lightning begin again as the Kulina family and the Czech Legionnaires settle down to wait for the train to leave. One last matter for Dunia is a better place to hang the family icon, deciding to hang it in the front left corner of the old baggage car, a secure location. Shortly after the express train departs, a whistle sounds, followed by a staggering lurch as the slack between cars is taken up. Neither the whistle, nor the lurch of the car disturbs Anya and Peter, now fast asleep. Nikolai and Dunia huddle in their corner, no tears, just sighs of relief to be on their way to an uncertain future.

* * *

In another part of Samara, the Kochergnas find their Ukrainian friends living near the juncture of the Samara River and the Volga. The children, Kochergna's eight and three from the family they are visiting, are asleep on the floor in one room of the small house. The Kochergnas and their hosts sip steaming cups of tea as Yuri entertains with an explanation of their travel permit. Laughing at his host's accusation he is a Bolshevik in farmer's clothing, Yuri protests. "No, no, my friend, I'm not Bolshevik, Menshevik, or Radish! You know Radish? They are red like Bolshevik on the outside, white like Czarist on the inside." Yuri pauses to see if they appreciate the metaphor. "My brother is a policeman in Khabarovsk. He works with the Bolsheviks, he helps them; they help him. Without the pass we would never have gotten this far. Since we are in White Army territory, it is not much help to us." He continues with stories long after the whistle of a departing train.

Chapter 3
Enroute to China

Near Pokhvistnevo, Russia
Before dawn Friday, 26 July 1918

Between Samara and the Urals lie some of the richest farmland in Russia and little villages dot the landscape. The engineer sounds his whistle at each crossing; Nikolai can't sleep. A Legionnaire cries out during the night. Anya stirs and watches sleepily as Nikolai removes the dimly burning lantern from its peg. He steps carefully over sleeping Legionnaires, and kneels, placing his hand on the soldier's feverish forehead. Holding the lantern over the man's bandaged leg, he looks for signs of fresh bleeding. The bandage is caked with mud and dried blood, no evidence of recent bleeding.

At Pokhvistnevo Nikolai and Dunia reexamine the soldier's leg. Dunia sends Nikolai to fetch boiled water from the station and gingerly removes portions of the bandage. They soak and remove the more difficult parts of the old bandage, then clean and dress the infected wound.

"Good job, Kulina," the watchful Rozacky comments as Nikolai finishes. "Will his leg heal?"

"I can't tell. The wound isn't deep, but it exposes bone and shows signs of infection. You should have a doctor look at him when we reach Ufa."

Station noises awaken Anya and Peter. "Are we in China?" Anya asks, rubbing her eyes as she looks out the door at new surroundings. "We've only begun our trip, Anyechka. Freight trains take a long time to get to China," Nikolai explains. For the first time Nikolai notices a small, ornate chest they brought aboard in Samara, far removed from the Kulinas. A soldier stands or sits near the chest. The *truhlici*, carrying their provisions, is near the door.

* * *

Before dawn, Bolshevik observers approach 7 Alexandra, taking up their post across the street. Parcels on the porch have disappeared, no one appears to be stirring in the house and they settle down for another day of watching. After sunrise and no movement, they become suspicious. The Yardmaster appears, walking slowly toward the house. They are familiar with Vali Kulina and his frequent visits. As they watch, he enters the house and can be seen moving about. He exits, locks the door and walks back to Dvoryanskaya and takes a street car to work. The female member of the team volunteers to check. She had met Dunia earlier. Approaching the house she raps on the door, no one answers. A quick inspection by the team confirms the Kulinas departed during the night. Some furniture remains but items they had seen on the porch have disappeared.

* * *

Ufa, Russia
Saturday, 27 July 1918

Crossing the Byelaya river bridge and entering Ufa as the sun rises, a tired and rumpled Nikolai sits sucking on his empty pipe as they brake to a halt. Frequent stops and tending the wounded interrupted attempts to sleep. Struggling to get his boots on, Nikolai hops down from the car and helps Dunia, then Anya, to the ground. Peter is already on the ground. "Papa, you said we could see the engine when we got here!"

"Might as well do it now," Nikolai responds.

Rozacky joins Peter and Nikolai as they amble toward the front of the train where the engineer is unhitching the engine from the rest of the train. "How long before we leave?" Nikolai asks. "Maybe two, three hours," the engineer guesses, "depends on the new crew. We don't have a firm schedule anymore," he shrugs and walks away. "No way to run a railroad," Nikolai comments to Rozacky.

Rozacky leaves to find a doctor for his men while Nikolai and Peter walk to the front of the engine. A cursory look does not satisfy Peter, he asks many questions. The engine is an S-class, 2-6-2, used for heavy freight loads crossing the Urals. An American built 2-10-0, is used on the Trans-Siberian Passenger Train. Finally coaxing Peter away from the engine, they continue to the station.

Dunia and Anya are waiting when Peter and Nikolai join them. It is a warm, sunny day, typical of late July. Ufa is not as large as Samara, but important for its location on the high right bank of the Byelaya. The town is about a mile south of the station. There is a good market in Ufa for precious stones from the Urals and steamboats regularly cruise the Byelaya and Kama rivers as far as Kazan on the Volga.

"We'll be here for a few hours as they change crews," Nikolai tells Dunia, "let's have some tea, and find food to take with us." Leading his family through the crowded waiting room and into the station restaurant, Nikolai stops at the service counter. Dunia seats the children at a table and joins Nikolai. The sandwiches appear dry, probably prepared for the express train preceding them. Dunia selects two after looking them over carefully, and Nikolai orders four cups of tea. Returning to the table a waiter he met on previous stops at Ufa joins them.

"What brings you to Ufa, Conductor Kulina?" Boris Kornodkin is a tall, smiling, balding, loquacious, and eternally curious waiter, using the same sour smelling, tea and coffee-stained cloth to wipe tables and dinnerware. "We are travelers," Nikolai replies guardedly, "and how are you doing?"

"Perhaps better if the railroad returns to normal. Since the revolution it is hard to make any money; and, the fighting doesn't help!" Kornodkin pauses in his nonchalant effort to clean the table while Nikolai and Dunia divide the sandwiches. "I think the Reds will make short work of the Whites once the Czech soldiers leave. Aren't you traveling with that bunch of Czechs on the freight train?"

"Yes, we are, very observant Boris. Can you tell me where I might find some cooked food to take with us, or something to prepare on the train?" Kornodkin looks around the dining room to see if anyone is listening, bends over and rubs the table once more with the stained towel and whispers, "If you want fresh food go to Mrs. Chevkin. You can't miss her house, down the tracks toward the Byelaya, with a yard full of kids. She's my sister! Tell her I sent you."

"I will and thanks, we'll go there after finishing our tea." Nikolai asks Peter, "Do you want to come along to Mrs. Chevkin's?"

"Yes sir!" he replies, jumping up smiling at Anya with a look of superiority.

"Bye Pot!" Anya calls out, wrinkling her nose at Peter.

Peter has earned a flattering or unflattering, depending on one's view, nickname of "Peter the Pot." Tolstoy's short story "Alyosha the Pot" is a favorite Dunia often reads to the children. It tells of a simple, but happy youth, who on one occasion dropped a pot of milk and was known thereafter as Alyosha the Pot. Peter liked Tolstoy's characterization of Alyosha and does not mind the nickname.

"We'll meet you at the train," Nikolai tells Dunia. "Finish your tea and don't rush. From the looks of things, we have plenty of time before the train leaves!" As they leave, Kornodkin walks over and whispers, "You're lucky to have those soldiers along as you cross the mountains. I hear Bolsheviks are stopping and looting some trains, even ambushing those with soldiers." Nikolai acknowledges the information and waves as they leave the restaurant.

Nikolai can hear the noisy Chevkin children before he sees them. They are fighting and playing behind a clump of bushes shielding the house from view. Mrs. Chevkin stands in the doorway, wiping swollen, red hands on a food-stained apron. A faded babushka covers her round head which rests on an equally rotund body, like a snow woman without a neck. Her cheeks and nose are shiny red in the morning sunlight. The puffiness in her face makes her nose appear flattened and her beady eyes squint continually as they are nearly closed by the fat on her brow and cheeks. She examines Nikolai and Peter as they approach. "Be ye hungry travelers?"

"We are, and come on recommendation of your brother," Nikolai replies. "What food do you have this time of day?"

"I've got potatoes, boiled or baked; corn steamed in its shuck; and boiled turnips and beets," she responds, in a quick, rhythmic recitation. All were probably home grown from the look of her garden. Nikolai and Peter turn to each other grinning, amused by the lyrical sound of Mrs. Chevkin's menu and her appearance. "What would you like?" Nikolai asks, stifling a desire to have her repeat the menu. "Some corn, Papa," he answers shyly, glancing at the size and girth of Mrs. Chevkin's shoe-less children who have gathered around them staring boldly at the visitors. "Good. Could we have four ears of corn, eight baked potatoes, and a couple of your boiled beets?" She is gone for a few minutes and returns with the vegetables wrapped in newsprint. She mentally calculates what Boris expects for sending her a customer and adds it to her charge. "Five rubles, mister," she says gruffly without blinking an eyelid.

"Five kopecks you say?" Nikolai asks innocently. "Five rubles mister," she is quick to reply. Her puffy red cheeks seem to get brighter. "We can't live on the Czar's charity anymore," she says! "This is robbery," he responds and grudgingly offers her three rubles. "Since my brother sent you, four rubles, but not a kopeck less!" Nikolai digs into a leather pouch containing their savings. Mrs. Chevkin avoids looking directly at the pouch, but out of the corner of her eye notices there is considerably more than the four rubles agreed upon. Nikolai counts out four silver rubles and places them in her outstretched palm. "Would you happen to know where I might find a fish for our meal?"

Eyeing his money pouch, she responds quickly, "I've got a big salmon, fresh from the Byelaya this morning. For you, the price is ten rubles, if I cook it, fifteen." He answers, "Your prices are steep, but we must have food for our trip. I'll give you eight rubles for the fish and not a kopeck more." She enters the house and returns holding a large salmon by its tail. "Here you are!" Nikolai hands the wrapped vegetables to Peter, counts out eight rubles and with his right hand takes the fish by its gill. The fish is a good size, maybe 12 pounds. One this size would cost two or three rubles (U.S. $1.00 to $1.50) in Samara before the war started. "Good day, Mrs. Chevkin," Nikolai says with a sour taste in his mouth for being civil to someone no better than a bandit.

In the rail yard, two more cars have been added to the train and Czech Legionnaires from Ufa are talking to members of Rozacky's platoon. Walking toward the train, Nikolai notices some of the Czech soldiers and their compatriots are already climbing aboard the empty freight cars. Dunia and Anya are making their way slowly from the station to the train. The engine has been rejoined to the train and a new crew is on hand. Preparations to depart are further along than expected. For unknown reasons the new crew appears anxious to depart, waving at the soldiers to hurry boarding. Holding the salmon at arm's length to keep it from brushing against his uniform, Nikolai pauses to get a fresh grip on the fish. Peter is walking at a fast pace trying to keep in front of his father. He turns for a moment when he can no longer hear Nikolai behind him. "Do you want me to help, Papa?"

"No, Petrushka, run ahead, just changing hands with this fish." Reaching for his handkerchief, he dabs his brow and eyes, then steps out a bit faster. The soldiers are climbing into the car and motioning toward Dunia and Anya to hurry along.

Peter stops, "Hurry Papa! The train is leaving!" Nikolai is jogging toward the train, holding the fish at arm's length. "I'm right behind you Peter!" There are five sets of tracks between Nikolai and the freight train, and about 200 feet angular distance to the baggage car, a blast from the whistle signals the train's impending departure. Dunia and Anya have reached the car and are being helped inside by the soldiers. Peter reaches the doorway as the train lurches. Rozacky jumps down and lifts Peter and his packages inside the door as the train starts to move.

"Hurry friend Kulina; we don't want to leave you and your fish behind," Rozacky yells as he swings into the car. Nikolai has crossed the tracks and is running alongside the freight cars as they slowly gather speed. Reaching the car, he slings the salmon inside on the floor. The soldiers yell encouragement as Nikolai runs on the rough ballast. Stumbling on the lip of a cross-tie, Nikolai catches himself by grasping a handle on the door of the car. Swinging by one arm from the handle, he nimbly regains his footing and leaps for the door, pulling himself inside next to the fish. Rolling away from the fish, he jumps to his feet. "I won't forget our stop at Ufa," he gasps, then grins broadly as a worried Dunia brushes the dust from his pants and blouse.

"Perhaps this will make the stop less painful," a clean-shaven Rozacky says as he smiles and hands Nikolai a pouch of pipe tobacco. "It's a gift from my men." Nikolai reaches for the tobacco, hesitates, and then hugs the big lieutenant before accepting the pouch. "Thank you, many times, my friend." He opens the pouch and smells the aroma, then pours a small amount into the bowl of his pipe, tamping it slightly. Striking a match, he lights the pipe. Taking a puff, Nikolai savors the taste and smell. "Excellent tobacco," he announces. The Czech soldiers applaud and pat him on the back. The guard at the chest remains at his post, but smiles and claps his hand. The soldier with the leg wound is not aboard.

As the train crosses the Ufa River and starts an imperceptible climb toward the Ural Mountains, Nikolai asks Rozacky about the other soldiers now on the train. "They are going as far as Zlatoust to get more weapons, and return to Ufa." The explanation is true, as far as it goes. The real reason for the other soldiers is protection against raiding bands of Red Army soldiers roaming the Urals.

Entering the Ural Mountains
Later the same day

Approaching Asha-Balashovskaya, the foothills encircle the town and force the tracks to follow the course of the Sima River valley. "A good place for an ambush," Rozacky remarks as he scans the hillsides. "I've heard bands of Bolsheviks are active in the mountains north of here," Nikolai comments as he savors the last draw from his pipe. Rising from the floor of the car, he walks to the door and looks up at the steep, wooded slopes tapping ashes from the pipe bowl.

"Bolsheviks or Red Army, they're hard to find in these mountains," Rozacky replies as both scan the rugged terrain. The train weaves back and forth across the Sima River and later crosses the Yuryuzan River in yet another valley. Sitting near the open door of the baggage car, the Kulinas eat warm potatoes and watch the scenery, enjoying the cool mountain air and warm sunshine.

Ahead a tree has been cut to fall on the tracks. Without warning the engineer applies the emergency brakes and as the train comes to a screeching stop, the Ufa crew abandon the engine and run toward trees bordering the tracks. Nikolai looks toward the engine and sees the crew running away. Rozacky and his soldiers check their rifles and look to Nikolai for an explanation. Suddenly shots ring out from the cliff above the track and from the tree line. "It's an ambush," Nikolai calls out. Remembering Kornodkin's warning, he wonders how much the fellow knew and if the crew was part of the plot. Rozacky's men dive beneath the cars of the train and return fire where they see movement. A long silence follows broken only by sounds of rifles being reloaded. Legionnaires crouch beneath the cars and scan the cliffs for movement. "We need to get to the engine and start moving while there is still steam in the boiler," Nikolai tells Rozacky.

Anya and Peter huddle at Dunia's side in their corner of the baggage car. Nikolai has thrown the mattress up in front of them and is crouched beside the door with Rozacky. "I guess we surprised the ambushers," Rozacky tells Nikolai. Rozacky and Nikolai drop to the ground and crawl along beneath the cars until reaching the engine. The Russian gendarme boarding with the engine crew in Ufa is dead.

"Can you operate the engine?" Rozacky asks. "Yes, with some help," Nikolai responds while staring at the cliffs. Rozacky takes charge, designating several Legionnaires to provide cover while others move the tree off the track. Four soldiers run forward and drag the log clear of the tracks. With a couple of soldiers feeding the boiler, Nikolai soon has the engine moving and an hour later they reach Vyazovaya.

Rozacky reports the incident to the Legionnaire detachment while Nikolai takes up the matter of a new crew with the Station Master. Several soldiers gather wood for the stove while Dunia takes the salmon and washes it at a water spigot outside the station. With permission of an oriental cook at the station restaurant, she cleans it and slices it into thick steaks. Returning to the baggage car with a half-kilo of Siberian butter and the salmon steaks, she is followed by several large alley cats.

Nikolai builds a fire in the pot-bellied stove and fashions wooden skewers from birch branches, then turns them over the coals. Dunia runs the fired skewers through the salmon steaks and holds them over the coals, wrapping her hand to keep from burning her fingers, occasionally coating the fish with generous portions of Siberian butter. (*Butter-making in Siberia is said to have started when the English wife of a Russian landowner insisted their servants learn to make butter, rather than using lard for cooking and eating.*)

A new crew is found and the train departs Vyazovaya. Dunia offers the Czechs some salmon as the train gets underway. It is more than the four Kulinas can eat. Quickly eating their rations, the soldiers help the Kulinas finish the remaining pieces of salmon. After the meal, a Legionnaire pulls a concertina from his pack, plays a few notes to test the instrument, and begins to play a lively polka. Anya and Peter are fascinated by the music and move closer to the young soldier. When he stops, Anya timidly asks, "Can you play 'A Cossack Was Stenka Rasin'?" (*Stenka Razin is a Russian folk hero who led a band of robbers on the Volga in the 1600s.*)

"Stenka Rasin? I don't know him," the concertina player says with a chuckle. "I do know Alois Rasin from my homeland, but we have no song for him!" The soldiers laugh. "If you sing, or hum the tune, I will try to play."

"Pot can sing it," Anya says quickly, pointing to her brother.

Peter ducks his head and blushes. "I won't sing!"

"Mama, you sing it for him, please," Anya pleads.

Dunia reluctantly hums the tune then begins to sing in a high, soft voice, *"A Cossack was Stenka Rasin; he was noble, true and good; and he guided his horsemen with boldness and fierce courage."*

The soldier has a good ear for music and picks up the tune quickly, playing it enthusiastically, if not skillfully. Anya stands and tries to dance, but struggles to keep her balance as the baggage car sways. Peter joins the dance, holding Anya by the hand while the soldiers clap their hands.

The train continues at a slow pace through the moonless night, climbing higher into the Ural Mountains. Inside the baggage car, exhausted from dancing and the excitement of the ambush, Anya and Peter fall asleep on the cotton mattress.

Zlatoust, Russia
Before Dawn, Sunday, 28 July 1918

Twenty hours and 200 miles from Ufa, they reach Zlatoust, until recently called "Armory of the Czars". It is now an armory for the White Army, producing an assortment of lethal weapons, including a vicious looking bayonet. In darkness and the dim lights lining the station platform, a group of Czech soldiers load a few crates of weapons into the Kulina's baggage car while the engine takes on water and a rare load of coal. The soldiers from Ufa have their cars unhooked from the train and depart with the local Czech unit.

As sunlight touches the peaks around them, the train departs Zlatoust climbing higher into the Urals until reaching Urzhumka. There, on the right (south) side of the train, Nikolai shows Anya and Peter a stone pyramid marking the boundary between Europe and Asia. Urzhumka is 1,850 feet above sea level, the highest elevation on the rail line between Samara and Omsk. From Urzhumka they descend the abrupt eastern slope of the Urals toward Chelyabinsk.

Chelyabinsk, Siberia
Mid-Afternoon, Sunday, 28 July 1918

It is noticeably cooler on the eastern slopes of the Urals, unusual for July. Chelyabinsk, however, has been giving Siberian travelers and settlers a cool reception for many years. Legionnaires now occupy several large wooden barracks near the station. The barracks were used by emigrants to Siberia during Czarist times. A motley group of uniformed Legionnaires are waiting for Rozacky and his men, waving excitedly as the train slows to a stop. Rozacky turns to Nikolai, "They've heard about the beer!" The crates of weapons are unloaded while Rozacky walks to the barracks to meet the local commander. Then soldiers check the other cars to find the beer Commander Cecek has sent them from Samara. The beer barrels are unloaded with much more care than the weapons from Zlatoust.

Rozacky returns hours later with ten more walking wounded for his platoon along with Dr. Josef Kopecky, an American army doctor of Czech descent, who will accompany them to Vladivostok. (*Dr. Kopecky was born in Ruttersville, Texas, in 1886. He joined the U.S. Army in 1917, and was sent to Russia, where he treated wounded American soldiers and Czech Legionnaires during the revolution.*) Several of these men were injured during a riot occurring in May and, now ambulatory, are on their way to Vladivostok.

During the stop, Legionnaires take turns guarding the mysterious chest. Nikolai and Dunia whisper their suspicions about the contents. The train is ready to get underway again and new arrangements have been made for the chest, moving it to an adjacent car along with six of Rozacky's platoon. Nikolai notices it takes four men to move the chest. Supplies in the car have been rearranged and some bundles moved to the car once containing the barrels of beer.

*** Kurgan, the Siberian Plains
Monday, 29 July 1918***

Each morning during their journey, the family continues to touch the icon and make the sign of the cross. It promises to be a warm day as they stop at Kurgan for fuel and water. Nikolai shows Dunia and the children a small railway chapel built from a fund established by Czar Alexander III. Only its front is still standing, because the rear of the chapel has been stripped to its wood frame by train crews desperate for fuel.

Kurgan is a collection point for shipping Siberian butter by rail to other parts of Russia. Most of it arrives by boat from farms along the Tobol River. Dunia, delighted by the taste of food cooked with butter (as opposed to lard), would like to take some with them to China, but Nikolai discourages her interest, "It will spoil," he insists.

Returning to the baggage car, the Kulinas huddle in their corner of the car and talk of plans for living in China. "I hope we will live in Harbin," Nikolai tells them, "In Harbin there are many, many Russians, and many Russian churches; and, for Anya and Peter the best Russian schools!" Anya and Peter make faces at their father and laugh.

During the stop, a soldier asks about the icon, "I've watched every morning, you touch the picture and make the sign of the cross, why do that?" Nikolai turns to Dunia, then back to the soldier, "It is our Catholic tradition, a sign of respect and worship as we start the day. The picture is an icon and has been in my wife's family many years." His answer appears to satisfy the Lutheran soldier's curiosity.

Omsk, Capital of Siberia
Tuesday, 30 July 1918

The freight train nears the end of its journey when it crosses the Irtuish River. It is early morning and steam rises like smoke from the river. The train enters the yards of the Omsk Railway Station as workers are arriving from the city. "This is where we leave you, friend Kulina," says the smiling Rozacky. "I'm glad we had you with us for this part of our journey." Rozacky kneels by Anya and gives her a small leather pouch. "It is a late birthday present, little Anya. Wait until we are gone before you open the pouch." Turning to Nikolai, "And, my good friend, it is a way of repaying you for taking good care of us."

Anya looks from Dunia to Nikolai in surprise to see if they will permit her to accept the present. Nikolai nods consent. "Thank you, Mr. Rozacky," she responds in a voice not much louder than a whisper and clasps her arms around his neck while he kneels beside her.

Rozacky and his men depart, escorted by the Omsk detachment of the Czech Legion. The Kulinas stack their belongings on a cart Nikolai commandeered and, with Dunia carrying the icon, Nikolai leads them into the passenger station at Omsk, with its high ceilings and stark interior. Settling his family in a corner of the waiting room he leaves to find Station Master Dushki.

Sergei Dushki is tall and pale, has a pencil-thin mustache, a pot belly, sagging chest and a fringe of black hair grows on his otherwise bald head. A

Czarist bureaucrat with an air of eternal boredom, Dushki dispenses favors and directs operations of the railroad for the new government. He also insures goods bound for Samara are not held too long because of petty squabbles between the two governments. Each morning, Dushki takes a *droshky* to Cywinski Prospekt from his apartment. From there he rides a branch line shuttle train to the main station, about two miles from the center of town. He must pay for the *droshky* ride, but the shuttle is free for railway officials. Dushki is sipping a cup of tea and shuffling through a stack of papers when Nikolai enters. "Sir, I am Nikolai Kulina of Samara, son of Valentin Kulina."

"Welcome, Vali told me you would be easy to recognize, you look just like him when we were both much younger and with more hair," Dushki remarks, rubbing the top of his head. "Have a seat and tell me what is happening in Samara." The look of boredom is gone. He is sitting on the edge of his chair, elbows on his desk watching Nikolai intently. Nikolai relays events surrounding their departure from Samara and the details of their trip to Omsk. Dushki asks a few questions about the Czech soldiers, and then asks Nikolai if he has papers concerning his appointment to the new job. "There was not time," Nikolai responds.

"Very well, I'll take care of it and include a letter of introduction to station masters on your route. And, if you want, get you a reservation on the next express leaving for the border," Dushki promises. "Where is your family?"

"In the main station waiting room," Nikolai replies. "We can find a better place for them to wait," Dushki says as they start down a hall lined with offices.

Hours later, Nikolai returns to his family with papers to work on the Chinese Eastern, letters of introduction, and ticket coupons to ride the express to Manzhouli, or Manchuria Station as it is sometimes called. Dushki offers use of a room near his office if the Kulinas want to wait in privacy. Deciding their luggage too bothersome to move, they keep their location in the waiting room.

Anya clutches the pouch from Lt. Rozacky in one hand and Botto in the other. "Can I open my present now?" she asks and Dunia nods her approval. Opening the pouch, a coin drops into her lap. "It's pretty," she exclaims. Anya passes the coin to her mother. It is gold and on one side is the word "LIBERTY" with a likeness of the goddess of freedom. The year 1914 appears in relief. The other side has "United States of America" and "Twenty Dollars" in raised letters, and the image of an eagle in flight.

"I knew something valuable was in the chest," Dunia exclaims. "That's where this coin came from, I'm sure. It is full of…" she stops, then in a whisper says "…gold coins." She examines the coin and returns it to the leather pouch, all of this observed by a secretive Bolshevik Station-Watcher.

* * *

In Samara the Bolshevik team assigned to find a fortune in jewels disappearing in Palekh, admits defeat. Their last link to the jewels has disappeared. Nothing of value was found in the Widow's home or in the home of Nikolai and Dunia Kulina. An operative at the train station heard they might have left on a freight train with some Czechoslovakian Legionnaires, but no one at the station can confirm. Reporting to their superiors, they are ordered to find the family!

A message to Comrade Kornodkin in Ufa confirms Conductor Kulina and family departed on a freight train with Czech Legionnaires, but escaped an ambush in the Sima River valley.

Chapter 4
The Trans-Siberian Express

Omsk
Wednesday, 31 July 1918

Rain has fallen intermittently all day and by mid-afternoon the station is filled with people and the sour smell of damp woolen clothing; some are meeting the train hoping to see a relative or friend, others to depart. Nikolai buys bread and cheese from a vendor and returns to his family as the public address system announces arrival of the State Express.

An hour later, the Kulinas board the train. A *provodnik* accompanies them to their compartment in Wagon-Lits sleeper #1841 (a first and second class sleeper with 10 compartments, built by the Upper Volga works at Twer). Dunia holds the family icon protectively and is first to enter. There are lamps by the window. The spring-cushioned seat is covered with dark-green velour and makes into a bed. Overhead are two fold-down bunks. A door leads to a lavatory shared with the adjacent compartment. Dunia notices every detail and her smile tells it all.

Nikolai watches Dunia's face brighten and hands the *provodnik* a five-ruble note. The *provodnik* has stacked their parcels in the aisle outside the compartment and Nikolai, with Dunia's guidance, stows their possessions. He is nearly finished when the first bell rings; the children dart to the window and count the cars of a local train as it moves out of the station. Ten minutes pass and the bell rings again. Dunia tells Anya and Peter to sit, "the train will be moving soon." Shortly afterward, the bell rings for the third time, and the train immediately lurches forward. "This is the way a railroad should operate," Dunia tells her family. They all agree.

As the train departs there is a rap on the compartment door. Nikolai opens the glass paneled door and the conductor presents him with a bottle of chilled

Abrau-Durso champagne. "We did not order this," Nikolai protests. A smile from the conductor, "I know, it is from Station Master Sergei Dushki and Wagon-Lits with good wishes for your journey. There are glasses in the lavatory cupboard."

"What will we do with this?" Dunia asks after the conductor leaves. "We toast the Station Master's health," Nikolai replies, removing the seal and loosening the cork. "Bring four glasses, Dunia." The cork pops unexpectedly and champagne spills from the bottle. "Quick, Dunia, the glasses!" He laughs as he pours from the foaming bottle and hands each of them a glass of champagne.

Raising his glass, Nikolai turns to Dunia and in a solemn voice says, "A toast to our happy past in Samara. May the future be as good to us, thanks to Sergi Dushki!" Anya and Peter watch as Nikolai and Dunia sip from their glasses. Anya holds her nose to the glass. "What are you doing, Anyechka?" her father asks. "I'm smelling the bubbles, Papa," she replies and puts her lips to the glass, making a face as she tastes her first champagne. Peter tastes the champagne and says, "It's bitter." Nikolai assures them, "Champagne is not to everyone's liking, don't worry about drinking it." He pours another glassful of champagne for himself and gazes comfortably out the window as heat from the steam radiator creeps into the compartment. Leaving Omsk behind, Anya is glued to the window of their compartment. Asking questions about everything she sees; her waking hours are spent absorbing the view.

* * *

Hampered by slow communications, a Bolshevik Station-Watcher reports indeed the Kulinas were in Omsk and assisted by the Station Master Dushki, but departed on an Express heading to China before an incident could be arranged.

* * *

Between Omsk and Krasnoyarsk
Thursday, 1 August 1918

During the night the express is shunted to a siding. Nikolai peers out the window and watches as a *Bronevik*, darkened except for its one running light, slowly passes the express heading east. The lights of the express cars clearly reveal the rows of machine guns and fortifications on the armored train. No one is visible on the *Bronevik*.

Morning sunlight filters through mile upon mile of dense, virgin forest (*taiga*). Occasionally, the Kulinas see a cluster of buildings nestled among the trees alongside the railway. There are no more marshes; instead, eagles soar in the clear blue sky as they cross the hilly country west of Krasnoyarsk. Along the Yaya River, mining camps built by gold seekers are still operating. Running at 35 miles an hour between stations, the express is making good time. As the train rumbles over switches and into Krasnoyarsk Station, a Czech *Bronevik* departs going eastward. The express leaves Krasnoyarsk at noon, Friday, 2 August 1918.

Toward Irkutsk
Saturday, 3 August 1918

They cross the Irkut River shortly before pulling into Irkutsk station. The station sits opposite the city on the south side of the swift, clear flowing Angara River. Sharp-eyed Anya, always at the window, spots a pontoon bridge spanning the Angara and points it out to Peter. The river is the only outlet for Lake Baikal. Railway clocks, which to this point have shown St. Petersburg time, now show Irkutsk time, nearly five hours ahead of St. Petersburg. At Irkutsk the coaches are exchanged. Once all their parcels have been moved to a new compartment, Dunia takes the children for a walk along the station platform. They see strangely dressed vendors and equally strange items sold in Siberia; wolf-fang necklaces, oriental objects and other souvenirs from the area around Lake Baikal.

A Czech soldier stands on a platform opposite them. "Mama; isn't he the man who played for us on the other train," Anya asks? Pointing the soldier out to Dunia and Peter she squeals, "It's him. It's him! Let's talk to him." As they walk toward the bridge between the two platforms the first bell rings announcing their departure. "We won't have time now," Dunia tells the children. "But it is the concertina player. Let's hurry back, or Papa will be worried."

Returning to their compartment with moments to spare, Anya excitedly tells her father about seeing the soldier. "Maybe they'll be on our train!" she exclaims. Nikolai nods and takes her in his lap. "You must keep your eyes open, Anyechka; who knows what we will see in this part of the Russia."

Lake Baikal

Baikal is a short train ride from Irkutsk and they arrive by late afternoon. The stay at Baikal is brief. A few passengers board at the station once serving as a transition point for those wanting to cross Lake Baikal on the ferry. Leaving Baikal, Nikolai points toward the lake. Barely visible in the distance is the hulk of the giant train ferry "Baikal", scuttled by the Bolsheviks at its special dock. It carried rail cars across the lake before the land route was built. Once the land route was completed, the ferry was still used when landslides blocked the tunnels cut through mountains ringing the shoreline.

Clear weather, a beautiful sunset, and Baikal Lake ringed by rugged mountains, provide spectacular views. Nikolai has traveled this route about once a month the past year. He points out slide areas which stopped the train on his previous trips. Anya asks if the mountains will slide on them, Nikolai replies softly and deceptively, "Maybe not if we are very quiet."

Lights are left on in the cars as the train is in and out of thirty or more tunnels protecting the track from landslides. Later in the evening, the train stops at Muisovaya, a town on the southeast shore of Lake Baikal. The Kulinas alternate leaving the train to eat in the station restaurant. Muisovaya station is crowded with the foulest smelling emigrants east of the Urals, many from the Trans Baikal district; the majority fleeing to China. Though pro-White Czech Legionnaires control most of the stations along this section of the Trans-Siberian, there are Bolsheviks at each stop working the crowds and causing trouble. Not only are Bolsheviks making problems for the emigrants, a renegade general named Semenov has assembled a version of the *Bronevik*. He uses it along the eastern section of the Trans-Siberian Railway, frequently stopping trains from the Trans Baikal area going to Khabarovsk. Semenov and his men rob passengers, harass the train crew, and kill those he suspects are Bolsheviks. Depending on his mood, the renegade general is said to kill passengers with no provocation.

The blackness of the night sky matches the mood of the passengers as they board the train to continue their journey. An abrupt weather change, common in the lake area, has brought clouds and the threat of rain. Before the train leaves Muisovaya, a steady rain begins to fall. The station clock shows ten minutes past midnight as the whistle sounds for departure.

Chita, Capital of Trans-Baikal Territory
Sunday, 4 August 1918

Train-weary and hungry, the Kulinas arrive in Chita, General Semenov's headquarters (and place of banishment for many Decembrists, early Russian revolutionaries). They again take turns leaving the compartment and exercise on the station platform in the brisk morning air. Boarding for the final leg to the China-Russia border, an air of apprehension and excitement can be felt among the passengers. Nikolai is unaware the Bolshevik spy network has alerted all agents to look for his family with intent to stop them from leaving Russian territory.

Kitaiski Razyezd (Kaidalovo) Junction is where the Trans-Siberian divides into the Amur line and the CER (Chinese Eastern Railway). The CER, built first, goes to Vladivostok via Harbin, China and is the shorter route. It is midday and dark under an overcast sky as the express slows for Kaidalovo Junction. The engineer brings the train to a stop. Ahead the main track is blocked by a *Bronevik*. Soldiers from the armored train are running to surround the express.

Watching from the compartment window, Nikolai sees a man leap from the express train and run toward a birch grove. A volley of rifle shots is heard, echoing in the valley; the man falls. He raises a hand for help as a soldier approaches him and plunges his bayonet into the wounded man several times. Anya and Peter, who have been playing on the floor of the compartment before the sudden stop, jump up to look out the window.

"Don't look children!" Nikolai warns and quickly lowers the blind.

"What is it Papa?" Peter asks.

"Some soldiers shooting," he explains. "The conductor will come by soon and we'll find out what is happening." But it is not the conductor who comes through the coach. A bearded man wearing an outlandish uniform, with a czarist cap perched on the back of his head, walks through the coach carrying a bayonet-tipped rifle. He orders everyone to exit the train and line up outside.

"Nikolai, what is happening?" Dunia asks quietly, eyes wide with fear. "Perhaps they check our papers and let us continue," he whispers with little assurance in his voice, and puts a protective arm around her shoulders as they leave the compartment. From all descriptions these are Semenov's men. As the Kulinas line up with other passengers outside the first-class car, several ragtag soldiers enter the cars and can be heard searching for valuables. The remaining men form a semi-circle around the passengers, rifles pointing at them menacingly.

A whistle sounds behind the express and brakes squeal. A second *Bronevik* appears. Soldiers clambering off the second train are Czech. The leader of Semenov's group stalks toward the newcomers, irritation plain on his face. A Czech officer meets him and they talk out of earshot of the passengers. While the officers argue, several Czechs walk among the passengers asking for cigarettes and stopping to talk. Unnoticed by the Kulinas, a Legionnaire has recognized them and is walking in their direction, smiling broadly. "Mama, it's the music man," Anya cries out, tugging on Dunia's sleeve as she spots the approaching Legionnaire. It is indeed the concertina player walking toward the Kulinas.

"I wondered if you would be on this train," he calls out. "Lt. Rozacky is on a *Bronevik* ahead of us. We split up at Irkutsk and I had to wait for the next group coming through," the Legionnaire explains, shaking Nikolai's hand. "Have you opened your gift from the lieutenant?" the smiling Legionnaire asks Anya. Anya, quick as a flash, pulls the pouch from Dunia's purse and shows it to the soldier. "See!" she exclaims. "Keep this in a safe place," he cautions Anya. "These cutthroats would kill for that coin."

"You arrived just in time," Nikolai interrupts. "Any idea what these men might be up to," he asks, nodding toward the motley group of soldiers surrounding the passengers? "Nothing good, they're standing there like a firing squad waiting for the order to shoot. Don't worry; they won't shoot anyone while we're here. I'll talk to our officer and see if he can do something." He pats Anya on the head and hurries back toward the Czech *Bronevik*.

The officers are still arguing as the soldier walks up and salutes. The Czech officer and soldier step away from Semenov's man to talk. Their conversation is short. The soldier salutes smartly and hurries over to the Czech *Bronevik*, returning a few minutes later with his rifle and a platoon of armed Legionnaires. They take up positions between the passengers and the soldiers of General Semenov.

Returning to the Kulinas holding his rifle, the soldier smiles and kneels beside Anya. "You can count this another birthday present from Lt. Rozacky. I told our officer you were the lieutenant's friends. Semenov's man had told him you were all Bolsheviks and should be shot. You'll be on your way soon!"

The officers end their conversation and, while the Czech commander watches, Semenov's officer stalks angrily back to the express. When his men are within earshot, he calls out for them to get back to their *Bronevik* and open the track. Nikolai embraces the Czech soldier and pounds his back. "You saved our lives; I don't have words to thank you, may God bless you Legionnaires!" Others crowd about, shouting their appreciation.

Walking across the field to the body of the man who was shot, the conductor retrieves the man's identification, and slowly returns to the train. "Everyone aboard," he yells. "Nothing more we can do here." The passengers begin to climb back onto the train. Nikolai and his family are among the last to board. Their compartment was thoroughly searched, many items were out of place and the samovar opened and on its side. Samovars are not the only place we Russians hide items, but it is the first place most thieves look. Fortunately, Dunia had removed their savings from the samovar while waiting in Omsk. The tin risa around the icon has been pried loose, some hide valuables beneath the risa. From their compartment window the Kulinas watch the Legionnaires return to their *Bronevik*. With noses pressed to the window, Peter and Anya wave until the last Legionnaire is out of sight. The engineer sounds a series of whistles, and the express moves slowly through the switch on its way to China.

The train gathers speed as it charges south toward the Chinese border. For the next few hours the train crosses rugged country, climbing and descending the watersheds of several rivers. Before entering China, there is a stop at Kharanor. Taking Anya and Peter to the edge of the station platform, Nikolai tells them to jump up and down rapidly. "Why are we doing this, Papa?" Anya asks. "You are shaking the dust of Russia from your clothes before we enter China. Off with the Russian dust, on with the Chinese." Passengers watch and laugh as Anya and Peter jump up and down with more vigor; Nikolai's relieved laughter can be heard the length of the platform.

Chapter 5
Welcome to China

Manzhouli, China
Later, 4 August 1918

Built as a customs check point by Chinese and Russians, Manchuria Station, or Manzhouli as the sign on the station reads, sprouted up almost overnight about the turn of the century with one main purpose, to support the Trans-Siberian and CER. Now, nearly 15,000 people live in Manzhouli, including colorful, camel-riding, nomadic Buriyats. At this juncture the rail tracks become narrower. Chinese have insisted on using standard width track. Russian railroads have a wider span of five feet between the rails. Before proceeding to Harbin, the Kulinas join other passengers to have their baggage inspected.

Along with tourists, the Kulinas exit the station and take in their first view of China. Tourists want to see the Mongolian people and the Mongolian people want money the tourists bring. Immigrants have a different view as Dunia clutches the family icon and grimly comments, "It is the end of civilization." Wooden buildings constructed by the railroad are weather beaten and aged after only a few years. Some new settlers have begun crude brick buildings.

"Mama look, a humped back horse!" Anya exclaims. A camel led by a turbaned Buriyat tribesman is plodding along near the railroad tracks with a load of wood strapped to its back. "That humped back horse is a camel," is Dunia's listless response after she has turned to look where Anya is pointing. "It really isn't a horse at all, but it can do the work of a horse. We'll probably see many more."

Chinese border guards go through the empty railway cars as the remaining baggage is dumped unceremoniously on the platform. Passengers jostle to grab their belongings and hurry into the station for inspection: 200 people are trying to get into a station which should, at best, hold 50 people comfortably. Settling Dunia and the children in a corner of the waiting room, Nikolai leaves to find the station master and hopefully news of a job in Harbin. It is warm and smoky in the waiting room with the passengers packed closely together.

The Chinese have completed their perfunctory customs inspection when Nikolai returns. "We'll not continue to Harbin," he tells Dunia. "Messages from Harbin and Vladivostok are the same, no openings. I can start here as a conductor once we are settled; the station master is having a porter take us to a boarding house for the night."

Wind sweeps the hard-packed earthen streets of Manzhouli as the Kulinas wait outside the station. A dour-faced Russian porter, accompanied by a smiling Chinese boy pulling a baggage cart, greets the Kulinas. Carefully loading their luggage in the cart, the boy steps between the shafts of the cart and starts jauntily down the dark and windswept dirt street. The Russian porter walking alongside Nikolai makes one attempt at conversation. "You will like it here," he says unconvincingly. He turns to look at Dunia and says nothing else. Dunia's un-smiling look and puffed eyes express her silent assessment of Manzhouli, and silences the porter. She holds the icon closer, and Anya's hand tightly, as the constantly blowing wind pushes them along the desolate main street of Manzhouli.

Wednesday, 6 August 1918

Two days later they are shown a log house owned by the CER, not as large as their home in Samara, but built like the log houses in Samara, in a square. A large stove for heating and cooking; a shaky but adequate kitchen cabinet; a dining table (the top deeply scarred with the carved signs and initials of previous occupants); and two chairs are the only furnishings in what will be their new home.

Dunia allows the luggage to be brought inside, but no farther until she cleans the house. There is dust, dirt, and smells she is unaccustomed to having in her house. Starting from the ceilings and down to the floors, everything is cleaned and furniture scrubbed. The ever-present samovar sits on the dining table. Eyeing her work, she sighs and takes the Donesyvna icon from its protective quilt. Dunia places the icon where it can be seen once one enters the house and, with ceremonial aplomb, touches it, makes the sign of the cross. "Now we can live here," she pronounces!

The first few nights, until Nikolai bargains for two beds, the Kulinas sleep on the floor. No one complains; the floors are clean. There are no forests as far as the eye can see, neither lime trees nor raspberry bushes, only scraggly brush that can grow quickly in the summer and survive the freezing winter. "But," as Nikolai says in encouragement, "we are together!"

The railroad's Chinese workers live in mud plastered huts with earthen floors, while Russians live as close to their old life style as conditions permit. The house is painted a pale green. Even the mud between the logs is painted green. There is a white picket fence surrounding the yard where Anya's first dog, a shaggy haired mongrel she calls "Peko," can play and not run away. To the rear of the house is a large yard, and beyond the yard, the rugged desert of northern Mongolia, extending eastward beyond Hulun Lake and the Argun River.

In September, Peter and Anya begin school in the Russian School of Manzhouli, housed in a new building built by the railroad. Teachers who fled Russian Universities for political reasons find ample teaching positions in China's expatriate Russian communities. The Russian children all have chores after school, everyone has a task, they play while at school. Dunia searches the shops of Manzhouli for furniture. The large iron skillet brought from Samara is used for every meal. Their main meal is Kasha (toasted buckwheat, boiled with meat or vegetables added when available). They hear nothing from Vali concerning their furniture. Several months go by before they receive a cryptic message from Vali:

"The Bolsheviks are back. After you left someone broke into your house and did much damage. I was questioned and moved there to prevent further looting, not much left to ship. There is much killing and many people disappear. I expect to be replaced very soon. Good health and God help Russia. V. Kulina"

* * *

As their lives return to some normalcy, Dunia finds part-time work in a clinic run by Catholic Nuns. She works only while Anya and Peter are in school. Nikolai has a varied schedule of runs between Manzhouli and Harbin until he gains seniority and is allowed to take the Manzhouli to Vladivostok run.

On his first trip to Vladivostok as a CER conductor he is determined to find Lt. Rozacky. A heavy ice fog coats the trees, power lines, as well as Nikolai's mustache, with layers of frost as he walks cautiously along Vladivostok's icy streets. An American officer, traveling from Harbin to Vladivostok, provided Nikolai the address of Czechoslovakian Legion headquarters. It is not far from the train crew's boarding house but the icy weather makes it a difficult trip on foot. Once inside the Czech's austere building, Nikolai easily finds Rozacky. The two traveling companions exchange greetings and arrange to meet for dinner at a Chinese restaurant serving excellent Russian kasha, according to Rozacky.

That evening Rozacky tells Nikolai the story of the chest. "It was once filled with gold coins, like the one I gave Anya. Czech and Slovak emigrants to America held rallies to collect money for our cause. They collected several hundred thousand dollars and gave us the money for the war effort. Before presenting the money to Tomas Masaryk, one of our revolution's leaders, they exchanged it for gold coins, gold being more easily accepted throughout the world. When Masaryk came to Russia the gold was to supply our army to fight the Germans. Bolsheviks upset everything after overthrowing the Czar. They signed the treaty at Brest-Litvosk and we could no longer fight from Russia. Masaryk left Russia in March, entrusting the chest of coins to my commander at Penza with plans to use the money for our transportation to France.

Our leaders used some of the gold for Broneviks. During the battle for Penza my commander ordered me to get the chest to Vladivostok. The Bolsheviks refused to let us use the port of Archangel and Vladivostok was our only way to rejoin the fighting. When we arrived here in August, I turned the chest over to the Czech Legion commander, who used the money to buy a ship. It is called the 'Legie' and was to carry us through the Panama Canal to France; since the war is over, we will use it to get back home the quickest way." (The Legie was the first merchant ship of the landlocked Czechoslovak Republic.) "Now, tell me about little Anya and the rest of your family."

"There is little to tell except your friendship perhaps saved our lives." Nikolai tells Rozacky the story of the incident at Kaidalovo Junction. They finish their meal and, bundling up in overcoats, scarves and wool hats, the two friends stumble along icy streets to Nikolai's boarding house. Rozacky wishes him farewell and asks him to visit again. "Next time bring better weather!"

* * *

Nikolai visits Rozacky frequently during the early months of 1919. Toward the end of March, Nikolai learns Rozacky and his soldiers have departed on the "Legie". In April, Dunia reads a notice the CER wants someone to wash linens from the trains transiting Manzhouli. Unable to find a full-time nursing job, and not one to be idle, she asks Nikolai to help her get the work. Nikolai brings home a list of items the railroad wants washed and approximate number of pieces required for each train. Not to be discouraged by the quantities on his list, Dunia figures the number of wash pots, irons and Chinese helpers she will need, convincing Nikolai and the station master she can run a laundry. In the meantime, Dunia plants a garden, adding another chore for Peter and Anya.

When the first load of CER linens arrives; Dunia discovers her biggest problem is the amount of water being delivered to the house. Each week an elderly Buriyat tribesman delivers fresh water to Company houses (those owned by CER). The two horses pulling the wagon are short and furry. Each visit Anya stands nearby looking into their big, brown eyes. According to Anya the horses smelled like "horse droppings" and the big brown eyes never looked at her. She suspects they are blind.

The 'water man' fills buckets at his wagon, attaches them to a yoke, and carries the water to a barrel inside each house. The process takes considerable time and, since his is the only railroad water wagon, he makes one trip a week. Each house gets a barrel a week, and, with Dunia laundering towels and linens from the trains stopping at Manzhouli, the Kulinas frequently run out of water. It takes seven buckets of water to do the washing, and each day the train stops they wash linens.

Anya describes the process in one of her school essays. "When the train stops, a Chinaman working for the railroad delivers Mama's freshly washed and ironed linens to the Head Conductor, and dirty linens come off the train into his cart. He pulls the cart to our house and the work begins again. With the money Papa makes and what Mama gets from washing, we have a good 'working peoples' life."

After school, Anya and Peter carry water to the house from a nearby well. Nikolai resolves the problem later; he gets another barrel and arranges for the water man to come twice a week to their house. Everyone finds the arrangement satisfactory, since the CER pays the water man and hires Dunia. The waste water is used on Dunia's garden.

The Buriyat water man is reluctant to make any other changes in his method of delivery and when Nikolai returns from a trip to Vladivostok with 100 foot of water hose and a hand operated water pump, the water man will have nothing to do with it. After some coaxing and a demonstration by Nikolai, he finally agrees to give it a try. The first time the water man uses the pump, he floods a house by not securing the hose to the water barrel. The irate Russian housewife flies out of her kitchen waving a skillet and shouting angrily for him to stop. It takes Nikolai a week to get him to try the pump again.

Dunia's laundry service for the CER opens an opportunity to get other customers. Her business grows and Dunia soon has three large black kettles for washing in one corner of the yard, the downwind side, and a crudely built stand holding four washtubs for rinsing nearby. From the middle of the yard to the southwest corner are several clothes lines and most every day there are linens flapping in the southwesterly breeze.

Dunia hires three Chinese women to work in her laundry, two in the yard to keep the fires going under the kettles and stirring the linens in the hot, soapy water. From the kettles the linens are wrung by hand then dropped into the rinsing tubs where the women poke the linens with paddles before wring them again and hanging them out to dry. As they dry, Dunia and the other Chinese woman take turns bringing in an armload to be ironed. Ironed linens and clothes are folded and stacked by customer number all over the house. She learns early in her business it is wisest to give each customer a number. Many Russians are not anxious to give their name, and some Russian names defy spelling.

Winter 1919-20

The Kolchak Government in Omsk falls; more Russians arrive in Manzhouli each day. They are protected from Bolshevik terror, but witness Chinese terror including weekly beheadings. The Chinese leave the heads of captured bandits impaled on tall posts at the northwest edge of town where travelers arriving from Russia can take note. Russians arriving now are often victims of Bolshevik revenge for siding with the White Russian Government, most escaping the Siberian prison system with only the clothing on their back. They stay in Manzhouli long enough to earn passage to more civilized parts of China. Some continue to other sympathetic countries, Australia being a popular destination.

In January, Hom Koopski's family is among refugees arriving in Manzhouli. They have been traveling since October, side tracked, forgotten, foraging for food, camping in the forests, watching as White Army generals flee the Red Army with a retinue of servants and heavily armed soldiers. The train is a string of heated boxcars used during Czarist times for carrying emigrants to Siberia, pulled by a rusting switch engine. For convenience, men and women are separated in different cars. Before continuing to Harbin, Hom leaves a message and package with the station master to hold for Nikolai. The message:

"Dear friend Nikolai. I had hoped to see you and tell you what little I know about Vali Kulina. The Cheka came to our office asking about you and took Vali for 'questioning.' (Lenin established the Cheka shortly after taking power. It later became the NKVD and, eventually, the KGB.) *I never saw him again. But, we had talked about what I should do if such were to happen. When the police left the office, I took a droshky to your house where Vali had been staying. There was not much there to save for you, only an album of photographs. I have placed it inside the package to be left with the station master. Perhaps your father is in a Bolshevik prison or Siberia. I do not know. I believe, and pray, he is still alive.*

"Our grand ride on the Trans-Siberian cattle car has been most difficult for me. I have lost maybe 30 pounds weight. There is nothing to eat when we stop. If there is something to eat, it is too expensive. In Ufa a former waiter in the dining room is now the station master, a fellow named Kornodkin. The Bolsheviks have put their people in place. We have waited weeks for an engine, hunting in the forest for food, and drinking melted snow. People are starving and some are dying on the train. I have not seen a medical person since we left Samara.

"I hope to find a job in Harbin or other parts of China. Inquire about me if you are in Harbin. I would like to see you."

(The note, signed "Hom Koopski," is attached to a package. Inside is Vali's photo album Hom managed to retrieve before Bolsheviks ransacked the house on Alexandra Street. Vali's album is a treasure of pictures from their home before the war. Some are in the photo section. Unavailable is a photograph taken in 1922 of the Russian Crown Jewels, most in that photo were imitation or paste. Bolshevik sleuths were still searching for the real jewels and had traced some to London, no one was looking for Crown Jewels in Manzhouli.)

* * *

On days when Nikolai returns from Harbin/Vladivostok, Anya and Peter are allowed to wait at the station after school for him to arrive. This particular day, school is over and the train will arrive soon. In the waiting room a girl with stringy reddish-blonde hair, light blue eyes and a dirt-smeared face, watches each person entering the room. She is dressed in several layers of rumpled homespun clothing and a small woolen cap sits on top of her head. A sign with the name "Lena K.", painstakingly printed in charcoal, hangs from her neck.

Tears have etched the smoke and dirt-darkened cheeks of Elena (Lena) Kochergna. She looks from face to face at the people in the room. Sent by her mother to live with a Russian pelt trader in Manzhouli, Lena was happy at first to be leaving the mud and cold of their Siberian farm. Little Lena never liked living on the farm in Siberia. A wagon store came by once a month, but there was no money to buy the candies Lena liked. Of the Widow Kochergna's eight children, Lena is the youngest and least able to help with family chores. Their first year farming in the Shilka Valley near Sretensk barely supported the family.

Last spring, "Viktor the Pelt Trader" offered to take Lena into his home. By the end of summer, Widow Kochergna decided it best if Lena went to live with Viktor. When her mother told her she was going to live in a town, Lena cried with happiness. When Lena boarded the train in Sretensk, she began crying, crying for three days until arriving in Manzhouli. She had never felt so alone.

Moved by the girl's helpless appearance, Anya is unaware she has seen her before and is about to speak when she sees a huge man pushing through the crowd heading directly toward Lena. "Lena, Lenachka," he calls and brushes people aside to reach her. "Don't cry Lenachka. Come with Viktor. We go home now!" He takes her hand and they leave the building.

Anya tells her father about seeing the girl and later tells her mother. "I understand it happens often," Dunia replies. "Families in the old country send their children out of the country when they can." A week passes and Anya finds she and Lena will be in the same room at school. When Lena is introduced to the class Anya offers to share her desk. Many students already share desks and Anya notices the new girl has had a bath and is wearing a clean dress, a rarity for some. The fur trader, Viktor Yeltzin, and his wife have no children. Lena is their 'adopted' daughter and helps Mrs. Yeltzin in the house. For her first day at school Mrs. Yeltzin had not only bathed Lena with perfumed soap, she had combed her hair and plaited twin pigtails, tying them with yellow ribbon.

Their teacher is Moscow-educated and reads stories to the class translated from English, American, French and German authors. When he reads, he seldom looks up and Anya quietly shows Lena the intricacies of their desk; where to place school supplies, a place for books, how to make distracting noises and not be caught, and to pass notes unobserved by the teacher. Lena watches Anya's demonstration of skills with a pained expression and without speaking a word. When Anya pauses to think of something else to draw out her new companion, Lena leans toward her seatmate and whispers self-consciously, "I need to pee!" Anya jumps up from the desk, like she was shot from it, and hurries to her teacher's side, whispering in his ear. The teacher smiles, nods his head and continues to read. Anya returns to the desk, takes Lena's hand and they leave the classroom.

* * *

A railroad family from Vladivostok moves into the house next door, among the first of a contingent of Wagon-Lits personnel moving to Manzhouli. The Tokmas are quiet people and stay to themselves. Dunia's new neighbor is pregnant. Nina Tokma's baby is born a month after they arrive in Manzhouli and several weeks early according to Nina's calculations. The night her baby is born, Nina sends her frantic husband to the Kulina's for help with the delivery. Dunia helps deliver the Tokma's baby daughter, Jenni. A lasting friendship between Nina Tokma and Dunia Kulina is also born.

Most Russians arriving in Manzhouli stay only long enough to find another home in Harbin. There is a large Wagon-Lits repair facility there for coaches operating between Manzhouli and Vladivostok. The dour-faced porter the Kulinas met when they first arrived in Manzhouli was unwittingly accurate; the Kulinas do like it here. They have a house of their own, live comfortably, and always have food in the pantry. Socially the Kulinas manage to keep up with a world that hardly knows where Manchuria is, much less their border town. Music at community dances is the latest from America, re-recorded in Hong Kong, and sold throughout Asia. The young people of Manzhouli dance the 'Charleston' as skillfully as their parents dance the waltz and Anya, now a teenager, is a sought after partner at dances.

* * *

Nina Tokma plans a surprise birthday party for Dunia in November 1927. Nikolai is scheduled to return from Vladivostok that evening and she asks Anya to meet him at the station, bringing him straight to her house. It is dark when the train arrives. As the passengers debark, Anya looks for Nikolai. White-jacketed waiters are leaving the dining car as she approaches, but Nikolai is not with them. Grasping the sleeve of a waiter she's seen with Nikolai, a worried Anya asks, "Where's my Papa, Nikolai Kulina? I have to stop him before he goes home!" The waiters exchange odd looks. The one whose sleeve Anya holds turns and says, "Ask the conductor, little Anya. He was not with us on this train."

Hurrying to find the conductor, Anya bumps into him as he leaves the station master's office. He puts a hand out to stop her wild charge across the platform. "Where are you rushing to at this hour, Anya? There are no more trains into Manzhouli tonight," he says soothingly.

"My Papa, have you seen my Papa? Nina Tokma is planning a surprise birthday party for Mama. I'm to bring Papa to the Tokma's house." Anya's voice is full of apprehension. "No, Anya, Nikolai was not on our train. He didn't show up when the crew was called and we got a replacement for him. Maybe your mother has heard something, don't worry," he adds. With that he turns from her and calls to the waiters to join him for a drink. They leave Anya standing on the platform, the dim light from two oil lamps casting long shadows. Glancing around as if Nikolai will suddenly appear out of the darkness, it must be a mistake, she thinks.

Shrugging dejectedly, Anya hops down from the platform and walks along the dark streets to Nina Tokma's house. Telling Nina what the conductor said, a frown spreads across Nina's usually happy face. She waits until Anya finishes the story and says, "I think you should get your mother and Peter. Bring them here."

Weeks later, Dunia discovers what happened to Nikolai, and then only through the news grapevine of railroad wives. He was arrested as he left a restaurant with other conductors in Vladivostok. A conductor in the group, knowing of Nikolai's friendship with Lt. Rozacky eight years earlier, reported him to a revolutionary committee. Whether the conductor did it to gain favor, or had a personal dislike for Nikolai, Dunia never knew. In Stalin's Socialist Republic, to be accused of collaborating with an enemy of the state is the same as being guilty.

Apparently, his arrest had nothing to do with the missing Czarist treasure.

Nikolai's arrest by the Soviets, and internment at a labor camp near Khabarovsk, begins a long period of decline in Dunia's health. To make matters worse for the two friends, Nina Tokma's husband is killed in a derailment between Harbin and Manzhouli. The Manzhouli Station Master allows the Kulinas and Tokmas to continue living in their houses but threatens to evict them if other families arrive.

* * *

The spring winds blow with unusual fierceness, and the air is filled with dust. Manzhouli is a town of masked people, everyone covering their face with a scarf to keep from inhaling the choking yellowish dust. People working outdoors wear goggles to prevent the powdery grit, blowing in from Outer Mongolia, from irritating their eyes. Anya's science teacher describes the dust as "loess," a loamy deposit found in Mongolia. The loess dries and gets picked up by the wind. It colors the sky, the buildings, the land, and gets into houses. Nothing escapes the yellowish-brown dust and it shuts down Dunia's laundry.

The miserable weather compounds Anya's hurt from the loss of her father. Her friends notice, but none can brighten the gloomy days for Anya. Even Lena finds Anya's mood difficult to penetrate. In her shyness, and still unaware of their chance meeting on the river landing in Samara, Lena hesitates to talk to Anya about Nikolai's disappearance, but makes an effort by visiting her at home.

Entering the house, Lena touches the icon and makes the sign of the cross, a custom she has observed Anya's family performing. "Anya, we've been friends for seven, almost eight years. I keep many things inside me we never talk about. Seeing you like this is not good, we need to talk."

"Go ahead and talk, I'm not stopping you," Anya replies sharply and steers Lena to the quiet of the laundry room. Lena ignores the cutting comment and tells her a story. "Your father was with you many years, and he's still alive. My father was killed when I was five years old. I hardly knew him, but I miss him always."

"Well, you don't show it," Anya replies. "You never talk about your father, or your mother!"

"That's because I never learned to talk about how I feel inside. Mama and Papa Yeltzin are good to me, and Papa Yeltzin treats me like a daughter, but I can't talk to him like he was my father." Lena chooses her next words carefully. "Do you want to know what happened to my father? I've never told anyone, or mentioned his name. But, I have dreams; scary dreams remembering what happened." Anya looks at Lena, suddenly interested. "Tell me what happened."

Lena stares at her shoes, and begins: "We left our farm during the war because there was much fighting. My father, Yuri, was tall—and strong, he would never use his strength to fight; he tried to reason with people. He had a brother in Khabarovsk and thought bringing us to Khabarovsk would get us away from the fighting.

"Papa was very excited as we drew near. 'The land looks good for farming,' he kept telling us. I don't know exactly where we were when the train stopped, but there was a big field, with wild flowers in the tall grass. Soldiers, they were Japanese, made everyone get off the train. We got off the train and Papa told us to stay near; he would take care of us. But the soldiers made all the children go into the field to pick flowers. I was small, scared, and the grass was taller than me, so I hid in the grass near my mother and father.

The soldiers argued with my father. Two of them hurt my mother. I could hear her crying and my father asking them to stop. I could see him standing above the soldiers, waving his arms. There was a shot and he fell out of sight. The soldiers were yelling and one of them raised his gun-knife high in the air and blood was running down the blade. I jumped up and ran through the grass to find my brothers and sisters.

"When we were told to come back to the train, all the men on the train had been killed and some women. Mother was crying, holding my father's hand. His eyes were open, but he was dead. After the soldiers left, a train from Khabarovsk stopped and took us to Sretensk. I wish now I had gone into the field to pick flowers and not seen what happened. None of my brothers or sisters had the scary dreams. But, I'll probably have these dreams the rest of my life."

During WWI, Japan sent army units to Russia supporting the fight against Germany. After the war Japanese occupied parts of Eastern Russia.

In the quiet of the laundry room, there are tears in the eyes of both girls as Lena finishes telling the story. Anya hugs Lena and the two friends sit quietly for several minutes. "I don't know why, but I think I feel better," Anya says, sniffing and clearing her throat. "I feel better having told someone," Lena sighs.

*   *   *

East of Manzhouli, about 20 miles in a straight line and not as the circling vulture flies, the Argun River bends sharply as it turns northward to join the Amur. A broad beach of sand and gravel is formed and attracts many of Manzhouli's residents for picnics and swimming during the short summer. Dunia and Nina Tokma often take Jenni and Anya to the beach during the summer. Although the beach is mostly pebbles, and the water is cold, it is a welcome respite from the confining life in Manzhouli. And, when the children are playing, Dunia and Nina plan how they will leave Manzhouli.

In June there is a school break. Dunia arranges for a car to take Anya and her friends to the Argun. The girls hold up straw screens to change into their bathing suits, then take their 'compulsory' dip in the cold, gray-green water of the Argun, then back to a windbreak and enjoy the real purpose of the outing, "girl talk." Still wearing colorful rubber bathing caps, made in Hong Kong, they talk about summer plans. Kahtia and Sara will be moving to Shanghai this summer. Kahtia says that she has heard that White Russian girls can make much money in Shanghai. "Doing what?" Anya asks innocently, her naiveté showing.

"Oh Anya, you know what girls do to make money, don't you?" Kahtia replies. "As friendly as you are, you could make more money than any of us," she states flatly with a mischievous twinkle in her eyes.

"I still don't know what kind of work you're talking about, and what's wrong with being friendly?" Anya asks, looking from one to another. Turning back to Kahtia, Anya jokingly threatens her. "You'd better tell me or I'll roll you on the beach and stuff sand down your bathing suit."

They laugh and Sara looks at Anya seriously. "It's whoring, Anya. You know, letting a man go to bed with you," she says. Anya looks from one to the other. They all act as though they know about girls going to Shanghai and working as prostitutes. Anya responds, "Well, I know about whores. Would you think about doing that? I'm saving myself for the man I'll marry, and that's that!" Kahtia looks down at the sand, embarrassed to answer the question, and draws some circles with her finger while thinking. Raising her eyes and squinting at Anya in the brilliant, unfiltered sunlight of the high desert, she says, "Maybe it would be fun. Maybe I could make enough money to leave China and go to America. I really don't know what I'll do when we get to Shanghai, but I'm not going to stay there."

"What are you going to do when we leave, Anya? Have you thought about that?" Sara asks. Anya has a ready answer, "I'm going to find someone to take me dancing at least twice a week. We'll take Lena dancing with us until she finds a boyfriend; right Lena?"

"That would be fun," says Lena hiding her smile.

* * *

Not long after Lena is offered a job in Tientsin by an English family, known to her fur trading foster parents. She will be a companion for their children. Tientsin, a major port on the Yellow River, has a large international settlement, major business center, and headquarters of the U.S. 15th Infantry

Regiment. On their last evening together, the two girls swear to be friends forever in a tearful goodbye.

One by one, Anya's friends leave Manzhouli. Kahtia's parents move only as far as Harbin, while Sara's parents continue to Shanghai. Anya helps Dunia with the house and laundry business, which has grown larger each year. Peter helps too, when not working at the station. Under Ma Chaing-su's tutelage, Anya is also becoming an adept seamstress. As summer turns to fall, Peter is offered a job in the ticket office at Harbin Railway Station, and moves there with the blessing of his mother.

Spring, 1928

With the coming of spring, new families arrive to work for CER. Nina Tokma and Jenni, still considered a "CER" family, are reluctantly evicted from their CER home and find temporary shelter with the CER Laundry Lady, Dunia. Nina scans the pages of Harbin's Russian newspaper, applies for a job as bookkeeper in a ladies shop and is hired. CER moves them to Harbin and helps her find an apartment. Jenni attends a school in Harbin run by Catholic Nuns and is tended by a Chinese amah when not in school.

Anya graduates from the Russian School of Manzhouli and is popular among the young men. She finds none 'romantically interesting' as she attends dances, goes to church, and works for her mother in the laundry. Fashion magazines from Europe and America mysteriously disappear from trains as passengers clear customs, reappearing in the bundles of linens delivered to Dunia's laundry. The year passes quickly and more Russians leave Manzhouli. Dunia is offered a job in the Russian Clinic of Harbin and Anya, a seamstress job where Nina works. She sells the laundry business to Ma Chaing-su and they leave the dust of Manzhouli behind.

Chapter 6
A New Life in Harbin

Harbin, China
Summer, 1929

The express train slows as it approaches the long, multi-span bridge crossing the Songhua River. A heavyset matron, dressed in black, sits in the first Wagon-Lits passenger coach facing a striking, young Russian beauty. The younger woman, fashionably dressed, reads from a small leather bound book. Dunia subconsciously smoothens the wrinkles from her black dress as she watches her daughter read, thinking Anya has never looked more beautiful. They sit on the north side of the salon car, avoiding the sun streaming in from the opposite side. Nikolai told them this bit of traveler's intelligence many years ago. It is hot in the car and small fans along the top of the car hum and whir with little cooling effect. In the seat beside Dunia is the Donesyvna family samovar and icon, not to be let out of her sight while traveling.

Nearly one-half million Russians live in Harbin. Most are refugees from Bolshevik Russia. Some are part of the railroad aristocracy moving to Harbin during the building of the Chinese Eastern link of the Trans-Siberian Railroad. Others are genuine aristocrats, titled Russians chased from Russia after the revolution. A large settlement of Russian Jews organized and became a fixture in the business and social life of Harbin long before the revolution, migrating during the early years of Czar Nicholas II's reign. The influx of White Russians brought changes in the social hierarchy; some businesses owned by Jews suffered. Buildings in the city's business section reflect West-European architecture popular in early St. Petersburg. Russian police patrol the streets; a Cossack colonel started the police force before the Revolution and Chinese have allowed it to continue.

The approach to Harbin is over a wide flood plain west of the Songhua. Noise from the elevated track reverberates inside the salon car as the train slows and the bridge appears. Anya looks up from her well-worn volume of Tolstoy's short stories. She closes the book and stares out the right side of the car as taller buildings of Harbin come into view. Kahtia moved to Harbin from Manzhouli last year. Her letters are filled with stories of dances, and parties on river boats. According to Kahtia, young men outnumber young women three to one. Peter has not written much about his social life, but seems to enjoy his work.

As the train comes to a stop in Harbin station, Peter, in his ticket agent uniform, greets them. Motioning to a Chinese porter to take their luggage, he steers Dunia (still carrying the family icon) and Anya (with the samovar) to the station entrance. Peter hails a taxi to take them to Shangzhi Street. Their new home is an apartment on tree-lined Shangzhi Street. The three-story, stone and masonry building sits on a cobblestone street and each apartment has a small balcony made of wrought iron. Most have potted flowers sitting on the balconies. "Don't bring anything in until I see the apartment," Dunia warns Peter. They leave the luggage in the taxi and go inside.

Peter has the keys and opens the door. The first floor apartment is very clean, to Dunia's surprise. An amah hired by Peter follows closely to insure it meets Dunia's discriminating eye. "This is nice, Peter," Dunia says slowly and with emphasis on the 'nice.' She walks to the window, opens it wider and looks out on the street. "I've never lived on a paved street before, I'll need flowers for the balcony and how is the water?"

"The water is good, Mama," Peter assures her and nods to the amah who is grinning broadly. "You are only two blocks from Toulong Street." Peter checks his watch and joins his mother by the window. "In a few minutes you'll hear the church bells on Toulong striking the hour." Their proximity to the onion-domed Russian Orthodox Church on Toulong brings another smile to Dunia's face.

"I'll wait and listen. Go get our things out of the taxi. Be careful with the icon and samovar," Dunia cautions Peter! True, from their apartment they can hear the bells of the church ringing the time of day. Peter finishes unloading the taxi while Anya pours water into the samovar. "Now where is the toilet?" Dunia asks.

"Outside behind this building, the amah will empty your "honey bucket" each morning. There is a bathtub and wash basin just down the hall to the left." As Dunia leaves to find the toilet, Anya prepares the samovar for an afternoon tea. "Mother likes it here, I can tell! She has smiled more today than all of last year."

Dunia starts work the following day at the modern, well-equipped Russian clinic, where Russian doctors and nurses supervise the aides and a few Chinese orderlies. For Dunia supervising aides is easy compared to running a primitive laundry in the high, desert climate of Manzhouli.

Anya, called by her childhood name as long as she remembers, is now Anna Kulina, a seamstress where Nina Tokma works. It is an exclusive shop. Only the wealthiest Russian society matrons living in Harbin can afford fashions shipped from Paris and London. Each item must be carefully tailored to fit bodies too large, or too small. After a few weeks, there is an opening for a stock girl and Anna encourages Kahtia to apply. She is hired, joining Anna and Nina in the dress shop.

Fall of 1929

While the world watches the start of the Great Depression in America, in Harbin pay is good and jobs are plentiful. Dunia occasionally attends mass on Saturdays, but always high Mass on Sundays and makes her offering to the Church. Anna goes because Dunia insists. The Church reminds Dunia of Russia, and family tradition, cobblestone streets help her forget the dust and house in Manzhouli.

Nina Tokma and Jenni live in an apartment building nearby. The building is similar, looks as modern, but has very poor facilities. Electricity is unreliable and frequently off. There is running water in the building, but the water must be boiled before drinking. Toilet facilities are outside the building. And, when a radio is being played loudly, it can be heard throughout the building. They, too, have a small wrought iron balcony outside their apartment and there Jenni has collected, and tends, an assortment of potted flowers.

Peter's sparsely furnished apartment near the station is in a predominantly Chinese section of Harbin. Studying Chinese, and playing soccer with a team of young Chinese from the station, brought derision from his Russian friends who think Peter has used his head on the ball too much. "Why else would one associate with the Chinese?" they chide.

Anna's skill with needle and pin ensures her popularity with the wealthy matrons as she adjusts their clothing to fit sagging figures. Her diplomacy in dealing with petulant ladies, who add pounds between fittings, is more of an asset than her seamstress skills. Before Christmas, she opens a bank account and moves into her own apartment, the floor above Dunia. Kahtia shares the apartment with Anna. Nina and Jenni take an apartment next door; the Russian expatriates are together again, with Dunia on the first floor to monitor their comings and goings.

Anna and Kahtia are invited to parties and dances given by wealthy patrons of the dress shop who wish to decorate their social events with attractive young Russian ladies. In the course of an evening they meet young (and old) men of financial substance, get flattering proposals, and find some who dance well.

The Russian Consulate sponsors a dance each November honoring the revolution; all members of the Russian community are invited. Anna goes in hopes she will meet someone having information about her father. It is a disappointment. Older Russians who decide to attend, more out of curiosity than anything else, are insulted and embarrassed by the crudeness of the young Soviets. Anna endures several dances with a member of the Consulate staff only to learn, when she finally asks about finding her father, the man is a member of the NKVD and not interested in helping find a "criminal."

* * *

Mikhail 'Misha' Voskovich and his brothers, Nikki and Sasha, arrive from Vladivostok in December 1931, their journey one of survival. An engineering student, but not a party member, Communists took Mikhail out of school and into the Army. After a few months of training, and before he was to be sent to an outpost on the Kamchatka Peninsula, Mikhail deserted the Army. Joined by his brothers, who were not in the Army, they made their way to Harbin, crossing the border with forged documents. Evicted from their first apartment in March, they move into an apartment building on Hongzhi and are immediately attracted to Anna and Kahtia living nearby. Finding the two young ladies a challenge to meet, they use an influential customer at the dress shop, and persistence, to arrange a formal introduction.

Like many young Russians passing through Harbin, Mikhail is eager to move on, forever looking over his shoulder, suspecting he is being followed. Tallest of the brothers with broad shoulders, narrow waist, and large, strong hands, Mikhail's rugged good looks attract Anna, and the fact he is from Vladivostok also interests her. He has a mustache, not unlike her father's, hanging like a horseshoe above his lips. As Mikhail explains to Anna, they plan to go to Australia to get as far away as possible from the Communists.

From their first date, Mikhail, who fashions himself a "Cossack" horseman, and Anna appear inseparable; they have intellectual chemistry mixed with physical attraction. Though often disagreeing about leaving Harbin, their quarrels are quickly healed. Mikhail considers Harbin a "…God-forsaken place in a God-forsaken country. It is crazy to stay here so close to the Communists, where they can kidnap you and whisk you across the border in a day's time."

In May, following a quick romance, Mikhail proposes to Anna with a bouquet of spring flowers in his hand, telling her they will live in Shanghai after they are married. Anna accepts and agrees to leave Harbin for Shanghai. Dunia helps plan the June wedding. Anna wants to be married in the church on Toulong Street and have a reception at the Yacht Club. The wedding dress is a gift from Anna's employer, a gown from Paris, too small to sell to her usual customers, but a perfect fit for Anna.

Chinese soldiers raid the Soviet Consulate the Friday Mikhail chooses to pick up his new documents, arresting everyone inside. The raid surprises most of the Russians in Harbin. Fortunately, Mikhail left the consulate moments before the Chinese soldiers entered. It would have been particularly bad timing for Mikhail to be in a Chinese prison with his wedding only a week away.

That evening when Mikhail and Anna return to her apartment, a note from Kahtia is under the door. "Meet me at Dunia's—Kahtia." As they enter Dunia's apartment Peter is excitedly telling Dunia, Kahtia, and Nina about the Chinese takeover of railroad operations, which occurred today. Russians will no longer have any control of the CER.

It is hot Saturday; the temperature over 90 degrees Fahrenheit at midday and tension is high between Harbin's Russian and Chinese communities. Nothing is moving along the entire railway system from Manzhouli to the Eastern border since the Chinese have taken control. Stations wait for instructions before letting trains leave. Repair crews walked off their jobs, taking tools with them. The new Chinese managers are unprepared for the chaotic situation. Peter and several other Russian employees are arrested by Chinese railway police, but allowed to go home. Top railway officials appointed by the Soviets are sent packing back to Russia. Peter is to report to the Chinese manager Monday.

Monday, May 30, 1932

"You can pet the fox, but keep one hand on your axe," Peter tells Anna and Dunia at breakfast. "Papa used to say that," Peter adds. It is unusual for Peter to come by the apartment in the morning. He is somber and subdued as Dunia tries to cheer him. Peter is going to see Mr. Fan, the Chinese manager who Peter compares to a fox, and is dressed for work, his worn gray suit neatly pressed and looking a size too small over his broad bony shoulders.

After breakfast, Dunia and Anna follow Peter down stairs. Turning and waving, he straddles his bicycle, pants legs tucked into sock tops, and departs. Dunia and Anna wave, worry plainly seen on their faces. Peter never returns from his visit with Mr. Fan. He is deported to Vladivostok.

3 June 1932

Anna and Mikhail are married in the onion-domed Russian Orthodox Church on Toulong Street. Kahtia is Maid of Honor, and Nikki, Mikhail's brother, is best man. Dunia, unable to afford the expensive Yacht Club, arranges a reception after the wedding in a restaurant on Shangzhi.

To Anna's surprise, Dunia gives her the Donesyvna icon as a wedding present. "It was my mother's, given to me before she died, framed by my father before he died. It must stay in the family; it is yours, my daughter and a story goes with the icon. Our family had the icon long before my father became a woodworker. My father made the frame while working with icon painters near Moscow. He was killed in an 'accident' at the icon painter's shop. The frame and icon survived and your grandmother brought it back to Samara. She gave it to me and told me to never let it go; it would bring us good fortune!"

Saturday morning Anna and Mikhail depart on their honeymoon, a trip to Dairen by train. Even with the turmoil about who is running the railroad, trains are running again. While in Dairen, Mikhail and Anna discuss their plans to leave Harbin. Mikhail wants to move to Shanghai immediately and with the Chinese taking control of Harbin, Japanese threatening to occupy all Manchuria, Anna agrees to leave. After a week-long honeymoon in Dairen, Mikhail moves into Anna's apartment. Anna gives notice at the dress shop she will be leaving the end of the month. Harbin is green, and the weather is pleasant the remainder of June.

Friday, July 1, temperatures in Harbin climb above 100 degrees. On their last evening before leaving, Anna and Mikhail attend a dance at the Yacht Club and afterward stroll in the park by the Songhua River. Many more Chinese soldiers walk the streets, and most of them are camped in the park.

The next morning Dunia and Anna have a tearful farewell as Dunia prepares to leave for work. "Write me often," Dunia pleads. "She will write, I promise," Mikhail assures her. Anna has her bags packed and notices Mikhail's bag is still open. She starts to close it and sees his revolver is inside the bag. Each of the brothers usually carries a revolver, as do many young Cossacks in Harbin. She leaves the bag open in case Mikhail might want to carry his revolver. Just then Nikki and Sasha arrive with their luggage. "You're early," Anna exclaims.

"We have some things to do before leaving," Sasha explains. "Would you mind taking our luggage down to the station when you go?"

"Not at all, did you see Misha outside?" she asks.

"Am I my brother's keeper?" Nikki jokes.

Just then Mikhail walks in, "Yes, little brother! We must take care of each other," he says with emphasis. "It's time to leave, so let's get started."

"Aren't we early?" Anna asks.

"We'll take you down to the station, get our tickets, and then I'm going with Nikki and Sasha to run some errands. We'll be back in plenty of time and you won't have to rush, or worry," Mikhail explains calmly, his voice condescending.

They reach the station nearly two hours before the train is due to depart. The brothers unload the luggage and deposit Anna, the icon, and the luggage in the waiting room. A young Chinese clerk is at the ticket window Peter once occupied. Mikhail purchases the tickets and brings them to Anna.

"Hold on to these for us. We'll be gone about an hour. I'm taking my bag with us to carry things Nikki and Sasha will pick up," he tells Anna as he bends over to kiss her. "Hurry back, my husband," Anna replies in a husky voice. She began smoking cigarettes after meeting Mikhail and her irritated throat plays tricks with her voice.

They are gone an hour and return, faces flushed, and breathing heavily. Nikki carries Mikhail's bag as they enter the waiting room and walk directly to Anna. "We hurried so you wouldn't worry. Has the boarding announcement been made?"

"I don't think so, haven't heard any announcement since you left."

"Sasha, find out if we can board, and hurry back." Mikhail's smile is forced and each word has a cold sharpness as his eyes dart around the waiting room to see if anyone is noticing their arrival. "Let me have the tickets now, sweetheart. I'll give Nikki his ticket and hold ours until Sasha returns."

When Sasha returns, they have approval to board the train. Nikki hurries aboard still carrying Mikhail's suitcase. In what Anna thinks is an odd sequence, she and Nikolai wait a few minutes and follow. Sasha waits outside on the platform. A quarter of an hour passes before Sasha enters the compartment. Once inside their adjoining first class compartments, connected by a lavatory, Mikhail pulls down the window cover and opens a bottle of vodka pouring Sasha and Nikki a drink. Opening a bottle of white Chinese wine, he pours Anna and himself a glass and raising his glass gleefully toasts "to our departure from Harbin and a new life in Shanghai."

Chapter 7
Shanghai

July 1932

The "Paris of the Orient" is hot and humid when Anna and Mikhail exit Shanghai's North Station. It is mid-morning and already the heat is intense. Despite the congestion of traffic around the station, Mikhail flags a taxi and gives the driver the name of their hotel. The hotel Mikhail has selected is more modern than any Anna has seen. Their room has hot and cold water, a private bath, ceiling fan, and a large, comforter-covered bed smelling of lavender.

Opening windows and turning on the fan to stir the stale, lavender scented air, the uniformed Chinese bellboy bows and backs out of the room. Mikhail steps carefully between luggage and furniture to reach a window and parts the draperies to look at the busy street below. Studying it with amusement, Mikhail turns to catch Anna looking in a full length mirror and frowning. "Why the sour face, Anna? Do you not like our room?"

"Don't be silly, Misha! The room is wonderful, but just look at me in this mirror. I'm a terrible sight. Don't you have something to do?"

"I must shave before meeting the Chief Detective," Mikhail mutters, rubbing his whiskered face.

"Good, now hurry, I want to bathe and put on something fresh!"

Mikhail is meeting the Chief of Detectives in the French Concession to ask about work. In Shanghai each international concession has a police force, or private army. Mikhail heard of the French Concession's "pock-faced" Chief of Detectives before leaving Harbin. Russian travelers from Shanghai told him to work in the French Concession. "You can make more money in a month working for the 'pock-faced' Chinaman than you can earn in a year in Harbin," one man said. "And, in the concessions, you pay no taxes unless you have a business then you pay 'taxes' to the Chinaman! Ha!"

Carefully shaving around his mustache, Mikhail rinses his face and dampens his hair, combs it and admires his image in the mirror. Buttoning his shirt and tucking it in around the waist of his pants, Mikhail is ready for his appointment with Mr. Huang. "I'm off to meet the Chief Detective, Anna. Wish me luck!"

"I wish you more than luck, Misha, I wish you success! We cannot stay long in a place like this, unless you have work," Anna responds as she mentally calculates the balance from her savings withdrawn in Harbin. "How long will you be gone?"

"Two, maybe three hours, and then we go to dinner at a fancy place." He walks over to where she is standing in her slip, puts his hand under her chin and tilts her head upward, delivers a kiss, turns and clomps out of the room, Cossack boots ringing on the marble floor. Finding the office of the French Concession's Chief of Detectives is easy. It seems everyone knows where to find the office of the Chief of Detectives. Huang's face is badly scarred from a pox when he was a child. Wearing a western suit and white shirt opened at the collar, Huang lifts his head as Mikhail enters the office, revealing scars from the pox extend to more of his body than just the face. The Chief Detective likes White Russians who do not mind doing a little dirty work.

Mikhail's interview does not take long. Huang was aware of the Voskovich brothers reputation before they arrived in Shanghai. His sources told him the brothers fit the description of three men boarding a train for Shanghai after robbing a bank in Harbin and he is to keep an eye out for them. The brothers are just the kind of men Huang wants on his "security" force. After questioning Mikhail, Huang notes Mikhail is deceptive in his answers about his past ("he will need to be monitored"). Not only is Mikhail hired, Huang offers to hire his brothers as well. They are "crooked enough" to be security officers in the French Concession, reporting directly to Chief Detective Huang and extorting bribes from Russian merchants in the Concession.

Back at the hotel, Mikhail orders a bottle of French champagne from room service, and hurries to the elevator anxious to tell Anna the news. Anna is dressed for dinner, adjusting her amethyst pendant and admiring it in the mirror when the door opens. Mikhail lifts Anna in his arms and whirls around. "Put me down, you crazy Cossack," she says with a squeal. "You're making a mess of my new dress!"

"I have a job, Anna, a good job. Tonight we celebrate." Mikhail tells Anna about the job and his interview with Huang. "They will give us a place to live. I go back tomorrow and get the address." The nagging concern in Anna's mind about Mikhail finding work is gone. A knock on the door interrupts their revelry as champagne arrives. The waiter, with exaggerated coolness, ceremonially uncorks the bottle. When Anna's glass is filled, she holds the glass to her nose. "We did this on the train when I was a little girl. I can still remember smelling the bubbles," Anna tells Mikhail, with a touch of melancholy in her voice.

Toasting everyone from "Pock faced" Huang to the waiter, Anna and Mikhail empty the bottle before leaving their room. A restaurant serving Russian food has been recommended by the hotel. The doorman hails a rickshaw to take them the short distance.

When they arrive, the only Russian working in the restaurant is the owner. He meets people as they come in and takes the money as people leave. Chinese do the cooking, serve, and clean tables. Each course is authentically prepared from thinly sliced cabbage, beets, and carrots in the borscht appetizer, served with a dollop of sour cream, to the "*keks stolichnyi*" (a Russian pound cake) and raspberries for dessert. Savoring each bite of food, Anna watches Mikhail devour his food as if it is his last meal. When the owner stops at their table Anna expresses her delight the Chinese cook mastered so many Russian recipes. He accepts Anna's praise without telling her about the hours his wife spent teaching the Chinese cook her recipes and secrets of preparation.

After the last bite of *keks stolichnyi* and raspberries, followed with strong coffee diluted with milk and sugar, they depart. Giddy from the champagne and elated to find such a good restaurant, they walk through jostling crowds to a park area along the river. They sit for a while, listening to ship's bells, a distant clock chimes the hour, and a cacophony of foreign tongues being spoken.

Returning to the hotel, Mikhail's arm heavy on her shoulders, Anna's excitement over her first day in Shanghai is more than she ever imagined. Preparing for bed she uses a little extra cologne, adjusts her gown to show more of her figure and steps into the bedroom. The overhead light is on and "Misha" is spread-eagled across the bed, fully dressed and snoring loudly. Anna removes his boots, turns out the lights, and snuggles close to her snoring "Cossack".

***

A small, sparsely furnished one room apartment, with a window overlooking an equally small interior courtyard, goes with the job. It is cramped; but there is electricity, running water and an indoor toilet. Bamboo curtains divide the room into three areas. "It is better than our apartment on Shangzhi," Anna comments as she surveys the room. "Don't unpack anything until I clean this place," she tells Mikhail and the concierge as they stand at the door. A brief argument ensues between Anna and the concierge about having a houseboy clean the room. Anna prevails, and the concierge grudgingly gives Mikhail a bucket, brush and soap. Changing into a smock, Anna attacks the job of scrubbing down their new home. Starting with the smoke encrusted ceiling, down the walls, and finally the floor, Anna scrubs, and cleans, and perspires. By mid-afternoon she is ready to unpack. Placing the family icon on a wall near the door, she touches the walnut frame, makes the sign of the cross and says a prayer for their first home in Shanghai.

The apartment building is on a narrow street reached from Avenue Joffre. There are shops on Avenue Joffre, and Anna sends Mikhail there with a list of food items she needs. Anna prepares kasha for their evening meal, starting with lard and buckwheat in her cast iron skillet, adding what she can find to make it tasty. "This is real Russian food," Mikhail boasts to their Russian neighbors who stop by to welcome the newcomers.

There are three Russian families in the apartment building, and they all arrive while Anna is cooking. She allows "Misha" to do the talking. Four empty Vodka bottles and a clean kasha bowl later, the neighbors finally leave. Turning out their overhead light and standing at the window looking down into the dimly lit courtyard, Anna points to several small children playing in the shadows of the courtyard. "It is good to have our own place," she says looking up into Mikhail's eyes. "I think I will like it here."

The next day Mikhail's brothers move in with them. Although Sasha and Nikki work for the French Concession, and should receive their own apartment, there is only one apartment currently available. Anna cooks, washes, and cleans as she did in Harbin. Now it is for four people.

The first letter received from Dunia is in two envelopes, one for Anna and Mikhail, and a personal letter for Anna which she conceals from Mikhail. Dunia covers everything in her letter, from the Japanese taking over most local government functions and stripping the Russian police of their power, to Nina Tokma moving closer in the apartment building. She writes:

"The Japanese are treating Russians no better than the Chinese treated us. Of course, the Chinese suffer greatly under the Japanese. Our people are still leaving Harbin and there are many empty apartments. Japanese families are beginning to move into our building and taking all the good jobs. Many Jewish families are moving to Tientsin and Shanghai, having lost their businesses to Japanese.

"Kahtia sends you greetings. She misses you at the shop and the dances. 'I have no one to talk with,' she tells me. I think she is interested in a young man working at a grain mill. They are together most of the time."

Mikhail finds the news boring and departs for work early. Anna continues to read the letter. After he leaves, Anna opens her letter. In it are details of a robbery occurring in Harbin the day Anna and Mikhail left for Shanghai. Harbin police questioned Dunia and other residents of the apartment house about the Voskovich brothers. Dunia warns Anna not to discuss the letter with Mikhail, "You can't tell what they will do. He might harm you." Dunia gives her the address of Aunt Sophia and Uncle Ivan Yetchekov. "Your Uncle Ivan is teaching in Shanghai. Contact them if there is an emergency."

The letter answers questions puzzling Anna since leaving Harbin. The brothers' actions before their departure from Harbin, the sudden abundance of money appearing on the train, it all fits. Money the brothers spent freely on the train to Shanghai must have been from the robbery. Their secretiveness boarding the train in Harbin was to avoid suspicion and, Mikhail's suitcase was where they put the money.

Anna destroys the letter after copying down the Yetchekov's address and makes a mental note to visit Aunt Sophia soon. It has been 14 years since Anna last saw her aunt and uncle, the day in Samara indelibly etched in her mind.

The summer heat is more bearable in September and the humid, steaminess that made Anna's first month in Shanghai a sweaty nightmare, appears to be over for the year. Uncomfortable with her new found knowledge of Mikhail's past, Anna, for the first time in her life, feels sluggish in the mornings and generally weak. It is nothing to see a doctor about, she reasons. The excitement of being in Shanghai and her concern about Mikhail must be the cause.

Later, Anna suspects she is pregnant. To be certain, she goes to a clinic operated by a German society and is seen by a lady doctor, Dr. (Frau) Kuentzler. Dr. Kuentzler confirms Anna's pregnancy and prescribes several medications to help her overcome the general anemia she is experiencing. Anna suspects Mikhail will be upset, but plans the occasion to tell him. Preparing a dinner for the two of them, she sends Sasha and Nikki out to eat. A candle on the table and French wine has Mikhail in a good mood.

"Anna, you make our little place so..." he pauses for a word, "...comfortable. This is very, very good for us, but soon it will be better. Soon," he lowers his voice and leans across the table taking her hand in his, "we will go to Australia."

This was not what Anna wanted to hear. "Misha, we must talk seriously," Anna jerks her hand away.

"Ah, my sweet Anna, you are always so serious! First you didn't want to leave Harbin, but see how much nicer it is in Shanghai? Now you don't want to leave Shanghai!"

"We can't go to Australia now, Misha. I'm going to have a baby, our baby!"

Mikhail is stunned. Rising quickly from the table, he kicks his chair across the room and curses. "You can't have a baby. It will change all our plans to have a baby now. We should leave for Australia now, a baby will delay us. Can't you have an abortion or something?" Anna rises slowly from her chair, her face a mask of pained fury. She walks over to Mikhail and puts her hand to his chest. "You sit!" She shoves him backward. "I don't want an abortion or something, Mikhail Voskovich!" Anna shouts back, undaunted by Mikhail's anger. "I want to have our baby. The doctor says I have anemia and shouldn't be traveling. When I am strong, and, if we must leave, I will go with you to Australia. So, no more talk about abortion, do you hear?"

For days following her outburst Misha, Sasha and Nikki rarely speak to Anna, except to ask, "When do we eat?" Writing Dunia her news is Anna's only pleasure, little realizing the letter will prompt Dunia to leave Harbin immediately to help Anna prepare for her baby.

In late September, as the first typhoon of the season blows into Shanghai, the Whangpoo and its tributaries overflow. South of Anna's apartment a drainage canal marks the southern boundary of the French Concession. It overflows and apartments on the ground floor are flooded. Shutters closed and without electricity, Anna and the Voskovich brothers ride out the storm in their apartment.

After cleaning up the mud tramped upstairs and into their apartment, Anna finds the summer heat, and high humidity left behind by the typhoon, are wreaking havoc. Linens mildew, the furniture (what little there is) warps and pulls away at the joints, and books and papers she brought from Harbin have mildewed. Turning to the family icon, she wonders where the good fortune is, or when it is coming.

Adding to Anna's misery, the anemia does not go away. At the clinic, Dr. Kuentzler prescribes a different medicine and tells Anna her health rules for survival in Shanghai. "Despite what they say, you should always boil your water. Don't eat any fruits or vegetables without first cooking them, the longer the better. If you are a guest and served raw vegetables, leave them on your plate and, with your fair complexion, you must always wear a hat in the sun." Anna writes Dr. Kuentzler's advice in a note book she started on arriving in Shanghai.

Meanwhile the Voskovich brothers have planned their departure from Shanghai without Anna. Bribing a ship's officer with drugs, they obtain passage on a freighter going to Australia. Making their usual weekday evening collections from merchants in the French Concession, the brothers meet at the Quai de France, disguising their appearance to avoid recognition by Huang's dock watchers, and slip on board during the dark.

Mikhail told Anna he would be late and not to wait up, or fix him supper. Suspecting nothing, Anna awakes the next morning and neither Mikhail nor his brothers have returned. Mikhail has spent the night out before, but not recently. Anna is worried and decides she will contact Aunt Sophia. Before she can leave the apartment, there is a knock on the door.

Opening the door she is face to face with several uniformed concession police standing in the hallway. Their spokesman is a stocky Chinese smartly dressed in a business suit. The Voskovich brothers' evening collections for "the Chief of Detectives" have not been received at the bank. Weeks before, when they had first started making collections, Mikhail neglected to make the drop off at Huang's bank and came home instead. The early morning visit by the police got the Voskovich brothers' attention then, and they promised it would not happen again. The Chung Wai Bank on Avenue Edward VII, a small brick building near their apartment with its name in ornate gold lettering, is where Mikhail makes his deposits.

Anna is confused by Mikhail not coming home, and frightened by the presence of the police. She answers their questions as directly as possible, but the spokesman insists on searching the apartment. (Why do they always look in the samovar?) They do not threaten her, but are reluctant to believe Mikhail could leave without her knowing. "Tell your husband, we come back," the stocky Chinaman warns Anna.

After the police leave, Anna replaces things moved during the search and does a search herself to see if Mikhail may have hidden a note or left a clue to explain what is happening. She finds nothing and immediately leaves to find Aunt Sophia.

The concession police allow Anna to stay in the apartment, not out of generosity. With her living in the apartment, they can watch her movements and visitors. Officially they are allowing her to remain in the apartment until other accommodations can be arranged.

In Harbin, Dunia ends her employment, packs her clothing and samovar, and boards a train for Shanghai. She arrives in Shanghai a week after the Voskovich brothers depart for Australia. Dunia notified the Yetchekovs of her arrival date and Anna insists on making the trip to North Station with them. Shanghai's North Station is no place for the timid, or ill, and Anna's fragile pregnancy, coupled with the hustle and bustle of Shanghai traffic, leaves her pale and nauseous as the Yetchekov's driver finally reaches the station.

Ivan Yetchekov has not changed much since the summer of 1918, except his thick thatch of hair is turning gray in streaks. Looking taller and a bit heavier among the crush of shorter Chinese, Ivan wades through the throng, leaving Sophia and Anna near the car. Sophia Yetchekov has lost the svelte figure Anna remembered, she is short, plump, and nearing her fiftieth birthday. On the crowded platform, it appears no one can get off the train as the masses of people press forward. Dunia, however, has managed to reach the platform and sees her brother-in-law. Holding the not-to-be-let-out-of-sight samovar cradled against her bosom, she waves to Ivan and forges a path directly toward him. Ivan corrals two Chinese porters to help Dunia with her bags and boxes, while he is entrusted with the samovar as they make their way to the car.

Dunia is unprepared for the shock of Anna's appearance. The healthy, robust bride who left Harbin only months ago is pale and thin. "Anna, what has happened to you?" Without giving Anna a chance to respond, Dunia continues. "We must put some meat on those bones!"

"Exactly what I've told her, big sister," adds Sophia, who has been standing unnoticed by Dunia. Turning to see who is speaking, Dunia gasps. "Sophie, you're as big as I am!" The sisters burst out laughing and, amid hugs and kisses, for the moment forget Anna and the jostling crowd around them. Ivan manages to get his entourage into the car, placing Dunia in the front seat with the driver. Her bags are secured on top of the sedan and the samovar is placed awkwardly, but prominently, in the space between Dunia and the Chinese driver.

Driving across town in a motor car is more excitement than the exhausted Dunia Kulina can stand. She fans herself furiously trying to ignore the careening maneuvers of the driver sending people scurrying for sidewalks. Peddlers grab their ducks and chickens, jumping out of the way. Rickshaw men wave their fists and shout wildly at the driver, who delights in sounding the horn and leaving confusion behind.

Turning west on Nanking and Bubbling Well Road they speed past the race course and turn north, finally arriving at the Yetchekov's house. It is on a quiet residential street in the International Settlement, south of Soochow Creek.

The driver stops partly on the street, partly on the sidewalk, in front of a tall, drab, gray wall. Large wooden doors, painted glossy black, protect an opening in the wall and swing wide as the driver sounds the horn. The doors are opened by an elderly servant, his hair in a braided pigtail extending midway down his back. Other servants stand behind him with hands clasped and shaved heads slightly bowed. They enter the Yetchekov's house through a small courtyard, shielded from the street by the doors.

"Welcome to 'Little Moscow' in the international concessions," Ivan announces with a hint of sarcasm as they enter the courtyard. "We have everything Moscow has, including hot and cold running Bolsheviks."

"Ivan Yetchekov, you are indeed a friend to help Anna and I on such short notice," Dunia exclaims after regaining her composure. "You didn't expect to have so many of Sophia's family descend on you, eh?" The implacable professor shrugs his shoulders, "It will be pleasant to talk about the joys of the past, rather than the problems of the present."

Servants take Dunia's baggage to another part of the house while Dunia glances discretely at the clean, comfortable surroundings. "Sophie, you must let me help with the house while I am here."

Sophia smiles, "There is nothing to do, unless your keen eyes spotted something I've not seen. The servants take care of everything. If you want Russian food, Mr. Singh can watch you prepare it once and, from then on, he will make the dish the same way. Already he has learned all our old recipes from Samara! Just sit and be comfortable; and, let's talk about Harbin. Mr. Singh, will you bring tea please." And, so, Dunia moves in with the Yetchekovs. "It is only temporary," she announces.

The Yetchekov's driver returns Anna to her apartment, she feels drained after the excitement. There is an envelope with an Australian postmark in her mail box. The postman had only moments before delivered it, and the inquisitive concierge has not had time to steam it open, as is his usual practice with Anna's mail. She takes the envelope to her apartment, closes the door, locks it, and opens the envelope. Inside is a letter from Mikhail and check for one thousand Australian dollars written on Barclay's Bank in Sydney. Mikhail's note is brief and written in Russian. "The money is for you. It will pay for a divorce and an abortion." Anna finishes reading the letter as there is a knock on the door. Quickly she looks around the room, furls the check and slips it down the empty heating chamber of her samovar, taking care to replace the cover. She tucks the letter back into its envelope and puts it in her purse as she goes to the door.

Anna pauses before unlocking the door, looks around, and decides to set her purse on a small table near the entrance. Only then does she cautiously open the door. The plainclothes policeman has returned.

"Mrs. Voskovich, have you heard from your husband?" he asks.

"Yes! How did you know this?"

"We know many things happening in Shanghai," he replies smiling. "Did he perhaps send something for Mr. Huang?"

"Nothing for Mr. Huang, but I can tell you where he is," she adds quickly.

"Australia, I suppose," the detective answers with a knowing smirk. "May I see the letter he sent you?"

Anna goes to the table, picks up her purse and removes the envelope. Handing it to the detective she asks, "Do you read Russian?"

The man's eyes close to narrow slits. "I can read many languages, Mrs. Voskovich," he hisses. Opening the envelope and removing the contents, then peering again into the empty envelope, his face is a mask of concentration. "Is this all that was in the envelope?"

Anna nods affirmatively, hoping he will overlook the mention of a check. She watches as he appears to read the letter. To distract him she wails, "He wants a divorce, and I'm bearing his child. How could he do this to me?" and begins sobbing.

"Mrs. Voskovich, I will ask you to stop crying. There is no need to cry. Your husband is a thief and wife-deserter. The Concession will take care of your needs. We have funds for such emergencies. Please to stop crying," he nervously asks, "I must go now!" The detective returns the envelope and letter to Anna and hastily departs.

Still nauseated from her earlier experiences traveling to North Station, Anna takes medicine Dr. Kuentzler has prescribed and lies down to rest. During the night, she becomes ill, vomiting, with chills and fever. Early the next morning she slips on a robe and carefully descends the stairs to the street door, where an omnipresent rickshaw driver takes her to the clinic. Dr. Kuentzler cannot be reached and a European doctor, who speaks Russian, examines Anna. He tells her she has suffered a miscarriage and they must operate to prevent complications. Anna asks if they could wait for Dr. Kuentzler and is told it would be dangerous to wait even for a few hours. She asks they call Dunia and have her come to the clinic. The Russian-speaking doctor performs the operation.

Dr. Kuentzler joins Dunia in the recovery room as Anna revives from the anesthesia. "I'm sorry I wasn't here when you needed me, Anna. I only hope everything was done properly. The people I work with at the Jewish center needed me, and no one told me you were here. How do you feel?"

"I feel like a horse kicked me in the stomach," Anna replies with a wan smile. "The doctor said it was a girl."

"There is plenty of time for you to have children, Anna. I'll be coming here every day to check on you. Your mother and I have worked out an arrangement with the clinic for her to be here beside you. She'll have a bed next to yours until you feel better." Turning to Dunia, Dr. Kuentzler says, "You'll be the best medicine she can have. Call me if she has fever or the pain worsens."

Anna is in the clinic several days and is finally released to recover at her apartment, under Dunia's watchful care. It doesn't take long for Anna to regain her strength. With Dunia at her side she removes Mikhail's check from the samovar and takes a taxi to the Bund. Making sure they are not followed, Anna opens an account at an English bank and deposits the check. Her divorce from Mikhail is final a few weeks later.

Chapter 8
Reunions

Fall and Winter, 1932-33

British and French have dominated the social and business life of Shanghai's International Settlement and to some extent the French Concession. Russian expatriates and Germans are newcomers to the scene after the end of WWI and the Bolshevik Revolution. As Anna's health improves, Dunia and the Yetchekovs pull her into the stream of social activities making Shanghai the "Paris of the Orient". A visit to the hair dresser, a pair of silk shoes, and matching silk dress, all encourage Anna's recovery.

To reach the Yetchekov's house in the International Settlement, Anna walks to Avenue Du Roi Albert and flags a rickshaw for the three kilometer ride crossing the busy thoroughfares of Avenue Joffre, Avenue Foch, Bubbling Well Road and Peking Road. Most mornings Bubbling Well Road is crowded with foul smelling "honey carts" and Anna is cautious when they are near. The most physically debilitated coolies in Shanghai end up pulling these carts, often stumbling and spilling the contents of the odorous carts on themselves and those around. Anna can close her eyes and tell by smell when the rickshaw coolie reaches Bubbling Well Road.

Residential streets north of Peking Road are quiet, tree-shaded refuges for Shanghai's affluent citizens. Behind the gates and walls, Anna can hear the noises of children playing; being scolded by watchful amahs; and occasionally a barking dog pierces the quiet. Automobiles are parked on the street, guarded by uniformed drivers or houseboys. The gate to the Yetchekovs' house opens as the rickshaw arrives. A servant helps Anna out of the rickshaw and, if raining, holds an umbrella over her head until she is safely inside. Anna feels spoiled by the attention, but openly enjoys it, as does Dunia. They have tea with Sophia then take a rickshaw to see a new part of the city. Their favorite haunt is the labyrinth of shops, temples and restaurants in the Old Chinese City.

The unusually hot summer with temperatures hovering near 100 degrees Fahrenheit, lasts through September. By early October, the days are pleasant and the evenings cool. Suddenly, in November, a cold wet winter sets in with temperatures near freezing. Shanghai is a miserable place to live when a person is ill. Ivan and Sophia Yetchekov insist Anna join Dunia as a guest in their home to preclude a recurrence of the anemia. She welcomes the change of address.

The new year, 1933 (Chinese year of the Rooster), starts with a round of international parties. Anna's beauty and wit, along with her mastery of English and German begun at school in Manzhouli, result in many party invitations. The Russian community has boisterous samovar tea parties, not to be confused with ritualistic Japanese teas, or staid British teas. The more affluent Russians serve the best caviar on Zakuska tables, accompanied by sturgeon in aspic, pate, pickled herring, varieties of bread, and large quantities of assorted vodkas. There is always a samovar with hot water for tea.

British have tea and pastries, and frequently binge on regular imports of Beefeaters gin (referred to by some as 'nectar of the gods'). Their cricket and soccer teams compete with other Europeans and a small Indian community. While Anna considers the British as Europeans, they quickly deny linkage maintaining they are "British."

Germans easily obtain imported schnapps, beer, wine, and sausages from a comprador, even when rice and other essentials are scarce. Their parties are most lively during "*Fasching*," following New Years and preceding the Lenten season. The carnival atmosphere, with party-goers wearing decorative masks and colorful costumes, adds a bright touch to Dunia's life as she chaperons Anna at the parties.

French celebrations for the New Year are somber affairs, with whispered conversations and anxious looks at new faces in their midst. A new administration in France is severing the opium cartel's French connection at its source in Shanghai. Their Consul General is being replaced along with the Concession's French police chief. To Anna's delight, she overhears the new police chief has fired all detectives suspected of being in the "Green Gang," including pock-faced Huang.

The Yetchekovs live well on a professor's earnings, entertaining modestly and frequently. Ivan teaches in an international school, and faculty members attending his parties come from many parts of the world. Some guests are diplomats, students, and many are intellectuals befriended by Ivan.

Summer, 1933

A letter from Lena Kochergna tells of her wedding to an American Army officer in Tientsin and that she will soon be departing for the United States. Anna takes a train to Tientsin, arriving three days before Lena sails to America.

She listens to Lena's story of meeting Captain Verval Smith, a self-described 'Ozark hillbilly' from Arkansas. "We met at a YMCA dance for an American Army commander who was leaving," Lena explains. "The Simpsons, my family, asked me to go with them. Mrs. Simpson bought me a new dress and shoes, took me to a beauty salon to have my hair fixed, and let me use her perfume. I felt beautiful whether I looked it or not. It was my first formal dance. Captain Smith brought an American school teacher to the dance; she had papers to grade for her class and left early. After seeing her home, Captain Smith returned to the dance and was introduced to me by Mr. Simpson. He asked me to dance and we spent the rest of the evening together, never once did he let the other young men cut in while we danced. I remember telling him I was leaving for England with the Simpsons in two weeks. He said I couldn't go, we had just met."

"Lena, why do you always refer to your husband as Captain Smith? You've said it several times," Anna remarks.

"He told me to call him by his first name, Verval, but it doesn't sound respectful, so, I call him 'my husband, Captain Smith'," Lena replies quietly, seeking Anna's approval.

"You can call him anything you like and I will try to remember his name is Verval Smith, right?" Anna is amused by Lena's continued use of her husband's last name.

"Right, Captain Verval Lloyd Smith," Lena persists with an understanding smile. "For two weeks we saw each other every day, often for a picnic on the parade ground in front of Army headquarters where he worked. He proposed to me while we were eating a picnic lunch I had prepared at the Simpsons. I was holding a soft boiled egg in my hand when he asked to marry me; I squashed it and made a drippy mess in my hand. I couldn't speak, I think I nodded yes. I don't remember saying anything until after he kissed me, wiped the gooey egg and shell bits and pieces from my hand with his handkerchief and said, 'Let's go tell your family'."

Lena continues the story, "The Simpsons liked Captain Smith and were sad I would not be going to England with them. I miss the children, but I knew I loved him, he knew everything to be done for us to marry before he left China. After the Simpsons left for England, I shared an apartment with a girlfriend. We married early in the morning in the Russian Orthodox Church across the river in the Russian Concession.

"A Greek monk, Captain Smith met in Peking, married us. Mrs. Simpson helped select my wedding dress and veil before leaving for England. She insisted on paying for everything. The morning of the wedding my roommate left for work before I finished dressing and I could not zip my dress in the back. When the Captain arrived to take me to the church, I had to ask him to zip my dress. I was so embarrassed, but he joked about it, and everything was all right." Her shyness had not gone away.

"We went in a boat across the river to the Russian Concession with a Chinaman rowing us. The morning smoke (fog) was still on the water. Captain Smith arranged for witnesses, an American he worked with, and a Russian language teacher. Our rings were made from a gold piece the Captain gave to the people who make rings." Lena shows Anna her gold wedding band delicately engraved with orange blossoms.

"After the wedding we went back across the river, all in one boat, and then to the American Consulate to file the marriage papers. From the consulate we went to a wedding dinner, very nice, and to this new apartment my husband rented for us. He left the next day for America. "My girlfriends told me to forget about Captain Smith since he had left me behind. Some of them had been left behind by American soldiers. But, I knew he would send for me. He is a Christian man, Anna." Lena's blue eyes are moist, and she dabs them with a handkerchief. "I received a call from the American Consulate last week to come and begin my passport application. They gave me shots, took my photograph and fingerprints, and here is my American passport," she shows it to Anna. "I went to American Express and they already had my tickets. He has taken care of everything."

Three days later the young women tearfully part. Lena, now Helen Smith, boards a small steamer for the trip to Kobe, Japan, the first leg of her journey to America.

* * *

Dunia scans each edition of a German language newspaper, "Ostasiatische Lloyd," finding several job opportunities for hospital workers. The paper is among several delivered to the house including an American paper published in Shanghai. In November Dunia is hired as a nurse's aide.

Summer, 1934

The Yetchekov's house is aglow with lanterns and the street outside filled with a variety of foreign automobiles. Anna and Uncle Ivan are standing by the Victrola, talking about music being a common language among his guests. A broad spectrum of Shanghai's international community is at the party. Dunia approaches with a tall young man in tow. "Professor have you met Gustav Boucher? This is the first of your parties he has attended and I know he hasn't met Anna, he's already told me."

Ivan Yetchekov extends his hand and smiles. Boucher shakes Ivan's hand, his light blond hair parted down the middle bounces with each pump of the arm. He turns to Anna. "Your mother insisted I come to the party. Now I know why. Would you care to dance?" Anna smiles and curtsies, "If my mother was still living in Russia she would be a village match-maker. I will be delighted to dance with you, Gustav Boucher."

While they dance, Gustav laughingly explains the circumstances bringing him to the dance. Dunia and his Uncle Herman met recently and, after dining at the Boucher's home one evening, Dunia mentioned her daughter was about Gustav's age. The conversation then turned to when Gustav, or Gus as he is called by the family, could meet Frau Kulina's daughter. "And, here I am," Gus concludes. The music stops while Gus is talking. "Now, may I have the next dance, Miss Kulina?" he asks with a slight bow.

"One moment while I check my book," Anna replies with mock seriousness. Pausing a moment and looking into her empty palm, "It happens the next dance is free, Mr. Boucher." His laughter is genuine, "Not only are you the prettiest girl I've met in Shanghai, but the wittiest."

Dunia and Ivan Yetchekov watch the pair dance and as Gus laughs, Dunia nudges him and smiles. "He's having a good time," she puts her hand to her mouth and whispers, "and, he's from a good family."

As the evening passes Anna learns Gustav Boucher has lived most of his life in Shanghai. His step-mother is Japanese and father, German. Gus is an engineer at the Siemens plant and plays soccer and tennis. Anna recalls seeing him at a "fasching" party earlier in February. He was easy to see because of his height, blond hair, and not wearing a mask.

As the guests leave, Gus asks Anna for a date the following evening. Anna again consults her imaginary date book and looks up smiling, "Wouldn't you know, tomorrow is free!" Gus smiles, takes her by the arm and they join Dunia who is sipping punch with Sophia Yetchekov and Uncle Herman. "Frau Kulina your daughter has agreed to go out with me tomorrow. I hope you have no objections?"

"My, my, Gustav, you certainly move fast for a German," Dunia responds laughingly while looking at Uncle Herman. "I certainly would not object if your Uncle would move as fast," she adds, as Sophia joins in the laughter.

During the following months and into the spring of 1935, Anna meets other young men from England and America. Of the young men she meets, Gus is more settled, the right mixture of work and play, serious about life; a crime in Shanghai where most young, unmarried men find the temptation to play exceeds all other interests. A very special young man in Anna's eyes, Gus is sure of himself and protective of Anna when they date. While his salary at Siemens affords him many luxuries, he persists in working long hours to the chagrin of the other junior executives. In the Russian School of Manchuria Anna studied German and English. With a little help from Gus, she becomes fluent in German.

Gus likes tradition, although his family is not a traditional family. Herr Frederick Boucher II came to China during World War I with his wife and first born son, Gustav. His wife died shortly after arriving in Shanghai. Herr Frederick took a Japanese lady as his wife, and their home is a mixture of the two cultures including seven more children: Marta, Frederick III, Franz, the twins Akihito and Atoshi, Yoshi, and Klaus. Klaus, the youngest, is twelve years younger than Gustav and a Boy Scout in a troop sponsored by German-

Jews. The family attends Roman Catholic services and Gus wants to be married in his church. To Anna it seems everything they do is part of a plan working perfectly. Even the church's annulment of her marriage to Mikhail is handled simply.

Dunia and Sophia work out a very acceptable routine to avoid conflicts in the wedding preparations. Dunia handles the arrangements and Sophia handles Anna. At Dunia's insistence, Nina Tokma and Jenni (she now spells her name Jenny) arrive in Shanghai for a visit in time for Anna's wedding.

Chapter 9
Pre-War Shanghai

Shanghai
June 1935

Anna becomes Frau Anna Boucher in June 1935. Siemens provides the newlyweds a large, and freshly redecorated, apartment near the Garden Bridge and German consulate. It is northwest of Soochow Creek, but within walking distance of the Bund. They move into the apartment in time to celebrate Anna's twenty-third birthday. The apartment is so clean Anna has little to do but place her things in the wardrobes and chests. One touch Anna adds to the apartment is finding the right place for her family icon. She asks Gus to secure it to the wall and they both touch the risa, making the sign of the cross. Dunia and Herman present them with a samovar decorated in silver, and ten matching silver cups.

From their apartment balcony, Anna can watch a constant stream of ships on the Whangpoo River. Sunday afternoons, Gus and Anna frequently stroll along the Bund, sometimes boarding the giant cruise ships anchored near the bank.

Nina Tokma, visiting Dunia since the wedding, likes Shanghai, finds a job, and returns to Harbin to arrange shipment of her belongings to Shanghai. She enrolls Jenny in a boarding school for girls.

Spring-Summer 1937

Five years have passed since Japanese last attempted to exert their influence over Shanghai. In early 1937, the Japanese Navy in a blustering show of force move warships up the Whangpoo. Anticipating trouble, Gus has Anna apply for a German passport. Shanghai's German Embassy processes her application and on May 8, 1937, she receives her German passport. Many foreigners are taking long vacations to avoid clashes between the Chinese and Japanese troops fighting over Shanghai, leaving servants behind to protect possessions.

13 August 1937, the fight for Shanghai begins in deadly earnest. From the roof of their apartment building, Anna and Gus watch Japanese warships in the Whangpoo shell Chinese settlements in the Hongkew district. Flights of Japanese planes swoop low over Hongkew dropping bombs and firing machine guns. Gus and Anna join their neighbors to watch the action from their rooftop. It seems unreal, like a movie set with spectators.

Fall and Winter, 1937

Dunia decides she can afford an apartment of her own and, with help from Uncle Herman, locates an apartment convenient to the Yetchekovs. Not only is her hospital pay adequate, Peter sends money from Russia where he has found Nikolai in a Khabarovsk Prison. With a job in the city and a new wife, Peter visits Nikolai each week.

As winter returns to Shanghai, Gus takes Anna on a business trip to Germany. It is a bitter, cold winter. Snow is piled high along the tracks as they travel across the Soviet Union in state-owned and operated carriages of the Trans-Siberian Express. Anna notices very little difference in service provided by the Chinese and Soviet conductors; both are equally indifferent to the needs of the passengers. The new route of the Express avoids Samara, taking a shorter path to Moscow from Omsk. The trip to Germany and back takes two months including a month at the family home near Weimar. Weimar was once the capital of the Republic before it was moved to Berlin.

Anna meets relatives of Gus in a succession of teas, parties, and outings. The matriarch of the Boucher family, Oma Marguerithe Boucher, finds Anna's beauty and wit captivating. Gustav's parents arrive from China a week before Christmas; the large estate house outside Weimar gradually fills with family. On Christmas Day the Boucher family gathers in the reception hall, freshly decorated with bright, red holly berries surrounded by dark green pine boughs draped from the walls. The strong fragrance of fresh cut pine penetrates the house. Near the fireplace colorfully wrapped presents fill a corner of the room.

Herr Frederick, the oldest male heir, passes out gifts before they sit to Christmas Dinner.

After dinner they discuss the "western wall" Hitler is building, occupying land west of the Rhine taken from Germany after World War I. Oma Boucher is seated in her chair near the hearth of the fire place, a lap robe tucked loosely around her legs and feet. "Here, Anna," she says, motioning with her hand, "come sit, and let's talk." As the rest of the family watches the blue flames of the *Feuerzangenbowle* (literally a "fire bowl" where a flaming, rum or cognac soaked, cone of sugar is suspended by crossed swords over a heated punch bowl until the sugar is melted) and talk about the present, Oma and Anna, however, tell stories of the past. Oma tells Anna about the Kaiser and her son who never came home from the trenches of Verdun. Anna tells the frail, gray-haired octogenarian, of the Kulinas' flight from Samara to China in 1918.

Although Gus and Anna were eventually to make one more trip to Weimar, this is their last Christmas with Oma Marguerithe Boucher. The visit is over quickly, as they are to return to China in January.

Shanghai is overrunning with Japanese soldiers when they arrive, their first stop is to see Dunia and pick up Barhotka, a black and white Shih-Tzu Gus gave Anna on her twenty-fourth birthday. Dunia is anxious to hear about the trip and, with excuses to Gus, they talk in Russian, Anna sitting on the floor and playing with Barhotka. After the visit, they hurry to their apartment. The first thing Anna wants is a bath to clean away the accumulation of grime from over a week of traveling. Filling her hand-painted porcelain bathtub with steaming water and medicinal salts, she soaks for an hour. While she bathes, Gus takes Barhotka for a walk. Though Gus makes a top salary at Siemens, he doesn't want Chinese servants. Normally a house boy would walk the dogs and tend the small flower garden on their balcony. Gus likes to do these things himself. Having a house boy would be a loss of privacy, and house keeping their apartment is easy for Anna.

When Gus returns from his walk, he grinds coffee beans purchased in Germany, and makes a pot of coffee. Anna bundles up in a heavy robe and follows Gus out onto the balcony. The peaceful, winking lights of ships anchored on the dark Whangpoo belie the dangerous cargos of the Japanese warships. It is good to be back in our world, Anna thinks.

They try often to have children, but Anna cannot get pregnant. Gus insists she see the best 'woman' doctor in Shanghai, an Englishman. To his credit, Dr.

Kuentzler also recommends him. After thoroughly examining her, the doctor tells Anna the surgery following her miscarriage caused uncorrectable internal damage. She is unable to have children. When Gus comes home that evening, Anna tells him the doctor's findings. Anna's tears are not for herself, but for Gus, his disappointment is easily seen. It is important to Gus the family name continues. "We will see another doctor in Europe," he tells her.

* * *

Little, if anything, changes for foreigners living in Shanghai's international settlements during the first years of Japanese occupation. The concessions private security forces, lavish entertainment, and pompous affluence of foreigners, stay the same. Only the Chinese suffer, particularly those east of Hongkew Creek.

Oma Boucher, in her late 80's, dies in the spring of 1938 at the family home in Weimar. After the funeral Herr Frederick and Frau Boucher return to China. Klaus decides to stay in Germany to finish his studies.

* * *

Instead of a cruise to Europe in 1939, Anna and Gustav again take the Trans-Siberian Express. At Omsk they leave the express and travel on a local train across the Urals to Samara; not a fancy ride, and definitely not fast. Anna wants to revisit her birthplace. While stopping in Ufa, Anna recalls Nikolai's story about buying a fish from an old woman near the train station. She looks for anything reminding her of that visit 21 years ago. It is disappointing for Anna; nothing is the same as her childhood recollection.

Arriving in Samara, now called Kubiyshev (named for a Red Army general), they stay in a tourist hotel. Anna asks the desk clerk to direct them to the street called Alexandra. He doesn't recall the street name but points to an elderly gentleman sitting in the lobby, deep in a Vodka stupor, and wearing a much abused carriage driver's cap. "He might remember, he was a *droshky* driver," the clerk tells her. Even in his drunken stupor the old timer recalls the street once known as Alexandra and tells them where to look. It has been renamed and paved. The house is no longer there. Apartment buildings line the street. Anna photographs the street with her box camera purchased in

Shanghai. It is not a particularly pretty street to photograph, but Dunia will find it interesting.

The city is large, but with fewer trees than Anna remembers. It is a major industrial center on the Volga and the need for hydro-electric power has brought about the construction of a dam upstream from Kubiyshev where the river cuts through the Zhigulev Hills. Boarding a cruise boat with cabins, they continue down the Volga to the Caspian Sea and Baku where they have a decent meal. Spending an extra day sunning on the Azerbaijan beaches, the sunburned Bouchers eventually board a train taking them through Armenia to the Black Sea.

In Turkey they board the Orient Express to Austria. Stopping for a few days in Vienna, Anna meets more of Gus' family. There, she also visits a Viennese gynecologist, is examined and hears the diagnosis she cannot have children reaffirmed. From there, a disconsolate Gustav and Anna take a less luxurious train to Weimar which stops at many stations along the way.

As their taxi enters the estate, Gustav comments about the grounds being neglected and the house seems empty of life. When the taxi stops, Klaus rushes past slow-paced Uncle Harry to greet them. Klaus is eager to return to China since Uncle Harry has assumed duties as overseer of the estate. The German Army is taking all unmarried men his age and he has made arrangements to return with them. Weimar is beautiful in the summer of 1939. During the warm, sunny days they ride horses in the hills north of the city and take leisurely drives in the family Mercedes touring car. Gustav appears to have forgotten the disappointment of Vienna; and Anna finds the German summer relaxing.

Leaving Weimar early in the morning, August 29, Klaus drives the touring car with Uncle Harry giving him directions and driving instructions. "You have lead in the foot. Slow down! Turn here. Follow the road signs." Leipzig is their departure point, taking a train for Warsaw, Moscow and then, by the Trans-Siberian Railway, back to China.

The Mercedes is a comfortable and powerful car. Klaus drives skillfully, but very fast. Anna begins to think it is a mistake to let him drive. Uncle Harry, who is sitting beside him in the front seat, fidgets and flinches, and between Weissenfels and Leipzig, the car overheats. Klaus is forced to slow down. Stopping in the village of Lützen for repairs, they limp into Leipzig with a sputtering engine and relieved passengers. (*Karl Meissner owned the only repair shop in Lützen.*)

At Leipzig Bahnhof they are informed tourists traveling through Poland for destinations in Russia or China are being rerouted. The Polish Army is causing problems, according to a police official at the ticketing office. The ticket agent arranges their return to China by way of Scandinavia. Saying farewell to Uncle Harry at the ticket kiosk, they have only a short wait until boarding a train to Berlin. There, they receive confirmation for the remainder of their route through Denmark, Sweden and Finland, to arrive in Moscow a week later than planned.

In Stockholm two days later, newspaper stories tell of Germany invading Poland. The invasion began the first day of September, about the time the Boucher's would have been in Warsaw had they not been rerouted. The return to China passes quickly, Klaus asks questions about everything he sees in the Soviet Union. Anna teaches him to pronounce Russian names and words to use with the conductors. Klaus learns fast and teaches Anna some new German phrases.

While Gus and Anna stop in Peking to visit friends, Klaus continues to Shanghai. Klaus wanted to see Peking, but Papa Boucher already has him a position with a German export firm in Shanghai starting immediately.

Fall and Winter, 1939

Gus buries himself in work at the Siemens office while Anna spends more time visiting with friends from Harbin, including the newly-wed Nina Tokma Wilson and Jenny. Nina's marriage to a British sea captain during the summer was a happy event. She frequently accompanies her new husband on his merchant ship as it plies the Western Pacific trade routes from Japan to Australia. As the Captain's wife she is allowed to go along.

Jenny attends a boarding school for girls allowing Nina and her new husband to travel. When Nina is in Shanghai, she terrorizes the rickshaw and taxi drivers, with her husband's green, 1936 Studebaker "President" sedan, maneuvering through the streets with intimidating speed. The four-door car has spoke rims on the wheels and a high hood line caused in part by the radiator-style grill. Nina must sit on pillows (a minimum of two) to see over the dashboard and steering wheel, giving the appearance of a vehicle operating *sans* driver.

Outwardly, nothing appears wrong between Gus and Anna. However, Gus talks privately with Anna about having an heir, eventually asking her if she would agree to a divorce. "It is a matter we must resolve," he says. She agrees and Gus takes a job with Siemens in Tientsin. Anna stays in their Shanghai apartment for the winter. In the spring, Gus tells Anna he has met a Japanese lady he wants to marry. Anna allows Gus to handle the divorce papers and receives a stipend each month adequately covering her expenses. Following the divorce, Anna and Barhotka move into Dunia's apartment.

Chapter 10
The War Years

Summer, 1940

The Bouchers offer Anna a room in the family compound. She declines but attends family celebrations, even when Gus visits from Tientsin. Eventually the closeness of living in Dunia's small apartment is overwhelming and she succumbs to the Boucher's offer. Her room opens out into a central courtyard, easy access for Barhotka. The courtyard is paved with stones and kept spotless by the houseboys "in their blue smocks and pigtails." The icon has a new resting place.

Klaus, an eligible bachelor, finds his former sister-in-law irresistible, looks for excuses being with her, and insists on sitting by her at the family table. They go out to dinner occasionally, but when the conversation turns dating Anna tells him to find himself a girl and get married. Klaus' response is, "No, I must stay here and take care of you." He is very attentive. Several times during May and June Klaus suggests they marry. "There is too much difference in our ages," she tells him. "I enjoy being with you, you're like a brother, but, in time I will look older and you will still be young. It is not a good idea." Despite Klaus' devotion, nothing changes Anna's mind and divides her time between visits with her mother and the Boucher household.

Winter, 1941-42

Anna's idyllic life in the international settlements is interrupted 8 December 1941 when Japanese shell a British Navy vessel anchored in the mouth of the Yangtze and news reaches Shanghai of the attack on Pearl Harbor. World War II brings a succession of harsh changes to Shanghai's international residents. Japanese are placed in charge of several large businesses, including the banks. Klaus keeps his job in the export firm's accounting department, and Anna's German passport, though frequently checked by Japanese police, draws a courteous apology. Items are now rationed, including gasoline. Nina's Studebaker is frequently without gas, though a black-market source is available; but the cost and risk of dealing with the black-market are greater than any luxury the car affords.

Klaus' concern for Anna's safety is paramount as Japanese paranoia about Caucasians brings new restrictions on foreign residents. He finally convinces Anna their age difference is not important to him, telling her, "Anna, it is you I love, you will learn to love me, wait and see." For Anna, it is a marriage of convenience. Klaus, 22, and Anna, 29, are married 4 January 1942 in a ceremony attended by those members of the Boucher family still in Shanghai. Dunia and the Yetchekovs, holding Russian passports, do not attend the Japanese officiated civil ceremony, but do attend the reception held in the Boucher compound.

Nina T. Wilson and Jenny attend the reception, leaving the large Studebaker at home and arriving in a less conspicuous rickshaw. Nina has a bad cold, but tells Anna all will be better when they can leave Shanghai. Her merchant captain husband has arranged passage for Nina and Jenny on a neutral ship operating along the Asian coast. The ship will take them to Singapore, the last remaining British stronghold in the far-east, and his current home port.

The newlyweds take a honeymoon trip to Japan, despite the war. "We will be there in time to see the blossoming of the cherry trees," Anna tells her friends. Their departure on a Japanese passenger ship is hurried. Nina smiles at Anna's enthusiasm. "We wish you health and happiness! And, we will write from Singapore. You must write us from Kyoto!"

A week later Nina is hospitalized with pneumonia, two days before her ship to safety is to depart Shanghai. Unable to leave the hospital, Nina and Jenny are left behind. When Nina is released from the hospital in March, Singapore has fallen to the Japanese. It is too late to join her husband. Russian-born with British passports, Nina and Jenny are marooned in Shanghai. A philosophical Nina tells her friends, "If you must be stuck some place in a war, there are worse places than Shanghai!"

After visiting Klaus' Japanese family, the honeymooners return to Yokohama the weekend before their departure to do some sightseeing. Their ship is scheduled to sail for Shanghai Monday, April 13, but a mechanical problem delays their departure a few days. When they arrive in Shanghai, everyone is talking of the bombing raid on Yokohama and other cities in Japan. A flight of American B-25 bombers bombed Tokyo, Kobe, Nagoya and Yokohama, April 18, their departure was timely. Bombers not shot down over Japan continued their flight into China.

Renting a new apartment in the International Settlement, north of Soochow Creek and not far from Nina T. Wilson's apartment, Anna and Klaus quickly settle into married life. The apartment was formerly occupied by Americans who left behind most of their furniture and other items too heavy and cumbersome to carry. Anna finds an appropriate place for the Donesyvna icon. A chest full of musical recordings left behind are a rare treasure for Anna, and she spends many hours playing the records on a Victrola Klaus has given her.

Fall and Winter, 1942-43

The Soviet-Japanese non-aggression pact allows Russians the option to stay in China for the duration of the war, or return to the Soviet Union. The Yetchekovs manage to enter Hong Kong at the end of the typhoon season where he finds employment teaching at the Crown Academy. Dunia gives up on Uncle Herman and decides the Soviet Union will be better than life under Japanese rule in China. Nina T. Wilson, Anna, and Jenny are dockside as Dunia boards a coastal steamer anchored in the Whangpoo. The trio stand on the Bund and wave as the small vessel turns in the current and slowly drifts downstream.

Arriving in Vladivostok several days later, Dunia takes a train to Khabarovsk and is met by Peter, his wife and Dunia's first grandson. Peter's news is bad. Nikolai has been moved and Peter cannot locate him. Winter has arrived and daylight hours are short, but Dunia uses the few daylight hours to visit the prison daily for a week. "We have no record of your husband, Nikolai Kulina," the authorities say repeatedly.

In Shanghai, foreigners are forced to register with the Japanese police. Those with passports from the allied nations will be interned. To insult and identify those to be interned, they must wear an armband with a letter sewn to it representing their nationality. Nina T. Wilson and Jenny are given red armbands by the British consulate with the letter "B" emblazoned.

* * *

Nina and Jenny meet with the British Relief Agency Monday, 11 January 1943, and receive instructions on what to bring and where to meet for their journey to internment. Isolated from friends who fear the Japanese, their only social contact is with British residents of the International Settlement. Even their neutral Jewish friends have begun to boycott American, British and Dutch residents of Shanghai. Anna discovers the plan to relocate Nina and Jenny and tells Klaus she is going to accompany them to the dock when they leave. Not wise he says, but realizing Anna's loyalty to her friends, agrees to go with her.

Two days later, with provisions they have been instructed to bring, they are surprised to find Anna and Klaus at their door to see them off. Arriving at the dock on Soochow Creek, a large group of British women and children are mustered there, British men were taken earlier to internment camps in the interior and haven't been heard from since. Japanese soldiers stop them as they approach, checking names and passports. Klaus and Anna are told they can go no further. After a tearful farewell they watch as Nina and Jenny are escorted to one of the boats tied up along the creek. A Japanese soldier escorting them appears helpful. Klaus and Anna wave good-by as the boat slowly moves out into the center of Soochow Creek and drifts toward the river. A small gasoline engine sputters to life and steers the boat along its way.

* * *

On board the boat, Nina and Jenny are confined to the main deck with 40 other women and children; the Japanese soldier who escorted them to the boat is an interpreter. He looks thin and weak, dropping his rifle while helping Nina move her packages out of the walkway. Smiling faintly as he picks up his rifle and swings it over his shoulder, Private Seichi Sakamoto apologizes for his clumsiness using very good English.

The fall of 1942 is particularly difficult for 25-year-old Japanese-American, Seichi Sakamoto. A seminary student in Tokyo, and naturalized American citizen, he is ordered to report to the registration office in Hiroshima, his birthplace, and be inducted by the Japanese Army.

To the Japanese government, he was Japanese and into the army he went. From Hiroshima, Seichi and a shipload of recruits sailed across the East China Sea into the mouth of the Yangtze River, then up the Whangpoo to Shanghai, arriving in November. Docking alongside the Bund, the recruits were fed and marched off the ship through the streets of the city to South Railway Station. They stopped several times along the roadside for tea (the Japanese army provided these tea stops because public water supplies in China were contaminated).

Seichi learns the Japanese phrase for "Don't drink the water" a day late. The gut-churning dysentery he suffers from drinking bad water puts him in the hospital for two weeks. Struggling to regain his health, as well as understanding instructions and orders barked in Japanese, Seichi falters in all phases of training. The camp commander decides to use Seichi as an interpreter. His first assignments is to accompany British and Americans to internment camps north of Shanghai, and one particularly located along the Grand Canal near Yangzhou.

Thanking him for his help in Russian, Nina turns away to find a place to sit.

He asks, "How many languages do you speak?" Taken by surprise, Nina at first will not answer. Jenny seeing her mother's confusion responds, "We speak Russian and English at home, mama also speaks some Chinese and German." Then with childish curiosity she asks, "How did you learn to speak English?"

"I lived in America and went to school there," he replies amused by her interest. During the three day voyage they are transferred to a small steamer on the Yellow River. Nina and Jenny have many conversations with Private Sakamoto deciding his story of being a missionary from Texas is too strange not to be true. Nina is suspicious; perhaps he is spying on their conversation with other internees. On the second day of their journey Nina tells Private Sakamoto she is Russian. That sparks immediate interest from Seichi whose next assignment will be in Harbin to study Russian. As he tells Nina about his future assignment, she becomes excited at the prospect of telling her Russian friends in Harbin where she will be interned and asks if he will relay messages through the Russian Orthodox Church. He agrees and Nina has one more request, "Will you tell my friends in Shanghai where I am?" He writes the address and says he will try.

Turning north on the Grand Canal, the boat moves slowly along the crowded waterway until reaching an American convent recently abandoned. A reception committee of Japanese soldiers meets them. They are told to carry their belongings into the convent. As Nina and Jenny leave the steamer, Seichi is standing at the gangway. "I will pray for you," he tells them.

Inside they are ushered to a bare, second floor room 20 feet by 40 feet, and told to become comfortable, for this is to be their new home. Except for exercise time in the convent yard, the women and children eat, sleep, bathe, and use the toilet in the same second floor room of the convent for the next two years. There is no privacy and, although it is difficult for Nina and Jenny, it absolutely crushes most of the proud English ladies to relinquish their privacy.

Duties are allocated to everyone in the compound, cleaning, cooking, and emptying the chamber pots. Nina cooks the first meal and is given a leg of pork and a bag of rice to prepare for 40 women. She cuts the meat into small pieces and puts it in a pot of boiling water. Using some condiments and vegetables she brought from Shanghai, Nina makes a stew and fixes a pot of rice. In typical British fashion, the women form a queue to receive their first meal, a ladle of stew, and a ladle of rice.

In the evenings, when chores are done, Nina and Jenny sit by a window overlooking the Grand Canal and watch the houseboats and sampans moving slowly along. Occasionally a lantern on board reveals a family gathered around a small cooking fire, eating their evening meal. Such scenes of family closeness she has never experienced, brings tears to Jenny's eyes. Each morning they are given a cup of hot water. Most of the women have brought tea from Shanghai. They savor the taste, knowing their supply of tea will soon run out.

Nina and Jenny receive Red Cross parcels of food and toiletries regularly the first year. Later, the parcels are delayed in Shanghai for as much as three months; then, no parcels at all.

* * *

Meanwhile, in Shanghai, Private Seichi Sakamoto finds Anna and Klaus living at 42 Prinz Heinrich Platz, and delivers the message from Nina while standing shyly in their doorway. He notices the icon and asks, "Are you Christian?" They respond, "We are Catholic!" He smiles, makes a slight bow, declines an invitation to have tea with them and departs. Anna and Klaus look at each other, "What an odd question," Klaus remarks. "What a strange young man," Anna replies.

They lead very normal lives as newlyweds, traveling and entertaining. German citizens are not hit as hard by rationing as other refugees from the war. They can even get gasoline from the Japanese, although they do not own a car. Klaus moves up in the export firm. Throughout Shanghai, most of the supervisory and management jobs are filled by Japanese, except within the German and Italian owned firms.

Anna frequently takes a rickshaw to Roy Roofgarden Restaurant, joining Dr. Kuentzler for tea. Since May 1943, all stateless Jews have been quartered in Hongkew. A German Jew, thus considered stateless, Dr. Kuentzler continues to practice medicine in a free clinic for the residents of Hongkew and occasionally sees some of her wealthy non-Jewish patients professionally.

During a visit in the spring of 1944, Anna mentions she has a frequent tooth ache and must find a dentist soon. Dr. Kuentzler takes her down the hall and introduces Anna to a Russian-speaking Jewess and dentist, Raya Rachlin, living in a Hongkew dormitory and working in the clinic. She studied dentistry in Germany and Austria and, in 1939, escaped Nazi internment through Latvia traveling across Russia to Japan, and then to Shanghai. Even in Hongkew's meager clinic, she has many patients from outside the district.

The two Russian-speaking expatriates, Anna and Raya, are unalike in temperament and appearance. Anna is small, quiet and unassuming, and Raya is large, robust, and outspoken. Raya's dental equipment is adequate, but the clinic is woefully short of anesthetics to reduce pain. To her credit, Raya works fast and is through with most patients before they faint. Anna is thankful only one tooth needed attention. Raya greets and leaves her patients with one word, "Shalom," Anna learns the word means "peace" and the proper response is "Shalom." It is both a greeting and farewell.

Anna's social associations are watched very closely and she is told to limit social contacts to only Japanese, Italians and non-Jewish Germans. As Klaus frequently warns her, the Japanese are extremely paranoid about the international mix of light-complexioned people in Shanghai. They suspect all Caucasians, even their allies, of being potential enemies.

As the war continues, even privileged Germans have difficulty getting delicacies, or petrol for their cars. The enclave of Jews in Hongkew is severely restricted and must have a pass to leave the district. Being a mixed household, the Bouchers are fortunate to have access to all rationed items. Anna is tempted to share rationed items with her Jewish friends, but Klaus' sister admonishes her, "Don't do it! If the Japanese find out they will cut off the entire family."

American bombers make frequent raids on Shanghai's military port facilities during July 1945. Anna is frightened by the thundering bombs falling in streams from the high-flying bombers, barely visible through the humid haze enveloping Shanghai. A frightened Barhotka escapes and is never found. Within a month the war ends for many Shanghai residents, and a strange transition begins. The exodus of Jews from Hongkew begins immediately. Dr. Kuentzler is on her way to America, while Raya Rachlin finds work in an American dental clinic. Her association there with a military dentist was fortunate. Through his help she was able to immigrate to the United States.

Harbin,
September, 1945

Seichi Sakamoto, still a private and Russian language translator, is in Harbin when the war ends. Entering Harbin quickly as the Japanese surrender, the Russians take thousands of Japanese prisoners of war, and intern them in Russian work camps. Seichi tries to convince the Japanese-speaking Russian Interrogator he is an American, but the Russian doesn't buy his story. He does keep him in Harbin to help translate while they dismantle the railway repair center and accompany the parts to Russia. There he and other POWs reassemble the equipment in Khabarovsk.

In 1946, Seichi is sent to a work camp west of Khabarovsk. Many of the Japanese POWs cannot exist on the diet of lard, stale bread and water and are buried in shallow, unmarked Siberian graves. Others fall at remote work sites and their frozen bodies become part of the tundra. Seichi survives.

While clearing a roadway in the forest he watches a swarm of bees and follows them back to their hive in a dead tree. Ignoring their stings, he gorges himself on honey. Before leaving the area he fills his drinking cup with honey taking it back to camp and sharing it with some of the weaker prisoners. For two days he continues to work in the area and returns each evening with honey to share. The third day after his find, the crew is moved to another location. In five years of imprisonment, the honey was Seichi's only supplement to his diet.

Understanding the Russian language has advantages and disadvantages. He knows the prison gossip from listening to the guards and gets to know some of the Russian prisoners. Sometimes he hears details of torture and death he would rather not hear. In 1949, Seichi and a tall Russian prisoner escape while working on a railroad track leading to a missile site. A week later and within a short walk of their destination, Nakhodka, a seaport northeast of Vladivostok, Seichi and Nikolai, his Russian compatriot, are captured and thrown into a nearby jail. The lice in the cell immediately jump on Seichi. Nikolai is not bothered by the lice. "We smell different," he tells Seichi. They are returned to Khabarovsk Prison and Seichi never sees Nikolai again.

Seichi is placed in solitary confinement for six months and in April 1950, is told he will be moved to another prison. Over hearing prison gossip, there he will be put to death. Fortunately a release program worked out between Japanese and Soviet governments goes into effect during Seichi's transfer. Seichi and other condemned Japanese prisoners are needed to fill the quota. Boarding a train in Khabarovsk, they travel to Nakhodka then board a ship sailing to a Japanese port on Western Honshu. When Japanese officials at the port release Seichi, he makes his way to Tokyo, anxious to tell his story to authorities.

At American Forces headquarters in Tokyo, he is instructed to talk to the intelligence staff on the fourth floor. There are no "coincidences", entering the elevator wearing a civilian repatriation suit he faces a young American soldier, who looks Japanese. The name tag on the soldiers pocket reads "Sako." It is his younger brother, now a sergeant in the United States Army, and assigned to the US Forces Headquarters in Tokyo. His family shortened the name during WWII.

After an emotional reunion, his brother accompanies him to the Intelligence office where for several hours Seichi describes with remarkable clarity, and precise directions, railway construction to strategic sites northeast of Khabarovsk and the approximate location of missile launch facilities.

Seichi recuperates at the missionary school where he was studying before the war. In September, 1950, he is inducted into the U. S. Air Force, getting the long-awaited commission in the Reserves from 1938, and boards a C-118 at Tachikawa Air Base for his trip home to the United States.

Shanghai,
Fall, 1945

Japanese military and civilians in China are returned to Japan through the Port of Shanghai. Papa Boucher moves the family to Japan along with many other mixed race families fleeing Chinese retribution. Klaus and Anna stay behind. As Klaus explains to his father, "I am neither Japanese, nor German. In my heart I was born here in China, in an international settlement. I feel like I'm an international citizen who happens to have a German passport. I'm not leaving China!"

Internees begin to return to Shanghai looking for their former dwellings and searching for property left behind. Nina Tokma-Wilson and Jenny come home to find their apartment much as they left it. The priests have protected the apartment and their personal items with great care. The following day, Nina contacts the British mission for news about her husband. Harry's ship was torpedoed by the Japanese in the South China Sea. There were no survivors. A settlement from her husband's estate provides funds allowing Nina and Jenny to live comfortably in Shanghai.

Anna hears of Nina's return and hurries to visit, hardly recognizing her as she opens the apartment door. Nina has lost more than twenty pounds while interned and was small before she left Shanghai. Her cheek bones rise sharply above pale and sunken cheeks. Her hands are rough and calloused from work at the convent as she struggled to grow vegetables in a small garden plot she worked by hand. Anna cries with relief, hugging the frail shoulders of her friend.

"What did they do to you?" she asks, holding Nina at arm's length and looking for a spark of the old Nina in this shell of a woman. Nina's eyes brighten at Anna's concern and she takes her by the arm, pulling her into the sitting room. "You don't need to know, Anna, and besides, it's over. We survived, and it looks like you did too!" Nina's voice has rustiness not there when she left Shanghai. "Jenny, your Aunty Anna is here," she calls out.

A tall, willowy, and attractive Jenny enters the room, her hair an awkward length from keeping it short for the two and a half years they were interned.

"How could you become so beautiful and grown up?" Anna asks. "I'm nearly 20-years-old, Aunty Anna. Mother made me exercise every day, and gave me some of her food," Jenny replies, her strong and self-assured voice pronounces the words in the stilted British English spoken daily during internment. "You look as pretty as I remembered, Mother often talked about you and Aunty Dunia in the evenings."

"And we thought of you, but there was little we could do. We knew where you were, a Japanese soldier appeared at our doorway one day and told us," Anna assures them. "Did your car survive the war?"

"The Japanese took it out of the garage where it was hidden and towed it away," Nina explains. "The priest told them it belonged to the church, as if any of the priests could drive. The soldiers took it anyway; it was on its last legs, but I sure enjoyed the old beast! Did you ever see it around the city while we were gone?"

"I don't think so," Anna replies. "I'm sure I would have recognized it," trying to recall vehicles she had seen the Japanese driving.

Anna and Klaus have an awkward and slightly diminished status in the newly reestablished business and social structure. German and Japanese-owned businesses are closed and reopened, often within days, under new names and new management. Some old employees are retained. Klaus is hired by the Chinese-American owner of a Sino-American import/export company doing business out of his old office.

In war-torn Shanghai romance can still blossom, Jenny Tokma meets an American naval officer assigned to the U.S. Consulate and becomes engaged. Navy Lieutenant Mark McMartin pulls strings to get approval for their marriage before his tour in Shanghai is over. Jenny and Mac, as he prefers to be called, are married September 17, 1947 in a civil ceremony and, later, in a church ceremony. The 21-year-old bride and her Mississippi-born husband leave the following week for the United States. A year later, after a tearful farewell with Anna, Nina T. Wilson sails from Shanghai to visit Jenny at a Connecticut Navy base. Nina's first granddaughter is born during her visit.

Summer, 1949

The San Francisco office of the company Klaus works for asks him to come there to work. Unable to get a visa from the American consulate since he falls under the German quota, Klaus and Anna decide in 1949 to leave China, return to Germany and apply. Klaus stays with the Shanghai office until they close their doors in March. Adding to the couple's plight, the Boucher family estate has been confiscated and reallocated in the East German land reform. Their return to Germany is complicated by division of the country.

Street fights between Chiang's remaining forces and communist cells keep residents of the settlements indoors at night. Dunia's letters take months to arrive. Her latest letter from Khabarovsk tells of plans to return to Samara (Kubiyshev) and her hopes someday Nikolai will return. Peter travels and Dunia dislikes staying with her daughter-in-law without someone to mediate their differences. Anna writes of their plan to return to Germany and promises to write when they have an address.

On their last evening in Shanghai, Anna prepares dinner while Klaus checks documents they need, their luggage, and systematically goes through the apartment looking at the furniture and clothing they will leave behind. They have sold the silver Samovar set, a wedding gift too bulky to carry. Despite Klaus' objection, Anna's icon is packed. family tradition is hard to break. The next day as their train departs North Station, remnants of Chiang's army are erecting barricades near the station, preparing to fight for Shanghai.

Chapter 11
Return to Germany

May 1949

The trip to Hong Kong is a nightmare. Constantly harassed by Nationalist soldiers and Chinese civilians who want their space on the train, they eventually arrive in Hong Kong on a train crowded with refugees. Holding German passports, they are not allowed to stay in the Crown Colony. Police escort them to a boat bound for Macao. They are unable to contact the Yetchekovs. Anna notices Klaus sweating profusely, and turning pale. His normally dark complexion is now white, and clammy. Klaus grips the boat rail with white knuckle intensity.

"Are you feeling sick, *liebchen*?"

"I think it's a fever. Sometimes I'm hot, and suddenly a chill runs through me."

"When we reach Macao, we'll see a doctor. You can't get sick on me now. We're so close to leaving."

"Don't worry Anna, I'll be all right," he responds, "but, right now I feel like I'm going to die!"

Clearing with Portuguese authorities at Macao, Anna arranges for a taxi to take them and their baggage to a doctor's office. The doctor suspects it is a tropical fever brought on by something he drank, or ate, during the trip. Prescribing a powder to be dissolved in water and taken twice a day, the doctor collects his fee and sends them on their way.

The taxi driver takes Anna, Klaus, baggage, and the family icon to the Bela Vista Hotel. Anna checks them in and helps her weakened husband to their room. The hum of an overhead fan blends with a chorus of night sounds, drifting through loosely closed, louvered shutters on the open window. The sounds are so different from the noisy, frantic crowds filling the streets during their last days in Shanghai.

The following day Anna begins to search for a way to reach Europe and Germany. Airlines and trains are out of the question. Passage on a ship is their only recourse and she finds passenger ships too expensive. However, cargo ships sail from Macao's port to Europe. She finds one leaving for Naples with a cabin for passengers.

Anna cannot sleep. They desperately need money to return to Germany, and Klaus could only draw a small advance from his company to get them as far as Macao. All Anna has of value is the amethyst necklace from her marriage to Mikhail, a diamond wedding ring from Klaus, and a gold American coin given to her many years ago by a Czechoslovakian officer. And, yes, there is the Donesyvna family icon which supposedly will bring good fortune. Collectively these items may be worth a few hundred dollars, not enough for their passage.

On the other hand, Voskovich Construction Company has prospered in postwar Australia. There is no other choice but to write him, she reasons. Having Mikhail's address is pure chance. Kahtia, Anna's girl friend from Manzhouli and Harbin, visited Australia in 1940. At a party given by her Russian host, Kahtia met Sasha Voskovich. The meeting was cordial, but nothing more. Before leaving Sydney, she got the address of the Voskovich Construction Company. Kahtia gave the address to Anna during one of their parties in Shanghai during 1941. "Since you're divorced, you may want to look him up. He's filthy rich and from what Sasha tells me, not very happy with his Australian wife." She had kept the address tucked away.

Stationary lettered "Bela Vista Hotel, Rua do Commendador Kou Ho Neng, Macao, Telefon 3821," a quill pen, and ink well are on a worn, but highly polished, desk. Years ago in Shanghai, Anna vowed never, never again to see or speak to Mikhail Voskovich. Here, 16 years later, on a steamy July night in a second-class Portuguese hotel, such resolve seems a lifetime ago and very ridiculous. The thought of returning to China when their temporary visas expire is disturbing. 'Sweet husband, you must not know of this letter,' Anna thinks, as she watches Klaus asleep in the dim light of the room. He lies on the bed curled up, facing away from the desk lamp, accustomed to her late night reading habits. A book is open on the desk within easy reach if he awakens.

Turning to the desk, dipping the pen in rich black ink and adjusting the stationary, Anna begins to write:

Dear Mikhail Voskovich,

Kahtia gave me your address several years ago. I have not heard from her since she returned to Russia, but then we have been traveling ourselves. She told me of your marriage and how successful you have been in the construction business. Congratulations! Are Nikki and Sasha still with you? If they are, you must tell them I wish them very good health. You may have heard I married a German businessman, Klaus Boucher. His firm has been forced from Shanghai by the Communists. Events have left us without funds to return to Germany and start anew. Company offices in Macao are closed and we need money for passage.

I have mentally exhausted all possibilities and there is no one I can turn to except to you. Believe me, I would not ask if it were only for me. Klaus has been a good and kind husband, protecting me through the war, accepting me as a woman who cannot have children and bringing me years of happiness. Now this is very difficult for me, asking you for money after years of bitterness between us. But, it is the result of understanding oneself better. I have forgiven you for what happened in Shanghai. Going to Australia with you was too much for me to consider at the time.

If you send money I will repay you as quickly as possible upon arriving in Germany. The passage to Europe grows more expensive each day. Many people want to leave here. There is a ship leaving for Naples in a fortnight. The captain will accommodate us for $2,000 (Australian). I need to stress our tourist visas expire in ten days and we will be sent back to China unless passage has been arranged.

I ask you to help, Mikhail. If you wire the money, please instruct the hotel to hold it privately, for my personal receipt. Klaus must not know.

Anna

Pulling an envelope from the desk drawer and addressing it, Anna carefully folds and inserts the letter. Tiptoeing over to the bed Anna checks to see if Klaus is still sleeping. His breathing is light and regular. Anna looks in the mirror and straightens her dress before slipping out the door into the wide, cool and dimly lit hallway. Clutching the letter tightly, she hurries down the hall.

A small Chinese gentleman at the desk peers over his gold-rimmed glasses at Anna, who has crossed the lobby and now stands impatiently before him. His look tells Anna she is interrupting his work. Anna ignores the look and hands him the letter, asking, "Can you post this letter for me as soon as possible?" He nods indicating he can. Glances at the address and lays it aside.

Anxiety gets the better of her. Anna asks, "How long will it take for the letter to get to Australia?" Anna gets a look saying 'how should I know,' and he shrugs his shoulders. "Do you understand German?" This time Anna gets a grunt from the reluctant deskman sounding like, "Ja."

"Is there a fast mail service to Australia?" Anna knows there is some way to get information from this man. Deskmen appear to know everything or nothing. Anna suspects this one knows everything, but wants privacy to do his bookkeeping at this late hour. Her persistence pays off.

"Madam," he says in perfect German, "if you want this letter to get to Australia any time soon, you must take it to the Australian Embassy. They have a courier service and will occasionally take personal mail."

"I am desperate! This letter must be delivered before the week is out. Is there any way you could help me get it in the embassy's courier service? I don't know the location of the embassy, and I don't know anyone at the embassy." The words roll out in a torrent of frustration. "I'm afraid they will not accept the letter from me, having a German passport. Can you help me, please? I will pay whatever you ask if only you'll help." Her eyes are brimming with tears, ready to unleash in a torrent as the stress of her worries is about to explode.

Adjusting rectangular, narrow lens glasses, he looks at Anna as if he sees right through her. There is something about his stare discomforting to Anna. She intuitively believes he will help her. "You are Frau Boucher, yes?" he asks, tapping the desk with his thin, bony fingers. There aren't many Germans left in Macao and the Bouchers are the only ones in the hotel. Anna nods, not trusting her voice. "I will see what I can do. You come here tomorrow night at this time and I will tell you if the letter is dispatched."

Wiping her eyes and attempting to smile, Anna tells him she will pay tomorrow. He smiles a half smile and nods as she turns to leave. Anna has dried her eyes by the time she returns to the room and eases the door open.

Klaus is still sleeping soundly as Anna turns out the desk lamp, undresses and joins him in bed. The sheets are cool and the room is now very cool. Getting back out of bed, Anna turns off the overhead fan and its grinding noise. Back in bed, Klaus turns and puts his arm over her as she lies facing him. Anna places her palm on his forehead and runs her fingers through his thick wavy hair. Caressing the back of his head with her hand she gently presses her lips to his. "Oh God, help us leave this place safely," Anna murmurs in prayer. Now she feels she can sleep.

The next night Klaus is some better but takes his powdered medicine and falls asleep quite early. Anna waits until she is sure Klaus is asleep then leaves the room with her purse in hand to pay the deskman. The deskman is friendlier as she approaches, smiles and greets her. "Good evening, Frau Boucher."

"Good evening," she responds, "I've come to pay you for posting my letter. Were you successful?"

"Of course, I arranged to have it sent in the courier pouch at some personal expense and with the promise of a favor. Your letter should arrive in Australia within three days." Anna's relief is readily apparent. "Thank you so very much. How can I repay you?" Looking around the lobby to see if anyone can overhear their conversation the deskman leans forward and says, "Perhaps you can repay me with a small favor, Frau Boucher. The gentleman who helped me get your letter in the pouch requested an opportunity to meet you. Would it be possible?"

"Here in the hotel?" she asks suspiciously.

"It might be awkward for you, Frau Boucher. He suggests an exclusive dining club. I can accompany you and make the introduction if you like." The deskman's smile is both disarming and uncomfortably insincere. Anna wants to thank the man but is leery about the arrangement. "I must be with my husband in his sickness. Perhaps when he has recovered this can be done," she replies with a forced, friendly smile. "But, I insist you take something for your service." She digs into her purse and from a small roll of Chinese Yuan notes extracts a bill and hands it to him.

Anna can tell from the look in his eyes her reluctance to meet his friend was unexpected. "My friend has much money," the deskman tells Anna. "He could arrange your passage to Germany if he enjoyed your company, Frau Boucher."

"You read my letter?" she asks with a gasp of surprise.

"Most certainly Frau Boucher, I could not ask my friend to put something in the courier pouch without knowing its contents." Anna's stunned silence prompts the deskman to continue. "My friend is patient and will consider his service to you complete if you do not wish to meet him. If, however, you change your mind, or if the money you have requested from Australia doesn't arrive, remember what I've said." Anna nods and is relieved when another hotel resident walks up wanting the deskman's assistance. She turns and walks slowly back to her room.

Several days go by and gradually Klaus shakes the fever immobilizing him. Anna receives nothing from Australia and is desperately trying to figure out a way to get passage on one of the vessels leaving for Europe in the next two weeks. The deskman on night duty watches her boldly as she and Klaus walk through the lobby in the evening. Their temporary visas are to expire in three days. A week has gone by since she wrote Mikhail. Surely by now, she thinks, he would have responded. Anna asks Klaus to go to a nearby pharmacy for a medication she takes. While he is out she walks down the polished hallway to the lobby and waits until the deskman is finished with a resident, then walks over.

"Have you heard anything from Australia?" she asks. The deskman smiles at her, "One moment Frau Boucher while I look." He thumbs through several stacks of letters. "There is nothing here. Perhaps you are ready to meet my friend?"

Anna looks at him, trying to figure her next step. "After I meet your friend, we would return to the hotel?"

"After you have a chance to talk and maybe dance with him."

Anna realizes this is a bargaining situation and is determined that if she prostitutes herself, it will cost the man dearly. "I will meet with him on the condition he purchases our passage on the freighter 'Twilight Sea' to Naples, Italy. He must have the documents with him when we meet, or I shall return to the hotel immediately, understood?"

"Frau Boucher, my friend is a patient man. But, he will not be pushed into such an agreement without knowing what he might receive in return."

"What does he want, except to talk and dance," Anna replies flippantly. "I can agree to those terms."

"Frau Boucher, my friend is generous. He only expects you to return his generosity." Anna notices it is about time for Klaus to return. "Then make the arrangements for tomorrow night. I insist he must have the travel documents and our passage confirmed when we meet. Understood?"

"Certainly, Frau Boucher," he replies with a half-smile.

The following afternoon, Anna checks with the steamship line ticket office and finds two passages have been purchased on the "Twilight Sea" for K. and A. Boucher. After an early meal with Klaus, Anna suggests a drink at a sidewalk bar. While Klaus watches a street disturbance, Anna drops a quickly dissolving powder into his drink. As they leave the bar and walk back to the hotel, Klaus suggests they get to bed early, feeling suddenly tired and weak.

As Klaus stretches out on the bed and the overhead fan whirs above them, Anna slowly undresses before her husband. Before she has undressed, Klaus is asleep. Anna waits a few minutes then changes into a black party dress, accentuating her white skin. Tiptoeing from the room, Anna walks into the lobby and straight to the deskman.

"I am ready to meet your friend. Shall we go?"

"Ah, Frau Boucher, you look lovely indeed. I have made the arrangements, but cannot accompany you. My friend's name is on this calling card. You can see he is an important business man. A taxi is waiting for you outside and will take you to the club. The driver will wait for you and bring you back to the hotel. When you arrive at the club give the doorman this card and he will take you to meet my friend. Isn't that simple?" he asks smiling.

"It would be simpler if you were there. You promised to introduce us!"

"Ah, so. But, it is too soon for me to leave the hotel. I'm very sorry." The glib responses worry Anna but she decides to proceed. Arriving at the Casino Club, Anna shows the doorman the card. He escorts her inside and tells the *maître de* to take madam to booth 14. As Anna and the *maître de* enter the glittering dining room, she is taken aback by the gaudy extravagance of the furnishings and the chandelier over the dance floor. Even in opulent Shanghai, such elaborate decorations were rarely seen. The oriental gentleman in booth 14 rises to meet Anna. Anna never hears from Mikhail Voskovich.

* * *

At Sea

The ocean voyage is not at all like Anna expected. Their accommodation is a small stateroom on the same deck as the ship's officers, her family icon rests against a bulkhead. Calling at every port, the ship wallows in heavy seas, and decks throb constantly as the big propeller churns night and day moving them into the South China Sea. Leaving Singapore in mid-September, and heading westward through the Straits of Malacca, the "Twilight Sea" enters the Indian Ocean. After a short anchorage off Ceylon, the ship continues across the Indian Ocean to Mombasa, Kenya, making several stops along the eastern coast of Africa reaching Durban, South Africa, on Sunday, 16 October 1949. A week later, they are anchored at Cape Town.

As the ship heads north from Cape Town, the weather becomes cooler. Passing through the Straits of Gibraltar during the first week of November, the ship is struck by a gale. The wind is cold and icy blasts of sea water make the deck a treacherous place to visit. When they finally dock at Naples, Anna clasps the icon to her breast and gives thanks for a safe journey.

Locating a family shelter run by Italian nuns, Klaus settles Anna there with half their money and the family icon. Hitchhiking to Germany in search of family, he proceeds north from Basel, systematically looking through telephone directories, police registration volumes, and, as a last resort, talks to concierges of large apartment complexes. The task appears hopeless.

Chapter 12
Post-War Germany

Winter, 1949

In early December, Klaus locates a cousin living in Darmstadt. Darmstadt is a completely new city, leveled and rebuilt after the war. Klaus gets a loan from his cousin and returns to Naples for Anna. Boarding a train, they arrive in Darmstadt Christmas week and accept his cousin's offer of a room. During the trip Anna pulls yarn from old socks and knits a sweater for Klaus' Christmas present.

Klaus is hired by American forces as a bookkeeper. Being multi-lingual, skilled in currency conversions, and multi-currency accounting procedures, Klaus advances rapidly. Klaus and Anna soon afford an apartment of their own. Anna unpacks the family icon, and sends their new address to her brother in Khabarovsk. Klaus repays his cousin's loan with interest and buys a house in a village near Darmstadt. It is their first home and both are excited. The garden needs work and the house must be painted. Anna locates the appropriate place for the family icon and tackles the garden. Klaus paints the exterior each evening until darkness.

Later, in a reflective mood, Anna writes her friends in America telling them life is again good. Her young husband is successful, the Boucher family is large and Anna welcomes them to their home.

In 1960, Klaus is hired by the Opel Works near Kaiserslautern. For several months he commutes. They move to a village in the Pfalzer Wald later. Anna buys a Pekingese puppy at Christmas and names her 'Cookie.'

During the '60's there are subtle changes taking place in the Boucher household. Klaus encourages Anna to get out of the house and find something to do. "Many women are working now and you would find it easier to meet new people."

"I'm not interested in meeting new people, Klaus. You have a big family and they come to visit often. I must be home to cook and keep the house. Besides, I enjoy the garden and fixing the dishes you like to eat. Cookie would be lonely. Those things take up my time and I'm happy, my husband," Anna smiles and brushes some imagined lint from his suit coat as he prepares to leave for work.

They build a home in Siegelbach, a village near the Opel plant. Their house is on the outskirts of the village, and behind the house is a large oat field. During construction of the house, Anna explains to the builder how she wants a special niche in the entrance hall for her family icon. There is much landscaping work to do and Anna, as before, eagerly attacks the project of designing a new garden.

The steep slope of the land lends itself to a terraced garden and is where Anna starts her work with Cookie racing between Anna and the gate to bark at villagers walking past. Klaus helps position the larger stones along the terrace in the evenings. For Anna it is an idyllic life.

January 1973, on their 32nd wedding anniversary, Klaus arrives home grim-faced, ignoring Cookie's welcoming leaps. Klaus has been preoccupied for weeks. Anna assumes his work is causing the tenseness between them. She has prepared dinner and set the table just for the two of them. Carefully, she lights the three white tapered candles in the silver candelabra, an anniversary gift some years before.

"What is bothering you, my husband?"

"Anna, you make it difficult, I waited to tell you, and now the timing is very bad. It is no use to try and mislead you. I want a divorce, the sooner the better. I'm no longer happy just to be with you. You seem happy staying here in this house. I need more!"

"What is it you need, my husband, a younger wife? You knew when we married, it would someday be like this; you, young and handsome. Me, I'm just an old *haus frau*. Is that the problem?"

Klaus is silent, trying to remember things he planned to say.

Anna continues, "Is it my fault, I'm not pretty enough? Or, maybe I'm not as interesting as the women you meet at work?"

"No, Anna, the truth is I've met another woman. We—she has the same interests as I and works in the building where I work. We seem to have much more in common than you and I ever had. She is a little younger than you (in reality, much younger). She thinks young! With her there seems to be so much future. Here, with you, the future is closing in on me. We don't go places like we used to, don't entertain family as much as before. Something is dying in our marriage. I am dying in our marriage and divorce seems to be the only answer for me."

Anna stands quietly, stunned; her blue-grey eyes are moist. "What will I do?" she asks. Accusing thoughts tumble through her mind, I need to get out of the house more, go with him to the office parties, make new friends, lose some weight, adopt a child.

Klaus wants to reach out to Anna, but having decided on a clean break, stands quietly, watching tears trickle down her cheeks. "You will stay here, in this house. I will provide a pension for you, enough for you to live comfortably. I think it is best I leave tonight. I'm going upstairs to pack some things. Tomorrow I'll come back to pick up what is left. You must take hold of yourself, Anna, find something to do."

Klaus leaves the room and hurries upstairs. While he packs, Anna stands in the living room, drying her tears as the impact of Klaus' action penetrates. She walks slowly over to the dining table and pulls out her chair. Easing into the chair, Anna looks at the food, ready to eat; the candles, still burning brightly; and Klaus' chair, empty. She looks through the open window out on to the dark street and the car parked by the gate. The sun has set and twilight is short during the winter months. Cookie has followed Klaus upstairs and now returns to Anna's side, ready to be walked. The emptiness seems to drain her body with every breath.

Klaus comes down stairs quickly, pausing at the entryway to look in on Anna. "You can reach me at the office if something is to be fixed in the house. A lawyer will call you, perhaps tomorrow. He can explain, better than I, details of divorce and prepare an agreement for you to sign. You will always be provided for, dear Anna. *Guten nacht*!" In the silence following, he walks out the door and to his car.

Anna can see a light inside the car as he hangs his suits over the door; then places a large suitcase in the trunk. He pauses, looks back at the house before getting into the driver's seat, starts the car and flicks on the car lights. Turning the car in the street and coasting down the slight hill toward town, Klaus is gone.

Anna lowers the roladen and returns to the dinner table. Taking the candle snuffer, she methodically extinguishes each flame. There is a sense of finality in each action! The following day a lawyer comes. Anna never cries afterward. The spring and summer are warm and good for Anna's spirits. She works in her garden, planting, moving, digging and thinking. The pension checks from Klaus are regular and adequate. Only the loneliness at night bothers her at first. A divorce after so many years of marriage changes many things. The Bouchers, who in China were so supportive after Gustav left her, no longer come to visit. The nephews and nieces have forgotten her. There is no sympathy from the neighbors. It seems Klaus took all their concern, or interest, with him the night he left. Casual acquaintances at the baker, butcher, or grocers, speak and smile; but, they do not know.

Anna reasons, if Klaus had left me a widow, I would still have the family and friends to help me get over losing him. Divorce is so different; no one helps an old woman with her grief. She writes Nina in San Francisco and invites her to visit. In her letter she says:

"Women of our generation were raised to focus their lives on their husbands, their husbands' career. I have done that and now there is nothing!"

November 1973

Winter arrives, and with it a letter from Nina Tokma explaining it will be impossible to visit this year, maybe next year. She encourages Anna to get out of the house and "find some work."

As Siegelbach's sole Russian resident, Anna is accustomed to winter storms having spent much of her life north of the 40th parallel and this storm is of no concern. The gathering storm is no exception, however the loneliness is deadly. She moves slowly, almost stealthily through her house, making arrangements to end her life. For several days snow has been falling like goose down—big soft flakes floating from the gray overcast sky, blanketing the hills and forests of the Pfalzerwald, an area west of the Rhein River and east of the Saarland. The wind begins to blow, bringing icy sleet mixed with snow. Lights from villages and farm homes twinkle then disappear as window shutters are closed. Roads between the villages are shut down and movement within each village restricted.

The heart of the storm is centered over Rodenbach, Weilerbach, Eulinbis and Siegelbach, the cluster of farm villages north of Kaiserslautern. Strong gusts of wind-driven sleet and snow batter the villages in this otherwise pastoral setting, rattling wooden slats of the roladen, a window shutter popular in Europe.

"Not a fit day to live or die," Anna mutters, her graying-blonde hair precisely combed and waved, and dressed as if she were going to a party. For a lady who spent the best years of her life enjoying the outdoors, her appearance is uncommon. She shakes her head to dispel the effect of the weather, but not a strand of the heavily-lacquered hair moves. With keen eyes she inspects each room of the immaculately clean house. "I cannot live in a dirty house, and I will not die in one," Anna grumbles in throaty, heavily-accented German. Her life has been spent running from events beyond her control, but never alone. Leaving Russia with her parents during the 1918 revolution, fleeing Japanese occupation of Manchuria with her Russian Cossack husband in 1933, and in the late 1940s hurrying out of Shanghai with Klaus Boucher, she has never faced them alone.

Months have passed since Klaus left for a younger woman. Well cared for financially, Anna stays trim for her 61 years, but the flesh on her face is sagging now and she appears older. She thinks younger than her years, a good sign, but moves more slowly. Wrinkles around her blue-gray eyes are not the only wrinkles she would like to erase. Examining personal treasures remaining in the house, Anna clearly remembers when, and where each became the property of Klaus and Anna Boucher. Cookie, her 12-year-old Pekingese, follows and watches as Anna walks through each room.

In Siegelbach few lights can be seen other than the Pils beer sign at Wagner's *Gasthaus*. Customers who braved the elements for an early round of drinking have drifted off to their homes, leaving the loud and friendly purveyor of propane and fuel oil, short and stocky Herr Dittman, to enjoy the warmth of Wagner's. He had a busy day, emptying his truck twice while making rounds on the icy streets of Siegelbach, satisfying the fuel demands of his American customers. His customers increased two-fold when the big American base at Ramstein expanded. The U. S. Air Force headquarters in Europe moved from historic and cultural Wiesbaden to rural Ramstein, settling thousands of American families in villages surrounding the base and making Herr Dittman a wealthy man. With a healthy belch and grumpy "*Wiedersehen!*" to Herr

Wagner, Herr Dittman staggers from Wagner's, the last customer for the evening. Small villages in the Pfalzerwald have been isolated by snow and ice for several days, but are accustomed to such solitude. Essential traffic has moved within the villages, such as Herr Dittman's fuel truck. Despite the snow and ice, autobahn traffic between Mannheim and Saarbrucken has been moving.

South of Siegelbach, snow removal equipment operates around the clock in Kaiserslautern. Klaus Boucher, takes the weather conditions as an excuse to depart the Vogelweh Opel plant an hour early for his new home in Kaiserslautern. Brushing accumulated snow from the roof and driver side door of the dark green 1954 gull-wing 300 SL Mercedes-Benz roadster, he slips into the white leather bucket seat and sighs contentedly as the gull-wing door silently closes. A smile crosses his face. His new, and younger, Frau Boucher is entertaining 'their' friends tonight. First they will visit the heated Swim-bad at Hotel Erika to have a drink and relax with their guests. Afterward they will dine at a restaurant followed by drinks in their home. Entertaining was never this easy with Anna. So much fuss, in and out of the kitchen, the rich aromas of her 'peasant' cooking filling the house, and Cookie yapping for attention when guests arrived made entertaining controlled chaos. A melancholy whisper, "Poor Anna," escapes his lips.

Meanwhile, a cold, penetrating loneliness fills the modern two-story Siegelbach house Klaus built for Anna in 1970. Since Klaus left, Anna has known nothing but sadness and loneliness. "This loneliness is like the breath of death," she barely whispers, not to disturb the silence settling around her.

Anna's hands tremble as she approaches the kitchen, she has spent the day planning for this moment, wedging towels snuggly around the doors, securing windows and lowering each *roladen*. Entering she turns on the gas burners of her range, but does not light them. Bending slightly and quickly sniffing the near-odorless propane, she turns off the overhead light and leaves, satisfied gas is pouring from the open burners.

In the entryway, she reaches instinctively to touch the Donesyvna icon. Carefully removing it from the wall, and with a final look toward the front entry, she nods to Cookie and climbs the stairs to her bedroom clutching the icon to her bosom. "It was supposed to protect me, bring me good fortune," she muses. At the top of the stairs she turns off the hall and stairway lights and, with a sigh, turns toward her brightly lit bedroom.

"I must leave a note," she says loud enough to break the silence and hear her voice again. From a drawer, she takes a tablet and pencil and begins to write: "In Samara, I was born. It seems like yesterday, but it was a lifetime ago. On my sixth birthday, events took place changing my life forever, it was 28 July 1918 ...."

The following morning

The bedside lamp is still burning and the suicide note Anna has written is propped against the lamp base. Cookie wakes her by licking her hand. Startled to be alive, and with a splitting headache, Anna moves slowly to sit up in bed. A wave of nausea comes, and passes.

From her bed, Anna reaches over to raise the roladen and open a window, aware she is still fully dressed. Taking a deep breath, she coughs uncontrollably for a minute. Head throbbing, the cold air like icy fire searing her throat and lungs, she carefully pushes herself from the bed and stands next to the window, still coughing intermittently. As her head clears the pain lessens. Looking out on the sunlit, frost-covered fields, she turns and walks carefully to the stairs. Holding to the railing, Anna descends the stairs and smells a faint odor of gas. She reaches up to touch the icon and realizes it is upstairs next to her bed. Puzzled, Anna looks into the kitchen and the smell of gas is a little stronger.

Three quick steps and her hand is on the range control knobs, turning off the gas jets. But, as she turns the knobs, she can tell gas is not coming from the burners. Confused, and her head pounding, she begins to raise roladen and open windows and doors. Cookie has followed her downstairs and keeps going right out the front door, vomiting in the driveway. The air is crisp, cold, and refreshing.

What a foolish thing to do, she thinks. Why didn't the gas do what it was supposed to do? Maybe I'm not ready to die. Anna notices the smell is downstairs and little of the gas could be smelled upstairs. She puts on several layers of clothing, afraid to light the heaters until all trace of gas is gone.

Taking two tablets from an aspirin bottle she keeps by the sink, Anna downs them with a glass of water. While she is standing at the sink, she hears noises and a man cursing. Looking out the window she sees Herr Dittman slipping and sliding on the icy driveway, exhaling clouds of frosted breath as he curses the ice, and people who don't clear their driveways. He stops in the middle of his struggle to pull his heavy hose up the driveway, looks up and sees Anna peering at him through the open kitchen window.

"*Guten morgen,* Frau Boucher!" He tips his hat. "How are you? I trust you haven't run out of gas. I've been unable to make it up your hill with all the ice." Not a word he says to her about the driveway.

"*Guten morgen*. I'm well, thank you. I noticed the burner would not light this morning, but I thought you came by last week."

"I would've, but my American customers in Weilerbach and Rodenbach kept me busy. The Americans must cook all day when it is cold! I had to change my route. Hope it didn't inconvenience you?"

"Not this time," she calls out the window, while under her breath she mutters, "the old coot saved my life." She watches as he grumbles and puffs and finally hooks up the hose to her tank. "When you finish, let me know; I want to make some tea!"

After the gas man departs, she makes her cup of tea and sits at the kitchen table, contemplating what happened during the night. "I will find another man," she mutters.

Part Two
Willi's Story

Chapter 13
Wilhelm, Born a Saxon

Lützen, Saxony
July 1912

Sweltering heat from the afternoon sun draws most of Lützen's convivial citizens outdoors. The farming village southwest of Leipzig has two public places where people gather, the square in front of the Rathaus next to Red Lion Inn, and the park in front of the Lützen Schloss (castle). Both are crowded Saturday, July 13, as people fan the flies and talk about the 90 degree (Fahrenheit) temperature.

Karl Meissner, the village blacksmith, short and muscular, coal-black hair a bit tousled from a long night awaiting the birth of a son, strides briskly along Kaiser Wilhelm Strasse pushing a wheel barrow. A sweaty shirt is not unseemly for Karl and he frequently stops to mop his brow with a soiled white handkerchief. Heat does not phase the blacksmith. Through the park, around the square, and at each house he stops, visits with people and tells them, "I have a son." He offers cigarettes, chocolates, or a drink from the keg of beer sitting in the wheel barrow. Karl does not drink beer, or smoke, but respects the choice, and custom, of those who do. He greets everyone in the same generous, gregarious manner.

His frau gave birth to a boy child this morning; after two daughters, finally a son. A fourth generation blacksmith needs a son to carry on the business and today is a special occasion. Normally Karl could walk the length of Lützen in 10 minutes. With a keg of beer in his wheel barrow, and stopping at every door, it takes the entire afternoon. Everyone in Lützen knows the Meissners, and Karl knows everyone in Lützen. So, from his house he walks each street celebrating and, by the end of day, everyone knows Karl has a son.

Karl can do things with metal other blacksmiths rarely attempt; "smithing" skills learned from his father have been passed down through generations of Meissners. An artist with metal, Karl can pound the rhythm of the "William Tell Overture" on his anvil, and mend machinery at the same time, perhaps why he named his son Wilhelm.

Wilhelm's mother is a Stolle, a family of tall and elegant looking people. Freda is nearly six foot tall, carries a little extra weight from three pregnancies, and has sharply carved facial features. She towers over her husband when they stand for hymns in the formidable Lutheran church on Kaiser Wilhelm Strasse, one block from the town square. The name Stolle means very little to the farm folk of Lützen. But, in Berlin, Hanover and Leipzig, Herr Stolle, Concertmaster of the Imperial Orchestra, is well known.

Karl respects the culture his Frau brings to their home in Lützen. But, some of Frau Stolle-Meissner's culture is foreign to rural Lützen. She is a product of abstract and expressionist schools of Berlin. In other words, she yells and screams.

In 1914 they move into a new house, closer to Lützen's *Hospital,* a residence for aged, indigent, or infirm persons, located on the edge of town. Appropriately, the cobblestone and crushed stone street leading to it was named Hospital Strasse. From Kaiser Wilhelm Strasse, the street becomes little more than a narrow lane after it passes the Meissner's at #15, barely suitable for automobiles.

Karl spends hours in his garden during the long summer evenings. From the rear of the house, to the small stream at the rear of his property, Karl digs and plants until every foot of earth is in use. When the "Great War" began in 1914, food was scarce in the cities. Not so in livable Lützen. Everyone has a garden and perhaps a pen for geese, or chickens. Barnyards (in town) are a cacophony of cackling, crowing, quacking, grunting and bovine sounds. Competing with the noise is discordant piano music flowing from the open windows of the Meissner's house. The daughters, Kristin and Ludwina, practice their music lessons and Wilhelm is surrounded by culture, a screaming mother and beginning piano students.

As the war progresses, all young men of Lützen are taken into Kaiser Wilhelm's army. Karl, in his mid-thirties, is one of the youngest men left in Lützen when the conscription law is enacted. Strikes at the shipyards and Krupp weapons plants begin to disrupt the war machine in January 1918.

Marxist-led laborers are sending a message to end to the war, but no one in the government pays attention.

During the final, miserably wet summer of the war, all men physically able to work in the strike-bound munitions factories and shipyards are conscripted. Karl is torn between his beliefs, as a "law-abiding" pragmatist, and duty to his country; he leaves Lützen for the shipyards at Kiel one week after Wilhelm turns six years old.

Steady summer rains have ruined Karl's garden. Seed potatoes planted in the spring, rot in the wet earth and there is very little to eat from the usually productive garden. Frau Stolle-Meissner's screams cannot encourage the garden, or keep the blacksmith shop running, but she keeps the family going by walking fourteen kilometers to Leipzig each day. She stands in line for a small piece of pork or horse meat, screams her frustrations at the butcher, and then walks back to Lützen, gathering wild plants and herbs along the railroad right of way.

Wilhelm thinks he has already lived through the worst years of his life; watching his mother take a small piece of meat, add dandelions, roots and all, to make a stew feeding the four of them. He is always hungry. One soggy August afternoon, Wilhelm returns from school and notices the piano is missing. Kristin, nine years older than her young brother, explains very patiently the piano has been traded to Herr Fleishmann, the grocer, for food. The pantry now has small amounts of smoked meat, sausage, potatoes and other vegetables. Each week Herr Fleishmann has food delivered to the Meissner household. Toward the end of October, the food quits coming. Slowly, the pantry empties. Frau Meissner again walks to Leipzig, returning with a portion of meat and wild plants to cook in a stew.

After school, Wilhelm takes his father's handcart and walks along the railroad tracks, scavenging for pieces of coal or firewood falling from a passing train. There never seems to be enough fuel, and the house grows colder, and colder, during the winter months.

An armistice is signed in November, ending the war. Karl returns in December, malnourished and pfennig-less, crushed by the incompetence of the country's leaders, his law-abiding pragmatism challenged. The conscripts were rarely fed, and received little pay for their work. Many are demoralized and unable, or unwilling, to work for a government treating them so badly. Unemployment grows as disillusioned Germans avoid the hard and undesirable work of rebuilding a destroyed nation. The family group falls apart in many homes throughout Germany. Despite the national sickness, Karl rekindles his blacksmith fire in poor health, but with a purpose. "My son will never fight a politicians' war if I can help it!"

Christmas Eve Service, 1918

The Lutheran Church on Kaiser Wilhelm Strasse is aglow with chandeliers and candle light. Wilhelm hears the sound of someone nearby sniffing during the pastor's prayer. Curiosity overcomes his fear of being seen and he cautiously turns his head in the direction of the sniffer and squints through half closed eyes. Tears trickle down his mother's cheeks, as the family attends Christmas Eve services, and Freda, her ranting and raving drove many others to tears during the war, is sniffing and dabbing her eyes with a small white handkerchief she always carries but never uses. Wilhelm ducks his head as the prayer ends. Opening his eyes and looking directly at his mother, it is as if she had never shed a tear. Many families in Lützen lost a son, or father during the war and there are not many dry eyes in the church. Wilhelm is unsure why his parents cried. His father survived, came home, and reopened the blacksmith shop.

Walking home from the service in frost laden air and early evening silence, their warm breath turns to frost as they exhale from beneath the layers of clothing holding back the biting cold. Turning down Hospitalstrasse, Karl puts a hand on Wilhelm's shoulder. "Run ahead, son, and get the fire started."

Karl laid out the wood and coal in the porcelain stove before leaving for church. Wilhelm dashes along the street and into the house, through the front door seldom locked. He strikes a match and holds it to the tinder strips. The flame catches and Wilhelm closes the stove door as his sisters enter the house. Very few words are spoken as everyone removes a layer of clothing, even though the house is scarcely warmer than outside. Wilhelm is still wearing two sweaters, his shirt and tie, two pair of pants and assorted underclothes, after shedding his jacket.

The Meissners gather around their small Christmas tree, decorated with ornaments from Christmases gone by, and wait for Karl to hand them their presents. Gifts are few, only what each could make for the other. Wilhelm has not bothered to wrap the wood carvings he made for each member of the family. Kristin bought Christmas candles with money earned working as a clerk. Karl lights a candle, places it in a window, and begins to sing "Silent Night." Freda and the children join in singing.

"It is not the same, singing without the piano," Wilhelm whispers to Kristin. A shrill whistle in the distance announces the departure of the train from Leipzig as it continues to Weissenfels.

They are startled by a sharp rapping at the door. Standing at the door with arms full of presents and a basket of sausages and fruit are *Opa* and *Oma* Stolle! *Opa* Stolle has his violin case under his arm.

The singing is much better with *Opa* Stolle playing his violin. Kristin and Ludwina make a fresh pot of linden berry tea before the presents are opened. "The house is still cold, but inside our hearts we are warm," Karl observes.

There are gradual changes in the Meissner household as prosperity returns. Frau Stolle-Meissner (a name she prefers to use) no longer screams. She becomes quietly mean. Wilhelm is first to notice as he is the principal victim of her mood change. Freda often locks him out of the house in the evening if he is late returning home. Only when Karl inquires does Freda allow Wilhelm to enter the house.

The only thing in the Meissners family life not changing is their regular attendance at the Lutheran church in Lützen. Each Sunday Frau Meissner insures the children bathe and dress in clean, if not their best, clothing for the services. Church attendance helps mischievous Wilhelm. Noting his regularity, the pastor asks Willi to assist in the services, lighting candles and ringing the church bell, a responsibility he enjoys.

By December 1921, Herr Meissner is again a prosperous blacksmith, opening a second shop in Leipzig with a loan from Freda's father. The shop is on the outskirts of Leipzig, scarcely 13 kilometers from Lützen. Karl drives a Daimler Benz between the two shops. On occasion, Wilhelm pedals his bicycle to the Leipzig shop, delivering a message, or a tool.

On his tenth birthday, Wilhelm receives a diary from Kristin, at nineteen the prettiest girl in Lützen and, to Wilhelm, the kindest sister a boy could ever want. He begins to scrupulously write his earliest recollections, including all he had ever been told by Oma and Opa Meissner about his childhood. On the first page of the diary he writes:

This is a very nice gift from Kristin, my sister. I am a Saxon, born at Lützen in Saxony, 13 July 1912. My diary is private. Not even Kristin can open these pages without my permission.

Wilhelm Meissner. He also gets a gift from Opa Stolle, tickets for the family to hear the Leipzig Symphony perform Bohemian Gustav Mahler's Ninth Symphony. They drive to Leipzig in the Daimler-Benz. Opa Stolle is concertmaster for this performance. It is Willi's first visit to the Symphony Hall and a memorable one.

Wilhelm's knowledge of Saxon history, and the sometimes divergent view he takes from the history books, interests his teacher. Actually, it is Karl's pragmatic view of the historic German events from the time of Saxony's King Otto I, until the fall of Kaiser Wilhelm II. Karl's view of Lützen's geographic location as a nexus of historic Saxon events has been passed on to Wilhelm who defends this view through use of two principal events, a critical battle fought at Lützen during the 30 Years War, and the defeat of Napoleon at Leipzig. *(Both events are described in detail in the current day Schloss Museum.)*

Wilhelm works in his father's shop after school, sweeping, picking up scraps of metal, fetching tools and listening to his father. Karl expounds on blacksmithing, history, religion according to Martin Luther, the post war attitude toward work, and the degeneration of family relationships:

- o "A 'smith must have a hot bed of coals to work the metal."
- o "Religion is like a pair of shoes you wear every day, not just on Sunday."
- o "No one wants to work. Everyone wants a handout."
- o "Young people have stopped listening to their parents. They follow every pied piper who comes to town."

Karl works like a man possessed. With post-war inflation, money is inconsequential now. His *Maschinen Arbeit* in Lützen and Leipzig are busy and he is being paid with livestock, vegetables, and dairy goods. What the family cannot use, he sells, or trades, for furniture, clothing and, yes, music lessons. The Meissners have a new piano and Wilhelm gets a horn.

Wilhelm's early interest in music pleases Karl; but, his practicing is barely tolerated by his mean-spirited mother. Both Wilhelm and the horn are frequently ejected from the house on Hospital Strasse. It is only a matter of time until he moves the horn to *Oma* and *Opa* Meissner's in Leipzig. And, since they are getting old, *Oma* Meissner frequently asks Freda to send Wilhelm over to help with chores. *Oma* Meissner always finds something in her pantry to feed the hearty appetite of the sandy-haired, gangly youth and allows him to practice his music. Wilhelm's diary eventually winds up hidden in a box at *Oma* Meissner's house, ferreted out during his frequent visits and, in the privacy of *Oma's* kitchen, he chronicles the best and worst of growing up.

Spring, 1927

Between Wilhelm's fourteenth and fifteenth birthdays he acquires the nickname 'Willi' and, with some reluctance, answers to the new name. At the same time, his interest in girls broadens. He now has girl acquaintants in many surrounding villages. On weekends Willi plays his horn with a group of local musicians organized, and originally directed (before Willi was born) by *Opa* Stolle. Saturday nights he plays his horn at a small dance place in Röcken, a circular village founded by Wends in the Middle Ages, less than two miles west of Lützen. The hall faces the main road between Lützen and Weissenfels and is a rendezvous for young people. Out of sight, and in the inner circle of the village, is the church yard where Nietzsche the philosopher is buried. Nietzsche was born in the parsonage, only a few yards from the church. Young folk come from as far away as Weissenfels to drink and dance to popular tunes. Very few come to see Nietzsche's burial place. The dances they like are waltzes, polkas and the Charleston.

One warm and clear Saturday night, a school mate and member of the band, clarinet player Frederic Schmidt, introduces Willi to a buxom young girl from Bothfeld. Alexis and Willi spend most of the evening eyeing each other and dancing when Willi is not playing his horn. Willi prefers the waltzes, and dances all of them with Alexis. Before the evening is over, Willi kisses her and swears his love (his first love).

The following weeks Willi rides his bicycle to Bothfeld at every opportunity, entering the village and circling left to the home of Alexis. Bothfeld, like Röcken, was founded by Wends and built in concentric circles, outer buildings surrounded by communal farms, and forming a wall of defense.

There is a large pond to the south of Bothfeld, near the home of Alexis. Farmers allow their horses to enter the murky green water for a drink, and pale skinned farm boys and girls swim there in the summer afternoons, wearing their work clothes if they do not have a swim suit. Willi and Alexis sit in the shade of a linden tree and toss stones into the water. When no one is looking they kiss and laugh. Willi carves their initials in the trunk of the old linden tree.

In July, hurricane force winds sweep across Saxony leaving 150 people dead, and the linden tree is toppled into the pond. When Willi visits Bothfeld, Saturday, July 16, the young lovers walk to the pond and, during the afternoon, have a quarrel. Willi suspects the downed linden tree may have had something to do with the quarrel, "I'm not superstitious," he adds, knocking on wood, however, their romance ends.

Willi completes formal schooling in Lützen and becomes an apprentice in a Leipzig trade school. During the week, Willi is awake by 4 a.m., dressing in the darkness of his closet size room. It is still dark when he leaves the house and walks past Kantzer's bakery. If the wind is from the north, Willi can smell the first trays of *Brötchen* coming out of the oven before he can see the bakery. Willi enters and, nodding to Frau Kantzer, sleepily mumbles, "*Zwei Brötchen, bitte.*" One he will eat now, the other later.

Turning left outside the bakery door, and taking a bite out of the warm bread roll, he walks west on Starseidler Strasse, passing the walled farm yard of Herr Fleishmann. Again, in the darkness Willi can tell where he is by the smell. It is a smell he likes, though others do not. The gates are open and six huge, snorting plough horses are in their traces, stomping on the cobble stone courtyard, ready for another day in the fields. Further down the street Willi observes the guard gate at the railroad crossing is down, and begins to jog toward Bahnhof Strasse. Taking a right on the tree lined street, his feet stir the fallen linden blossoms as he sprints the remaining distance to the station. Fumbling in his pocket for the commuter pass he uses, Willi holds it out for Herr Finck, the gray-haired, stoop-shouldered, station attendant. Herr Finck clips the ticket and perfunctorily says, "*Morgen.*"

Weekdays Willi takes the train to Leipzig, attends classes and works as an apprentice machinist. Each weekend he practices with the band and plays at dances. In 1930 he passes the journeyman examination and has another year of work before becoming fully qualified as a machine mechanic.

Summer, 1931

Willi is certified as a mechanic in June, a combination of blacksmith and mechanical skills. But, the job market is declining. There are very few jobs for any craftsman, including mechanics. Meissner's *Maschinen Arbeit* in Leipzig has only one man working full time. Karl keeps the shop in Lützen open, but spends many afternoons in his garden. Willi has not planned to work for his father, and does not ask him for work. Besides, he reasons, the worker in Leipzig has a family to support.

Notices are posted in Lützen's post office concerning the police academy examinations. Willi applies. He easily passes the physical test, but has some difficulty with the academic tests. There are over a thousand young men in the Leipzig area testing for 100 training slots. Willi is notified a week later of his acceptance in the police academy at Burg, northeast of Magdeburg.

Karl and Freda are not pleased with Willi's choice of a career and show their displeasure by failing to even see him off at the train station. A girl friend, Gisela from Leipzig, accompanies him to the station. Willi has dated her often since breaking up with Alexis. He has never been kissed like Gisela kisses; she kisses with her mouth open and an active tongue. Promising to come back on his first leave, Willi boards the train and races to a window leaning out for one more kiss as the train begins to move. It is July, the week of his nineteenth birthday and Willi has severed ties with his family.

Discipline at the academy is what the rough and tumble son of a blacksmith needs. Nearly every town and village in Germany had experienced some aspect of the "Weimar Period." Most had seen family discipline break down. The strict schedule of exercises, uniform inspections, and inspection of each cadet's living area, turns Willi into a disciplined young man. Attendance at chapel services is voluntary and few cadets attend. For reasons Willi does not fully understand, years of Lutheran church services have woven a strong habit and Willi enjoys the peaceful hour spent in the chapel on Sundays.

The spit and polish of academy life challenges Willi. Never one to put his clothing away at home, he now must have every item of clothing folded, and in order in his *Schrank* (a foot locker.) Willi can perform the uniform change drill as fast as anyone in his class. It works like this, as the cadets come in from a work out on the sports field, the instructor blows a whistle, and starts his stop watch. The cadets run inside the barracks, change into the uniform of the day, or one the instructor specifies, and scramble back outside. Once they are good enough at this exercise, the instructor goes inside and inspects their *Schrank* to see how well they put everything back into place.

In 1932, the rebellious spirit in Willi finds expression; each police cadet must participate in a sport. Max Schmeling won the adulation of Willi's generation of German young men by winning the world heavyweight boxing championship from an American boxer, so Willi chooses boxing. Six feet, one inch, and weighing 198 pounds, broad-shouldered Willi enters the boxing program as a heavyweight (light-heavyweights came later).

The academy's boxing coach sadistically enjoys getting in the ring with his novice boxers; pounding them around when they make mistakes. Willi learns to absorb the punishment, and is surprisingly fast for a heavyweight. A week after his first pounding at the hands of the coach, Willi unleashes a flurry of punches sending his teacher to the canvas, much to the delight of the other young boxers. He is immediately a hero to his classmates. The coach, although his dignity and body are bruised, thinks he has found someone to bring a trophy back to the academy in the next round of police competitions.

In quick succession, Willi wins his first eight fights in the police district and is a master boxer (champion) with a broken nose to show for it. While fighting the police master heavyweight from the state of Prussia, Willi discovers slugging and taking punishment can cost a decision. He is narrowly out pointed by the Prussian, a loss hurting far more than physical punishment. The taunting calls from the partisan Prussian crowd ring in Willi's ears. A long standing dislike between Prussians and Saxons is fueled by such competitions.

A month later the boxing team travels to Berlin to participate in the All-German Police Master Boxing Competition. Willi's first bout is against a battle scarred veteran of many boxing contests, a police sergeant from Berlin. The fight ends Willi's police boxing career. A new invention called flash bulbs (Germany 1932) has revolutionized photo taking. Each bout has camera men circling the ring flashing their cameras at the boxers. Willi's attention is distracted each time a flash occurs and his opponent uses the opportunity to score a hit. One camera man particularly gets behind Willi's opponent and flashes the bulb at every opportunity, almost blinding Willi.

After another encounter with the flash bulb, Willi is staggered with a hard right to his nose and left eye at the end of the third round. His coach stops the bleeding between rounds, but notices loose cartilage as he packs Willi's nose.

"I think your nose is broken again, Willi. I've stopped the bleeding, but any punch landing on your nose will start it bleeding again." The coach examines Willi's bruised and swelling face carefully. "Do you want me to stop the fight?"

"I fight," Willi mumbles, spitting into a tin can at the edge of the ring. Willi squints across the ring and leaves his corner at the bell. The throbbing in his nose is a distraction, nothing to keep him from continuing the fight. As Willi circles to his left, looking for an opening, the flash bulbs go off again and his opponent lands a left hook to the head, starting Willi's nose bleeding again. He tastes the blood and attempts to wipe it away from his mouth, smearing it on his glove and over his face. Guarding his nose, he continues to circle and jab.

Another photo flash at ringside momentarily blinds Willi and the next moment a thousand lights are going off inside his head. The ring lights are in an unusual position, or so it appears to Willi lying on the canvas. Dazed and bloody, his body glistening with sweat, Willi struggles to regain his feet, but his arms and legs will not respond. The referee bends down as he counts, watching Willi attempt to rise. The count is finished and Willi still cannot get to his knees. His coach and the team manager enter the ring and carry Willi to the dressing room.

Willi's head begins to clear as he lies on a dressing room table. A doctor is examining him and talking. "I'm afraid you've had a bad concussion, young man. It would be dangerous if you fight again and receive another blow to the head," the doctor explains. "Your brain could be damaged, I have seen it happen."

The boxers stay in Berlin until the contest is over and Willi watches the remaining fights, learning more about boxing than his coach had taught him. Each time a boxer from Berlin is in the ring, a photo flash appears to blind the opponent before the bout is over. The Berlin boxer seems to anticipate the flash and delivers a flurry of punches while his opponent back pedals and covers his head.

Willi's classmates are waiting as the bus arrives and cheer as he sheepishly gets off the bus. "Why do you do this? I lost the fight." Willi is confused and embarrassed by the attention. "You are Saxon! You never gave up! You are one of us and we are proud!" They are yelling and pounding his back as they escort him to the barracks.

Boxing career finished, Willi completes his training at Burg and moves to another barracks to wait for his duty assignment. He asks the training school bandmaster if he can practice with the band, but his nose has not healed and blowing the horn is uncomfortable. A month after his injury Willi is performing with the Police band in Leipzig and throughout the district. His parents never came to see him fight, but, at Karl's insistence, are usually in the audience when the band performs. Willi can hardly believe his mother would travel across Lützen to hear him play, much less to Wittenberg and Leipzig. He marvels at how much his "parents have changed" since he has been at the academy.

Freda and Karl are equally amazed at the change in Wilhelm's appearance and manners during his year away from home. "He even plays the horn better," Freda whispers to Karl during a concert.

30 January 1933, Adolf Hitler becomes Chancellor of the Reich. Goering establishes an auxiliary police force on 22 February 1933, combining 40,000 SA and SS militants with 10,000 of the existing state police. Later, in March, the Enabling Act is passed giving National Socialists (Nazis) broad powers, essentially to do as they wish in the name of "removing the communist threat" and continuing their revolution. As Nazis are placed in key positions throughout Germany, state police units are neutralized. To remain a policeman one must agree (volunteer) to be a member of Hitler's National Socialist party.

Willi telephones his father from the barracks in Merseburg and tells him about the Nazis plan to take over police functions. Herr Meissner, an active Social Democrat, has watched leaders of his party depart Germany; those who remain are interned in prison camps. He tells Willi, "You must make your own decision, but, the National Socialists are bad people. They will lead us into war!"

Willi decides not to join the National Socialists. When a notice is posted in March ordering the young policemen to pick up forms to join the National Socialists, Willi empties his *Schrank*, folds his uniforms and turns them in at the quartermaster's window. Walking to his chief's office he tells him he is resigning.

"Why do you do this, Meissner? You have a good record, this will change things."

"It is simple. I cannot be a National Socialist."

"Have you talked about this with your friends in the barracks?"

"No. I decide for myself. They must decide for themselves."

"You still have a year on your labor service contract. What will you do?" the chief asks.

"I will find something, sir. May I go now?"

Police records show Wilhelm Meissner (not related to Dr. Otto Meissner of political fame) was dismissed from the police force in May 1933; his record annotated "politically unsatisfactory." In the Nazi political purge of the police many good men left. As terms of his "rehabilitation" Willi joins the labor service (*Arbeitsdienst*) orchestra for one year.

The summer of 1934, after finishing his year with the *Arbeitsdienst*, Willi returns to Lützen and looks for work. In spite of his *Arbeitsdienst* service, Willi's state papers remain stamped "Politically Unsatisfactory." He rides into Leipzig and checks the union halls, reads notices posted for workers, and follows every lead trying to find work other than in his father's shop.

The day Hindenburg dies, 2 August 1934, Willi is near Wittenberg, north of Leipzig, inquiring about a job. Shops close at noon to pay homage to Germany's postwar leader. Willi decides to visit a girl he had met during his year with the *Arbeitsdienst* Orchestra. Tall, blonde Katarina Schwartz, from Wittenberg is interested in music and Willi dated her when performing near Wittenberg. Stopping at a flower shop, he purchases a small bouquet and rides his bicycle to the Schwartz' home to call on Katarina.

Katarina is surprised and flirtatious, anxious to please Willi. Strangely to Willi, her parents seem equally pleased to see him. They insist he stay for the evening meal and Willi, predictably hungry, accepts the invitation.

Later, sitting outdoors and talking in the lingering summer twilight, Herr Schwartz suggests Willi spend the night and not try to return to Leipzig. Willi finds the idea agreeable, his parents will think he is at *Opa* and *Oma* Meissner's house in Leipzig and no one will worry. After everyone has gone to bed, Katarina comes to Willi's bed and gets in beside him. "Do you mind?" she asks. It is the first time he has been in bed with a girl. "It was a very good feeling," he later records in his diary.

Taking leave of the Schwartz family the next morning, his face flushed with memories of the night spent in Katarina's arms, Willi pedals wildly to the Wittenberg train station, carries his bicycle on board and is in Leipzig by noon time. He has lunch with *Oma* and *Opa* Meissner, who suspect something is amiss by Willi's light-hearted answers to their questions about the job in

Wittenberg. "The boy has something else on his mind, Papa," *Oma* Meissner says as Willi leaves.

Willi returns to Lützen and helps his father in the shop, working late into the evening and cleaning up after father leaves for supper. "I tell you Freda, the boy is sick or going crazy. He has never missed a meal at home when he's in town." Karl decides it is pressure from the S.A. causing the strange behavior.

Weeks go by and then Willi receives a letter from Katarina. She is pregnant and Willi is the father. Unable to talk with his parents about this development, Willi muddles through the events as he recalls them. Not knowing much about these things, he remembers Katarina introducing him to the way babies are made. He answers her letter promptly and tells her he will do the "honorable thing."

The evening comes when he must explain to his parents why he is leaving home. His father says, "Now I know why you've been acting strange." Freda's face clouds and her voice is shrill as she tells him, "You've disgraced the family! When you go, take your bed with you." Willi knows why it is difficult for them. A Lützen girl he has known since childhood is the one they had picked to become their daughter-in-law. Loading his bed roll, suitcase, and box of music books on his bicycle, Willi leaves for Wittenberg. Katarina's parents allow Willi to live with them and work on her father's farms until the wedding.

Surprising to Willi, his mother and father attend the wedding. They call to tell "Wilhelm" they are coming. He meets them at the station, shakes his father's hand, kisses his mother on the cheek, and says very little as they walk through town. Karl finally asks, "Is that the suit you will wear for the wedding?"

"*Ja,* is the only one I have."

"You can't get married in that thing," Frau Meissner responds. "Show us to a tailor shop, Wilhelm, the least we can do is get you something decent to wear." They take him to buy a new suit for the wedding, have it fitted, get the tailor to throw in a shirt and tie for the price, and stay for the wedding. Standing aloof from the Schwartz family, Karl and Freda look like they are attending a funeral, not their son's wedding.

After the wedding, Willi's father-in-law takes him aside. "One day all that we have will be Katarina's. You stay with Katarina, be a good husband, and this will be yours." Willi works for his father-in-law and lives in his father-in-law's house. But, he gets only five marks a week and any inheritance is years away.

Six months later, in January 1935, Katarina gives birth to a baby girl they name Christel. Willi is sure it takes longer for babies to come, but Katarina and her mother say that the eight and one-half pound girl was early.

After working for his father-in-law nearly a year, Freda writes "Your father needs someone to help him at the shop in Leipzig, would you be interested." Reaching out to him is unusual for Freda, Willi is pleasantly surprised. In June 1936, Willi and Katarina go to Lützen and move in with Willi's parents. He travels to Leipzig on his bicycle and works as a mechanic; in the fall he takes the Master Mechanics examination and passes. Karl turns the shop in Leipzig over to Willi to operate.

Willi and Katarina's search for a house near the shop is time consuming; Katarina is difficult to please. Houses she likes, they cannot afford. Houses they can afford, she does not like. In January 1937, they move into a remodeled apartment with a private entrance on Eisenbahn Strasse, near the center of Leipzig. There is a small garden in the rear, two bedrooms and a toilet upstairs, and a large kitchen and small living room downstairs. A large metal tub in one corner of the kitchen is used for bathing. The apartment is two miles from the shop. "Meissner's Mechanic Works" is painted on the shop building, easy to see from the highway one would take from Leipzig to Weimar. Although located inside the city, farmers have little difficulty bringing equipment into Willi's shop. And, there are more and more automobiles to fix. His business is good and he has not been conscripted, he suspects because of the "entry" on his papers.

August 1937, Gestapo officials arrive in Lützen looking for Willi. They are told he is in Leipzig and before he can be warned of the visit, the Gestapo men find him at his shop. As a politically unsatisfactory German, he must join a civilian labor force building the west wall, the Siegfried Line. The Gestapo wait while Willi packs his suitcase, then trundle him off to the Bahnhof where a group of "unsatisfactory" men are herded aboard a train and sent to an area near the French border. They build bunkers. While Willi digs defensive fortifications along the Siegfried Line in November, Katarina gives birth to their second child, Ingebord, another girl. Willi is allowed to return to Leipzig.

September 1939, Willi is finally called up by the military, issued a uniform and Soldbuch, and told to report in October for training in an infantry unit at

Leitmeritz in the Sudetenland. (A Soldbuch is the Wehrmacht soldiers identification, to be carried at all times, containing: photograph, unit identification, authorization for leave and pay, travel, and other records. Annotations in the book were, but not always, to be made by an officer. Willi's Soldbuch has been stamped **Unsatisfactory**.)

Chapter 14
Off to War

Leipzig, Saxony
September 1939

Oma Meissner's dining room is filled with the aroma of real coffee brewing, and the warm brightness of autumn sunshine. How she gets real coffee and not the ersatz mixture from the grocer, surprises Willi, but *Oma* is full of surprises he recalls. Rich mahogany shines through the lattice work of the lace table cloth. A bouquet of red and yellow peonies Willi brought her are now in a Kaiser Porcelain vase in the center of the table. Puttering about in the kitchen, *Oma* makes clucking noises; the house is a happy place for Willi, a peaceful place, a sanctuary since his youth. Tomorrow he leaves for basic training in the Sudetenland.

Earlier Willi visited his parent's in Lützen, much easier on his emotions. Freda and Karl had already finished breakfast when he arrived. They sat in the kitchen and drank coffee at the same table they were using in 1918 to sip ersatz coffee made of roasted corn grain. In 1939, it is ersatz coffee made from barley seeds. When it was time to leave, Willi stood while dry-eyed Freda hugged him and kissed his cheek, his father shook his hand with tears in his eyes and said, "I hoped this would never happen again," choking on the words.

Saying '*auf weidersehn*' to *Oma* and *Opa* is difficult, Willi has not looked forward to facing *Oma's* penetrating gaze and *Opa's* helpless gasps and wheezes. The U*nterfeldwebel* (sergeant) for recruits told him it will be many weeks before he can come home again, months possibly. Willi's emotions are mixed, happy to have the time with Oma, but sad thinking she may not be around when he returns from the war. His worn and bulging diary, with clippings and mementos from his tenth birthday, lies on the dining table.

Oma enters with a cup of coffee and slice of strawberry *'kuchen'.* "Wilhelm, put down your diary and talk to me!" Wiping her hands on her apron and looking at the table, she returns to the kitchen for some cream. "*Ja, ja,* when you quit puttering around in the kitchen,*"* he joshes her and puts the diary aside. *Oma* calls him Wilhelm, though everyone else now calls him Willi. "If I don't come home from the war, you must give my diary to the girls when they are older." Returning from the kitchen and setting the cream on the table, *Oma* scolds him, "Don't say such things. It will be a miracle if *Opa* and I live through the war. But, you are young and strong and you will come home! I know! Now, tell me again where you are going and when you leave."

"The Sudetenland, *Oma,* and I leave tomorrow. I take tests there and get more uniforms, then I will be a Wehrmacht infantryman." Adding cream to his coffee and stirring it slowly, he watches *Oma* ease into her chair, carefully smoothing her apron. With hands in her lap, she waits for him to take the first bite of her 'kuchen.' He knows she's wants an opinion and never disappoints her. "Tastes good!" he says, rolling his eyes.

"You always say that Wilhelm, but when you roll your eyes, I know you mean it." She pauses then asks, "Do you think you could be in the army band like your *Opa* Stolle? Wasn't he a general?"

"*Opa* Stolle was a concertmaster, not a general although he looked like one," Willi adds. "The Kaiser had many bands, but Hitler has a few musicians and many noisemakers. Anyway, Hitler is looking for men to fight, not play music."

Finishing the *'kuchen'*, he pushes back from the table and leans over, gently kissing *Oma* on each cheek. "Now I must say goodbye to *Opa*." Placing the diary in a wooden box *Opa* made, he walks to the pantry and slides it behind the flour barrel where it has been placed for safe keeping ever since Kristin gave it to him.

His visit to *Opa i*s cut short by *Opa's* labored wheezing. As he wheels his bicycle from the house on *Bunde Strasse,* his eyes are suddenly tearing and he pulls out his handkerchief. "Must be the smoke," he calls back to *Oma* Meissner as she stands very straight and fragile in the doorway. Dabbing both eyes, Willi calls out, "*Wiedersehen Oma, Wiedersehen.*!"

Parking his bicycle in the walkway between the apartment buildings on Eisenbahn Strasse, Willi can see the busybody neighborhood wives peeking from behind their curtains, always spying. He takes the five steps to the door in two big leaps, turns and bows to the spying ladies, careful not to stumble in his new boots. "Good afternoon *Frau* Bohnen, *Frau* Miklaus, and *Frau* Cohen," he says loudly. "Katarina, I'm home!" From the doorway he can hear her in the kitchen. *Ach*, she is a good cook! If only her disposition was as good as her cooking.

"Willi, you are married and a father, yet you treat the *Hausfraus* on our street as if you were a teenager. Why did you yell at them when you came in?" Katarina asks, as she strides toward him, wiping her hand on her apron. She is very tall when she is mad. Her blonde hair is braided and pinned atop her head making her look taller. The tip of her small, pointy nose is glowing pink and her large, round doe-eyes appear to bulge slightly in her anger. Otherwise, she is remarkably pretty when not wearing a frown.

Willi puts an arm around her waist, and pulls her close, kissing her cheek as she turns her lips away from him. "What is wrong, *Liebchen,* I thought you like me in a uniform?"

"You're changing the subject Willi, but never mind." She leans back against Willi's arm to look. "It doesn't look as nice as your police uniform with all the brass buttons. But it will do," she says, running her fingers over the rough twill of his gray Wehrmacht jacket. She pushes out of his grasp and stands, hands on her broad hips, looking at him critically. "It is good you are going off to fight for the Reich. The neighborhood will be more peaceful without your bellowing. And, because you are a soldier, we get extra rations at the *Kartenstelle* even though you are not a party member."

Willi knows the Bürgermeister has been generous to let Katarina have extra blue cards for meat. Since early this year Hitler started a rationing program, first for food. He suspects it is because of the emergency repairs Willi makes on city equipment in his blacksmith shop. And, there were other things Katarina managed to get others could not. When Willi asks, "Where did it come from?" Katarina gets sullen and will not speak to him for hours.

Out of the corner of his eye there is a blur as the girls come running down the stairs and right into his arms. "Papa!" they cry out as they each try to fasten their arms around Willi's neck. "Girls, you are fine young Saxon ladies. Why do you run so fast on the stairway? You could hurt yourselves and," pretending to gasp and wheeze, "…choke your Papa to death!" The first time they played this little game, the girls released his neck immediately, worried they might hurt Papa. Now they only squeeze harder. Katarina is already talking of putting them into a Hitler Youth program. They do not need Hitler Youth training Willi keeps telling her. They need to learn to be little ladies and grow up to be good mothers, Willi thinks.

Katarina begins to set the table as Willi removes first Christel, whose arms are still wrapped tightly around his neck, then his blouse. Inge is sitting on his boot, arms wrapped around his leg, waiting to ride his foot to the table. It is to be his last meal at home for a while. "Ah Katarina, where did you get the goose liver?" he asks as she brings out a large dish of his favorite food. He knew as soon as the words left his mouth he should not have asked.

"There you go again, always asking where this came from, or where that came from. You never give me credit for being able to go to the market and find a bargain," she snaps back angrily.

Quickly Willi clasps his hands and bows his head, the signal to the girls and Katarina for silence as Willi blesses the food. Willi includes a little extra blessing for his 'loving' wife and daughters and peeks at Katarina to see if she is listening. He cannot tell.

Willi always enjoys his food and, even with an angry wife and foreboding thoughts about tomorrow's departure, this meal will not go to waste. Katarina is over her pout and the girls ask questions about the army, and when he will be coming home from the war. They talk nonchalantly as if his departure for the army will be only a short excursion away from home. Finishing the meal Willi smacks his lips, nods his head, and pats his stomach in approval. Leaning back in his chair he watches as Christel tries to imitate him and almost slides out of her chair when she leans back.

As Willi gives the girls instruction on how they are to behave while he is gone, Katarina gives a sniff of her nose and gets up from the table. She moves noisily about the kitchen getting things put away and muttering under her breath she can 'manage this all much better once Willi is gone.' Willi pretends not to hear and asks Christel to get the checker board. It is time to play their evening game. Inge watches and helps Willi with his moves.

Finishing the dishes, Katarina wraps the remaining goose liver pate and leaves it out for Willi to take with him in the morning. Out of the corner of his eye Willi can see Katarina watching as they play, frowning occasionally as they vigorously slap their checkers on the board. For Willi, part of the fun of checkers is getting emotionally involved in playing. Christel finally corners his remaining king.

"I win! I win! Mama I beat Papa!" Christel is excited.

"You were too much for me tonight, Christel. When I come home I want a rematch!"

"Let's play another game tonight, Papa," Christel demands.

"Papa let you win, Christel," Inge states with a pout in her voice. "We could have beaten you."

Katarina has finished. She sits on the sofa with her sewing bag, watching to see what they will do.

"It is time for bed," Willi tells the girls. "You'll get your chance to beat me again when I come home." Katarina takes Christel by the hand and starts upstairs. Taking a final look around downstairs, Willi stoops over and picks Inge out of the chair where she is about to fall asleep. Holding her in his arms, he presses the wall switch with his elbow and follows along.

All is quiet at 788 Eisenbahn Strasse in Leipzig.

Chapter 15
Basic Training

In the Sudetenland
Tuesday, 24 October 1939

When Willi arrives in the annexed Sudetenland for basic training his first impression is there are only Germans living in this border area. The street signs are German, the cinema advertisements are in German, everyone speaks German and when he actually meets a Czechoslovakian, he looks like a German. There are Nazi black shirts (Gestapo) in every town. The first day in camp Willi gets two grey field uniforms and another pair of boots. There are at least 200 infantry recruits going through the line. The second day they are taught military courtesy, who to salute and when. The third day they are given written and physical endurance tests.

The fourth day Willi is told to report to the *Unterfeldwebel* (sergeant). "Your soldbuch is stamped Unsatisfactory, Meissner," the sergeant grumbles. "We are training for the real army! You should not have been sent to this camp. We are sending you to Munich for radio operator training and, if you are lucky, you will be in an expanded unit."

"What does expanded unit mean?" Willi asks.

"For one thing, Meissner, you use horses, not tanks or trucks," the sergeant replies. "And, if the panzer units go beyond Poland, they still won't send your unit. You'll be too slow to keep up!" (Expanded units are comprised of politically unsatisfactory men and those who did poorly on the written and/or physical tests.)

Boarding the train for Munich with other politically unsatisfactory soldiers, he also learns how the mighty German army travels. They are loaded twenty soldiers in one box car. The master sergeant in charge of transportation says the car will hold over 100 prisoners. What kind of prisoners, he did not say.

Arriving in Munich Bahnhof fourteen hours later, cold and stiff from riding in the unheated car, a portly sergeant, buttons on his shirt straining to contain the girth, meets the train. He marches them to the training school, part of the university complex south of central Munich. The Alps are maybe 30 miles away.

Student radio operators live in a dormitory building and train in a classroom nearby. Each day they have two hours of physical training (PT). A ski instructor is their PT leader and the first day of class asks what sports they play. Someone behind Willi (perhaps someone who knew Willi had been a boxer) says, "boxing." The ski instructor turns to Willi and asks, "Private, you like to box?"

"Not me," he responds!

"Someone said boxing. Who said boxing? We have gloves and it is a good sport to start with. What is your name, private?"

"Meissner, Wilhelm Meissner. But, I do not like to box you."

"Private, the first thing you will learn here is everyone participates. If we race, everyone races. If we swim, everyone swims. And, if we box, everyone boxes. You will be first. I won't hurt you. Come, put the gloves on! You're a big lad and I'll take it easy." He strips to the waist and motions for Willi to do likewise.

It is chilly on the exercise field and a light wind bends the tops of the ankle deep, green grass. Willi shrugs and removes his exercise top, then picks up a pair of gloves and slips them on his hands. Turning to a student, Willi asks him to tie the laces and instructs him to pull the laces tight.

Meanwhile the instructor has the sergeant help him with his gloves. The instructor is tall, about Willi's height, thin, and very quick in his movements. Once his gloves are laced, he dances around the makeshift grass covered ring, shadow boxing while waiting for Willi to join him in the circle. He is a little older than Willi, perhaps thirty years old.

As the instructor circles and jabs, hitting Willi's gloves, he watches the instructor's eyes and when the eye movements quicken Willi knows he is ready for the attack. The instructor jabs with his left and starts to swing his right. Willi catches the punch in midair with his left glove, pushes it aside, and plants a healthy right jab squarely on the instructor's mouth and nose. Stunned, the instructor slips and falls to the grass, blood spurting from his nose. His lip is cut and blood runs from the corners of his mouth.

The instructor sits up, propping himself with his gloved fists. A medic, on standby for injuries, bends over him cleaning away the blood. "Where did you learn to box?" the instructor asks.

"I was a police master boxer," Willi replies calmly.

"Why didn't you tell me?"

"You didn't ask!"

The instructor, noticing the smirking faces of the students, spits blood from his mouth and says, "Enough for today. Go with the sergeant and do your exercises." He leaves the sports ground with the medic.

"I think you hurt his pride more than his face, Meissner," the Bavarian sergeant tells Willi as he unties the gloves. He yells, "Okay, boys! Let's go behind the barn and get to work." They walk around behind a big barn, once a stable for the University equestrian team, and the sergeant says, "Now you boys can exercise if you want, but you look in pretty good shape to me. We'll just have a rest back here and I'll make the officer think we are hard at it." Walking back to the corner of the barn, he sees the officer is still on the exercise field. Then he yells out, "Okay, now run in place, left, right, left, right!" Meanwhile the trainees relax in the sun, blocked from the cool breeze by the barn.

Every day the Bavarian sergeant is in charge of exercise, the same thing happens. This is one of the few good breaks they get in school. The ski master never asks Willi to box again, but insures Willi gets his share of licks in other sports.

During the second week of school, Hitler comes to Munich and speaks to a reunion of the *Alte Kampfer* (Old Fighters), Tuesday, 8 November 1939. In the evening, Willi hears an attempt has been made on the Führer's life at the Bürgerbräukeller. A bomb practically destroyed the hall where Hitler was speaking only minutes after he left. Willi thinks if he had spoken as long as he did in Leipzig, Hitler would be dead now.

Perhaps it is Willi's music training helping in his communications class. He easily picks up the difference between dots and dashes. Mastering Morse code is a little more difficult for Willi. But, the final phase of the course is sending and receiving messages using a telegraph key. Willi's instructors are surprised at his speed and accuracy tapping out the messages. Willi meets the required speed for sending and receiving messages and is excused from practice. He uses the time to visit *Oberschütze* (senior private) Frederic Schmidt, his clarinet playing friend from Lützen.

Frederic is in a different part of the communications school, living in the same dormitory as Willi, but sharing a room with a Nazi senior private. Frederic's roommate takes the same course as Willi. One day while visiting Frederic, the roommate comes in from class and tells Willi, "Private, don't you have something better to do with your time, like cleaning your pigsty of a room. And, if you're going to visit this room you'll speak proper German, not Saxon gibberish."

Willi looks up from where he is sitting. "Go away and bother someone else," Willi says dispassionately.

"You can't talk to me that way, Private."

"Don't make trouble, boy private. We are two friends talking. If you need someone to talk with, talk to your Nazi friends." The senior private, face flushed and intimidated by Willi's size, turns and leaves the room. "Willi, you took a big chance, he is snot, but his party connections can make things bad for you," Frederic says thoughtfully, "and for me!"

The next day Willi's telegraph instructor calls him aside; Willi figures the young Nazi has reported him. But the instructor tells him he has passed all the tests and need not return to class. While others are still in training, Willi is told to report to his unit, an expanded artillery battalion in Army Group C, near the French border.

Willi joins the unit in the Rhineland, March 1940. It has been the coldest winter in years, even the Rhine has been frozen. Fortunately Willi spent most of it in Munich. But, spring has still not shown itself in the fortified trenches of the Siegfried Line. Willi knows the area from his earlier experience as a laborer building the west wall. Shortly after he arrives, snow begins to melt from the shaded northern slopes of the bunkers and they begin training exercises.

For four weeks Willi practices signaling with the company telegraph communications equipment while other soldiers dry fire their cannons. The artillery men in the expanded unit do not load real shells because it is dangerous, and must conserve ammunition in case the 'French start a war'.

9 April 1940, Willi is still sitting on the Siegfried Line while Germany invades Denmark and Norway. A month later, at 5:30 a.m., 10 May 1940, the German army moves across the borders of Holland, Belgium and Luxembourg.

Willi's unit is alerted to pack up and be ready to move. The last of May they finally move by rail to Holland. It is Willi's first time to see homes destroyed, people living in the streets, burned-out carcasses of trucks and cars piled alongside the road, and rows of freshly dug graves in the cemeteries. When they finally arrive in Zeeland, artillery pieces are unloaded at a railway siding near Vlissingen. The weather is warm and the unit spends the night encamped by the railroad.

The Dutch have already surrendered and the next morning Willi awakes to the sound of a rooster crowing in the distance, not the sound of artillery. Spending their first full day in Holland positioning the unit's artillery pieces with teams of horses, the men return to their camp by the railway siding, tired and ready for the evening meal. After eating a thin soup soaked in chunks of black bread, they sit by camp fires and talk about the things they saw today, destroyed canal bridges and other sabotage aimed at slowing the German advance. Willi's NCO tells his men tomorrow they will be moving to a forward observation point.

Following a breakfast of cheese, butter, bread and marmalade, washed down with weak, hot coffee, Willi and the other artillery spotters gather their bed rolls, mount their horses and follow the NCO and *Hauptmann* (Captain) Rischmann, their commander, to a small village on the North Sea coast. Captain Rischmann looks very funny on a horse for he is built like a Gouda cheese, round and hard. The Bürgermeister, a Nazi sympathizer, welcomes Captain Rischmann and offers to provide anything they need.

The Bürgermeister places the men in houses throughout the village. He takes Willi to the Harbormaster's house and knocks on the door. It opens slightly and first one head appears in the opening, then two, three and four. The mother, the son, the father and daughter are looking out the door with only their surprised faces showing.

"You will give this man a room in your house," the Bürgermeister tells them and leaves Willi standing at the door, embarrassed. They give Willi a large room, a comfortable bed, the windows let in much light, and the Harbormaster even has a stable for Willi's horse.

Willi's observation post is on a small spit of land extending out into the sea. An even smaller village (called Spitzbruggen) is there, and a light house. To reach Spitzbruggen by horseback or on foot, he must cross canals and narrow footbridges. By sea, it is much shorter, and in the Harbormaster's power boat, much faster. Willi will travel to Spitzbruggen every day to look for ships, listen for bombers, and decode British weather signals. His orders are to send a coded message to the artillery communications center if he sees or hears anything.

On his first visit, and to help Willi locate the best place to set up his transmitter, Captain Rischmann accompanies him in the Harbormaster's boat. It is only a twenty minute run and the Harbormaster assures Willi the horse will take much longer. From a few hundred yards off-shore the swells make it difficult to see Spitzbruggen. It is barely above sea level, with a few houses, windmill, lighthouse, and lots of black and white cattle for making milk and cheeses.

A small group of people watch as the Harbormaster brings his launch in toward the beach. The Captain has a little difficulty getting out of the boat and on to the beach without getting his boots wet. Once on firm footing he immediately draws himself up to his full five foot two inches and demands to know who lives in the large house nearest the shore. Herr Polter, a large Dutchman, about Willi's size, steps forward and introduces himself as the owner.

"When Private Meissner comes to Spitzbruggen you will feed him and assist him with whatever he asks. Do you understand?" Captain Rischmann demands. Herr Polter nods agreement. Willi shoulders his telegraph pack and starts toward the lighthouse, the best place to watch for ships. Willi climbs the narrow, curving steps inside the lighthouse and Captain Rischmann follows, puffing and wheezing along behind. When they reach the top, and Willi sets his pack down, there is no room for Captain Rischmann. Willi opens a window and the wind whistles through the small space, and down through the winding stairwell. Captain Rischmann sits on a step below the platform and gasps for breath. His face is red and he looks like he is ready to collapse.

"This looks like a good place, eh Captain?" Willi asks.

"*Ja!*" Captain Rischmann exhales and sits with his chin on his chest.

Willi squeezes around the reflector, finds a better place to put the batteries and antenna, then begins to unpack his wireless telegraph set. While Captain Rischmann gets his breath, Willi tunes his set to the unit's frequency and attempts to tap out a signal to the communications center and tell them he is at Spitzbruggen. There is only static on the receiver.

After Captain Rischmann gets to feeling better he says, "We go now!" Back down the steps they go and reaching the bottom the Captain turns to Willi and says, "You, Private Meissner, stay and be on look out. Listen for Englanders talking on their radios. The Harbormaster will return for you at the end of the day." Then he climbs back in the boat while the Harbormaster and several men from Spitzbruggen push it into the surf.

Willi walks back to the lighthouse and climbs the stairs. First he inspects the telegraph key, then his headset, to see if there is a problem. Rechecking the frequency, he moves his antenna to different positions around the reflector. Deftly he taps out a message, "This is Willi at Spitzbruggen. Do you read?" The sound of dots and dashes confirms contact has been made with the center. Excited, Willi looks down to see if the Harbormaster's boat has departed. It has gradually moved out into more open water and is turning south toward Zeeland. Willi waves and shouts from the window as loudly as possible, "I've made contact!"

Captain Rischmann, now some distance away, turns in the boat to see what all the commotion is about. He sees Willi waving and raises his arm and shouts something back. Willi cannot hear what the Captain says but it must have been 'Heil Hitler.' The wind is blowing and whistling around the lighthouse. Some gulls are circling and squawking, adding to the noise.

As soon as the Captain is out of sight in the haze, Willi rechecks his equipment and clambers back down from the light house, his boots ringing on the spiral metal staircase. Herr Polter, who has been standing outside with his neighbors, asks, "What do you need from us?"

"Do you have work for a blacksmith?" Willi replies with a broad smile. There are six families in Spitzbruggen, twenty-three people. They are all looking at Willi. Herr Polter speaks German and Dutch and tells them what Willi has asked. They look at each other with puzzled expressions, whispering and gesturing. Then Herr Polter says guardedly, "We will see. For now, you tell us what you need. We will cooperate."

"Good," Willi says, "I'm hungry from my trip and my last real meal was in Leipzig. Have you some cheese and bread?" he asks, putting his folded fingers to his mouth for emphasis. The soup and one pot meals he has lived on for the past week is causing him to lose weight and feel a bit weak. Perhaps it was the climb up the lighthouse steps. Herr Polter's wife, a thin, sharp featured woman, in a white bonnet and black dress, motions for Willi to follow her.

Frau Polter leads Willi to a clean, white-washed kitchen. A cool breeze billows her hand-embroidered curtains, as she motions for Willi to sit at a scrubbed wooden dinner table. The top of the table is made from heavy planks at least three inches thick before being worn smooth, and thinner, by daily scrubbing. Opening the pantry, she brings out a fresh cheese, a loaf of bread that has already been broken, and some butter.

Hungry, but remembering Oma's instructions to be courteous, Willi waits to see if Frau Polter will join him at the table. When she steps back from the table, Willi thanks her and bows his head to bless the food. She is silent until Willi finishes his prayer then says her first words to him. "Would you like something else, soldier? If not, I have other things to do." Willi dismisses her with a nod of approval and is left alone to eat and mull over his good fortune.

The weeks go by very quickly as he travels the 12 kilometers on horseback, back and forth to Spitzbruggen. Sometimes the weather is bad and Willi stays at Spitzbruggen overnight. More than once he has stayed with Herr Polter helping him with his cattle. He also does blacksmith work for the other people of Spitzbruggen. Willi is accepted more as a neighbor than a German soldier.

There are times when Willi almost forgets there is a war. The Dutch are good to him. He builds a small forge on Spitzbruggen with parts scavenged on the mainland. In turn, they help him with the communications equipment Captain Rischmann sends over to be tested. He moves the equipment to various locations on the spit of land.

New listening devices are installed Captain Rischmann says will make it easier to pick up British radio broadcasts and ship reports. If it were any easier, Willi would do nothing but eat and sleep. What the captain did not say was once the devices were operational, Willi would be sent to other duties.

Letters from Katarina are not as frequent as Willi had hoped. Yet, the news is good. Everyone is healthy and Leipzig is not a target for the British bombers. During a November visit to Spitzbruggen, Captain Rischmann tells Meissner he can have leave at Christmas. Willi writes Katarina, *Oma* and *Opa*, and Papa and Mama in Lützen, telling them he will be home for Christmas.

In December, Willi's sergeant tells him to report to the orderly office and pick up his leave papers, he can start leave the next day, but must return Christmas Eve. The Harbormaster's family is very excited for Willi and plan a surprise farewell party.

As Willi packs his bags the people he has befriended from Spitzbruggen and Zeeland bring gifts for him to take to his family, a wheel of cheese, bars of chocolates, wooden shoes for Ingebord and Christel, sugar, beer, tea and real coffee. He gets an allotment of tobacco when he arrives at the orderly room to pick up his pass and tickets. This will be a good Christmas.

Chapter 16
Home for Christmas

Leipzig
December 1940

Willi is unsure what to expect from Katarina. It is cold and dreary as Willi steps from the train. He stops to survey the crowd of people, hoping there might be someone to greet him. Walking past the small clusters of families and on through the station, he hails a taxi. Willi gives the driver the address on Eisenbahn Strasse and sits back in the old Mercedes, enjoying the trip home. His pack is heavy with gifts from the Dutchmen. It rests on the seat beside him.

"You are home for Christmas?" the driver asks.

"*Ja*. It is the first time home in over a year!"

"How is the war going?"

"I don't know. I haven't seen much of it. But, I can say my horse is getting fat and the Dutchmen are friendly people."

The driver pulls up and stops in front of the house on Eisenbahn Strasse. Christel and Inge are standing by the window, watching the street. They wave and disappear.

Paying the taxi driver, Willi looks up and down the street. Not much has changed except the neighbor wives are not leaning out the windows talking. Shouldering his pack he takes the steps one at a time, and, as he reaches the door it opens and three-year-old Inge grabs him about the waist.

Christel and Ingebord are talking at the same time. Willi puts his pack on the dining table and sits on the couch between the two girls. They tell him about school, their mother and the Bürgermeister's sergeant, and their grandparents. Katarina is at the market shopping and will return soon. Christel wants to play checkers, demanding a rematch Willi promised before leaving for the Sudetenland.

Willi makes a mental note to ask Katarina about this sergeant in the Bürgermeister's office; he promises to play checkers with both girls, and then telephones *Oma* Meissner. They are still talking when Katarina enters the house.

"You're home," Katarina says flatly. She puts her shopping bag on the kitchen counter, then walks over and plants a kiss on Willi's forehead. "Who are you talking to?"

"*Oma* Meissner," he says holding his hand over the mouthpiece. "I'll be through in a moment."

After Willi finishes talking with *Oma* Meissner, he rises from the chair and reaches for Katarina's hand, "And, for you, my wife, a more appropriate greeting." As he kisses her she starts to object, telling him the girls are watching. It is no use.

Katarina has tickets for a concert to celebrate his return. Christel and Ingebord stay with a neighbor as Willi and Katarina take the trolley to the Bahnhof and walk down Goethe Strasse toward the opera house. It is a beautiful, clear, cold evening. The war seems far away. Willi hears the rapid footsteps behind them. It sounds like a person is about to run into them. They step aside. A high-pitched voice says, "Soldier, show me your Soldbuch *bitte.*"

Willi turns and is confronted by a small man with a mustache, trimmed carefully to look like the Führer's mustache. A red armband with a black swastika encircled in white is pinned to the left sleeve of his civilian overcoat. "Why do you ask?" Willi responds.

"Do not question me, just hand over your Soldbuch. I want to see if you are a deserter." To keep from causing a disturbance and ruining their evening, Willi pulls his Soldbuch from inside his military blouse and hands it to the man he now recognizes as Gestapo.

Squinting at the Soldbuch, and determining Willi is legitimately on leave, he says, "Very well, Private Meissner," raises his hand in a salute and shouts, "Heil Hitler!"

Willi does not think it necessary to return the salute and reaches for his Soldbuch.

"One moment, Private, why didn't you return my salute?"

"You aren't a soldier and I didn't think it necessary," Willi replies.

"I am an officer of the government and you will salute me, do you hear?"

Willi nods silently looking at this "cockadoodle" of a man. The Gestapo agent takes out a pencil and writes Willi's name and unit on a piece of paper, drops the soldbuch on the sidewalk and stalks off.

Willi picks up his Soldbuch and sticks it inside his coat pocket. Shrugging his shoulders, they continue walking to the opera house. The incident bothers Willi, but he soon pushes it from his mind once the concert starts. The sound of violins in the final movement is very restful. It is an enjoyable concert, and there are no air raids. As Katarina and Willi leave the opera house, Katarina smiles and waves to a sergeant who is standing near the exit. "Who is he?" Willi asks.

"The Bürgermeister's sergeant, he got us the tickets for tonight," is Katarina's snippy response.

"The girls tell me the sergeant comes to the house often. Is true?"

"No! It is not true. He only comes when the Bürgermeister has something to send us. Since I am being cooperative with the officials, we have food one cannot get from the grocer and the girls are doing well in the youth program. If only you were not so stubborn, we could have much more. You deliberately provoke people, like the Gestapo man!"

"The Gestapo shouldn't stop me on the street like a suspected criminal when I'm home on leave," Willi tells her. Over the next few days the argument festers.

Willi takes Christel and Inge, by train, to Lützen to deliver gifts from the Netherlands. Arriving before noon, a light snow is falling, just enough to see their footprints on the station platform when they leave the train. Freda and Karl are there to meet them. Willi looks inside the station for Herr Finck, waves to him, and leaves with his family.

As they walk beneath the naked limbs of the Linden trees, Freda tells Willi the bad news. Kristin's husband and oldest son have been killed while fighting in Poland. She is living with her mother-in-law at Weissenfels, and raising two younger sons.

Ludwina lives in Lützen while her husband is away in the army. Leaving the girls with their grandparents, Willi walks a back pathway to Ludwina's house. Ludwina is critical of Willi's uniform and lack of medals. "I think Mother has lunch ready and I must go. It was good to see you have not changed," he says, excusing himself.

After lunch, Willi gives his parents presents brought from his Dutch friends. Freda has made a scarf for Willi, and Karl gives him a belt buckle made in his shop. The family walks back to the station and Willi and the girls board the train, waving to Freda and Karl. Herr Finck hobbles out on the platform as the train slowly leaves Lützen, waving to his friend, Willi.

The snow is heavier as they return to Leipzig. Willi finds a taxi to take them to *Oma* and *Opa* Meissner's house. The smell of coffee from *Oma* Meissner's kitchen is not the same as before the war. The richness has gone from the smell.

"*Oma* you have changed your brand of coffee," Willi says with a chuckle as he wraps his arms around the frail lady. "You'll like what I've brought you from Holland, the real stuff." Willi has brought her a bag of South American coffee beans, another of the gifts from his friends. Her eyes show her pleasure, as she alternately hugs Willi and the girls. *Opa* Meissner is still bedridden. After a short visit at his bedside, Willi knows *Opa* will not suffer much longer.

Oma Meissner gives Willi several handmade items as gifts for his Dutch hosts. They sit at the dining table and drink the watered down coffee *Oma* has prepared. Receiving their presents, Christel and Inge are anxious to return home. The weather worsens; snow mixed with sleet covers the streets. Willi apologizes to *Oma* for not visiting longer and takes the girls home.

Returning to Eisenbahn Strasse, Willi decides to leave for his unit tonight. Arguing with Katarina has spoiled the holiday for Willi. Katarina is in the kitchen preparing the evening meal when they arrive. Willi plays a game of checkers with Christel while waiting for dinner. Inge pouts as Christel wins quickly, taking advantage of Willi's half-hearted play.

After dinner, Willi gives the girls their presents to open and tells Katarina of his decision to return to his unit early. She accepts the news coolly, offering to help him pack his bags. Snow is falling steadily as Willi leaves the house on Eisenbahn. The rooftops and streets are blanketed in white. His taxi is waiting at the curb. Inside the house, Christel and Inge hold candles in the window and wave. Katarina is nowhere to be seen.

The Netherlands, 20 December 1940

On his return, Willi is called to Captain Rischmann's office. "Private Meissner, sit down. Now, tell me, why is it you come back so soon? Your leave is not over."

"It is nothing, Sir. The weather was bad, and the wife fusses a lot. So I come back early."

The fat little officer looks at Willi, puzzling over his answer. "A soldier cannot be worried about his home and be a good soldier, Meissner. You tell me if anything is wrong!"

"*Ja,* will do Sir."

Three days after Christmas, Willi receives a message on the telegraph while he is at Spitzbruggen. He is to come to company headquarters and see the *staff-führer* (adjutant) immediately. The company sends a man to replace Willi. Willi asks him if he knows what the adjutant wants. The new man shakes his head, no, and ads, "They said, 'hurry'." Willi arrives at company headquarters in the afternoon.

The adjutant, stern and intimidating behind his desk, asks Willi, "Why did you return from Leipzig early?"

"I explained to Captain Rischmann; it was family troubles," Willi responds with a strained expression on his face.

"You lie, Meissner," the adjutant snaps, almost jumping out of his chair. "You were in trouble with the Gestapo! We have heard from Leipzig. Why didn't you salute the officer?"

It suddenly dawns on Willi what the adjutant is excited about. He starts to explain and is interrupted as the adjutant springs from his chair and pounds the desk.

"No excuses, Private. You are under house arrest for lying to the Captain and failing to salute an officer."

"What do you mean I lie?"

"You didn't tell the Captain the truth about returning early. When you get in trouble with the Gestapo, everyone gets in trouble."

"But this is impossible! I was walking with my wife to hear a concert and this 'officer'…"

"Watch what you are about to say, Private." The adjutant cuts him off sharply, smirks, and says, "All it takes to put a politically unreliable person away in a camp is a word from the Gestapo. The captain has suggested we punish you here, light punishment. Do you understand what house arrest means?"

"*Ja!*"

"We have a house in this village. Come, we go now!"

Willi follows the adjutant and his sergeant, despairing of any chance to defend his actions. There is a house nearby used for such purposes. A Dutch family resides in part of the large house and one wing is used to confine German officers and enlisted men accused of minor violations. Willi is placed in a room with only a straw sack for a bed; otherwise it is empty.

"Someone will come later to feed you," the adjutant remarks as he checks the door and then locks it. About dark, the door is opened, and a corporal from headquarters enters and tells Willi he can go to the toilet and then return to the room. When Willi returns, a piece of bread and cup of water are on the floor. The corporal locks the door and leaves Willi alone.

After the first full day of house arrest, Willi is pacing the floor. He is allowed out to go to the toilet in the middle of the afternoon and returns to find bread and water on the floor for his meal. During the evening as he sits on the straw sack, Willi hears a key in the lock. It is the daughter of the man who owns the house. "This is no good for you," she says. "Come; eat with us in the kitchen. No one will know."

After the meal, the family gives Willi some cheese and bread to take back to his room. The daughter, about the age of Christel, gives Willi a small block of chocolate.

The house arrest only lasts three days. Willi is needed at his radio post.

France, autumn, 1942

After nearly two years in the Netherlands Willi's unit packs and moves through Belgium to France. Joining the expanded artillery units, they spend several months in exercises along the northern coast. Willi's unit leaves France in February 1943; their destination, Italy. Skirting Paris, the train travels through southern France, almost to the Mediterranean. Artillery pieces are on flat cars near the front of the train and the soldiers ride in boxcars at the end of the train. Passing through the French Alps and crossing the flat plains of northern Italy, they reach Rimini on the Adriatic coast. The unit unloads and stays in Rimini until the end of March.

Then, it is back on a train for Taranto, where they board a ship for Tunis. Anchored in the Gulf of Tunis in early April for several days, Willi spends his free time sun-bathing and getting sunburned. The unit goes ashore, but before all their artillery pieces can be offloaded, orders are changed. Less than a week in Tunis and Willi is helping to reload the equipment.

Landing in Salerno in early May, the unit entrains for a trip across the boot of Italy to Foggia. The train is strafed by American planes, and several artillery pieces are damaged. Other than bruises incurred leaping from the train, no one is injured.

Summer in Southern Italy is not as good as Willi has been led to believe. There are mosquitoes, bad water, and some Italians hate the German Army. But, the wine is good, and a little wine is good for the stomach. They camp near Foggia until September when the Americans land at Salerno. Willi's unit is put on alert to move at short notice. The mood of Italians changes drastically after 8 September 1943, their government calls for an Armistice with the Allies. Concealed animosity once prevailed, now the Italians want nothing to do with Germans.

The artillery battalion is ordered to move September 23rd, the day the Americans land at Bari, less than 75 miles away. Their column is strafed by fighter planes twice the first day. Each time Willi finds a ditch to jump into. They lose much time due to the strafing. The next day is worse. As the unit moves further north, more German and a few remaining Italian units join them. An entire division of the German Tenth Army is moving toward Pescara where a new defensive line is being formed called the "Gustav Line".

Once they arrive, Willi thinks this is where they will surely make a stand—mountains from one side of Italy to the other and the Volturno and Sangro rivers blocking valley approaches to the Gustav Line. Willi's unit is north of the River Sangro, between Ortona and Pescara. The heaviest defense works are on the eastern side of the Gustav line, reinforcing what General Kesserling has called "an impenetrable barrier."

The British come within range of Willi's artillery unit 20 December 1943. Willi is a mile forward of the artillery when he spots German infantry retreating toward his position. Somehow British units have crossed the rain swollen

Sangro and are advancing toward Ortona. Willi spots British foot soldiers, moving up the coastal highway, shielded by tanks, and followed by trucks. He taps out coded coordinates quickly and gets a "repeat" signal back from his command post. He taps out the position of the British tanks again and waits.

The first blast and whistle of German 88mm artillery sends the Englishmen running for cover. From Willi's vantage point he sees the first barrage is off target, but slowing the advancing soldiers. He sends corrections back to artillery control and another salvo of 88mm artillery fire descends on the advancing British units.

A thick gray pall of acrid smoke settles over the scene. This is Willi's first smell of war. During the next few days he moves between the lines, carrying his telegraph set with battery pack and earphones. The four batteries can last two or three days before recharging. In this "no man's land" Willi has seen his British counterpart moving about. They have even waved at each other during lulls in the fighting.

Christmas Eve, Willi crawls back to his observation post with a fresh battery pack and a loaf of black bread from the unit mess. In the darkness he is surprised to see the outline of a soldier reclining comfortably in his fox hole and smoking a cigarette. Willi calls out in German, "Who is there?"

The cigarette is doused and an English voice responds nervously, "I am Ian, who are you?" (At least the man understands German. Although Willi has never had a good look at the enemy forward observer, he suspects it may be him.)

An artillery barrage, called in by another unit, begins to drop shells nearby. It is obvious to Willi they are firing in the blind and no telling where they may land. An explosion 30 meters away makes the ground heave beneath Willi and showers him with mud.

"I am Willi! Don't shoot; I'm coming in there with you!" Willi drops his gear into the fox hole and falls down beside the Englishman.

The English forward observer, Ian, has become disoriented and gone further than his usual position between the lines. When he found Willi's apparently abandoned position, he decided to hunker down for the night. "Any port in a storm, ol' chap," the English-born Canadian quips.

The two trade bread, English canned bread for thick crusted German black bread, and munch while artillery shells whistle overhead. When the adjacent sector barrage stops, Ian crawls back to his position about fifty meters from

Willi's fox hole, turns, waves, and disappears. Only after taking time to reflect on this unorthodox visit does Willi realize they exchanged presents on Christmas Eve.

For the next two nights the two meet and exchange food items. On the third night, as Willi returns with a new pack of batteries and more food, a new officer assigned to his unit accompanies him. During the night Ian signals he is coming over. Their signal is a warbling whistle, no particular tune. Willi returns the signal. The officer, startled to see the low charging silhouette coming from the direction of the enemy, scrambles from the fox-hole and, half-crawling, half-running, retreats to the German lines.

When Ian reaches Willi's foxhole, Willi is chuckling at the lieutenant's hasty departure. He shares the lieutenant's rations with Ian and both have a laugh as Willi tells about the lieutenant.

"You are a good bloke, Kaiser Willie."

"You are a good one of those too, Ian."

"I cawn't tell you what might happen, ol' chap. But, I must caution you about returning here tomorrow night." He pauses for the information to sink in. "Now what will you do after the war?" The two men talk, helmet to helmet, for a half hour. They clasp hands then Ian crawls back to his foxhole.

The next morning German infantry withdraw from Ortona under a heavy attack by British artillery. Willi is told to join his artillery unit within the fortifications of the Gustav Line. As he falls back, keeping the coastal highway in sight and avoiding German mine fields, Willi stops frequently and, raising his binoculars, scans the area he has just left. Was Ian warning him, or trying to conceal troop movements, are questions in his mind? He liked the chance to use his limited English there on the battlefield and felt the Englishman had been honest with him. Early in the afternoon Willi sees an enemy unit approaching Ortona from the West. Whether it is a New Zealand or Canadian unit, he is uncertain. Ian had given him a warning.

The British appear to stop at Ortona. There are only a few probes of the Gustav Line north of Ortona; then the forces appear to dig in. A few days later, Willi's artillery unit is put on a train and moved north to Ravenna.

From Ravenna, the men march, while their artillery moves by train, to La Spezia. The port at La Spezia sheltered U-boats earlier in the war; and, most recently ships of the Italian Navy were anchored in the deep-water port. After the Italian government declared an Armistice in September, several battleships, light cruisers and destroyers made their escape at night from La Spezia intending to surrender to the Allies in North Africa. Most of the ships made it to safety.

When Willi arrives, the artillery pieces for the coastal watch are already in place. Wireless operators are positioned along the coast to monitor ship movements. Willi is to man a site on Montemarcello, an island just offshore. An Italian fisherman ferries the operators back and forth. Steep steps are carved in the rocky cliff to reach an observation point 150 feet above the landing. Willi climbs the steps carrying his 80-pound telegraph pack. Upon reaching the top for the first time, Willi is winded, but in awe of the beauty and loneliness of the spot. He sits down to appreciate the panorama of coastline and sea spread before him. A few small fishing boats, their sails filled with the strong breeze, move slowly through the choppy waters.

Alternating shifts, Willi is billeted in La Spezia with "duty on the rock," as he calls it. The sea is rough during February, and often, the operator on the island must stay there until the weather improves. Willi is granted his second leave of the war and returns to Leipzig in March 1944.

Leipzig
Spring, 1944

A crisp breeze is blowing as Willi arrives in Leipzig's bomb-damaged Bahnhof. He notices gaping holes in the roof as he hurries through the station and walks to his home on Eisenbahn Strasse. No one is home; Willi waits, impatience growing. When Katarina finally returns, the Bürgermeister's sergeant is escorting her; both surprised to find Willi. The sergeant, fat, flustered, and somewhat shorter than Willi, decides to make a prudent and hasty retreat.

Alone in the apartment with an angry Willi, Katarina freely admits her infidelity, knowing Willi will not harm her. She tells him their daughters are living in a Hitler Youth Hostel. Anxious to see his daughters, Willi gets the address of the hostel, and asks Katarina if any of the neighbors have a car. Kurt Blocker is home, convalescing from wounds received on the Eastern Front. His car is operable, and he has enough gas to make the trip.

Driving through the blacked-out streets, Kurt and Willi arrive at the hostel as the young people are finishing their evening meal. The headmaster is easily convinced to allow Christel and Inge go home with Willi, since he has only a few days of leave showing on his Soldbuch; Willi promises to return them.

The next morning Willi takes the girls to Lützen, arriving early enough to have tea with his parents. Hospital Strasse has not changed; only the people who live there have grown older. Karl and Freda are not surprised to learn about Katarina's unfaithfulness. They agree to have Christel and Inge stay with them until Willi returns from the war; any reluctance is because of the interruption of schooling for the girls. Willi is surprised by his parents support, but many things have changed. Freda insists he stay the night, sleeping in his old room, and catching up on news of the family.

The saddest news is again from Kristin. Her sons, 14-year-old Stefan and 13-year-old Kolt, have been taken into the army. Their infantry training was completed in three weeks and they are now en route to the Eastern Front. It is more than Kristin can stand, and Freda fears for Kristin's health. "She seems to be doing well, some days when we visit. But, other days she hardly knows who I am, her own mother."

Taking the early train back to Leipzig the next morning, Willi catches a ride in an army truck from the Bahnhof to *Oma* Meissner's neighborhood. He hops out of the truck a block from the house and walks the remaining distance to the house. He raps on the door, peering in the side window for movement inside the dark interior. *Oma*, always frail looking, now uses a cane and Willi can hear it tapping the floor as she comes to the door. She pushes aside the curtain and peeks at the uniformed man, then opens the door slowly.

"Wilhelm, is it you?"

"*Ja, Oma,* it is me, Wilhelm. How are you?" he asks, as he kneels and hugs the waist of his grandmother. "I have missed you." There are tears in his eyes, but she can no longer see them. His father had told him *Oma* Meissner is fast losing her sight. "I was sorry to hear about *Opa*, but now he has peace." A letter from *Oma* told him of *Opa's* death the past winter.

Willi spends the night at *Oma* Meissner's house, leaving early the next morning to return to Italy. He stops by the apartment to pick up his remaining personal items, and is in and out of the apartment before Katarina is fully awake. The return trip takes much longer. There are air raids near Munich and damage to the railroad tracks. A late March snow storm delays the train in Austria and northern Italy.

Willi's unit has moved to Livorno, a coastal city farther south. When he reaches Livorno and locates his unit, there are new people in the command positions. Willi tells the new adjutant about the family situation, his wife's infidelity, and the Bürgermeister's sergeant. The adjutant, eager to show ability to handle such problems, writes an angry letter to the Bürgermeister of Leipzig decrying the morale problems such behavior causes men fighting the war.

Mail is slow and it is several weeks before the adjutant receives a response from the Bürgermeister. In the meantime, Willi's artillery unit has moved forward to a position near the Anzio beachhead, becoming part of the 92nd Infantry Division, under General von Mackensen's 14th Army. The first week of May, Willi is summoned to the adjutant's office, a room in a farm house. The adjutant accuses Willi of lying and embarrassing him. Both the Bürgermeister, and the sergeant have written and claim their innocence in the affair of "Frau Meissner." They accuse Willi of being an anti-Nazi trouble maker. An entry is made in Willi's *Soldbuch* docking him three day's pay and service credit.

Rather than confinement, Willi is sent back to his post on the coast, watching for enemy ships and occasionally directing artillery fire into American positions at Anzio. Hitler's radio broadcasts from Berlin are received daily and relayed by field radio to the units at Anzio, praising the men of the Tenth and Fourteenth Armies for their efforts to drive the Americans into the sea. He never ends a broadcast without berating them for allowing the Americans to land.

Scuttlebutt is they will be moving soon, although from Willi's vantage point north of the beachhead, the Americans seem to be pretty well confined. A week later, May 27, Willi accompanies a battery of 88's moving east along the front to reinforce the First Parachute Corps at Velletri. Willi rides in a truck pulling one of the artillery pieces. Other units of the 92nd Infantry get orders to pack up and move north of Rome. This time they are going to a new defensive line to be formed near Florence.

Reaching Velletri late on the 29th of May, the unit is told to withdraw northeast on Highway 7, then set up their weapons to fire against tanks. After digging in for the night, Willi manages to find a field kitchen with some cold, thin soup still in the pot and dry bread in the cook's wagon. For the next two days they wait, training their guns one day on Monte Artemisio and then back on the approaches to Highway 7. June 1, Willi's artillery unit is ordered to rejoin the 92nd Infantry near San Severa, along the coastline north of Rome. They move out during the night. A peasant's horse is confiscated and given to Willi to carry his heavy gear during the march.

Retreating northward along the highway they encounter a traffic jam of retreating units, stalled vehicles and craters from air raids. They take offensive positions near the outskirts of Rome June 2nd. The artillery pieces have been configured to fire as anti-aircraft weapons (as the 88mm was originally designed to be used).

Those who can, sleep during the day. Willi finds shelter from the sun near a railroad embankment after feeding his horse and stabling it in the ruins of a nearby house. At nightfall they march through Rome. There are many deserters. There is much confusion during the nighttime march through Rome; artillery is being pulled by horses and tractors, anything they can find. The following morning, June 3, they make camp off Highway 1, north of Rome. Nearly half the unit fails to muster for rations. The next night they continue along Highway 1 until reaching the forward units of Group Goerlitz, a provisional organization including the 92nd.

The camp is hit by American fighter airplanes during the day. One bomb lands near Willi's shelter, killing several horses. As officers survey the damage, they accuse Willi and the remaining soldiers of not taking time to camouflage the artillery pieces and protecting their horses. Willi expects partisans may have broadcast their position.

Before sunset June 4, units of the Goerlitz Group begin moving north to prepare a defensive line near Orbetello. Willi and remnants of his artillery unit cover nearly 40 kilometers during the night before halting near Tarquinia. When it grows light Willi discovers his horse is lame. The horse had stumbled several times during the night as Willi followed the dim shadows of the others in the column. Examining the horse, he notices all four hooves are cracked and bleeding. Facing another hard night traveling the darkened back roads along the coast, Willi decides to leave the horse behind.

5 June 1944

As they break camp, Willi shoulders the radio pack and leads his horse out of camp. An officer observing his departure shouts, "Use the horse or let me have it!" Willi shifts his pack and swings it up over the back of the horse and joins the retreat. As soon as it is dark he stops, removes the burden from the horse, and continues the march. Crossing a stream north of Tarquinia, soldiers take a brief rest stop to water their animals. Willi's horse has been stumbling frequently in the darkness. He decides it is time to release the horse. Telling the soldier nearest him, "Toilet," he leads the horse along a dim path running east, away from the road, following the course of the stream. Willi follows it several yards, stopping when he can no longer see the column of soldiers, nor hear tractors pulling the artillery pieces.

"This is where we say goodbye, my friend," Willi says as he rubs the horse's nose and drops the telegraph pack from his shoulders. Leading the horse further up the trail, Willi removes the halter so the horse will not become entangled, then spanks it on the rump. The horse moves ahead a few feet and stops. As Willi turns to pick up his pack and rejoin the march, the horse follows him. When Willi finally reaches the road the column of soldiers has passed; all is quiet.

Chapter 17
Taking French Leave

Near Tarquinia, Italy
6 June 1944

Rather than face another reprimand from the Lieutenant for falling out of the march, Willi decides to wait for the advancing Americans, and surrender. It is not worth the trouble to try to catch up with his unit. Backtracking, Willi finds his horse, hides his telegraph pack under a brush pile, and together they continue to follow the climbing trail as it leads eastward away from Highway 1. After walking perhaps 15 minutes, the path joins a rutted dirt road. Willi continues eastward on the narrow road, putting as much distance between him and Highway 1 as he can.

When the dirt road joins a secondary road, Willi stops and waits for dawn not wanting to run into a German patrol after this much trouble. When the sky turns a bright blue in the east, he sees a small cluster of farm houses and a barn about two kilometers along the secondary road and perhaps 100 meters off the road. Willi cautiously leads his lame horse from the trees, out onto the road, and toward the buildings. Pausing frequently to listen for motor vehicles, Willi reaches a point near the barn and scans the area as it gets lighter.

There are no soldiers or military vehicles around the cluster of houses. As the sun begins to break the horizon, an old man opens the door of the nearest house. The man is stoop shouldered and walks with a limp. His dark clothing is rumpled and patched. As he approaches where Willi is standing, he stops and leans forward squinting in the early morning light to get a better view.

Willi calls out to him and steps forward, leading the horse behind him. Reaching into his pocket he pulls out a white handkerchief. A smile flits over his face as he thinks of a comment he once made about the 'Wehrmacht parachute,' carried for such occasions, then waves the handkerchief over his head. He approaches the white-haired Italian slowly.

"I'm a German soldier. I want to give up to Americans. Can you help me?"

The old man shakes his head indicating he does not understand. Willi repeats his words, slower and louder.

This time he seems to understand, but waves Willi away. Willi stands his ground. "You can have my horse," he says, holding out the reins toward the old man. The old man hobbles over to where he is standing and says a few words in Italian Willi cannot understand. He points to the barn and at Willi. Willi walks over to the barn, the horse plodding behind him. He enters the barn and looks around. There is a pile of straw near the door. Tethering the horse to a crib, Willi sits down in the straw, removes his boots, and quickly falls asleep with his head resting on his bedroll.

Willi awakes suddenly to the sound of loud voices in the yard outside the barn. Two women are speaking Italian rapidly and at full volume, while a man is speaking German, equally loud and excited. Willi sits up, brushes the straw from his hair and uniform, puts on his boots and creeps over to the open barn door. The women are standing in the door of the nearest house and a Waffen SS man, young, maybe 20 years old, has his gun out and is waving it at the women. He is yelling in German, "I'll shoot you if you don't give me eggs and sausage. I know you have food in your house, out of my way!"

Willi thinks the young man might be foolish enough to shoot and walks out of the barn toward the trio at the door of the house. As he draws closer the women see him and point in his direction. The soldier whips around pointing the gun at Willi in his Wehrmacht uniform. Drawing himself to his full height, Willi continues to walk toward the group and, as he nears, puts his hand to his lips. "This is the sleeping quarters for the commander. You must go to the next house for food."

The young man holsters his pistol and says, "Why didn't these stupid peasant women say so!" He turns and hurriedly stalks away, not to the next house, but toward the road leading away from the settlement.

Willi and the two women watch him leave. When he is out of sight, the older of the two women beams a toothless smile at Willi and goes into the house. The younger woman meekly thanks Willi for interceding. Her German is broken but understandable. The toothless old woman returns bringing Willi some bread and milk.

"You can stay in the barn today," the younger woman tells him. Willi takes his food and returns to the barn. The bread is hard and dark, but when it is soaked in milk it is very good. Willi leaves no crumbs for the field mice, and, adding more straw to the pile he has been sleeping on, resumes his position on the floor of the barn and is soon asleep.

The old man, Willi first saw in the morning, and a younger man stand near his feet when he awakes. The old man holds a lantern his weathered face reveals no emotion. Through the open barn door, Willi can see it is night already. The younger man is wearing dark clothing, a large floppy cap, and has a rifle slung over his shoulder. The young man is smiling, as Willi sits up quickly.

"The women say you chased away an SS man today. He had a gun, you didn't. Is it so?" the younger man asks.

Willi rubs his hands through his hair and nods. "*Ja*, is true."

"You are brave! Why did you do it?"

Willi gets up from the pile of straw and stretches, looking away from the lantern, while trying to see the faces of the two Italians better. Squinting as he looks past the lantern toward the younger Italian, Willi says, "I want no more war, no more killing. The SS boy might shoot the gun and hurt someone. So, I did what came to mind. It worked!" Willi flashes a smile back at the two Italians.

"Come to the house. Eat with us. We will help you find American soldiers," the young Italian tells him. Meanwhile, the old man hobbles over to the crib and unties Willi's horse. Leading it into a stall and removing the bridle and bit, the old man pats the horse on the flank and closes the gate to the stall.

"Thank you, I was too tired. The horse is lame," he says apologetically. "With a little care, he'll be okay!" The old man nods and leads them out of the barn, holding the lantern by his side as he limps along in front of Willi and the young partisan soldier. The house looks dark and empty from outside.

"You can wash here," the young Italian says, pointing to a basin sitting on a wooden stand next to a pump. Willi pumps the handle a few times, and a stream of cool water trickles from the spout. He catches it in his hands and throws it on his face. Pumping again he fills the basin and washes his hands and face for the first time in three days. It feels good. The old man hands him a remnant of a towel to dry with.

Ducking his head as he enters the low ceilinged house, Willi smells meat and pasta cooking. There are lamps in the large kitchen, and heavy, dark cloths cover the windows. Both women are working at the stove, turning to nod as he enters. The young man, Sergio Raimondo, swings the rifle from his shoulder and motions for Willi to take a chair at the table. He is still smiling as Willi sits down. "Mama, bring our guest some food. He looks hungry," Sergio calls out.

The toothless older lady brings a platter of sausage and a bowl of pasta to the table and pats Willi's shoulder. "Now you eat!"

The men join Willi at the table, fill their glasses with a heavy red wine from a jug sitting on the table, and begin to eat. Sergio tells Willi their plans for the next day. Allied soldiers are not far away, but this area is still under German control. Willi will need to stay out of sight, or get out of his uniform. As they are talking, two sharp raps on the door are followed by two more. The older woman goes to the door and two men enter. Two shabbily dressed men enter the room. They stare at Willi silently until Sergio speaks, identifying Willi as a deserter. The men are British officers dressed as peasant farmers.

Sergio takes glasses from a cabinet and pours more wine for everyone at the table. The British, Willi learns, have been with the partisan group operating from this settlement for several months, having parachuted into the area in March. The night Willi arrived, about 40 of the partisans were setting up an ambush for retreating German units. They could not return until this evening, and are coming back in groups of two and three to avoid notice.

The partisans decide to get Willi into civilian clothes immediately. The presence of a German soldier in their midst could scare some of the returning partisans away. They outfit him with pants and a shirt. The old man finds a pair of sandals for his feet. His boots would be a dead giveaway should German soldiers come looking.

Once Willi has changed into his new clothing, everyone is more comfortable, except for Willi. "The clothing is too small for me to wear comfortably." The British ask Willi about his unit and look at his Soldbuch. During the evening, other members of the partisan unit arrive and have big news, the Americans and British have invaded France. They received the news over a radio the commando unit uses for coordinating their movements. After eating and celebrating, Willi returns to the barn and finds they have a cot for him to sleep on.

"But first you must put some straw on the cot to make it comfortable," an Italian tells him.

Willi piles some straw on the cot and puts his bedroll on top of the straw. Having slept the major part of the day, Willi can't sleep and hears every noise of the night. Finally he falls asleep.

Thursday, 8 June 1944

Willi has been with the partisans twenty four hours. Units of the retreating German Fourteenth Army have moved north of Tarquinia, leaving only the 20th Luftwaffe Field Division blocking Highway 1 south of Tarquinia. "The allies are getting closer," the partisan Sergio tells Willi.

At dawn the partisans prepare to leave and work in the fields. Working in fields along the roads used by the retreating Germans, they can identify units, their size and condition as they file past. Willi is told to remain in the barn. Four partisans also stay behind with him.

By noon, their water bucket is empty; Willi walks across the yard to draw some fresh water from the well. As he returns, two German soldiers drive up in a truck. Willi knows they have seen him and stops in the yard, not wanting to lead them into the barn where the partisans are taking a nap.

The truck stops in front of the house. A German soldier yells at Willi and asks if he has seen any German soldiers. Willi points to his ears and mouth, pretending he is a deaf-mute. Meanwhile, Sergio's wife has come out of the house and asking them in Italian what they want. The soldier who yelled speaks Italian and explains they are "looking for deserters."

"There is no one here but me and my brother," she replies, pointing at Willi.

"Then you won't mind if we look around just to see for ourselves," he tells her.

"I do mind. We have work to do and I don't need any more soldiers poking around the house and stealing our food," she exclaims, taking her apron and waving for them to go.

A low flying American fighter plane appears overhead and circles when it sees the German truck sitting in the yard. The German soldier driving the truck puts it in gear and careens the truck around the yard forcing Willi to jump aside. He accelerates out of the settlement leaving Willi, Sergio's wife and the four partisans, who are now awake with their guns trained on the departing truck, staring in disbelief. It had all happened so fast, Willi can't remember if he had said anything or not.

"When angels travel, the skies are clear." So went a proverb Oma Meissner had often quoted to Willi. Willi had modified it to "When a good man travels, angels clear the path." To him, it explains his extraordinarily good luck for staying out of trouble. After nightfall, Willi is told to put on his Wehrmacht uniform. The partisans have met allied ground forces and will escort Willi to the nearest unit to surrender. A French unit occupies a neighboring farm and uses a sheep stable for an interrogation office. The commander of the French unit speaks German.

"Your Soldbuch, please."

Willi hands it to him.

"You are a radio operator according to this. If you are a radio operator you know the code used for messages. Why not cooperate with us and tell us the code?" he asks.

"I can't," Willi says.

"If you are a deserter you no longer care for your comrades. Tell us the code."

"I can't," Willi repeats.

The French officer picks up a pistol lying on the interrogation table and menacingly points it at Willi's forehead. "Tell me the code Private Meissner."

"If I tell you the code you will use it to kill many German soldiers. For that reason I can't tell you."

The partisans behind Willi move up to the table and stand behind him. The French officer's face breaks into a smile. "The kind of answer one expects from a good soldier." Turning to the partisans he says, "Keep him under guard until the morning, and I'll have him delivered to the American authorities."

The next morning, very early, a tall, black French soldier, larger than Willi, and armed to the teeth, arrives to take Willi to the nearest Italian garrison. Parking his Jeep in the village square, the soldier goes inside the Gendarme office and returns with Willi. Bound and thinking he will soon be in the hands of American forces, Willi sits in the Jeep in the middle of the square. When Sergio's wife arrives in the town square to sell her eggs, she sees Willi and goes directly to the Jeep. Raising her voice, she happily calls out to the townsfolk, "This is the man who saved my life." A curious crowd gathers, and when the French soldier returns with an Italian gendarme, Sergio's wife asks what they are going to do with Willi. "He is to be turned over to Americans," she tells them.

"He will be held here," the Italian gendarme retorts.

Sergio's wife turns to the gathered crowd and begins pleading with the people of the village to take her side in the matter. The French soldier, angered by the crowd and delay, hauls Willi out of the Jeep and pushes him toward the gendarme. Before the gendarme can get Willi out of the square, his path is blocked by shouting villagers who have heard the story of Willi intervening for Sergio's wife.

"All right, all right! I will hold him until the American soldiers arrive," the gendarme agrees.

"We will bring some Americans here soon," Sergio's wife assures Willi. And, within two hours, Americans from the 5th Army arrive at the village gendarme's office, led by Sergio, to claim Willi. The American soldiers take him to a truck loaded with German prisoners going to a POW holding area. The holding area is in a marble quarry near Naples, several days journey by truck. There are perhaps 4,000-5,000 prisoners in the quarry, no shelter, no beds, just the clothing and packs they had when captured. Willi is held there for about a week, then, with 500 other German POWs, taken to the harbor at Naples where they board a coal tender used by the American Navy to carry coal for their ships.

"*Allesman in die Keller*!"

"Everyone in the bunkers," they are told, as they climb down into the dark and coal encrusted hold of the ship. For two days the ship moves slowly through the Mediterranean Sea, finally arriving in Algiers. On deck the sea breeze provides a little coolness for the sun-drenched shipload of POWs. At Algiers another hundred POWs, most from Rommel's desert forces, are put aboard, and the ship weighs anchor for America. Sailing through the Straits of Gibraltar at night, the ship follows the Moroccan coast line out into the Atlantic Ocean.

The POWs sleep on the floors of the large cargo holds, forward and aft "like fish in a box." The floor is cleaner than when they first boarded. Their clothing is black with coal dust (the ship carried a load of coal to American destroyers in the Mediterranean and was turned into a "passenger ship" on its return). Because of the flammable coal dust, the prisoners cannot have a fire to warm their food. After a week eating cold beans and ham from the C rations, the German POWs find the only items they have an appetite for are biscuits and preserves included in the rations. Since everyone is hungry, very few get seasick.

Once in the Atlantic, they join other ships, forming a convoy to cross the Atlantic, with two destroyers for escort. After waiting four days at anchor off the Moroccan coast, the convoy sets sail 2 July 1944.

Chapter 18
Off to America

Somewhere in the Atlantic
July 1944

Early in the trip an alarm sounds; a U-boat has been sighted. Willi is on deck exercising. "Just my luck," he thinks, "to finally get away from war only to be sunk by a German submarine." The prisoners crowd against the railing, looking for torpedoes.

The speaker horn blares out, "All prisoners below deck!" There are over five hundred German prisoners of war on this cargo ship. All were on the on deck when the order is given. Five minutes later, the decks are cleared. No more submarine alarms; however everyone stays below deck.

From then on, the prisoners have deck-time in shifts. Most everyone takes their turn on deck, although a few are too weak to climb the ladders. Those prisoners staying below walk from one bulkhead to another, trying to get a breath of fresh air when the sea breeze whips down through the large opening overhead.

Some nights are very hot in the closeness of the cargo hold. The convoy swings far south to avoid U-boats following the North Atlantic convoy routes. "July and August are good months to cross the Atlantic," according to a well-traveled German officer resting near Willi in the hold of the ship. Willi smiles in the darkness, any month is a good month for a POW to cross the Atlantic.

Expecting to see the Statue of Liberty as they arrive in the United States, Willi learns from an American sailor they will be going to Norfolk, Virginia. Perhaps the Nazi officers were right for once. (The Nazi grapevine has been telling prisoners New York has been bombed by the Luftwaffe, and their ship cannot go there.) The bright sunny days for the crossing have given way to a dull gray, overcast from horizon to horizon. Squalls drenched those who climbed the ladders to exercise earlier in the day.

August 19, the freighter's steadily rumbling engines change to an irregular, low-pitched grind. Willi wants to be on deck to see the end of the voyage. But, no one is allowed on deck while entering the harbor at Norfolk, Virginia. Nothing, except other ships in the convoy, not even a tiny island, have they seen since leaving Gibraltar.

A nauseous knot grows in Willi's stomach. The ship is rolling gently in the channel and there is no horizon to fix his eyes on. "Must be a little excitement in my belly or maybe more hunger pains," he thinks. Hans Berber, a chemist from Kaiserslautern, squeezes in beside Willi. "Excuse me, Willi. I must go up the ladder and see the doctor. Do you need anything?"

"*Ja*, some fresh air!"

"I'll bring some back," Hans responds with a chuckle as he starts up the ladder.

After forty-eight days of zigzagging across the Atlantic, another load of POWs prepares to debark in the United States. It is a relief when the throbbing engine stops. "All prisoners, Achtung!" the speaker blares. Willi jumps every time the ship's speaker system is used. After six weeks of unexpected announcements, his neck still prickles at the sound of a loud speaker.

A German officer uses the speaker to announce, "You must gather your belongings and be prepared to debark within the hour. We will be boarding an American train on the dock. As soon as you have your kit assembled, you may go to the main deck. We will form ranks and march off the ship like true soldiers of the Third Reich. Heil Hit…!"

The speaker clicks off before he can finish the sentence. A few men could be heard shouting "Heil Hitler!" Willi knows there are Nazi's on board, more than will admit it. He cannot figure the big fuss about gathering up belongings. All he has is the Red Cross kit given as they boarded ship and the clothing on his back. And he still has the cap given him by the Italian partisans.

Only officers brought their suitcases to war, and then, on to POW camp. Willi had watched with amusement as the new prisoners boarded at Tripoli. A young officer, bringing his suitcase on board the ship, dropped it to salute an Oberst. The case broke open, revealing civilian clothing and an expensive silk robe and slippers. One might think he was expecting to be captured, or had planned to avoid capture as a civilian!

At Norfolk, Willi is among the first to arrive on deck. Railcars recently painted with a thin coat of olive green and "U.S. Army" stenciled over what appears to have been Atlantic Seaboard, sit on a siding extending on to the wharf. Willi's first view of America, dockside at Norfolk, is not what he had expected. After all prisoners arrive on deck, they are formed into squads of 20 men and marched across a ramp and into a building on the wharf. Although it is still overcast, the temperature has warmed up enough Willi is sweating as he waits.

An American soldier orders the POWs to get their "Soldbuch" in hand and spread their belongings on the floor. All personal things can be kept and are sprayed. They are then marched into a large bath hall to wash off the dirt and coal dust from their long journey. There are big bars of soap; Willi feels clean again. As they come out of the shower, the POWs are given new clothes. Another soldier comes down the line, wearing a mask over his nose, and spraying a cloud of white smoke on everyone and on their gear. After four weeks at sea, sleeping in the coal dust, and wearing the same uniform, Willi feels appropriately deloused.

After the delousing, a clerk checks Willi's Soldbuch against a list of names and then sends him out to board the first of two trains parked on the dock. There is another line and, while he waits, the clouds part. The sun bears down on the POWs as they wait to board the train. Moving up the steps on the heels of the prisoner in front of him, Willi can see through the door two rows of green upholstered seats. "This train must be for officers," he thinks. A Military Policeman is sitting at a table at the top of the steps and asks, "What is your name? Namen!"

"Wilhelm Meissner, you can call me Willi."

"I'll call you Kraut! Go on in and take a seat."

"Thank you, sir!" Willi learned to say 'thank you, hello, and goodbye,' in English on the ship. As he enters the car another American soldier is directing people to their seats. The man in front of Willi is a German officer. Maybe they send me to another car, he thinks. Instead the officer is directed into a group of facing seats where another man is already sitting. He points to a seat in the same little cubicle for Willi. Four seats, three men. Each man has room for his bag of personal belongings in the rack above the seat.

Stowing his bag of Red Cross items, Willi looks around to see who else is on the car. A senior German officer sits at the front of the car and has a little table between him and the facing seat. There are others he has seen on the ship, but no one he knows. Sitting down and looking out the window is a disappointment. The windows are dirty, hard to see through. But, since he is the last man in, and sitting on the aisle, he can stretch his legs out in front of him and be very comfortable. An hour drags by in the uncomfortably hot car as gradually each car is filled with freshly deloused POWs.

While they are waiting, an American soldier enters, speaking slowly in very good German, "You will remain in your seats unless you must go to the toilet. There can be only one person waiting outside the toilet at any time. Your meals will be brought to you at your seat. You must stay in this car until you have reached your destination. You will be informed when you have reached your camp. Are there any questions?"

An officer asks, "What is our destination?"

"I don't know. Just keep your shirt on; somebody'll tell you when you get there. Any more questions?" He walks on through the car.

The second train departs first, filled with the many officers who were the last prisoners to get off the ship. A short time later, there is a jolt, and Willi's train moves backward a few feet. Then a rippling sound as the cars start moving forward, smoothly and quietly. They leave the dockside platform, glide through an industrial area and into the countryside. Only the clickety-clack sound of the wheels disturbs the quiet, and many POWs are soon asleep.

The car is very comfortable. Surely it must be a mistake to put POWs on a train like this, he thinks. The train windows cannot be opened, Willi discovers when he has a chance to sit by the window. A few rows in front of Willi, sits the POW senior officer, Oberst Hauptman, an officer in the Afrika Corps and a Nazi. Willi met him once on the boat. Hauptman told Willi to salute him with a proper "Heil Hitler." Since we are prisoners here in the United States, there is little he can do, Willi thinks, but what will he do after the war? Willi hopes the Oberst will forget their conversation and makes it a point to avoid him as much as possible.

There are two guards in the car, standing at each end of the car. The guards rotate, going somewhere else to sleep. Lights are on in the car day and night. Willi is quite content to stay in his seat and, when necessary to go to the WC, raises his hand until the guard nods he can go.

In Atlanta, Georgia, the prisoners stay on the train for about an hour. Then the guards allow each cubicle of three men to get up, walk to the end of the car, step out on the station platform, and walk to the other end of the car and reenter, returning to their seats. The guards watch the prisoners very closely. No one attempts an escape. Where else can they get three meals a day, a place to sleep and no one shooting at them?

Birmingham, Alabama, is another long stop. The POWs are again allowed to exercise. On the platform at Birmingham, Willi can tell it is a big Bahnhof. He thinks they do this to impress German prisoners. "We have a big Bahnhof in Leipzig, but not this big," Willi tells the young officer who is his seat partner. Some prisoners are taken from the train in Birmingham to be sent to a military base in Alabama.

Back on the train, Willi has a seat by the window all the way to New Orleans. There are many cars and trucks on the highways and at the crossings. Occasionally he spots a brown military truck or Jeep. At night there are lights in the towns they pass. There are no blackouts. Willi can see city lights glowing on the horizon for almost an hour before they finally arrive in New Orleans.

In New Orleans, the prisoners are allowed to exercise on the station platform. The air is warm and sticky, even at this early hour. Nearly half the prisoners in Willi's car are marched off to board military buses parked at the end of the platform. Willi sees Hans and some prisoners from his car being marched to the waiting buses. "Where are they taking you, Hans?" Willi yells.

"We are going to Arkansas!" he yells back. "See you after the war!" he yells before he is out of sight.

Waiting on the platform outside the train is like taking a steam bath. "It cannot be healthy to live in climate like this," Willi thinks. The guards allow the prisoners to use the station toilet while they are waiting. As Willi stands in line with maybe a hundred prisoners ahead of him, he notices another toilet marked "colored" with no one in line.

"Officer," Willi calls out to the guard and when he approaches, Willi motions to the colored toilet. "Is OK?"

The guard shakes his head and says, "White folks don't use colored folk's restrooms."

When the guard isn't looking, Willi uses the restroom. There is something strange about Americans. It is a problem between the black man and the white man. They are from the same country, but treat each other different, like some Germans treat Jews different.

Oberst Hauptman is pacing the platform while they wait to go back on board the train. No one will tell him where the train is going. An MP guard says, "It's gotta be west from here!" Willi hopes it will be the Wild West he has seen in motion pictures.

Finally the prisoners board another train; Southern Pacific is written on the cars. The sun is almost overhead when they leave New Orleans and cross a river. The bridge is much longer than any Willi has seen.

A guard tells them it is the Mississippi River; Willi recalls the name from his geography studies at Lützen. He leans over to tell the German soldier sitting next to him, "It is the longest river in the United States!" The soldier does not seem to care what it is they are crossing.

A few days later they arrive in Tucson, Arizona. There Willi is in a group of about 100 prisoners put on board yet another train, with only two passenger cars going north to Camp Florence, Arizona. They arrive at Camp Florence, Arizona, with one thought on their mind, "real food!" The prisoners are hungry for food which does not come from a can.

Chapter 19
What Is This Place?

2 September 1944

Camp Florence, Arizona, is hardly an oasis in the desert. But, to Willi and the German prisoners arriving there in the fall of 1944, it is destined to be their most comfortable assignment of the entire war. The camp rests peacefully and hot in the Arizona desert not far from the Superstition Mountains.

Bound on the south by the Gila River and to the east by Arizona SR 79, Camp Florence is served by a small railroad depot near the Gila River. South of the river is the town of Florence. The 400-acre camp was approved for construction in 1942, and developed at a cost of $5,000,000. It houses 7,000 American soldiers and includes a hospital along with the internment camp for prisoners of war.

The first POWs arrived in 1943, mostly Italians captured in northern Africa. They came off the U. S. Army-operated passenger train with their hands held over their heads, expecting punishment. From the desert sand of North Africa to the desert sand of Arizona there is not a great climatological difference. But, for the prisoners, there is a great sociological difference. The Italian prisoners overcame their fear and many did not wish to return to Europe when the war ended. They did everything possible to improve the camp, lining walkways with rocks, cultivating small gardens between barracks, reporting prisoners who destroyed property, and starting cultural activities lasting until the camp closed in 1946.

Among the other prisoners eventually finding their way to Florence were Japanese and German POWs, plus American soldiers accused of offenses, from damaging government property and desertion, to disrespect. A collection of four compounds comprise the POW area of the camp. Four barracks and a mess hall are in each POW compound. The hospital compound, motor pool and barracks for the American soldiers are on the north end of the camp. The camp is encircled by a barbed-wire fence defended by one man guard towers, each equipped with a 30 caliber machine gun and flood lights. The lights remain on all night.

The afternoon Willi and the first German soldiers arrive at Camp Florence, a group of local residents gather in the shade of the small station to see the "Germans". As they climb down from the train into the late afternoon heat of the Arizona desert, they are confused by the attention they draw and bewildered by the vastness of the horizon. The translators meeting them are mostly Jewish, first and second generation German immigrants. They wear U. S. Army uniforms and tell the arriving prisoners to form into four columns. Willi can see guard towers ahead as they start walking toward the camp.

The men walk casually at first, and a bit clumsily. Many still wear their Wehrmacht jack boots and stagger in the loose gravel of the roadway. Some locals watching shout, "They don't look like a conquering army." From Willi's position in the column of train-weary prisoners, he cannot see who started it, but suddenly the ranks get in step and the men are throwing their shoulders back. A German sergeant major shouts cadence and those who still have the energy "goose step" into camp.

The distance they march is several hundred yards and, when they arrive, all are sweating profusely, even Rommel's desert soldiers. An American guard, Bud Gomes, observed the arrival from guard tower 15 at the southeast corner of the camp, closest to the depot. He could hear the taunting of the locals watching the event and saw the loosely assembled prisoners began walking toward the searching area, forming up and begin marching. "It made goose bumps rise on the back of my neck to see the pride of those Germans marching into Camp Florence," he told a newsman later.

In the search area they are told to remove their clothing, receive inoculations from a medical corpsman and Willi gets his second shower in the two months since capture.

More clothing is issued: two pair of cotton trousers with PW marked in yellow on the seat, a pair of work gloves, a belt, a pair of new shoes, four pairs of socks, four under drawers and undershirts, a cap and a long sleeve cotton shirt with PW marked in yellow on the back. After everyone is dressed, they form into small units and are marched to their compound where barracks and beds are assigned, 40 men to each barrack. It is less than 200 feet from the processing center to the barracks, just far enough for Willi to feel the late afternoon sun in his face and take a few deep breaths of clean air not tainted by the smell of a deloused uniform.

Their wooden barracks were once used by Italian POWs and in the afternoon heat are hot and stuffy. Windows are hard to open. Willi drops his PW clothing on the bunk assigned him and turns to raise a window. A POW named Kreutz is watching, "It won't do any good, soldier, they're nailed shut. I've already tried."

Willi acknowledges the comment, looks for nails, sees none, and gripping the window handles, begins to lift. As he strains the screws holding the handles start to come out. Suddenly the window slides up with a bang, shattering a pane of glass.

"You're in trouble now, private," another POW yells.

Willi looks at him, "Are you talking to me?" Willi asks quietly, shrugs and begins to fold his new clothes and stack them in a foot locker at the end of his bunk. He makes a mental note to watch out for the one who yells, probably a Nazi trouble maker. Kreutz speaks up, "Leave him alone," he says to the trouble maker, "he was just trying to make it more bearable in here."

A fat American soldier, hardly old enough to shave and speaking very poor German, enters the barracks and tells the men to raise the windows and get some fresh air inside. He says nothing about the broken window.

"When you have your stuff put away, come outside," he tells the prisoners. Willi thought surprises were over for the day, but, when they walk outside the barracks, the translator tells them to line up. "You will now go to the mess hall. You may eat what you want, and as much as you want, but don't leave any food on your tray. Follow me."

Willi cannot believe human beings could eat so much; they all suffer later from eating too much. Most cannot lie down or sleep, so bad is the pain in their stomachs many stay in the toilet area, groaning. As he tosses and turns on his bunk, despite the stomach ache, Willi finds many positive things to think about. He now has an issue of PW clothes actually fitting him. The "*luft*" is good. He quickly learns not to confide much with his fellow prisoners. There is a Nazi network among both the officer and enlisted soldiers. It is dangerous to say good things about Americans. He also learns Americans think all Germans are Nazis.

The next morning, and every morning thereafter, a bugler wakes the camp. A clock over the entry door of the barracks is dust covered and hardly readable. Willi squints and sees it is five in the morning. The new POWs fall out in front of their barracks for a head count and then march to breakfast. After breakfast, the fat American translator asks if anyone wants to volunteer for details. They have garbage detail, farm detail, cleanup detail, and more details than Willi can remember. (Initially prisoners consider the details demeaning; however, the boredom of being a POW, with nothing to do, makes it more palatable.)

Willi soon volunteers for the farm detail, Kreutz also. Kreutz has never been on a farm but wants to get away from the camp. The translator needs 20 volunteers from their compound, 16 volunteer. The POWs cannot be made to work, just encouraged. The volunteers follow the translator to an assembly area where maybe 100 POWs are waiting to go the farm, a mixture of Germans and Italians. Coming through the gate is a big truck pulling a trailer. The driver, a dark skinned man, pulls up in front of the POWs and stops. "Farm workers on the truck," the translator yells out. "When the truck is full, the rest of you get on the trailer." The translator and a guard are standing by the truck.

A skinny, black soldier, carrying a semi-automatic Garand rifle, is the guard for Willi's group. The guard smiles, a gold tooth glistens as he speaks to the POWs. "Mawnin! Watch yo step! Listed men to de back o' de bus! Check yo tickets an' make sho you on de right truck!" Willi returns the black man's smile as he gets on the truck, and wishes he understood all the guard said; he gets a translation later and it brings a smile to Willi's face. The guard and translator accompany the POWs on the truck.

Leaving Camp Florence by 7:30 a.m., they ride for several miles through a stretch of desert and cactus. The farm is not far from Camp Florence, but the road goes north before turning west. Shortly after turning west Willi notices an irrigation ditch, the dry bottom covered with a white chalky substance. Beyond the ditch, row after row of cotton stretches to the distant mountains rising on the horizon. Willi has never seen cotton fields before.

The truck pulls into a farmyard and Mr. Bud, owner of the farm, a tall, gaunt man, with skin like tanned leather, meets them at a shed near the fields. The translator tells the POWs to stay on the truck while he finds out where they will be working. While the translator and Mr. Bud talk, Willi notices smaller, dark-skinned men, wearing big hats and no shoes, coming from a long, low building with many doors. The Mexican laborers, equally curious about the POWs, stop to watch the exchange between the translator and Mr. Bud. Eventually, the translator and Mr. Bud climb into the cab of the truck and the truck starts across the field, bumping across rows of already picked cotton, stopping at an irrigation ditch.

"Everyone off the truck, and gather around!" the translator yells. A wagon is parked by the ditch with a pile of long sacks stacked underneath. Speaking through the translator, Mr. Bud tells the POWs to "pick up a sack and start picking cotton." The Italians, who have done this work before, did as they are told. But, the translation does not make sense to Willi and the German POWs who stand there confused, looking first at the translator, then Mr. Bud.

"Didn't they understand you, boy?" Mr. Bud asks the translator. "Let me tell 'em," he says loudly. Stepping in front of the remaining POWs with his straw hat tilted back on his sunburned forehead, Mr. Bud grabs a long sack from the pile on the ground beneath the wagon. "This here's a cotton pickin' sack. Now y'all get over there and find one for yourself." He points to the pile and the POWs all pick up a sack. Mr. Bud looks at the young translator with a superior grin, "You just gotta know how to talk to these folks. They understand what we're sayin', just say it louder."

"Now foller me over here to this fust row o' cotton and watch whut I do with the sack." Taking the sack by its strap, he swings the sack over his head so the strap crosses his right shoulder, allowing him to carry the sack with both hands free. When he gets to the edge of the field, the first thing he does is reach over and break a stem off the cotton stalk. "See this heah cotton boll?" he waves the stem in front of the POWs. He repeats the question louder and gets a few "*Ja*", "*ist goodt*" comments. "OK, now we're gettin' somewhere. Now, don't y'all go breakin' of these stems, jes' reach into the husk of the boll and grab the cotton like this heah!" Mr. Bud puts his fingers around the wad of cotton hanging from the stem and pulls it out, dropping it into the cotton sack. "See, I didn't get any stem or husk, just cotton," he says, beaming at the POWs. "Let's see if y'all can do it." He waves his arm toward the cotton field and then points at the POWs.

Getting the strap from the cotton sacks over their heads and shoulders is the easy part. Unfortunately, when the POWs get to the cotton stalks they all reach over, break off a stem and proceed to pluck the cotton very daintily from the boll husk. Then with great aplomb, drop the wad of cotton into their sack, exactly as Mr. Bud had shown them.

"Naw! Ah shit." Mr. Bud is red-faced. "I tole you not to break off the stem and you can't do this standin' up straight. Now watch me again." He points to Willi's eyes and then to himself. Bending over, Mr. Bud starts going down a row picking cotton. After picking each stalk clean for about five stalks, he straightens up and turns to the POWs and says, "Now y'all do it like that!"

Willi is the first to step up and begin picking. "Right," exclaims Mr. Bud, "y'all do it just like the big feller. What's your name boy?" Willi continues to pick cotton. The boy translator waddles down the row and taps Willi on the shoulder and shouts, "*Namen? Namen?*"

Straightening up to his full height and looking down at the translator, Willi responds with mock dignity, "Private Wilhelm Meissner! You can call me Willi," he adds with a smile. The translator waves for Willi to continue with his cotton picking. Willi gathers from the conversation between Mr. Bud and the translator Mr. Bud is late getting his cotton picked. Italians have been picking for him, but many of them were released when Italy surrendered. The newly arrived German soldiers working in the cotton fields have very little experience, are slow, and tire quickly in the hot sun.

Willi sees brown-skinned men from the farm house are picking in the same field. Some pick the husk and all and throw it in their sack. It is obviously easier and faster to pick cotton in such a way because the tip of the husk is very sharp and pricks the ends of Willi's fingers each time he grasps the cotton. Willi's hands, once tough and calloused from hard work, have grown soft in the two months he has been a POW. Still it does not bother him as much as his erstwhile friend, Kreutz, who must have had an easy job. Kreutz' finger tips are bleeding from the stabs of cotton bolls.

For Willi and the POWs, lunch is a welcome break from the heat of the cotton field. They sit under a shed and eat a boxed lunch prepared at Camp Florence. Kreutz has a pair of gloves Mr. Bud gave him for his soft hands. They talk very little. Everyone is suspicious. Mr. Bud brings the translator to the shed and tries to get the POWs to talk. He calls the brown-skinned Americans, "Mes-cans" (Mexicans). They come from Mexico to pick cotton, he says. Everybody gets paid by the weight of the cotton they pick. For POWs it means a credit at the POW canteen equal to the money they earn. Mr. Bud says it will get cooler during the winter, but this part of Arizona stays pretty warm. The POWs agree, it is very warm in Arizona in September.

"Can any of you boys drive a tractor?" Mr. Bud asks through the translator. "I need someone to move trailers in the cotton field." No one volunteers. Willi looks at the tractor sitting under the shed. It looks like those he drove in his father-in-law's fields near Wittenberg and he has driven them around the shops in Lützen and Leipzig. "I am a farm worker and machinist in Germany. I think I can drive your tractor," Willi claims.

"What'd he say, boy?" Mr. Bud asks the translator.

"He said he 'can drive your tractor'."

"Good boy, Willi. Get your cotton weighed after lunch and come over here. We'll get you started on a higher payin' job."

When Mr. Bud leaves, Kreutz comes over and sits down beside Willi. Making sure no one will over hear their conversation, Kreutz whispers: "It is not wise to cooperate with Americans so easily. There are those who will remember and report you when the Americans are finally beaten."

Looking Kreutz eye to eye, Willi responds, "Would you?"

"I don't know, Meissner," Kreutz replies, still in a whisper. "Just be careful."

Willi drives the tractor and for the next few days is allowed to stay on the farm, sleeping in the bunkhouse with the Mexicans. Mr. Bud signs a custody agreement which allows Willi to stay outside the camp. Rarely are German POWs allowed the freedom Willi has at Mr. Bud's. During Willi's second week at the farm, a fire in the barn brings an end to his stay.

On the evening of the fire, while waiting for a bus to arrive to take them back to Camp Florence, Willi grabs the tongue of a cotton trailer and pulls it into the barn to be taken to the gin the next day. He doesn't need a tractor for such a light job. Kreutz follows him into the barn and spends a few minutes talking with Willi.

After the bus leaves, Willi and the Mexicans are called into the farm kitchen to eat. When they finish their dinner it is dark. The sky is clear and Willi relaxes, looking at the stars. Some of the constellations are familiar. A rotund Mexican takes a seat on the porch and tunes his guitar. His fingers pluck the strings slowly, gradually picking up speed, and then in a flurry of chords he stops. Then he begins to sing softly. Others join him singing a few verses and then the singing dies out.

The night air becomes cool and Willi walks into the bunkhouse to get a blanket. Throwing the blanket over his shoulders as he comes out of the bunkhouse, he smells smoke. It is not wood smoke. The Mexicans smell it too, the guitar player stops. Everyone looks toward the barn about the same time and can see smoke pouring out of the loft.

The next thing happening is best described as a "German-Mexican fire drill!" A Mexican worker runs to tell Mr. Bud, while others yell in panic. Willi grabs a bucket but cannot prime the water pump. Several Mexicans grab cotton sacks and run toward the barn. Willi follows and pulls open the barn doors, only to get his eyebrows singed as flames lick out into the night air.

The Mexicans try to get close enough to beat on the flames, but it is too hot. Mr. Bud calls the volunteer fire departments at Florence and Olberg for help. Both show up after the barn is nothing but a smoldering, black shell; it had burned too fast to save anything. Luckily the tractors were in a shed away from the barn, and the Mexicans were able to beat out the small fires started by sparks from the barn.

By morning, remains of the barn are still smoldering; and the cotton trailers have burned to their metal rims. A fire inspector from Florence, and one from Camp Florence, arrive early and inspect what is left of the barn. They tell Mr. Bud arson is suspected. Mr. Bud asks Willi if he saw anything suspicious before the prisoners left the night before. Willi recalls the conversation with Kreutz as they stood by the trailer. "He was smoking a cigarette, but I think he put it out," Willi adds. Deep down Willi is not sure until the crew truck arrives and Kreutz is not on board.

"Take 'em back to the Camp," Mr. Bud tells the driver. "If I can't trust 'em, I don't want 'em!" Turning to Willi he says, "Willi, can you stay and help us clean up this mess? I'd be much obliged."

"*Ja, ja*, I can help," and looking over at the POWs ready to get back on the truck, "maybe they can help. I will talk to them, okay? There's much work to do." Willi has the crew working hard, but not happily. There is grumbling among the men. Turning to the grumblers he says, "I hear you mumbling. I'm a worker all my life and I don't understand people who complain about work when they are paid." When they finish stacking the remains of the barn to one side, Willi attaches a grading blade to the front of a tractor and begins to push the remaining debris into a pile. Mr. Bud is watching as Willi finishes the cleanup, parks the tractor and removes the blade. "You are one hard working man, Willi. When this war's over, stay here in Arizona. I'll give you a job."

"Thank you, Mr. Bud. We will see." Willi does not speak to Kreutz that evening, nor does Kreutz approach Willi. During the night Willi finds it hard to sleep thinking about the fire. Next morning, Willi tells the translator he wants another job. "Good, I need a man at the hospital. Go see Corporal Jepson at the hospital kitchen right now!" Corporal Jepson is in charge of garbage detail at the hospital dining hall. Jepson welcomes Willi as a volunteer for an unpopular job.

Chapter 20
A Model Prisoner

October 1944

Willi has two others helping him with the garbage detail—Helmut Winkler, a white-haired POW and former patient at the hospital, and the young black man who was a guard when Willi first went to Mr. Bud's farm. Helmut had black hair when he arrived at Camp Florence. Trying to be a cooperative prisoner, he was frightened by Nazi NCOs who told him his family in Germany would be harmed if he continued to cooperate with the Americans. Worried about his wife and family in Berlin, he had a dream one night, in the dream he saw his wife walking from a prison camp with the look of death about her. As Helmut was taken to the hospital the next morning, his hair was completely white.

Learning new English/American words helped Willi become a trustee at the hospital. A German/English dictionary is Willi's first purchase at the canteen. Some words he learned at Mr. Bud's are not in the dictionary and the Mexican farm hands used a version of English that defies definition. He notices things at the hospital that puzzle him. Three black military nurses wait outside the dining room until the other hospital personnel have eaten. Occasionally one of the nurses looks inside to see if the "white folks" have left. It is all very puzzling to Willi and spends much of his time at the hospital mess hall waiting for a crew to be called.

One day he has company as he sits in the shade near the back door. The black American guard from his first day in camp is now on garbage detail and eager to talk. Willi does not know the black soldier's real name; the name he likes to be called is "Zoot Suit." German POWs are told not to "fraternize" with Americans. But, Zoot Suit is not like other Americans, he is a prisoner too. Sitting together on the garbage platform, legs dangling over the side and brushing at flies buzzing their faces, Willi chuckles inwardly at the odd pair they make. Maybe this is "fraternize," he thinks. Willi is a big man, many kilos heavier and a foot taller than Zoot Suit. Also, he is very white and does not tan easily. Even when he worked for Mr. Bud, he would get sunburned but never tan.

Zoot Suit is short and skinny, a kinky-haired very black, black man in a dirty white T-shirt, a braided leather string hanging from his dog tag chain, and grease stained fatigue pants. He began at Camp Florence as a guard. Several weeks after Willi's group of POWs arrived, Zoot Suit mouthed-off to his supervisor and was transferred to the motor pool. A week later he decided to borrow a truck and drive to Phoenix for what Zoot Suit describes as "lights an' action." He returned to Camp Florence the next morning a "pris'ner third-class" (his description) and escorted by MPs. What he means by "pris'ner third-class" Willi does not understand.

Between swatting flies and spitting in the dust below their dangling feet, Willi asks, "What do you mean, Zoot Suit, pris'ner third-class?"

"Will-helm," he drawls, accentuating each syllable, "sho you know de diff'nce fum fust-class an' sec'un-class?"

"You tell me, what is difference," Willi replies, shaking his head negatively.

"Man, you know dat white s– a– Clem? Him a pris'ner fust-class. All dem white boys in trouble is pris'ners fust-class. Nex' come you Germans and Japs. Y'all pris'ners sec'un-class. Us niggers, we de third-class pris'ners. Ever'body heada us."

Willi mulls over this explanation while fanning at a persistent fly, and says slowly, "How can that be? You are American. We are not!"

"Where you been, man?" Zoot Suit looks at Willi suspiciously. "Doan yo got colored folks in Germ'ny?" Before Willi could answer, he continues. "Ast dem white boys who dey hate de mos', you Germans or us niggers. I bet dey'll all say 'niggers.' An' dat redneck Clem? Him soon bash my haid as look at me!" He flicks his ear and mutters "damn fly" under his breath.

"*Ja, ja.* I know what you mean. Clem calls me names, some I understand and others no. He is always mad, why?" Zoot Suit lies back on the garbage stained floor of the platform, and looks straight up at the bright, clear blue Arizona sky, straining his eyes as if he were looking in the sky for an answer. Willi thinks he may be in a trance, he is thinking so hard. Then his thick lips break into a wide grin as he sits up and looks at Willi with the devil in his gleaming eyes.

"I know, Will-helm! By damn I know! He think all us pris'ners de same! I'll bet dat's it. Hot damn, wait'll I tell ever'body! He think since we pris'ners, we all de same an' he mad 'cause he jus' like us!"

Not many days after Willi's conversation with Zoot Suit, the Camp Plumber, Elmer Davis, asks for a volunteer to help him. Since Helmut seems happy on the garbage detail and there is so little work, Willi volunteers. Davis, a short and wiry Arizonan, whose legs are a little bowed in the knees, interviews Willi and likes the way Willi looks him in the eye when he talks. Willi knows how to work with his hands and understands enough English to accept instructions.

Willi is a quick learner and soon is fixing leaks, unplugging drains and working on the several septic systems serving the camp. There are many plumbing jobs at Camp Florence, most of them in the different mess halls. Willi still gets to see Zoot Suit and they "fraternize" a little bit, talking on the back stoop of the mess hall where no one else hangs around. Occasionally Willi is rewarded with a container of ice cream for doing a good plumbing job. He shares with Zoot Suit who can eat more ice cream, faster, and without getting a headache, than anyone Willi knows.

A newly arrived POW, Ernst Becker, has replaced Willi on the detail. Becker was a German private in World War I, but never a POW, he tells Willi. "After the Great War I went home and became a baker. Bakers always have bread," the elderly POW explains. "Now I am 57-years-old, a POW, and no more a baker!"

One day after cleaning a drain in the mess hall at his compound, Willi tells the Chief Cook, "If you like good German bread cooked in your kitchen, get Ernst Becker from garbage detail at the hospital."

"What's wrong with the bread we get from central bakery?" the cook asks.

"Your American bread is soft, and good, but Ernst's bread is hard, and good. German soldier likes hard bread. Ernst speaks poor English, but he is a good baker." Ernst gets a job in the kitchen the next day and begins to bake small quantities of hard crusted rolls. Willi gets a bag of rolls each morning from Ernst, sharing them with his boss and others around the camp.

Davis finds Willi is quick to pick up the details of the plumbing trade. Not only is he strong enough to carry all the tools, which is Davis' first concern, but Willi remembers the tools needed for each job and is always learning. Among the first things he teaches Willi is to drive the plumber's truck.

On one occasion Davis sends Willi to fix a faucet leak at the officer prisoner compound. Willi has no difficulty getting past the guard at the officer's compound carrying his plumbing tool kit. But, Oberst Hauptman stops Willi at the front of the barracks building and orders him to leave the officer area. Willi tries to explain he has come to fix a faucet leak. The Oberst said, "Not while I am the senior officer." Returning to the plumbing shop, he relates the story to an understanding Elmer Davis.

Davis calmly says, "We'll fix that German sausage." They return to the officer area, Willi driving. Davis gets out of the truck very leisurely, stretching to look his tallest in the cowboy boots, adding two inches to his height. Nodding to the guard as they enter the compound, he says, "Willi, come with me." They enter the officer's quarters and Willi fixes the leak. Oberst Hauptman glares at Willi but says nothing.

The next morning Oberst Hauptman carries his complaints to Colonel Shannon, camp commander. "Private Meissner is being allowed too many privileges, and the other prisoners may do him harm." Shannon, an army reservist called to active duty from Tucson, 50 miles south of Florence, made his peacetime living building bridges over dry creek beds and other types of highway construction. He listens to the senior prisoner and assures him he will look into the matter.

Shannon understands violence among the prisoners and deals with it swiftly when it occurs. He calls Davis' office. "Elmer come over, we need to talk about your German helper." Colonel Shannon calls most of his people by their first names. When Davis arrives at Colonel Shannon's office, he carries a German roll with him, still warm, and offers it to the Colonel.

"Where did you get this, Elmer?" he asks as he bites through the crust and smacks his lips. "Your wife make this?"

"No sir," Davis tells the camp commander, "I couldn't make somethin' like that if my life depended on it, and the wife makes biscuits, not rolls. My helper, Willi, he got one of the prisoners a job fixin' rolls at his mess hall. Makes the prisoners happy and I think they're pretty damn good myself! He brings me some every morning."

"This helper of yours, Willi, what all do you have him doing?"

"Colonel, Willi is a fast learner and good worker. That's why he gets to do so many things. There's not a thing around here I wouldn't trust him to do and do it right!"

"Well, our Nazi Colonel thinks Private Meissner might get hurt by some of the other prisoners."

"Only if they catch him by surprise, Colonel," Davis responds. "That boy can whip any three of them at the same time. Four might be a little tough, but he's tough. He tells me he did some boxing when he was in Germany."

"You just tell him to be on the lookout, Elmer. Don't want him getting hurt like that German kid they hung at Papago. (Papago Park is a German POW camp near Phoenix. Twelve of the POWs held a kangaroo court and found one of their men guilty of treason. They sentenced him to death and hung him in the bathroom. The twelve men were moved to Camp Florence and placed in a wing of the hospital, guarded 24 hours a day.) You watch out for Meissner, I'll take care of the Oberst."

In January 1945, Davis gets approval for Willi to take the truck to Litchfield Airfield and get supplies from the Post Engineer. Before Willi can drive outside the camp, Davis takes him to get an Arizona driver's license. Returning to the motor pool to have Willi's temporary Arizona permit entered into his military driver records, Willi spots Zoot Suit, no longer a "pris'ner third class" and back working in the motor pool.

"Will-Helm, dis is good t'ing to hab. I kin getcha job drivin' fo de mob when de Wah ovah." He chuckles like it is a big joke.

"I never have a driving license before," Willi tells him. "In Germany to have a driving license is to have job. Of course, you need something to drive, and I never had a car."

"Well, jus' you 'member whut I say. When de Wah ovah, Zoot Suit get his frien' Will-Helm a job back east an' doan go donkey-shining me."

"What is 'donkey-shine,' Zoot Suit?"

"Doan you heah good, tha's whut you Germans say fo' 'thank yo', Will-Helm."

Willi shrugs, smiles and leaves the motor pool muttering under his breath, "donkey-shine, donkey-shine. *Danke Schoen*?"

Willi tells his barracks mates he is going to Litchfield. Someone in the barracks, possibly Kreutz, tells Oberst Hauptman. A Nazi captain arrives the next evening to escort Willi to the officer compound. Willi suspects trouble.

He has not been summoned to the officer compound before. Others have and it is usually for a reprimand or punishment. Willi is ready to fight if they start anything. Entering Oberst Hauptman's room in the officer barracks Willi salutes, but does not say 'Heil Hitler.'

Oberst Hauptman returns the salute and says "Heil Hitler," ignoring Willi's omission. Hauptman pretends friendliness and interest in Willi's camp activities. Willi tells the Oberst he is learning much from the camp plumber and now has an Arizona driver license. Hauptman asks to see it. Willi is proud to show it, and hands it to him. After Hauptman looks at it and shows it to the other officers. They pass it around. "Why do you have this license? Are they going to allow you to drive outside the camp?" Hauptman asks.

It dawns on Willi why the Oberst is so friendly. Hauptman must have heard about the trip to Litchfield. "*Ja*! I will get to drive outside the camp. The plumber, Mr. Davis, wants me to take the truck to Litchfield and get supplies."

"Private Meissner," his tone is very friendly, always before it is 'Private Meissner', with an unfriendly growl. "I've been trying to think of a way to improve the quality of life here in Camp Florence. We have arranged through a contact at Litchfield for a few supplies to have a surprise '*Fasching*' party. We have no way to get the supplies here without the Americans knowing about our plans. Perhaps you could bring the supplies back with you?"

This is first time Willi has heard of any *Fasching* party. Something about this smells like dead fish, he thinks.

"Herr Oberst, why do you need my help?" he asks. "There are others who go to Litchfield, to the clinic."

"We need your truck because there are many supplies to bring back. Also, the person who has our supplies just happens to work in the Post Engineer compound. Is that not where you are going?"

Willi nods.

"Need I remind you of your duty as a German soldier to help improve camp morale? It is a worthy cause!"

"I don't suppose it will hurt, Oberst Hauptman. The Americans trust me. I only want to do what is right."

"And I would not ask you to do something wrong, Private Meissner. Our contact man will be looking for you at Litchfield and will load the supplies in your truck himself. All you need to do on returning to Camp Florence is to stop on the road where you see a handkerchief in a tree. We will be there to unload the supplies before you get to camp. Understand?"

"*Ja. Ja.* I can do it."

"You must tell no one about our little surprise, right Wilhelm?" This is the first time a German officer calls Willi by his first name.

Willi nods his head in agreement. Hauptman pats Willi on the shoulder as he turns to leave. "You forgot something, Private Meissner."

Turning around Willi sees Oberst Hauptman raise his arm in a salute and quickly raises his arm with a click of his heels. Conditioned reflex, Willi thinks. As Willi starts back to his barracks, he fumbles around in his pocket for his driver's license. Thinking he dropped it at the officer quarters, he retraces his steps. Walking alongside the officer building he hears Oberst Hauptman talking, "through Meissner's good fortune we can still be heroes of the Third Reich. There are many airfields nearby and from what I hear they are not well guarded. With the use of his truck we can sabotage the Americans flying program."

Quietly Willi turns and leaves the officer's compound. The license is not important now. It is important he tell someone about Oberst Hauptman's plan.

Willi does not sleep well that night. Tossing and turning in his bunk, he gets grumbles from the upper bunk. So, he gets up, goes to the toilet, and sits there thinking about his options. The toilet is the only place in the barracks with a light at night. The light bulb is near the sink so the POWs can see to shave when they get up early in the morning. There is a line of stools across from the urinals. Willi sits on one by the window and looks out into the dark night. The latrine is on the north side of the barracks and, despite the light, he can see the big dipper, low in the sky and pointing to the North Star about 30 degrees above the horizon. A cool breeze is blowing in the window. "What is it like in Leipzig this January day? Is Katarina still living in our house? What can I do about this predicament?" His thoughts are rambling. He sits there for maybe an hour and nothing is resolved, except now, he is sleepy. He decides to talk with Davis in the morning.

Willi has his talk with Plumber Davis. Davis tells him to take the truck and drive over to the officer quarters and get his license like nothing has happened. Pulling up in front of the officer quarters in his truck, Willi sees a lieutenant who was in the room with Oberst Hauptman yesterday, walks up and salutes him. "Sir, have you seen my driver license?"

The Lieutenant points toward the door. Willi goes to the door and looks inside. His license is on their notice board. Taking it from the board, Willi scans the hallway. It appears no one is around. He turns and walks quickly back to his truck and leaves for Litchfield.

Willi's trip to Litchfield is good for his sagging morale. He has made the trip with Mr. Davis many times before. The road is straight through the desert. Cactus, the kind his boss calls prickly pear, have many yellow blooms. Willi wants to stop and look more closely at a variety of cactus they do not have in the camp. He slows down, but decides to drive on. It is good Willi did not stop. A military police Jeep passes him going toward Camp Florence. At Litchfield, Willi gets the plumbing supplies at the Post Engineer's compound.

Willi looks for the man with Oberst Hauptman's supplies. While he is waiting, he watches the American training airplanes circling the field. Standing by the truck, he feels important because of the trust Mr. Davis has placed in him. The truck, of course, is not his, but "I am the driver, the *wagen-führer*," he rationalizes. "What would Katarina think if she could see me here in Arizona, driving a truck and helping the chief plumber?" While waiting, a POW walks up and puts a package in the back of the truck.

"*Guten tag*! I have more packages if you will wait a little longer," the POW from Litchfield says with eyebrows raised.

Willi nods as the fellow walks away, only to return a few minutes later with yet another package. In all there are seven additional packages of supplies in Willi's truck when he leaves the post engineer compound at Litchfield. Driving through town and out into the desert, Willi is careful of other traffic and finally there is no traffic, only the 1939 Ford pickup used by the plumber. Willi mulls over his situation, "Can this really be happening to me, a POW?" Nearing the camp he begins looking for Oberst Hauptman's handkerchief. Not seeing a handkerchief, he continues to drive on up to the front gate and is immediately waved into camp.

Pulling up in front of the plumber's shop, Davis comes outside smiling and asks, "Did you get the supplies, Willi?"

"*Ja*, I have supplies. What we do with them?" he asks, looking at the packages loaded by the POW at Litchfield.

"We have a 'Fasching' blow out, Willi, that's what we'll do! Wait 'till the camp commander sees the surprise your Nazi colonel was cooking up."

"Why didn't I see Oberst Hauptman's handkerchief?"

"Colonel Shannon decided today will be a 'training day' for all prisoners. Even those who were sick had to show up in the auditorium for training. He still has them in there, and it must be a hundred an' ten degrees inside. You're the only prisoner to miss training. Ha!"

They unload the truck. Mr. Davis puts the '*Fasching*' packages in his private room and locks the door. "Go on to the auditorium, Willi, the commander is holding everyone there until he sees you."

"I am going!"

When Willi arrives at the packed auditorium, the guard motions Willi to go on inside. It is very hot inside; everyone is sweating. The officers are arguing with the training officer they do not have to stay for the training, something about Geneva Convention.

The telephone in the auditorium office is ringing. Finally someone answers it. "It's for you cap'n," a soldier calls out to the training officer.

The training officer climbs down from the stage and walks to the rear of the auditorium. Willi can hear him talking to someone on the telephone and then cradles the receiver. Turning to the officers, including Oberst Hauptman, he says, "Oh, very well! You're all dismissed!"

Willi is among the first prisoners out of the door.

"Wilhelm, you lucky stiff, you missed all this," calls a barracks mate.

"*Ja*. They make me come here as soon as I get back. How long did it last?"

"The camp commander had a roll call at noon chow and marched us all to the auditorium. That training officer kept everyone in the auditorium until just now. Almost four hours. Whew, was it hot!"

Willi spots Oberst Hauptman coming toward him and braces himself for a reprimand. The Oberst's forehead is creased with worry lines.

"Ah, Meissner. Were you able to bring anything with you from Litchfield?"

"*Ja*, Oberst Hauptman. I brought back the *Fasching* supplies, but I don't see a handkerchief."

"I know Meissner. The stupid camp commander decides to train today. We couldn't get away to meet you. Where are the supplies? Were you able to get them into the camp?"

"Mr. Davis put all the supplies in his plumbing shop," Willi replies truthfully.

"Our supplies?"

"All the supplies," Willi responds.

"Did he ask you any questions about our packages?" Oberst Hauptman asks with a worried look on his face.

"No, he just dumped them in his private room and locked the door."

"Dumped them, you say?" Oberst Hauptman looks even more worried.

"*Ja*. I suppose you can ask for them tomorrow," Willi responds innocently.

"*Wiedersehen.*"

As Willi walks back to his barracks, Kreutz, who has not talked with Willi for several months, hurries to catch up with him and asks what happened. Willi tells him about the trip, the blooming prickly pear and the training planes at Litchfield. "Anything else?" Kreutz asks.

Willi looks out of the corner of his eyes to see if Kreutz is as nervous as he sounds. "No, nothing I can think of except …."

"Except what?" Kreutz interrupts.

"I promised Oberst Hauptman I wouldn't tell, and I better not," Willi says with all innocence. Kreutz walks along in silence until they reach the barracks. There they sit on the steps, each deep in his thoughts, and wait for the call to supper.

The next day Oberst Hauptman, a captain and lieutenant are transferred to another POW camp. Kreutz is very nervous when they tell the POWs there is a new senior officer. He corners Willi afterward in the barracks and demands to know what has happened to Oberst Hauptman. "You knew something Hauptman was doing. You said he told you not to tell. Tell me!"

"I honestly know nothing about what happened to the Oberst. It surprises me as much as it seems to surprise you. I do know he was planning something, nothing bad," Willi tells Kreutz, calmly, reflectively. "If the Oberst tells me not to tell, then I don't tell," he adds emphatically. Willi is beginning to suspect Kreutz has some part to play in all that has happened.

A few days later, Mr. Davis asks Willi to join him at his house in Florence for dinner, "A home-cooked meal for your good work." Willi wonders if the invitation has something to do with the '*Fasching*' party. The supplies from Litchfield are never seen again. As Willi and Elmer climb into Elmer's battleship-grey, two door, 1941 Ford sedan, and drive out of Camp Florence, Willi shows the guard at the gate a pass signed by Colonel Shannon.

Crossing the nearly dry Gila River and entering the town of Florence, Davis talks about the weather and about the mountains changing color into a fire ball of color as the sun goes down. Then he looks over at Willi and asks, "Willi, aren't you just a little curious about what you brought back from Litchfield? Or, what your colonel had in mind with those packages?"

"*Ja*, I'm a little curious."

"We better talk about this before I get you to the house. Don't want the little lady to be worried. When you told me what Colonel Hauptman said, I knew you could be trusted. Remember I said, 'Just go on to Litchfield like nothin' happened.' We knew through the intelligence guys you Nazis had a communications network between Litchfield and Florence."

Willi interrupts him. "Mr. Davis. I have told you we are not all Nazis. You call us by that name, but only a few POWs at Florence are Nazis."

"Yeah, right Willi. I keep forgettin' you don't like to be called Nazis. Anyway, the intelligence guys also told us something was being planned. What they didn't know was exactly what your German buddies were up to. That's where your bit of information helped and, to find out who was helping Hauptman, you had to make that trip to Litchfield. I didn't want you to worry or have any problems, so I didn't tell you what we knew. Hauptman contacted that POW at Litchfield who managed to get dynamite out of the Post Engineer's supplies. That's what was in those packages, dynamite."

"Whew, was it dangerous?"

"Not really. But, it could've been dangerous in the hands of Colonel Hauptman and his buddies. I called the camp commander soon as you left my shop that morning and told him what was happening. He approved your trip to Litchfield, or you wouldn't have gotten off the base. He also took care of calling the commander at Litchfield. You were watched the whole time you were there. They took that little sneak who was stealing the dynamite into custody soon as you left. The commander didn't want to risk something happening on the public highway so he made sure all the prisoners would be in training 'til you got back. That night, after you got back, Hauptman and the others who were in on his little plan, came down to the plumbing shop and were trying to break-in when the MP's got'em. What do you think about that?" Willi frowns, "I think I could be in big trouble!"

"Naw, Willi, you're lily-white in the whole thing. Fact is, the commander wants to give you a commendation, but the OSI guys say it could make trouble for you later. That whole bunch is gonna spend some time in one of the big prisons."

They arrive in front of Davis' house. "Not a word of this to the missus," he says. One thing for certain, all this was not going to spoil Willi's appetite. Willi has been growing vegetables in his garden outside the barracks and has learned vegetables can grow year around in Arizona. Davis takes Willi behind his house and shows him "a real Arizona garden." After looking at the garden, Willi tells him, "I think you are a better gardener than plumber." He has fresh tomatoes, green beans; all those summer vegetables, and it is January.

Mrs. Davis is a small lady, wears metal rim glasses and fixes her brown hair in a bun at the top of her head. Her white socks are rolled down to the top of her Mexican sandals and the dress she is wearing she calls her "flour-sack dress." She shows Willi where he can wash his hands and, then, where to sit. On the table are vegetables from the garden plus chicken she calls "Indian-style." The conversation is about ration stamps. They have stamps for meat, sugar, shoes, and they raise their own chickens, she says. "That's why we eat a lot of chicken," she laughs. After the meal Willi offers to help clean up, but Elmer says they must get back to camp. It is dark as they drive back to Camp Florence and Willi is a POW again.

Chaplains at Camp Florence hold services every Sunday for the prisoners. Italian POWs helped build the chapel and formed a choir. Very few German POWs attend, but Willi goes and is a helper in early Sunday Lutheran services. An oddity to Willi is the separate service black people have at the chapel. They hold their church service before and after the protestant service. Willi arrives early and stays after the Lutheran service just to hear the black people sing. He asks for an explanation. "I can try to understand making the black man use a different toilet, or waiting to eat until the white people have eaten; but the church, why have a separate church?" The chaplain's explanation leaves Willi more confused. Did the blacks not want to share their religion with the whites, or vice versa?

13 April 1945

The Americans are very sad today, Willi recalls. It was announced on the camp loudspeakers their president has died. Some prisoners applauded.

Chapter 21
Repatriated

Camp Florence
7 May 1945

At noon, the camp loudspeakers announce Germany has surrendered. Willi is in the barracks to wash his hands before going to lunch. He sighs, "I'm glad it's over."

"When will it be over for us?" Kreutz asks from his bunk. No one has an answer. The new senior officer, Oberst-lieutenant Keeler meets with the camp commander often to "demand" their return to Germany. Keeler is in the first group to leave Camp Florence in January 1946.

In February, Davis asks Willi if he wants to stay in America and be a plumber. "I must go back to my home," Willi tells him. "There is not much left between Katarina and me. But, I must go back."

When Willi leaves Camp Florence, he considers himself a rich man in many respects. Mr. Davis, his boss, is a good friend and has given him many gifts to take back to Germany. There is a letter from the new camp commander saying he is a "good worker," an Arizona driver license and military driver license, tobacco, many changes of underwear, extra clothes, and two pair of shoes. Also, Willi has money earned from work details and from the canteen fund.

Willi is among 50 men from Camp Florence selected to go by train to Fort Eustis, Virginia, Monday, 18 February 1946. He leaves Camp Florence with $115 in his pocket, once again escorted by MPs.

Fort Eustis was designated in December 1945, to receive some 20,000 trustworthy German POWs and put them through a crash course in democracy. The first group had completed the course when Willi's group arrived. He joins about 2,000 other POWs in the Special Projects Center. An officer tells them they will spend six days studying democracy, and how it could work in Germany; then they will be on their way home.

Cheers break out from the assembled POWs at this bit of news. Everyone in Willi's group appear enthusiastic about going home. Each day, the POWs divide into two groups of about 1,000, to attend lectures, see a film and then participate in discussion groups about the lectures. In the evenings they can see another film, or have a choice of other activities. Willi uses the time trying to find out about his family in Lützen, now in the Russian sector of divided Germany. (*A detailed account of the course at Fort Eustis can be found in "Stalag USA" by Judith M. Gansberg, Thomas Y. Cravell Company, New York, NY, 1977.*)

Willi listens to lectures on democracy; however, he finds it difficult to absorb all he is told, or why he is being told these things. He understands they are being prepared for their return to Germany, and, attending the training course at Ft. Eustis will help them get good jobs. Attendance is voluntary, they are told, but by attending the lectures there will be no further delays in repatriation. (Over 30,000 German prisoners were sent through specialized training at Ft. Eustis, and other installations, before being repatriated. They were selected because of their cooperative attitude while POWs.)

After Fort Eustis, the men are sent to a camp in North Carolina for relaxation. Willi tells the officer accompanying them he does not need to relax, he needs to get home. It appears to Willi they do not know what to do with the prisoners. After several days of swimming and playing soccer, Willi's group boards a train for New York, spending two nights in a camp near New York City. From there they board a troop ship, "with hammocks and lockers," for their return to Europe.

It is mid-March, and the ship takes only seven days to reach Le Havre, France, much quicker than his forty-eight days on a freighter en route to America. An American officer accompanies Willi and the other Ft. Eustis-trained prisoners back to Germany. Their first night in France, all the prisoners are taken to Camp Bolbec, a French army camp. During the night, the French commander accompanied by several armed guards, enters the former POWs' building at midnight, waking everyone up to form a work detail. They grumble and make considerable noise about having to get out of bed in middle of the night. The American officer escorting them hears the noise and comes over to where the men are staying.

"What are you doing to my boys?" he asks the French captain.

"We have much work to do in the camp. These prisoners can help!" The French officer stood nose to nose with the American officer.

"You will not use my prisoners for your details tonight. Tomorrow morning we can discuss this at your office. Tonight they rest!"

The American officer stands there with his arms folded until the French officer leaves. "Back to bed, boys," he says, "tomorrow is a long day."

The next morning, Willi and the Fort Eustis group leave the French camp. There were other German POWs at the French camp kept behind. Willi's group is getting the special treatment they had been promised back at Fort Eustis. Their train avoids Paris. It is a very slow trip to the German border. The train moves along for maybe two hours then stops as they wait for another engine. The train stops at Forbach, and the damage is worse than pictures Willi saw at Fort Eustis. The former POWs, who have been talking and joking during the trip, are suddenly silent as the train rolls through the rail yards of Saarbrucken. Women in ragged clothing are standing beside the tracks, coal dust on their faces and hands, holding small buckets containing bits and pieces of coal or wood.

Crumbled walls and empty buildings with glassless windows looking like hollow eyes are all they can see as the train slowly passes through Saarbrucken. The countryside a year after the surrender is looking untouched by the war. But, each city along the way, Karlsruhe, Stuttgart, Ulm and Augsburg, all show the scars of war, and the people mirror the defeat. Darkness has long since fallen as their train rolls through Munich and into Bad Abling, their termination point.

The American lieutenant, who has accompanied them the entire way, turns the group over to a Wehrmacht officer. The good treatment Willi and his group have received on their trip ends at Bad Abling.

Wednesday Evening, 20 March 1946

The first thing the German officer does is have them empty their duffel bags on the floor of the billets. He inspects items the Fort Eustis trainees have brought with them from the United States and takes things from each man, puts them in a pile and goes to the next person. When he gets to Willi, he takes an extra pair of shoes and two shirts along with half his American money. What little hope they had of fair treatment from the German Army is stifled by their reception committee.

There is no food to eat the night they arrive at the German camp. Breakfast the next morning is a hot broth. Standing in line for his discharge papers, Willi is told there is no back pay for being a POW. From there, they board a train for the Munich Bahnhof and receive directions to the American employment office in Munich. Willi walks ahead of the group and into the office first, "I go quickly for I want to make money to return to Leipzig."

Willi reports to the American director of Munich's public services. The interview is quick. "What was your civilian work?"

"I was a policeman and a machinist. I drove a truck at Camp Florence and helped the plumber."

The interviewer looks at his list of jobs. "Do you want to be a truck driver?"

"No."

"Do you want to be a policeman?"

"Not really."

"Do you want to work in the Stadelheim Prison?"

"Perhaps."

"Good. Report to the supervisor at the prison this afternoon, here are your instructions."

Willi begins work as a guard at Stadelheim Friday, 22 March 1946. In little more than a month, he has gone from being a POW in Arizona, to being a guard/spy in a prison for suspected Nazi collaborators. He has a sleeping room at the University and eats his meals at the prison. His pay allows him to save a few marks and to buy extra food.

Months go by, Willi listens to the prisoners talk, trying to determine from their conversations, the falsely accused, and who the real Nazis are. All someone needs to do in Post-war Germany is accuse a neighbor, or perhaps someone they owe money to, of being a Nazi, they are sent immediately to Stadelheim Prison.

Some prisoners are moved to Nuremberg for trial and in September, and Willi is called to testify about conversations he overheard in the prison. Willi arrives in Nuremberg September 6, and later meets with a translator, an Englishman named Frank. Some American lawyers are called in to discuss his testimony.

After giving his testimony Willi thinks seriously of returning to his *Heimat* (home) in Saxony. It should be easy, he expects, to sneak across without being caught and take the train to Leipzig. Having heard nothing from Katarina, or his parents, in two years, a great deal of pent up anxiety overrules his practical concerns about life under the Russians.

Thursday, September 12, Willi goes to the office of the American lawyers to see if there is any further need of his services. A German lawyer working for the Americans tells him he can return to Munich; his work in Nuremberg is complete.

Willi has a briefcase filled with cigarettes, soap, tobacco and other rationed items, and the duffel bag he had brought from America. The duffel bag contains clothes bought since returning to Germany. At the Nuremberg Bahnhof, Willi does not hesitate. He steps up to the ticket window and asks for a ticket to Rodach. The train departs at noon, and Willi has a good seat by the window, to see the changes in Germany since he left. A young man sitting nearby asks him for a cigarette and Willi provides one.

"Where are you going?" he asks.

"Rodach," Willi responds.

"Rodach is a good place to cross the border, if you are interested in that sort of thing," the young man adds.

Willi sits back and folds his arms. He nods at the comments of the younger traveler. They arrive in Rodach late in the afternoon. The train turns around and will return to Coburg. The border is closed to trains. "Everyone must get off." Willi gathers his briefcase and duffel bag, which he throws over his shoulder. Stepping down from the car to the platform, he cautiously looks around. There are no German guards, only train people and an American MP. The MP is standing at the station platform exit and is checking papers. Willi pulls his identification papers from Fort Eustis out of his wallet and shows them to the MP. The MP waves him through the gate.

From Rodach it is only six kilometers to the East German border. The railroad tracks are the best indicator of the direction to walk. Willi studied the *plan* (map) at Nuremberg. The sun is getting very low. He can still be at the border by nightfall.

The civilian clothes Willi received at the Munich Repatriation Center are a dead giveaway he is a German soldier, coming home. "I will get new clothes in Leipzig," he tells himself. Several repatriated soldiers approached Willi during the train trip to ask where he was a prisoner. They know the repatriation suit. One soldier also told him that crossing at Rodach is the best way to get into East Germany without getting caught.

People in Rodach glance casually at Willi, they have seen many ex-soldiers step off the train and start walking north along the railroad track. There is nothing in that direction except the border. Willi is happy to finally be going home, regardless of what he might find. Being a Saxon, "it is natural to want to return to Saxony," is Willi's mindset. A man from the station is now following him, discreetly at first, and when Willi goes beyond the last house in Rodach, the man calls out to him. "Friend, either you are lost or going to cross the border. I'll guide you over the border for five marks!"

Willi stops. If he refuses, the man might turn him in to the Rodach authorities. If he says OK, maybe the guide can keep him away from patrols. "All right, but I won't pay until we are across the border safely."

The road to the border is narrow and winds through forests, passing an occasional clearing. There are no houses along the road after Willi leaves Rodach. He can glimpse the setting sun, a deep-orange fireball with rays of light filtering through the green leaves on the trees. There is a quiet coolness in the woods of Lower Saxony. Fog is beginning to form in the hollows as the sun goes down. Within a kilometer of the border signs warn the border is ahead and not to proceed beyond that point. It is dark and the fog is heavier. The guide points to a trail that runs east. They follow it until reaching a small creek.

"We have come to the border. Follow the creek and when you reach a bridge you will be one kilometer inside East Germany. You pay me now!" the guide demands.

Willi pays the guide and they part company. Following the creek seems a safe way to avoid detection. There is no semblance of a path or trail guards would watch. After what seems an interminable time, Willi stumbles out of the dark, foggy forest near the bridge and steps on to the road to Hildburghausen. Despite the darkness and fog, Willi feels someone is watching him.

Walking quickly and trying to make very little sound, Willi becomes more confident. There are no lights or traffic along this road. After perhaps two minutes a voice behind him orders, "Halt!"

Willi turns around and a flashlight cuts through the fog, shinning in his eyes. Two Russian soldiers, border police, approach him.

"Papers!" is the next command.

Willi has placed his identification papers in his shoe. Now he must sit on the road, remove his shoe, and show the Russian he has papers.

"Why are your papers in your shoe?" one of the Russians asks.

"I put them there for safe keeping. At night a man could be robbed."

The Russian with the flashlight takes Willi's identification papers and shines the light on them momentarily. "Come with us," he tells Willi. They turn and walk back along the road to their checkpoint, about ten meters south of the bridge where Willi had stepped onto the road. A half hour later a car pulls up with a Russian officer inside. He asks many questions Willi cannot understand.

Frustrated, the officer has the men put Willi in his car and drives him to Hildburghausen, accompanied by a soldier.

Willi is taken to a small office in a house. First they empty his bag and look at American cigarettes, cotton underwear made in USA and the toilet items he is taking to Katarina.

"You empty your pockets on the table please," orders the squatty Russian soldier who stopped Willi on the road.

The marks he has saved from his first few months of pay are counted carefully by the soldier, along with the American currency he has kept. They examine everything, even the ticket stub from the train to Rodach. Although they speak German, Willi is now certain they are Russian soldiers.

"Remove both shoes!" The officer tells him. He is a smaller man.

With the identification papers Willi had placed in his shoe were the certificate from Fort Eustis, a letter from the camp commander in Arizona, his driving licenses, Zoot Suit's address, and a letter from Mr. Davis inside his shoes. Although he dreaded explaining all the documents, it is a relief to remove them from his shoes.

"We trust you can explain all this in your shoes?" queries the Russian officer.

"*Ja*! *Ja*! I can explain."

"Good. You will explain to our interrogation team."

"That is good. I can answer their questions. I am not a spy, I am a Saxon."

"Then you won't mind waiting in our Saxon prison," the Russian officer says with a cynical smile. "Take him out back."

Behind the house is a pig barn, the Saxon prison. For three days Willi sits in a pig pen with five others captured crossing the border. They must wait for Russian interrogators to come.

Finally on the third day they are taken one by one before an interrogation team. Willi is the second prisoner called. He enters the room and behind a large table are four Russian officers. One of them is a woman. Behind the officers a Russian soldier is standing.

"What is your name?" an obese officer to Willi's left asks in English.

"Wilhelm Meissner. You can call me Willi," Willi responds in German, trying to be friendly.

"You understand English," he says.

"*Ja*, I was a POW in Arizona for three year."

The Russian officer nods and writes on a paper before him.

"What was your Wehrmacht service grade?" the woman officer asks.

"I was a private."

"Why did you illegally cross the border?" she asks.

"My home is Leipzig. Like I say, I was prisoner of war in Arizona for almost three years and now I am coming home."

"Where in Leipzig is your home?"

"Eisenbahn Strasse, 788."

The female officer nods to the soldier behind them and he leaves the room. Another officer, very tall and thin, begins questioning Willi.

As he answers the questions, Willi can hear a voice talking like on telephone. But cannot hear what is said. The soldier comes back and whispers something in Russian to the female officer.

The tall, thin officer asks, "Why do you hide these papers in your shoe?" He is holding the letters, the Camp Eustis certificate, and Willi's Arizona driving license.

"I wanted to be sure I didn't lose them," Willi responds quickly.

"What are these?" he asks holding up the letters.

"They are nothing except papers saying what kind of work I do in prison camp. The other card is a license to drive truck."

The officer slowly and methodically tears up the papers while looking directly at Willi, then picks up the driving license and rips it into small pieces. "You are in Germany now. You do not need these papers," he says calmly.

"What did Americans tell you about Russians? Did they tell you we would steal from you, put you in prison?

"No-o-o," Willi responds cautiously.

"Is this your bag?" he asks, as he points to Willi's bag on the desk.

"*Ja*, it is mine."

"Check to see if everything is inside."

Willi looks inside and everything appears pretty much as he remembers, even the American cigarettes. He removes a package of Lucky Strike cigarettes from a carton and offers it to the officers.

The tall, thin Russian officer holds up his hand and says, "*Nein, nein*! Here, try a Russian cigarette, they are better." Taking one of his Russian cigarettes and lighting it, Willi can barely keep from choking. They are very strong and taste bitter. The Russians watch as Willi smokes the cigarette.

"It is good, better than American cigarettes," Willi responds diplomatically.

"See, Herr Meissner, we Russians would not take from you. We give to you." The officers are smiling and nodding their heads.

The fat officer on the left says, "I will try one of your American cigarettes, if you insist." He takes the pack, opens it, and pulls several cigarettes so they fall on the table. "Oops, here take your package. I only wanted one to compare." He takes one from the table and lights it, then puts the others in his jacket pocket. Willi nods and smiles, hoping he can finish the Russian cigarette without coughing.

"Your wife still lives at 788 Eisenbahn Strasse, Herr Meissner," the female officer interjects. "Unless my comrades have other questions for you, we can give you a permit allowing you to travel on the train system absolutely free. A soldier will take you to the train station. Is that what you want, Herr Meissner?" the Russian officer asks.

"*Ja*, that's what I want." Willi is suspicious of the treatment he is receiving. But, he is excited he will soon be on his way to Leipzig. He asks if he can wash up before leaving for Leipzig and they point to the toilet. It is good to get some stink of the pigsty washed away. Outside the house he climbs in a truck bed for the ride to Schwarza. They no longer have train service from Hildburghausen to Leipzig.

Chapter 22
Saxony, Home Again

Monday, 16 September 1946

The Russian driver delivers Willi to the Schwarza train station late in the afternoon. Showing the permit provided by the NKVD, Willi boards the train at eight o'clock in the evening and two hours later is in Leipzig Bahnhof. Evidence of destruction is everywhere, from American bombers, or maybe it was Russian or British bombers. The war has been over more than a year and nothing has been done to repair the roof of the Bahnhof. Only heat-scarred metal columns are left standing, like jagged steel fingers pointing toward the dark sky.

As Willi steps out of the dilapidated railway coach, all the uncertainties about coming back vanish. A policeman stands at a gate on the platform and checks everyone's papers. Waiting with the other passengers, Willi attempts to start a conversation. His comments are met with silence. Willi shows his NKVD permit to the policeman.

"Step aside and wait until I'm through," he tells Willi. When he finishes checking every person leaving the train, he takes Willi to his car and they go to the police station. There Willi gets new identification papers. It is after midnight when Willi finally gets in a small police car for the last leg of his trip home.

Getting out of the car at 788 Eisenbahn Strasse and reaching for his bag, the first thing striking Willi is the darkness of the street. There were many street lights on Eisenbahn Strasse before the war. In the dim light provided by the running lights of the police car, he steps tentatively toward the house, remembering it is two paces from the curb to the steps of the house. Next he counts the five steps and can see the outline of the door. Standing on the landing he gropes for the metal knocker beside the door. It is not there. Using his fist he raps sharply on the door. Katarina is a sound sleeper, Willi recalls. The neighbors will hear him knocking before Katarina awakes. Willi raps on the door again and from inside he hears a baby cry. What is this? The baby crying must have awakened Katarina for she sleepily calls from inside the house, "Who is it?"

"It is I, Wilhelm. I'm home!"

The entry light is turned on and the door opens.

"Willi," Katarina gasps, standing barefoot and dressed only in her robe. "I think maybe you never come back!" She looks beyond him to the police car at the curb.

"I'm home from the war," is all he can think to say, dropping his bag inside the door and holding out his arms to her.

Putting one hand to his chest and the other to her forehead she exclaims, "You heard the baby crying, I can explain."

"You don't need to explain now. We can talk about it later."

Katarina is in a state of panic. She backs away from Willi, talking rapidly and not daring to look at him except out of the corner of her eyes. Turning and nodding toward the police car, Willi pushes past her and closes the door. Standing in the doorway is not a good place to have a long conversation at one o'clock in the morning.

"The baby is from a Russian officer," Katarina blurts out. "He still comes to the house sometimes. I had to sleep with him or I would have starved. There is so little food, I would cry myself to sleep with hunger. Now I cry myself to sleep with a full stomach."

"I will tell him he can't come here anymore," Willi states, with understanding in his voice.

"Your mother, father and the girls are dead!" Katarina glances out of the corner of her eyes to see how he reacts. She gets cruel satisfaction from seeing the look on his face. "A bomb from an airplane, the only one to fall on Lützen, did it. If the girls had been with me they would be alive. You took them there, away from me. If anyone is to blame, it's you. It is the only bomb to fall on Lützen during all the war and it hits their house. They were asleep in their beds when the bomb fell. It was in the middle of the night and the damage was terrible. I didn't know how to get word to you. Not that you could do anything!"

(In the early morning hours on 14 February 1945, a crippled Lancaster bomber returning from a raid on Dresden jettisoned a high explosive bomb hung in its bomb bay, over the village of Lützen.)

Willi slumps forward, his head bowed and tears streaming down his cheeks. He sits down as Katarina continues to divulge all the terrible things that happened during the war, Willi is not listening. The baby starts crying and Katarina leaves Willi sitting stone-faced in the chair, his tears eventually stop.

Sometime later Willi goes upstairs to their bedroom. Katarina is sitting on the edge of the bed holding her Russian baby. They sleep in the same bed but do not touch.

The next morning Willi is downstairs at the light of dawn to see the changes in his house. Opening the front door and stepping outside, he takes a deep breath and looks at the houses across the street. They are all there, more dingy perhaps, but in one piece. Turning he looks where the rapper once hung. It is gone and in its place, a little lower on the wall is a button. He presses it out of curiosity, and a buzzer sounds in the house. The baby starts crying and Willi hurries inside. Katarina calls out, "Who is it, Willi?"

"It is only me. I press the button by the door and it makes a buzz noise inside. This is new, *ja*?"

Katarina acknowledges it is new and quiets the baby. She is buttoning her dress as she comes down stairs and goes to the kitchen. "I have coffee, if you like some?"

"*Ja*, I would like that. Do you know that we have coffee at the POW camp in Arizona? We also have eggs and pork in the mornings!" He sits down at the kitchen table as Katarina boils the coffee.

Later in the morning Willi has an opportunity to talk to Katarina's Russian officer. The buzzer rings and he goes to the door. Standing there in a Russian uniform, shorter than Willi by several inches, but stocky, is Katarina's lover. Willi stares at him for a moment then says, "I am home from the war. My wife has told me about you. We wish to be left alone, understand?"

The Russian nods and asks to see Katarina and the baby. Katarina brings the baby downstairs and Willi watches as the Russian takes the baby and plays with it for a few minutes. "I think it will be better if the baby is placed in a home for Russian babies and you can visit the baby there," Willi tells the baby's father as he prepares to leave. Nodding his head and smiling pleasantly, the Russian leaves the house.

Later in the morning, Willi walks down the street to the shop. He finds the shop stripped of equipment, not even the workbenches are left. Katarina tells him the Russians took everything. Later Willi rides his bicycle, miraculously saved from the war effort, to the street where his grandparents once lived. He pokes about in the ruins of the burned house hoping to find some remembrance. There is no diary, only ashen fragments too small to recognize.

Sunday, 22 September 1946

Sunday Willi and Katarina take a bus to Lützen. They carry flowers for the graves of Christel, Ingebord, Freda and Karl. They step off the bus at the Schloss, walk across the park in front of the Schloss, then north on the back road to Tollwitz. Willi carries the flowers; Katarina carries guilt from not coming earlier.

Less than a half kilometer from town, they enter the cemetery and pause for a moment, looking at the chapel. Turning to the left and crossing a foot bridge, is the older part of the cemetery. Willi locates the headstone with the names of his daughters and parents. The date of death on the headstone is 14 February 1945, only three months before the end of the war in Europe. He then notices the graves of Kristin and her husband are nearby. He adds fresh water to containers near the headstones and divides the flowers among the graves.

Willi stands awkwardly for a moment, sniffs, wiping his eyes with the back of his hand, then turns away, walking toward the entrance. His eyes are moist, but there are no tears. "Saxon men do not cry," Willi has heard since his youth. The aftershock of the war numbed the emotions of many Germans, men and women. There are no tears in Katarina's eyes; only a vacant stare denying any of this is real.

As they leave the cemetery and walk slowly toward town along the narrow lane, Katarina follows Willi, her eyes to the ground. Nearing the first buildings of Lützen, they turn left and walk toward Karl's blacksmith shop. Willi notices the door to his father's shop is open, walks over and enters. Inside a young man is making a large metal collar for a piece of farm equipment.

"Good day," Willi says, clearing his throat as he speaks. The young man is an apprentice and looks up at the interruption. "We are closed today." The young man frowns as he looks at Willi, trying to place where he might have met him. "I only use the shop on weekends for the odd job, you know. If you want some work done, you must see the council."

"I have no work for you. My father owned this place before the war. Did you work for him?"

"*Ja*!" he says excitedly. "You must be Willi Meissner. Your Papa told me about you. You were a prisoner in America, yes? He was teaching me to be a blacksmith when the bomb came." He lays down the tool in his hand and, wiping his hands on his black apron, comes over to greet Willi. "It was a bad thing to happen. Herr Meissner was a good man." Willi shakes the hand offered and silently looks around the shop, seeking the familiar order of things and the tools used by his father. Nothing is the same.

"You can see nothing is new. I can't repair the shop equipment as fast as it breaks. Things are in pretty much of a mess!" The young man's conversation rambles on as Willi looks around the shop where he had learned the blacksmith trade. The state has taken over the property and operates it for essential farm machinery repair twice a week. There are not many skilled machinists remaining in the area. An apprentice is all the state can find to keep the place open. It is worse than before the start of the war. Willi thanks the young man for telling him about the shop and taking Katarina by the arm they leave.

After a few days sorting things out, Willi petitions the Leipzig District Socialist Unity Party to reopen his father's Leipzig shop and become a machinist again. The shop has been neglected and unused since Papa Karl closed it and moved his business to Lützen during the war. The property has little value and has not been confiscated by the Russians. Through inheritance Willi has title.

The Communist People's committee agrees to let Willi operate the shop in exchange for him working six days a week at a state owned farm equipment repair shop. The tractors and other farm equipment from the large state owned farms are repaired in this shop. The arrangement does not leave Willi much time for rebuilding the Leipzig shop. But, it gives him a little income to begin repairs. Working on weekends, Willi takes over the shop and soon has three apprentices working. Willi's salary from the state owned shop is hardly enough to buy food. But, weekends are another story. With Willi teaching his apprentice helpers, Meissner Machine Works does emergency repairs for small farmers each weekend. Their pay is in food from the farmers.

A United States Government check for $482 arrives in the mail Saturday, 9 November 1946. It is addressed to Wilhelm Meissner (serial number), 788 Eisenbahn Strasse, Leipzig. Willi takes the check to a bank in Leipzig, but is told the only place to cash the check is in the American sector of Berlin.

Monday, November 25, Willi takes a train to Berlin. It takes twice as long as before the war to get to Berlin. He arrives at Friedrich Strasse Station. The subways are still flooded, so Willi walks south on Friedrich Strasse to the American sector and cashes his check for American dollars in an army finance office. After counting the bills again in front of the clerk, Willi asks how they were able to find where to send the check.

"When you left the POW camp, they must've asked you for a forwarding address and sent it to that address."

"*Ja*, they did. What if I hadn't gone home?"

The clerk shrugs and Willi turns away from the window. The money comes from settling the assets of canteen sales to POWs in America. Willi notices a sign on the wall they exchange the dollars for five Reichsmarks on the dollar. Taking a trolley to Alexander Platz, Willi walks along Rathaus Strasse looking for people exchanging money. The sky is a dull grey and the wind is chilly.

A young woman is exchanging money for an American soldier and talking with him. Willi waits until the soldier leaves and walks up to her. "Excuse me, please. Do you exchange money, dollars for marks?"

She turns and her eyes assess the intent of the man in front of her. Willi passes the quick assessment. "Yes. How much do you have?" Her reply is short and crisp as she reaches into her purse and pulls out a cigarette. When she opens the purse, Willi can see a large roll of dollars and a large roll of Reichsmarks. She is shivering as she tries to light the cigarette. "I have only a hundred dollars, but how many marks do you give me?"

The young woman has lit her cigarette and, exhaling a puff into Willi's face, says, "One thousand, twice what the Americans give you." Willi pauses, looks around the street, notices that many others are doing the same business, and tells her, "I think I will try for a better exchange, thank you. *Wiedersehen*!" As he turns to walk away, she reaches out and grasps his coat sleeve. "Wait a minute. Don't be in such a hurry. Maybe we can still do business, say 1,500 marks for your hundred dollars." Willi looks at her and down at her bulging purse. "I think two thousand marks for one hundred dollars is good exchange, OK?"

"OK, but that's the best you're going to get!"

Willi takes the 2,000 Reichsmarks, recounts the money, folds it and puts it in his pocket. Tipping his hat, Willi walks over to a bench and sits down. He opens the bag he brought from Leipzig and digs around inside. Looking in each direction and over his shoulder, Willi removes a sock from the bag and, rolls the marks into a tight wad of bills and deftly puts the roll of marks in the toe of the sock. With eyes darting in each direction, he ties a knot in the sock and stuffs it inside his shirt.

Converting only a small amount each time, Willi's roll of Reichsmarks grows. After each exchange he hides his marks in the sock and stuffs it inside his shirt. The Leipzig exchange rate would not be so good nor would the items he plans to buy on the black market be as good.

Walking between the sectors, there are signs to identify the sector one is entering. Willi finds a restaurant open on Waisen Strasse. Entering, he sits by a tiled stove in the front room. After examining the small menu he orders oxtail soup and a pork cutlet. The food is excellent, better than any of the Leipzig restaurants are serving with rationing and other problems endemic to the Russian sector.

In the Russian sector of Berlin preparations are being made for celebrating Soviet National Day. He cannot understand why Germans should celebrate a Russian holiday when all the soviets seem to be doing is pillaging their sector of Germany.

Crossing the River Spree and walking along Unter den Linden to Freidrich Strasse, Willi is back at the Station and checks the schedule of trains. The last train of the day to Leipzig has been canceled and there will be no trains Tuesday. Before the war there were maybe six trains a day from Berlin to Leipzig. Now there is every other day service, and some of those trains are canceled. He asks a kiosk keeper where he can sleep. While they are talking, an old woman stops and listens. She interrupts to tell him he can sleep at her house for 20 marks. Her house is a cellar with a couch, the only piece of furniture. After a fitful nights rest on the couch with the old lady sitting on the floor counting and recounting her marks by candle light, Willi decides to sleep in the Bahnhof the next night.

It is the winter of 1946 and Russian soldiers are black marketing sausages from Poland, and anything else they can get their hands on. The black market trading in Berlin surprises Willi. Everyone is selling or trading items, even the American soldiers.

With extra time on his hands, Willi sets out to find an old friend from Camp Florence, white-haired Helmut Winkler. He finds Helmut living in a crowded apartment building off Leipziger Strasse near the American sector, ill with pneumonia and confined to bed. Helmut's wife did indeed die during the war and as nearly as his sick friend can determine, she died the same time Helmut had the dream at Camp Florence.

Helmut has also received a check from the U. S. Government, he confides in Willi, but does not know how to get it cashed. The daughter Helmut lives with works each day and is afraid to meet Americans because of her job in the Russian sector. Willi looks at Helmut's check. It is smaller because he was a prisoner for less time. Willi tells him to write his name on the back of the check. Taking Helmut's identification card and the check Willi walks back to the American sector down Wilhelm Strasse, turning right on Leipziger Strasse and into Potsdamer Platz. There he cashes the check. Again, Willi takes his time and gets a good exchange rate for his friend.

Returning to Helmut's apartment, Willi makes sure they are alone and then counts out 7,500 Reichsmarks into the hands of his old friend. Helmut cannot believe his good fortune. The two friends laugh and cry as Helmut counts the money several times. That was the last time Willi saw his friend. He later learns Helmut never recovered from his bout with pneumonia and died the following spring.

Before returning to Leipzig, Willi buys Katarina two pair of nylon stockings and some French perfume. He buys a money belt and in the privacy of a nearby toilet removes the sock from his shirt waist and stuffs nearly 9,000 Reichsmarks in 100 and 50 mark denominations into the belt. To round out his purchases, Willi finds a sidewalk delicatessen on the Alexanderplatz and buys a kilo of choice pate.

* * *

Wednesday, 27 November 1946

Returning from Berlin, Willi finds work has piled up. Nothing was done while he was gone. Apprentices only work when there is a master machinist in the shop. The two extra days Willi spent waiting for a train in Berlin, are two days of vacation for the shop. Willi is charged with vacation for the time he was gone.

* * *

March-April 1947

Through the early months of 1947, Willi works six days a week, 12 and 14 hour days. He saves a little money and adds to the money belt. Tuesday, April 15, the agriculture council sends Willi and a party member to buy farm machinery at an exhibition north of Berlin. The western built tractors and combines are parked in a field where they were unloaded. Because of Russian security the operators were sent back to the west. Willi asks the exhibitor to demonstrate the equipment, as do some Russians attending the show.

"We have no one to operate the machinery," he complains. "Your military would not let our people stay."

Willi inspects the machines and decides he can operate the tractors, but does not understand the workings of the combine. He cranks up a large tractor and drives around the field. The exhibitor attaches a hydraulic lift plows and asks Willi to demonstrate how it works. After the demonstration, Willi and his party accomplice prepare to buy some equipment. Russians attending the show tell the exhibitor they want all the equipment prepared and shipped to Russia immediately. The Leipzig agriculture committee is furious when Willi and his party chaperon return empty handed.

Bartering flourishes in Leipzig. Willi gets food for their table and furniture for their house by bartering. For example, a farmer needs his tractor fixed on a Sunday. Willi opens the shop and works on the tractor. The farmer gives Willi a sack of flour or a basket of eggs. Sometimes a farmer will give Willi a pig, if the job takes much time. Willi will take the pig to the butcher, who slaughters and prepare the pig into swine cutlets and sausage for a quarter of the pig. For a kilo of sausage, the baker will trade Willi three loaves of bread. With one loaf of bread, Willi can get a half kilo of butter and the trading continues.

One of the irksome tasks for managers of East Germany's small shops is the frequency and length of worker's council meetings. Willi must go to first one meeting, then another. Attendance at the meetings is necessary for the few who still operate private businesses. To make progress in life, one must work long hours for the state and longer hours in private pursuits. In the Russian sector, under their socialist government, Germans are learning to be lazy, Willi observes. They are content to accept the slight improvement in lifestyle peace affords them, though the economic hardships they suffered in war have not changed much.

During August, the busiest time for repairing harvesting machines, Willi is called to attend a meeting of the Worker's Council Farm Committee. The repatriation suit, his only suit, is at home and to such meetings Willi wears a suit. So, leaving the shop in the hands of an apprentice, he goes home to change clothes.

Reaching the house on Eisenbahn Strasse, there is a Russian Army car parked outside. Entering quietly, he hears noises upstairs. What Willi suspects, is true. The "honorable" Russian officer is in bed with Katarina. Willi bursts into the bedroom and sees the Russian and Katarina trying to cover their nakedness. As Willi stands there, the Russian major rolls out of bed and grabs his pants. While he slips them on he looks at Willi and says, "Your woman is good!"

Glaring at Katarina and the Russian, Willi yells, "Out! Take the 'good woman' and get out of my house, now!"

The Russian glowers back at Willi. "Your woman stays here or I shoot you." He makes a gesture similar to pulling a pistol and says "Bum, bum." Grabbing his boots and the rest of his uniform, the Russian walks past Willi and down the stairs.

Willi watches him leave then turns to Katarina. She is trying to dress hurriedly and is cursing Willi. "Why have you done this to me?" he chokes on the words. "A woman who has once been with a Russian has no joy anymore from a German man," she smugly responds!

Removing a suitcase from over the Shrank, Willi fills it with her clothes, grabs her coat and escorts her down the stairs. They take a taxi to the Bahnhof. Nothing is said between the two of them. When they reach the Bahnhof, Willi pays the driver, takes the suitcase and carries it inside. He sits it down near the ticket kiosk and turns to Katarina. "Go someplace, I don't want to know where you are. Never let me see you here again," he tells her quietly and bitterly.

Leaving her at the Bahnhof, Willi skips his meeting, goes immediately to an attorney and instructs him to start a divorce. From the attorney's office, Willi wanders aimlessly through the streets of Leipzig. The sky is now fully overcast. It grows dark and Willi suddenly realizes he has walked to Bunde Strasse and is standing, staring blankly at the pile of rubble where Oma and Opa lived and died. He has not been here since the day he returned. Katarina's betrayal is only a small part of the hurt. The thought paining him even more is there is no one left in his family, only his youngest sister, Ludwina, and she has fled with her husband to the American sector. Vines have crept over the ruins of the house as sadness now creeps like an entangling vine into Willi's thoughts. Willi does not recall walking home.

Kurt Blocker calls to Willi as he walks past the Blocker's house. "*Wie gehts*, Willi? Judith tells me that Katarina left this afternoon. Is something wrong?" Kurt has been a neighbor since Willi and Katarina bought the house on Eisenbahn Strasse. Judith nods to Willi as he walks over and sits down on their steps. "It is the Russian again," Willi admits. "I came home to change clothes for a meeting and he is here with Katarina. No more!" Kurt was wounded on the Russian front in 1943. He was returned home to convalesce and later demobilized.

Willi talks with the Blockers until it is dark and there is the smell of rain in the air. He bids them goodnight. Walking from room to room and turning on the lights, Willi stops to pick up the small checker board he and Christel once played with. In the kitchen he finds some cheese and cold beef tongue. He makes a sandwich and sits at the table to eat. Emotionally weary, Willi turns off the lights and goes up stairs. He removes all the bed covers and disgustedly tosses them in a corner. Finding clean linens, he makes the bed, turns out the light and prepares for bed. The house is quiet except for the sound of rain. A long time has passed since he prayed before bed, tonight he prays for direction in his life.

Chapter 23
Escape to the West

Leipzig
Thursday, 14 August 1947

Early the next morning, before leaving for the shop, the doorbell buzzes. "Moment," Willi calls out, while buttoning his shirt and rubbing his hand through his hair. Opening the door, two Russian soldiers in rain coats are standing there and another outside in a truck.

"Herr Meissner?" a soldier asks.

"*Ja*, that's me."

"Come with us now!"

"Moment, while I get my cap and coat," Willi replies. "Where are we going?"

"To see the commandant," the older of the two replies.

Willi and the younger soldier climb on the back of the truck while the other sits up front with the driver. They drive to a state office building and usher Willi into a room with the city commander, a Russian officer. "Meissner, Wilhelm. Master machinist, correct?" he asks looking at some papers on his desk.

"*Ja*, that's me."

"We are sending you to Russia to work as a machinist. You will leave Leipzig in ten hours. My men will return you to your home where you may pack one suitcase to take with you. We have a special train leaving this afternoon and, Herr Meissner, you will be on it. Understand?"

"Why is this, commandant? I've done nothing wrong. I do good work. If it is because of my wife, the major can have her. It is all over with us, kaput!"

"Ah, Herr Meissner, you misunderstand. We need men like you working alongside our Russian machinists. In Russia you will have a better working place than you have here and the people are friendlier."

With a wave of his hand the commander signals the meeting is over. Taking Willi by the arm, the soldiers lead him out of the office and stay by his side, on the truck, back to his house. During the trip back to his house he plans a way to escape, the plan is simple, get the Russian soldiers to relax and make his break. Now he must make it work.

Opening the door, he asks the soldiers to step inside. "I think this is a good change for me," he tells them. "I like to learn new things, travel, meet people, come in my house while I pack." Looking around for something to occupy them while he makes his escape, Willi recalls a bottle of schnapps in the living room cabinet. Removing it from the cabinet he says, "Here, drink some schnapps while I go upstairs to pack. I can't take it with me." He places the bottle in front of them and pours each a glass full. They look at each other, then around the room, suspicious of Willi's generosity. Shrugging their shoulders, and seeing no way Willi could leave the house without coming through this room, they sit down to drink while Willi goes upstairs to pack.

Willi makes loud noises in the bedroom as he rummages for money and papers he can take with him, stuffing everything into a small bag. While slamming doors and drawers about, he eases the window open a bit wider so he can get through it quickly. Next he drops the bag out the window and calls to the soldiers, loud enough they will not hear the bag hit the ground.

"Toilet and then I'll be right down!" Entering the toilet, Willi makes appropriate noises and then flushes the toilet bowl. The plumbing is very loud and Willi is able to step to the bedroom window and leap to the yard below without disturbing the schnapps drinkers. Fortunately the ground is wet and soft enough to absorb the sound of his leap. He retrieves his bag and runs through the back garden, then down a passage way between the houses. Reaching the street behind his house, he slows to a walk and nonchalantly crosses the street. Very few people are out in the rain and after walking another block he finds a hiding place in a ruined building.

Within minutes after discovering Willi's escape, the Russians have cordoned the area around 788 Eisenbahn Strasse and are stopping everyone in the street asking about Willi. For two days Russian soldiers search everywhere for Wilhelm Meissner. On the third day after his escape, Willi ventures out in the evening. He later tells Kurt Blocker, "They can't find me because I hide very well, even though I am a big man. Once they get close enough I smell them, a Russian smell." With Kurt's help he manages to get new identity papers, then returns to his hiding place.

Monday evening, August 18, the fourth night since his escape, Willi crawls from behind a false wall in the cellar of the vacant building and, following the dark alleys and shadowy walkways, leaves Leipzig. Walking along the railroad tracks leading to Halle, Willi reaches the city northwest of Leipzig early the next morning.

The streets of Halle are beginning to fill with workers, and Willi walks unnoticed with the workers as they go to their shops. The smell of a bakery calls to him and he buys a loaf of bread, and next door buys cheese and milk. Stuffing the items in his bag, he continues to the western outskirts of town and finds a barn appearing unused. Looking through the barn he discovers a sleeping vagabond and sits down to wait for him to awake.

Willi dozes but sits up quickly when he realizes the man in the ragged clothing is moving. He is crawling toward the door. "Where are you going, friend?" Willi asks. The man spryly jumps to his feet and pulls a knife from his belt. "I don't have friends and it's none of your business where I'm going," he spits out the words. "Are you Polizei?" Willi looks at the man carefully, relaxes his position and says, "No, not Polizei, not Russian, not NKVD, just a blacksmith looking for work."

The knife-wielding vagabond folds the knife and sticks it back in his belt. "You scared the hell out of me, you know! Why did you sneak up on me?"

"I need a place to sleep and it looks safe in here. Thought I'd join you. Do you have anything to eat?"

"Does it look like I've got something to eat? I haven't eaten a good meal in two days. You got something in your pack?"

Willi pulls out the bread, cheese and milk and sits them on a board. "I'll share," he says and breaks off a chunk of the bread. They eat silently and the vagabond cleans up each crumb falling on the board.

There is nothing left for the field mice when the man rises and grudgingly shakes Willi's hand. "*Wiedersehen*," he calls out as he leaves.

Willi makes a comfortable bed of straw, gathered from the field outside the barn, and quickly falls asleep. It is late in the day when he is awakened by the sound of a tractor. He lies there half awake and thinks over the routes to take to the border. When it is dark he leaves the barn and picks up the road that leads west through Eisleben, Sangerhausen and Nordhausen.

Walking at night on footpaths just off the roadway and sleeping during the day, Willi finally reaches Nordhausen. Two weeks have passed since Willi escaped his Russian guards. In a village west of Nordhausen, Willi stops at a train station in the evening to eat and get a drink of water. There he meets several other people with the same destination, but no plan to avoid the border guards. They walk along together and plan how to make their crossing.

Willi begins to think it is not wise to be in such a large group. There are seven and as they get closer to the border, the excitement begins to make everyone jumpy. A cow moves in the darkness and everyone dives into a ditch alongside the road. They plan to skirt the village of Gudersleben and cross the border between Mackenrode and Walkenreid. Reaching the crest of a hill north of Mackenrode they can see the distant lights of Walkenreid due west of their position. The road descends sharply to the south about five kilometers, into Mackenrode. Toward Walkenreid the ground drops off to a wide valley. Four kilometers of rolling farmland and forests are between the group and the border.

"This is where we leave the road," Willi tells them. "If we get separated, look for the hunter in the sky, Orion. He's going the same direction we are. I've shown you the stars and there won't be a moon tonight. That's an advantage. This close to the border, we can expect patrols by the border police on any road or path. So, stay quiet. If you see something moving, freeze until you can tell what it is. We'll keep about five paces distance from each other. Does anyone want to lead?"

"You lead, Herr Meissner. You know the stars better than we do," says a woman in the group.

Willi turns and starts down the hill following a tractor road between fields. As they descend from the hill the lights of Walkenreid disappear. The tractor road comes to an abrupt end and Willi looks for a path. Finding none, he strikes out across the field, keeping low so there will be no silhouette for someone to spot in this flat area. Ahead, the lights of bicycle patrols along the East German side of the border flicker in the darkness of the night. Everyone is wearing dark clothing and it is difficult to see the person ahead or behind. As Willi slows the pace, moving more cautiously, the group suddenly bunches up. Willi can hear those behind him and stops. Motioning them to spread out and keep quiet, Willi creeps forward to the first of the bicycle paths. Grass and underbrush have been cleared for about ten yards and the path is a pale stripe down the middle. To Willi's right, a member of the group starts to cross without waiting to see if there are guards nearby.

A flashlight cuts through the darkness and catches the border crosser in the middle of the clearing. There is a shout to "Halt!" and pandemonium breaks loose. Willi drops to the ground and crawls under some bushes, blaming himself for attempting a crossing with a large group. Others run, some toward the border and others toward Mackenrode. Guards fire at those headed for the border, some are captured. By the sounds and yells Willi hears in the night, perhaps all the others are stopped.

For two hours Willi scarcely breathes, guards are crisscrossing the area, some on bicycles, others on foot. He has no idea what has happened to the others. Waiting patiently, Willi can tell from the sky there are several hours of darkness left and knows it is best to wait to make his move. A guard is coming. Willi can hear him puffing as he pedals his bicycle along the path directly in front of the brush pile Willi has burrowed into. The carbide light on the guard's cap flashes up and down, left and right as he rides along and then he is gone. In the darkness Willi listens until he can no longer hear the labored breathing of the guard. Creeping from his hideaway, he crosses the path and follows a cow trail leading westward. The trail ends in a shallow stream smelling of cow dung. Easing himself into the muck and water on his hands and knees, Willi crawls and wades the last kilometer to the border.

By Willi's own estimate, he should be across the border. As the first light of dawn turns dark shadows to gray outlines, Willi can see a barn and house directly ahead. He pulls himself out of the shallow stream bed near the barn and crosses the barnyard toward the house. As he walks toward the house, a door opens and light from inside the house spills out into the yard. A farm woman stands in the door and stops as she sees Willi, an apparition covered with mud and smelling like the barnyard. Holding his hands over his head to show he is unarmed, he asks, "Where is the border."

"Beyond that fence," she says pointing to the fence bordering her yard. Willi thanks her and hurries through the gate and onto a dirt lane. He follows the lane until it runs into a larger road. Looking down the road toward the east, Willi sees a barricade and Russian soldiers. To his left the road leads to

Walkenreid. Hoisting his pack he turns toward Walkenreid. It is only two kilometers and by sunrise he is walking the village's cobble stone streets.

Among the first people he sees is a policeman. Tall, muddy, and foul smelling, Willi is asked for his papers. Showing his forged papers from Leipzig, he tells him "my real name is Wilhelm Meissner." The policeman explains he will need new papers to get work and live in West Germany.

"First, I must have a bath and get cleaned up," Willi tells him and is allowed to proceed; he smells worse than the barnyard. Using a public bath and washing his clothing, Willi catches a train to Northeim intending to work in the coal mines.

Chapter 24
A New Start

British Sector, North Germany
Friday, 29 August 1947

It was common knowledge among those fleeing to the western sectors of Germany people without residence papers can work in the mines. And, those who work in the mines get more to eat than most other workers. Willi arrives in Northeim asking for directions to the personnel bureau for the mines. Walking along the busy streets of Northeim, he notices the difference in the two Germanys. Here people are working, there is food in the shops, more automobiles on the road, buildings have been repaired, and people hold their heads up. Though both Germanys must ration items, in West Germany there is food to be bought. In East Germany there is nothing in the store.

The personnel bureau is in a small building outside the fence of the mine works. Inside the well-lit office Willi offers his papers to a clerk and asks for work.

"You are from the East," she says, half as a statement and half as a question.

"*Ja*. I cross the border yesterday and come here for work."

"You must first get a new identity card, Herr Meissner. These papers from the East are no good," she says with a glance at a man sitting in a corner of the room.

"But, at the border they say you will hire me. I am strong. I am a good worker. I was a soldier and POW."

The young woman will not look at Willi. She stares at the papers he has given her and pushes them toward him. "You must get new identification, I'm sorry."

"Okay. Where do I get new identification?" Willi asks in a tone of exasperation.

The man in the corner speaks, "It is not the fault of the *Fraulein* you cannot be hired. British authorities insist refugees must first go to a displaced persons camp. There they have the staff to check your identity and provide you with a new passport. We can no longer allow people to work here without proper identification. Understand?"

"I understand, maybe, but where is the refugee camp?"

"The closest one is in Westfalen," the man says as he rises from his chair. "It is several hours from here. But, it will not be a matter taken care of quickly. Do you have money?"

"*Nein*, only a few marks I had in my pocket when I left my home in Leipzig." Willi does not want anyone to know about the money belt full of Reichsmarks. The man looks at Willi carefully. "After you get your papers, come back. We can use you." He holds out his hand.

Willi nods and says, "Maybe." He shakes the offered hand and leaves the building. A light mist is falling from the darkening clouds. Lights from the mine pit are eerie in the half light of day. He trudges back toward the train station fingering the coins in his pocket. Stopping at a cafe, Willi orders his meal, goes to the toilet and, removing some bills from his money belt, he returns to his table. After the meal, Willi orders a cup of coffee and asks the waitress if it is real coffee. She smiles and brings him a cup of the "real coffee." Willi sips the coffee and decides his next move.

The displaced persons camp, is east, near the Rhine River. Willi spends the winter of 1947 in the camp, waiting for new identification papers. Monday, 15 March 1948, brings Willi the long awaited passport, his *"Persilschein"* a slang term, clears the bearer from having been a member of any Nazi organization during Hitler's reign. Persil is a brand of toothpaste, the bearer of such a certificate is therefore clean. Along with his paperwork is a job offer working for a narrow gauge railroad. The railroad runs from a small village in the American Zone of occupation, near Siegen, to Aachen, in the British Zone. Although the route is short, the train operates in all three of the Western sectors of Germany, entering the French Zone near Siegburg and the British Zone southwest of Bonn.

The job with the railroad includes a good ration card. "Not the best, but good," Willi comments to his companions in the camp. A job in the mines would have given him one of the top two ration cards. But, his new job pays 220 Reichsmarks a month and the work is not hard. The amount of food he can buy with his pay is adequate. However; there is little left to buy new clothes. In the camp he showered in his clothes, returning to his bunk to undress, and hanging his clothes up to dry. It was always a chance they would not be dry by morning. Now he finds the only way to bathe and not spend any money is to swim in the Sieg River after work. He also washes his clothing there.

On one trip to Aachen each week, the train crew must spend the night. The other trips are all made during the same day. During one such layover, the crew is joined at their Gasthaus table by two Germans and an American. While they eat the subject turns to the price of food and other rationed items. To get a loaf of bread on the black-market cost 100 to 120 RM. Price controls permit bakers to charge only a fraction of the amount for rationed bread. (Aachen was the center of black-market smuggling on a huge scale. Across the Dutch and Belgian borders, columns of Germans smuggled goods in bulk for the home black-market.)

"I think we can help you if you can help us," one German tells them. "Are you willing to take a little risk?" Willi and the other train crewmen look at each other, shrug their shoulders and nod consent. "Can you deliver some packages for us to a friend in Siegburg and avoid the customs check between zones (French, British and American zones of West Germany)?"

"*Ja*, we can do that," the engineer assures the trio.

"When do you return to Aachen? What day?" the American asks.

"We'll be back next week, this same day," the engineer replies. He is the one with the master schedule and the train doesn't run unless he is there.

"Good. We'll meet you here next week, have dinner, and go for a walk. We'll tell you more when we see you again. Okay?" The Germans have picked up on the American slang and respond with a loud "Okay!"

Chapter 25
A Criminal Enterprise

West Germany
Summer, 1948

The following week, Willi and the crew show up at the Aachen Gasthaus early and are waiting at a table when the trio arrives. While they are eating the German who is the leader of the trio explains a little about their "walk" this evening. "We will cross the border into Belgium and follow the road to Aubel. Somewhere along the way we will meet a friend from Belgium who will lead us the rest of the way to our destination. Understand? Then we'll each get to carry a heavy knapsack back to Aachen. Now isn't that simple?"

It sounds simple enough to Willi and the train crew, but "What happens if we get stopped?" Willi asks. "If anyone stops us, I do the talking," the American tells them. "I'll tell them we've bought some grain for our cows. I'll have a knapsack filled with grain and if they want to look, all they'll find is cow feed."

They leave the Gasthaus and a man from Aachen, with a truck, drives the four trainmen and three smugglers to the outskirts of town. It is a dark night, no moon, and the few stars that show are visible only through a thin layer of clouds. On foot for two hours, they cross into Belgium. Another two hours walking in silence passes before the Belgian friend greets the leader. They follow him to a small barn and inside find the knapsacks.

"First we have some coffee," the Belgian tells them and pours coffee from a thermos into mugs that he has set out. The coffee is still hot as Willi sips from his mug. "It is real coffee," he exclaims.

"What did you expect, trainman? There is more like this in your knapsack."

"How many kilos?" Willi asks.

"About thirty kilos in each knapsack," the Belgian responds.

Willi rolls his eyes and smiles. "That would make a man rich on the black-market!"

"How much would you pay for a kilo of coffee in Siegen?" the Belgian asks.

"Maybe 500 marks," Willi guesses.

"More like 800 marks," the brakeman on the crew chimes in.

Willi hastily calculates the value of his load. "I'll be carrying 24,000 marks on my back. *Ach*!"

They down their coffee and depart. "Remember, if we are stopped by anyone, let me do the talking," the American tells them. "Now, let's keep it quiet!"

The return trip is uneventful, and, when they arrive back at the truck, it is 4 a.m. The driver takes the crew to their hotel and pays each man 1000 marks in crisp 100 RM notes. "I'll meet you at the Gasthaus for breakfast and we'll plan the next step."

Three hours later they are up and dressing for the return train trip. "What do you think we'll be carrying to Siegen?" Willi asks. "Coffee?"

"Maybe," the engineer growls as he tries to shave without cutting himself, "and maybe not. Those guys are bringing more than coffee out of Belgium. The Belgian guy said he can get chocolates, sugar, nylon stockings, just about everything that's rationed."

"Where can you hide stuff without the customs people finding it?" Willi asks.

"We'll show you, Willi, when we get to the train. Now quit interrupting while I'm trying to shave."

When they get to the Gasthaus, the truck is parked outside, and a tarpaulin covers some boxes on the truck bed. Inside, their German contact man is eating a roll and sipping the watered down coffee served in most German Gasthaus'. They join him, and, as they eat, he tells them what he has on the truck to be delivered to Siegen. "Some coffee brought across the border last night will be going to Siegen and some chocolate, maybe a hundred kilos altogether."

The engineer explains the routine inspections they go through at each check point starting in Aachen before they leave. They leave the Gasthaus and drive to a shed near the rail yard where each man is given another suitcase filled with packages of coffee and chocolate.

"We get paid for this in advance?" the engineer asks.

"That's not the way we do business," the smuggler says with a smile. "When you get the merchandise to Siegen, you are paid."

"Sounds fair." The engineer nods to his crew and they leave for their train carrying the extra suitcases. Taking the suitcases into the engine cab, he tells Willi to check the couplings on the cars and see if the doors are sealed. (Customs seal) While Willi is doing this, the fireman starts building a fire in the engine, with pine and oil. After the fire has started, he shovels a hole in the coal pile and places a suitcase in the hole before the coal can shift and fill the space. He does this for each of the four suitcases. It takes about an hour to get up steam.

They depart Aachen and cross each of the checkpoints, British and French, without a problem. When they leave the train, each man is carrying a coal encrusted suitcase along with their own suitcase. The engineer calls the number given him by the contact man.

"There is a green truck parked by the Hessen Gasthaus. The driver's name is Heine. He has your money." End of conversation.

The crew walks toward the Hessen. A green truck is there and a man sitting in the cab. The engineer walks over to ask the driver his name. He waves for the others to join him and as they deposit the suitcases in the cab of the truck, Heine hands the engineer an envelope. Looking inside, the engineer nods to Heine and turning to his crew says, "Let's go inside for a drink boys, I'm buying."

Inside the Gasthaus they find a table in a corner of the room, place their order, and, while the innkeeper is getting their drinks, the engineer takes 5,000 marks from the envelope and divides it among his crew. Willi, smiling broadly, takes his money and puts it in his wallet, amazed at this change in his fortunes.

Each week the scene is replayed. Willi rents a room in Kirchen and cannot find a safe place to hide his accumulating wealth. He opens an account at a bank in Siegen. By early summer he has accumulated nearly 40,000 RM. Unable to spend any of his black-market profits, Willi looks for a house, or apartment, to buy. The people with property are not interested in selling it.

Friday, 18 June 1948, the U.S. and British governments announce a sweeping currency reform. Every man, woman and child residing in the British and American zones of Germany is given 40 of the new Deutsche Marks printed in the United States and shipped to Germany under the code name of "Bird Dog." Willi's 40,000 marks are worthless.

The result on the economy is miraculous. The result on Willi is disastrous. The black-market is wiped out almost immediately. Profiteers have only their goods and 40 of the new marks. Shopkeepers overnight start stocking their shelves and windows with food and goods only available through the black-market previously. Confidence in the new currency is immediate.

Deposits can be converted if the depositor can prove the legitimate source of the money. Willi can convert only forty marks he has in his wallet and is afraid to claim any portion of his black-market nest egg.

On their next trip to Aachen, the train crew waits in their Gasthaus meeting place until it closes. None of the trio of smugglers shows. When the crew returns to Freudenberg, the green truck is noticeably absent.

Willi is forced to find a job where he can get more food in order to survive. A farmer he met during his work with the train crew offers Willi a job. The pay is simply three meals a day, a roof over his head and a pouch of tobacco each week. The farmer gives Willi a blue work suit to wear, the only change of clothing he has. Willi is happy to have a roof over his head at night and something to eat. But, he cannot help thinking there is not much difference in his circumstances than that of the Mexican laborers on Mr. Bud's cotton farm in Arizona.

After the harvest is in, and the farmer is able to sell at a good price, Willi is given five marks each week, with his food. The farmer also gives Willi a large wooden tub for his use. Now Willi can bathe each Saturday. If the weather over the weekend is good for drying his clothes, he washes his work suit. When the weather is bad, he starts the week wearing a dirty work suit.

From the fall of 1948 until January 1950, Willi works on the farm and regains his health and weight. On May 23, 1949, the Federal Republic of Germany is created, comprised of the French, British and American zones. The capital is in the nearby town of Bonn. Bonn is not a big city like Frankfurt, Munich or Berlin. Willi and his employer join in the festivities, driving over to Bonn to hear Mr. Adenauer speak. The economic upturn of the new Federal Republic is immediate. Funds for construction are available. A dam is being built on the Mosel near Koblenz, and the construction company is advertising for mechanics and pipefitters.

Leaving the farm and the camp behind him, Willi takes a bus to Koblenz, applies for, and receives a job working on the dam. He lives for several weeks in a shack at the construction site. Saving the money from his payroll envelope, Willi again deposits some in a bank. Some he buries under the shack in a jar.

Frugal living is taking its toll and sleeping on the floor of the construction shack is making him irritable. Through inquiries, he finds an empty garden house in the neighborhood of the dam. No one knows who owns the small plot of land; it has been sitting unoccupied for several years. Willi moves into the secluded house, and, over a period of a week obtains a bed, chair and table. He can even run an electric line from the construction site to his new home. There is only one room, about four meters by three meters; but, for Willi, it is sufficient space.

Willi lives there a year, saving enough to buy a garden plot and build a house. He builds it by himself except for having a carpenter make the doors and windows. It is not necessary at the time to have a licensed carpenter do the construction and Willi has learned many skills he is not licensed to perform. The three years Willi worked on the locks brought good wages. Not only does he have a house, he now owns two suits, three pair of shoes (one pair with crepe soles) and can go out among people.

When work on the Mosel locks is completed, the company moves on to another project in Frankfurt. Willi is offered a job in Frankfurt, but decides to stay in Koblenz. Responding to an advertisement, Willi becomes a seller of medical books, gets a trade license and is in business for himself.

After two days training, Willi is earning money again. There is something about this kindly, giant of a man, the easy flow of his Saxon dialect, and his earnest and honest appearance makes door to door selling an easy and profitable experience. The books, or booklets, are a series of publications relating to different medical problems. Combined they form a comprehensive home medical library. The advantage in post war Germany is the low cost of buying the books separately and the rising cost of medical care. In less than a year, he is offered a new territory, Mainz. Reluctantly he sells his house and moves to Mainz.

In Mainz his job is organizing and managing a sales office. Having to train new sales people, plus managing the office, proves to be more than Willi can handle. He is fired. Fortunately, he finds work at a shop making precision pneumatic tools in nearby Mannheim where he can use some of his early blacksmithing skills, and plumbing skills from Arizona, along with his knowledge of machines.

In Mannheim during the summer of 1964, Willi met and married Klara Keitel, an unusual woman. Losing both legs below the knees during an air raid in 1943, Klara survived the war. A friend fashioned wooden peg legs for her and, by using crutches to assist her walking, Klara kept her children and their hopes alive, scavenging and trading after the war. In the 1950's a group of American servicemen collected money to provide Klara with a set of orthopedically designed prosthesis. Her new legs allowed her to do most anything she had strength to do, and she could dance. The servicemen also got her a job working in their American GI canteen.

Klara and Willi met at a dance in Mannheim, and a year later they were married. Not long after they were married, Klara's youngest son, Pauli, became bedridden with pneumonia. Klara quit her job at the American army post to spend her time caring for Pauli. From 1966 until he died in 1967, the son was chronically ill and unable to get out of bed except for short periods. After Pauli's death, Willi and Klara resume their social activities, going to dances, and visiting Klara's relatives and other children. Taking short walks around a lake near their apartment is the way they spend most evenings. Despite her physical limitations, Klara had a positive attitude telling Willi, "as long as we have each other and can work with our hands, we can be happy." They were happy, picking fruit in a nearby orchard, working in their small garden near the apartment building, repairing a friend's garden house.

During a physical checkup in 1970, Willi is diagnosed as having lung trouble and sent to a sanatorium to recuperate for a few months. Klara visits Willi each week. After the third month the doctors decide Willi's condition is chronic and limits him to light work. The owner of the plant offers Willi a job in building maintenance, a job usually performed by "guest laborers." He works for another year in the low paying maintenance job and, during the year, Klara is diagnosed as having cancer. Klara's treatment in 1971-1972 is limited to radiation. She suffers through the treatments, but is too weak to use her artificial legs. Being carried from room to room by Willi, Klara often jokes with him, "I'm 20 kilos lighter without those legs, and you're getting off easy." The cancer spreads, and, on a November afternoon in 1972, as Willi sat by her bed, the pain ended. As Willi explained to several American servicemen who continued to correspond with Klara, "Klara is no more!"

It has been several years since Willi worked with his hands. Taking care of Klara, as cancer drained her life, has taxed his lungs. He has grown progressively weaker. "There must be something I can do with my hands other than making useless fists and pounding the table." Rudy, Klara's older son, suggested Willi take a job as a night watchman in one of the many warehouses around Mannheim and Ludwigshafen. Willi wants a job where he can use his hands, these hands of a musician, machinist, blacksmith, and telegrapher.

Mannheim, West Germany
Winter, 1972

Weeks have passed since Klara Keitel's death; Willi has mourned her passing each day. A winter storm west of the Rhine has brought icy rain and sleet to Mannheim. Ignoring the foul weather and contemplating suicide, Willi is a solitary figure standing on the Rhine River Bridge, watching debris float by, swirl in an eddy, then drift slowly on downstream. This bridge over the Rhine points to heaven, some people say. Perhaps the slate gray water boiling along below is the entrance to hell. Nothing heavenly about the pollution and grimy barges passing beneath. Looking upward at the cables and the stainless steel wishbone of the bridge, a solid gray overcast forms a backdrop. "Heaven is having a gray day, too," Willi thinks. "If I jump, would He know? I think not."

Reaching into his pocket he removes a folded piece of paper. It is a note Klara wrote days before she died. He has memorized the words. *"Dearest Willi,"* it reads, *"when I am gone, and it will be soon, you will find this message and wonder why I could not tell you these things. It is because the words I write will last, and the words I say will soon be forgotten. I want you to remember what I say. In my lifetime I saw many good things and survived many bad things. We have been happy. You seem to always find a way to make me happy. It is your nature, perhaps your Saxon nature. This is important for you to know, and remember, as long as you live, I live in you. Take care of our life!"*

As Willi carefully refolds the note a gust of wind takes it from his hand and it sails over the side of the bridge. He tries to recover it as it floats and tumbles in the air. Before it reaches the water the note settles on a barge moving north with the current. Willi can do nothing but stare at the speck of white rapidly disappearing on the barge. "As long as you live, I live in you,"

Willi repeats Klara's message. "I will not forget, Klara Keitel. I will remember your words," he shouts at the now distant barge. "I will have a life!"

Straightening his shoulders and turning his back to the gray-green water of the Rhine, Willi steps away from the railing and walks east toward Ludwigshafen. He continues to walk through the city streets as a break in the overcast allows a sliver of sunlight to brighten the late afternoon sky.

* * *

In not too distant Siegelbach, Anna Boucher, a Russian lady divorced from her German husband, has decided she too will have a life!

**Part Three
Their Story**

Chapter 26
The Last of Life, the Best of Life

Rhein-Pfalz
Summer, 1975

Dawn on a cool, clear June morning and inside Herties' large, Ludwigshafen warehouse a night watchman, slowly and methodically, checks the truck entrances. Willi has been working at the warehouse several months. He dislikes the hours, from 10 p.m. to 6 a.m., but likes the solitude associated with the work, time to read without anyone interrupting, and time to think.

For several months, he has read a column in the Sunday newspaper "Sonntag Aktuell". Called Die Menschliche Bruecke (The Human Bridge), the column is more an advertisement for men and women looking for companionship than a source of news or entertainment. Not to infer the column lacks news or entertainment. Some of the personal information placed in the column is racy, and newsworthy. The paper is widely circulated in the Rhein-Pfalz. After looking at many sample advertisements, Willi placed his own advertisement on the first of June:

Saxon man, widowed, 63 years old, 180 centimeters tall, do not smoke or drink. Looking for wife. (349)

"Today's the big day, eh, Willi?" the relief watchman asks as he enters the warehouse. "Ja, today I see if anyone answers my lonely heart," Willi responds with dejection in his voice. "The newspaper office tells me, 'wait a week and come back.' It is a week, so I will check today." His breathing is short and rapid as he signs the checkout sheet, then turning over the keys and alarm device each guard must carry. In anticipation of what the day may bring, Willi is hyperventilating and alert enough to recognize the condition. He pauses, takes a few slow deep breaths, and walks slowly over to his aging Vespa.

The newspaper office will not be open for another two hours so Willi returns to his apartment, changes clothes and has coffee with Rudy and Renata. Later, parking his Vespa by the office of "Sonntag Actuell," Willi has another of those (what may best be called) anxiety attacks. Removing his helmet and wiping his glasses, he enters the office and smiles at the receptionist. "Please, I would like to see if you have received any answers to my advertisement. Would you look for me? My name is Wilhelm Meissner, number 349." The receptionist returns his smile and buzzes another office on her intercom. "Do we have anything for 349?"

"One moment, please," the female voice at the other end answers. After a short pause, "Yes, we have several. I'll bring them up. I want to meet this man!"

A few minutes pass and a short, stoutly built blonde woman approaches the desk holding two bundles of letters held together with rubber bands. The letters are all addressed to "Sonntag Actuell," #349, and there are nearly sixty responses! "Here you are, Herr Meissner. You did very well," the blonde woman tells him.

Surprised at the response, Willi thinks it must really be true women of my generation outnumber the men two to one. Returning home he carefully reads each letter. Only three seem to have common interests. Writing notes to all of the women, he thanks them for answering his advertisement. To the three ladies sharing common interests; he also includes his work schedule. This protocol works and they respond with dates for Willi to visit.

Saturday, June 21, Willi boards an early morning train for Pirmasens to meet with Frau Winifred Schmidt. Schmidt sounds like a good Saxon name to Willi and the lady is a widow with much money, according to her letter.

Arriving in Pirmasens mid-morning, Willi likes the town immediately. Nestled in the Pfalzer Wald about 20 kilometers from the French border, Pirmasens is unlike the gently rolling farmland surrounding Lützen. It has its own flavor, he thinks. Frau Schmidt's house is easy to find, a huge two level house. "All of this house for one person?" Willi mutters under his breath.

Ringing the bell, he steps backward, holding behind him a bouquet of flowers he bought in Ludwigshafen. The sound of heavy footsteps can be heard from deep inside the house, growing louder as they approach the door. The footsteps stop and the door opens, revealing a smiling 'Rubenesque' figure, wearing a black dress with white polka dots. Other than her ample bosom, that is all Willi can see in the darkened entry way. "Frau Schmidt?"

"Ja-a," she drawls out the word. "You must be Herr Meissner, please come in." Deftly he removes the paper wrapping from the flowers and with a slight bow offers her the flowers. "Thank you, Herr Meissner. They are lovely!"

Entering the house, she leads Willi into a sitting room and asks him to make himself comfortable while she takes care of the flowers. Looking around, he is uncomfortable in the dark room cluttered with expensive furnishings. His first thought is, she is not expecting company to leave things in such disarray. There are several half eaten chocolates in a silver tray on the marble coffee table, an empty wine glass on top of her television (a big screen), and the place has not been dusted in weeks. So? She is a messy housekeeper; that is not the most important part of a relationship, Willi rationalizes. If she has money, she should have a *Putzfrau*.

"Herr Meissner," she drawls, entering the room with the flowers in a vase, "you must excuse the place. My housekeeper is on vacation. Sit down, please, and tell me about yourself." Her voice is pleasant, almost musical. "I am a Saxon, but of course you knew that from the paper." Those were his first pleasantries, and the conversation continues for more than an hour. He learns she wants to travel with a man who will appreciate and protect her as she spends money left by her late husband.

They talk about food and she asks, "Are you hungry?" He nods and says, "Yes, a little."

"I've prepared lunch for us, come to the kitchen," and she leads the way. Her perfume is very strong; either she uses a strong, expensive perfume, or too much of a cheap perfume, Willi thinks, and it smells like she took a bath in it. She nods for him to take a seat at the kitchen table as she serves a bowl of steaming potatoes, dishes of meat, gravy and carrot salad. Willi rises, helps her into her chair, then takes a seat and waits for her to bless the food, or start serving. She immediately begins to put food on her plate, fingering a piece of sliced beef and stuffing it into her mouth. She looks up quickly, sees Willi staring at her, smiles, winks, and resumes preparing her plate.

Willi takes the food he thinks good manners will allow, smiles at Frau Schmidt, and begins to eat. The food is good and he tells her so. There is a grunt from the opposite side of the table. Looking up, he notices gravy sliding from the corners of Frau Schmidt's mouth as she concentrates on the job at hand, eating. She is an ambidextrous eater, using both hands to stuff food into her mouth. It is a very efficient way to eat, but, Willi concludes, "The woman lacks table manners." Once is enough for Willi to eat at the same table with her. After their meal, Willi is in a hurry to depart.

"When will I see you again, Herr Meissner?"

"I must make some more visits Frau Schmidt and I will call you," he says over his shoulder as he quickly departs for the train station and leaves Pirmasens with no regrets. The shock of this first experience is disquieting for Willi. He wonders what others on his list are like. You cannot judge by their letters, he opines.

The next visit Willi makes is to Frau Anna Boucher on Sunday, June 29. Her home is in Siegelbach, a village near Kaiserslautern. He takes the train to Kaiserslautern; then, by autobus, to Siegelbach. Frau Boucher's house on Sonnenstrasse is the last house on the block, standing next to an oat field soon to be harvested. It is comfortable looking, semi-detached (a duplex), with a garden and fenced yard. The fenced yard is to keep her Pekingese dog from attacking visitors, he soon learns. Her house is remarkable for the well-kept garden. Although there are many nice gardens along the street, Willi notices the variety of flowers and the skill in landscaping her sloping yard. The house is smaller and less pretentious than Frau Schmidt's.

Ringing a bell at the gate, he glimpses a face in the window. The door opens, and a dog shoots out from behind a petite lady with graying hair, standing in the doorway. Willi likes animals and holds out his hand, wondering if this will be the one dog to bite. He is not so sure until it sniffs his hand and then licks his fingers.

"Good morning, Frau Boucher. I'm Wilhelm Meissner from Ludwigshafen." He tips his hat.

"Do not worry about Cookie, Herr Meissner. She likes to bark, but doesn't bite." She pushes a button inside the door and the gate unlatches automatically. "Won't you come in?"

This Frau Boucher is a nice woman, he thinks, her voice is soft and friendly, something about her says she is a good person. Again, he has brought flowers from Ludwigshafen and gives them to her as he reaches the door.

"This is nice of you, but you needn't have," she murmurs with an appreciative look in her eyes. "Please, come in and have a seat. Cookie, come!"

Cookie is sniffing Willi's pant leg and is between him and the door. At her command, the dog turns and runs inside the house. Willi follows.

The house is like Frau Boucher, neat and clean. Her furniture is modern and adequate. There is an old icon in her entryway; Willi pauses to admire. The frame is unusually large and deep for the thin silver-looking covering and small picture of the Virgin Mary. "Is this from Germany?" he asks, thinking it must be a part of her past. "*Nein,* Herr Meissner, it is from Russia. I am Russian," she answers with a straight forward candor Willi finds appealing. "It's a family keepsake. Where are you from in Saxony?" she asks.

"I'm from Leipzig, but, before that, Lützen." Willi's pronunciation of Leipzig sounds like Lipe-sisch. Anna seems a little confused by Willi's pronunciation. "Where is this town you speak of? Show me." She pulls an atlas from a shelf and lays it on the coffee table. Opening it to the page that shows most of Saxony, Willi points to Leipzig.

"Oh Leipzig, I was there once before the war with my husband. We were returning to our home in China. It was many years ago." She pauses a moment, meditating, then continues, "As I recall we had some difficulty there with our travel arrangements. Yes! I've been there."

The two sit and talk, then stroll in Frau Boucher's garden. It is mid-afternoon when she asks him if he would like "tiffin." Willi nods affirmatively and follows her toward the kitchen. "No, Herr Meissner. You sit in the dining room. I will have it ready very soon," she says as she gently pushes him out of the kitchen. It is only a few minutes until Frau Boucher returns with a coffee dispenser, China cups and saucers, and a strawberry torte. The strawberries, she says, are from her garden.

"I have not had coffee and fresh strawberry torte at home for a long time, Frau Boucher. My late wife, Klara, did not like strawberries; they made her break out in hives. But, my *Oma* in Leipzig made many strawberry tortes. In recent years I have my coffee and cake at a bakery. It is much better at home."

Anna watches as Willi eyes the food and then comes around the table to seat her. "Thank you, Herr Meissner." Anna takes a plate and puts a large slice of kuchen on the plate, handing it to Willi. Pouring coffee, she asks if he would like cream and sugar.

"Both," he replies, watching her ease in serving, much as *Oma* used to do. Sipping his coffee, Willi asks Anna if she could recall her visit to Leipzig, "I have a feeling we have met before. My memory is not so good that I can say exactly when or where, but I think we have met." Anna suspects he is making too much of her earlier admission to being in Leipzig. "I don't think so," she replies cautiously. "We left Germany to return to China in August 1939, so it must have been August and we were there for only a few hours."

The time passes quickly as Willi and Anna eat and talk about their families, and what they did during the War. The allotted time for the first visit is long past and Willi prepares to leave. He asks if he can visit again. Anna smiles as she assures Herr Meissner another visit would be quite proper, and thinks to herself 'this man is a keeper'.

Willi can scarcely contain himself as he travels back to Ludwigshafen, pacing the aisle in the railway car. Arriving at his apartment after dark, he puts a bottle of milk in the refrigerator and hurries over to the next apartment building, anxious to tell his stepdaughter and her family the news of his visit. He can see their lights are still on; they are expecting him.

Ringing the doorbell he gives the door a gentle push and it opens. His grandsons run to the door to meet him followed by Renata and Rudy. The boys are like 'his' children, he carried them on outings when they were babies, took them for walks and brought presents. "You will not believe what has happened to me," he says breathing heavily. "The lady I visited today, Frau Boucher, I think I've seen her before. She is very nice! Your mother, God rest her soul, would approve of our meeting. It is a miracle."

"Opa, settle down. Have you taken your medicine? Is your heart okay? You're out of breath and your face is flushed. This is not good for you. Here, sit in this chair and be quiet for a few minutes," Renata points to Rudy's recliner. Leaning back in the chair, Willi can feel his heart beat is too fast. The exercise is only part of the cause. The events of the day and the thought of seeing Anna Boucher again, have excited him.

Rudy takes the boys outside while Renata fixes Willi a cup of coffee. Soon he is breathing normally and able to relate the story to Renata.

"Is this going to be a serious relationship, Opa?" she asks. "I don't know about Frau Boucher, but, I think it is serious," Willi replies. (We know what Frau Boucher thinks!)

For Willi, the week seems never to end. Saturday he is on the train for Kaiserslautern and then by bus to Siegelbach. The bouquet of flowers he brings is larger than last week. He also has a biscuit for Cookie. On this visit he wants to show Anna his skills around the house, repairing a sticking roladen, and, shedding his coat (revealing bright red suspenders), he shovels some compost around plants in the garden.

Anna cooks while Willi putters in the garden. As they sit to eat, Anna bows her head as Willi says a prayer of thanks for their food. Eating slowly, Anna and Willi talk about problems they would face if their relationship continues. Anna will lose the house if she marries. The divorce settlement allows her full use of the house and a monthly allotment while she is unmarried. Willi's pension as a former military man and disabled worker will not provide enough for them to rent a nice apartment, much less buy a new home.

The only reasonable relationship, one allowing Anna to maintain the lifestyle she is accustomed to, is for them to live together, but not as husband and wife. The thought is difficult for both to accept. Finishing their meal, Willi helps Anna with the dishes while continuing their talk. It is getting late and nothing has been decided. Willi asks if he may return for another visit. Anna says it is fine with her. Then, as Willi prepares to leave that evening, Anna helps him with his coat and almost as an afterthought says, "When you return bring your things!"

Surprised, Willi grasps Anna about the waist, lifts her off her feet and twirls around. "You make me a happy man, Frau Boucher!" Cookie is barking and jumping on Willi's leg.

* * *

Willi quits his night watchman job and moves to Siegelbach. He writes the one lady remaining on his list to visit and explains he will be unable to visit. Willi calls Frau Schmidt in Pirmasens telling her of his decision, the call didn't go well. Anna's homemaking skills and Willi's desire to do things with his hands makes their relationship a comfortable one. Their financial situation is satisfactory, enough so that they can squander 10 DM a week on the lotto.

Anna's neighbors in Siegelbach are surprised when they discover the living arrangement. She is snubbed at the bakery, grocery store, and butchers. When she meets someone for the first time, she does not hesitate to tell them up front "the man I'm living with, he is not my husband." It bothers Lutheran Willi they cannot afford to marry. He prays often for God's forgiveness. In time they seem to enjoy their exclusion from social activities in the neighborhood. It allows them more time together.

Riding his aging Vespa motor scooter, Willi finds odd jobs in neighboring villages. Repairing plumbing in Rodenbach one day, some loose gutters on a house in Weilerbach the next, Willi gets to know his way around.

After attending a Catholic Mass in Weilerbach one Sunday, they ride the Vespa to Eulenbis. Well, not all the way. The steep and winding road slows the Vespa to near the stalling point. Willi stops and they dismount, walking the remaining distance. Eulenbis is perched on the south side of a steep hill. At the top of the hill on a summer day you can almost reach up and touch the soft white clouds sailing by. The land is farmed, undulating downward into tree covered ravines and valleys. West, along the crest of the hill, is an old, ruined tower. Anna has packed a picnic basket; near the tower is where they have their picnic.

"I would like to have a house here, near the fields," Willi says wistfully. "It would take much money we don't have, Anna. But, wouldn't it be nice to see the hills and valleys of the Pfalzer Wald each morning, watch the farmers in the fields, and have our own place?" Anna pauses, looks at Willi, "You are dreaming Herr Meissner, "but, it would be nice."

Packing up their picnic basket, they walk along the farm road at the top of the hill. At the east end of the village is a cemetery. Trees shade the entrance and a small chapel sits in one corner. It is a peaceful, sunny day and many people are in the cemetery watering flowers and tidying up around family graves. As they walk beyond the cemetery, Willi notices some wild blackberries growing beside the road. He picks a few and offers some to Anna. They nibble the berries and continue their walk to a bend in the road. There they turnaround and with the afternoon sun in their faces return to where the Vespa is parked. Anna looks up at Willi, her eyes squinting, and says, "I like this place."

August 1977

Cookie dies in her sleep the first Saturday in August. Willi buries the 16-year-old Pekingese in a corner of their garden and promises Anna she can have another dog as soon as they save the money.

Picking lotto numbers during the following week, both talk of winning enough to buy another pedigreed Pekingese. "How much does one cost?" Willi asks.

"About 800 DM," Anna replies, shrugging her shoulders. Willi shakes his head negatively and starts selecting numbers. Their multiple sets of lotto numbers the following week include this series on one card:

7 – the month they were born.
12 – the year they were born.
23 – the day Willi was born.
25 – the day Anna was born (Western calendar).
39 – for the year Anna visited Leipzig.
47 – the year Willi escaped from East Germany.

Watching television Saturday evening, the two can hardly contain themselves after the first three numbers are called. One card has matched each number drawn. Slowly, as the remaining numbers are pulled from the machine on stage, Anna frowns, it is not good to be so excited. With four numbers they may win enough to buy another dog. When the final number is called they are standing in front of the television with disbelief on their faces, they have four matching numbers on one of their cards. Willi turns and clasps his arms around Anna, whirls her off the floor and around the room, and knocks over the lamp. Anna cries with happiness; Willi laughs with her. Strollers looking through the raised roladen Saturday night, stop and watch, mutter to themselves, then walk on, shaking their heads.

The winning numbers of the state lotto on a Saturday in 1977, in the order they were drawn are: 12, 23, 47, 2, 59, and 25. Anna and Willi have a share of the pot with four of those numbers. After taxes they receive a check for 826 DM. The following week they buy a dog for Anna paying 800 DM for a registered Pekingese. Three months later Anna determines the dog is untrainable and mean tempered. They give the dog away and sadly cross off the loss to experience.

Chapter 27
The Secret of the icon

Siegelbach
Winter, 1977

Ice and snow blanket the area making trips on Willi's Vespa hazardous. He bundles up to walk to the village center. At the *Bakerei*, he buys a loaf of bread, and, at the *Metzgeri*, a pint of milk. Inside his coat pocket he has a string bag used for shopping. With both purchases in his bag he returns to the house on Sonnenstrasse, making his way carefully up the hill.

Entering the house, the soles of his shoes are wet and he slips on Anna's well-polished floor. Falling against the wall, he knocks Anna's family icon from its protective niche, sending it crashing to the floor along with Willi's bag of groceries. Anna, hearing the noise, hurries downstairs and sees Willi sitting dazed on the floor, a pool of milk spreading around him; the icon with a cracked frame is in the middle of the mess.

"What happened Willi, are you hurt?"

"I slipped, I think," he mutters straightening his glasses and slowly getting to his feet, and checking his limbs. "Nothing broken, except the milk." He sees the icon on the floor and its frame is cracked, "Your Russian religious painting is okay, but the frame is cracked. I can fix, but I can't fix the bottle of milk."

"We won't worry about the milk if you are alright; here, let me look at you," Anna replies in a soothing voice. "Give me the bag, and I'll clean up the milk. You take off your coat and go sit by the fire."

Willi hands her the string bag and removes his coat. Picking up the icon he checks the frame. The corners of the frame are joined by a combination of intricate interlocking grooves and pegs. The frame maker must have spent many hours making the corners fit so precisely around the painting. One corner of the frame is smashed, the wood is splintered and will need to be replaced.

Almost unnoticeable before, Willi can now see two carved initials in the corner of the frame, overlapping *Cyrillic* D's (those were the initials carved in the Czar's frame). "Anna, there is something carved here!"

She looks, "Those are my grandfather's initials in Russian!"

Taking the icon with him, Willi sits by the fire place to study the damaged frame more thoroughly. Carefully he removes the first peg, a short one tapered like a cone. The second peg is more difficult to remove, is cylindrical in shape, and is much longer than the first peg. As it finally works loose, there is a fragment of cloth and a pair of green stones can be seen in the opening.

"Anna, can you come here?"

Anna has finished cleaning up the milk and glass; she comes into the living room, wiping her hands on her apron. "What is it?"

"Look what was in the frame of the icon," he holds up the two stones. "What do you know about this?"

Anna takes the stones and holds them up to the light. "My mother told me a story about the icon years ago in Harbin. As I recall, Grandfather Dimitri made the frame in a village where icons were made for the Czar, Nicholas the first, or Alexander the first, I can't remember. Anyway, I think they gave him the painting; he made a new frame for it and, before he could leave, there was an explosion in the painter's shop. My grandfather, the painter, and a jeweler were killed. My grandmother recovered the icon from the ruins and returned to Samara."

Anna pauses, "The only other thing I remember her saying is—'the icon would bring good fortune,' and that's been questionable." She returns the stones to Willi and he places them on the coffee table. The round peg is about three-quarters of a centimeter in diameter and the stones are slightly smaller.

"I'm going to take this frame apart and rebuild the damaged corner. There could be more stones in the frame, and valuable if hidden like this." Taking the frame to the dining table, he begins disassembling it, first removing the painting and tin *risa* overlay.

"While you do that, I'll fix tiffin," Anna tells him and returns to the kitchen. She steps outside to have a cigarette, then walks along the patio, thinking of the icon and the little green stones Willi has found. She shakes her head, and looking out toward her garden covered with snow, draws deeply on the cigarette. Smoke bothers Willi, and, except when she first started smoking in Harbin, Anna has always gone outside to smoke.

An hour later, the frame lies in four separate pieces. On the table, among strips of cloth, is a collection of green, yellow, red, purple and clear stones of varying sizes and shapes. If the frame had not been cracked exposing the structure of the interlocking groves and location of the pegs, the secret of the frame would never have been discovered. In each piece of the frame a cavity had been drilled and gemstones placed inside. Whether the stones are semi-precious, or of great value, Willi can't tell. He removes the pieces to the coffee table and gathers the stones in his hand, taking them to the kitchen to show Anna.

While they eat, Willi and Anna discuss what to do with the gemstones. They decide such a find of gems would need an explanation and determination of the rightful owner. The stones could only have been placed in the frame before it was assembled. Willi concludes Anna's great grandfather had possession of the stones, either legally or illegally. And, if they were his, why would he hide them from his family? Doubting records would exist concerning such a transaction, Willi suggests they take the stones to a jeweler in Kaiserslautern and have them appraised. Agreeing, Anna pours another cup of tea for Willi, then fills her cup.

Willi divides the stones into two piles of equal colors, places one pile in a pouch and the other in a small box. Calling his POW shipmate, Hans Berber, now living in Kaiserslautern, Willi asks him to recommend a jeweler. Hans knows one with an office on Richard Wagner Strasse, not far from the Bahnhof. They arrange to meet for lunch the following day, and Hans will go with Willi to the gemologist's office. After the telephone conversation, Willi hides the pouch and box in his bedroom. They still maintain separate bedrooms.

The following morning, with the pouch of gems tucked inside his jacket, Willi walks to the bus stop and takes a bus to Kaiserslautern. The snow has begun to melt; streets are wet, not a good time to ride the Vespa. Sunlight glares off the ice-topped crust of snow, and Willi puts on his sunglasses when he exits the bus near the marketplace. Hans' chemist shop is on a pedestrian way, a short distance from Kaufhaus. He waves to Hans as he enters and waits for him to finish with a customer. The two old friends shake hands and Hans tells his assistant they are leaving for lunch.

Both like to eat at the restaurant in Wertheim's, a nearby department store, serving good food quickly and cheaply. While they wait for their meal to come,

Willi motions Hans to move closer and removes the gemstones from the pouch. Cupping them in both hands he holds them out for Hans to examine.

"How did you come to possess these?" Hans asks after examining several of the stones. "You might say I fell into them," he jokes. "They were hidden in the frame of an icon belonging to Anna's family, probably there for nearly a hundred years. I slipped, knocked the icon off the wall and cracked the frame, then found the stones."

"If the stones are genuine, you, or Anna, have a small fortune," Hans whispers to his friend.

"Good, with the way things have been going, we need a fortune to make up for the misfortune following us. Anna lost her dog a few years back. We bought another dog after winning 800 marks in the Lotto, only to find it had a bad temper. Anna gave it away, and we haven't been able to afford another dog. She only likes the expensive ones," Willi adds with a chuckle. Finishing their meal and paying the check, Hans leads the way out of Wertheim's and across the downtown area to Richard Wagner Strasse.

The jewelry company Hans recommends was originally from Idar-Oberstein. Their resident gemologist and jeweler is a customer at Hans' pharmacy. After Hans' introduction, they proceed to a corner of the display room. Willi produces the pouch of gemstones for examination. The gray-haired gentleman is mildly surprised to see the number of stones and their color. Only after careful examination of the first stone does excitement show in his voice. "Herr Meissner, this is an emerald," he says holding up one of the green stones Willi had first discovered. "If the others are as genuine as this, you are a wealthy man. Would you mind telling me where you obtained them?"

Willi relates the story of the frame and how Anna received the icon. The jeweler takes them to his work area in the rear of the store and continues to examine the remaining stones. He records measurements, and weights, of each stone and places them inside a velvet-lined case.

"Herr Meissner, I think you might need a lawyer" the jeweler responds cautiously. "I have not seen a collection of cut stones like this before. I can only speculate, but sold individually, the stones could bring several thousand marks." He pauses for the impact to record in Willi's face. "Sold as a collection, in the right market, they could go for as much as a million marks. Again, I think you might need a lawyer!" Willi gasps at the jeweler's estimate.

Hans looks at his friend to see if he is surviving the shock. Patting Willi gently on the back, Hans asks, "Are you alright, Private Meissner?"

"*Jawohl*, Corporal Berber, but I'm about to wet my pants. I have more jewels I did not bring, where's the toilet?"

"If you are serious," the jeweler answers, amused by the use of rank between the two men, "we have a toilet in the back of our office."

"I'm serious," Willi replies, walking hurriedly to the rear of the office.

A relieved Willi returns from the toilet to find Hans and the jeweler discussing options available to Anna and Willi for disposing of the gems. He asks to use the telephone to call Anna and tell her the good news. Anna finds the excited Willi is too difficult to understand and asks him to let the man from the store talk. The jeweler describes the stones as diamonds, rubies, emeralds, topaz, amethyst and alexandrite, and tells her their approximate worth. Anna is silent for a moment, and he asks if she is alright.

"*Ja*," practical Anna replies, "I'm just thinking how I'll spend all that money! Tell Herr Meissner to hurry home."

Arrangements are made to sell the gems, but before publicity, lawyers for the firm handling the sale want proof of ownership. They arrange to meet with Anna and Willi to go over the "acquisition". Anna describes the story of the icon told her by her mother now deceased, the icon being a wedding gift to Anna is vouched for by Nina Tokma Wilson now living in the United States, and Klaus affirms the icon being in Anna's possession from the time they first met and he has no claim to the icon. Aunt Sophia Yetchekov and her husband lived out their lives in Hong Kong and are buried there. The only other living relative Anna is aware of his her brother Peter who lives in or about the city of Kuibyshev in Russia and was never in possession of the icon. A courtesy request through diplomatic channels to the Russian government finds its way into the hands of a researcher named Yetchekov who can find "no record of the jewels in question". Satisfied, the lawyers give approval to proceed.

Deep in Russian archives there are reports from teams sent to retrieve Czarist treasures. In the village of Palekh a team recovered the Czar's icon with its gold and silver risa and expensive painting, but no jewels. That team report is missing, but was mailed to Frau Anna Kulina Meisner, Eulenbis, W. Germany, with a note: *"Thought you might like to have this."* Someone remembered.

Anna's first purchase is a dog, a Shih-Tzu she names Chi-Lin, literally translated it means "generations of happiness." Next they buy land in Eulenbis and begin planning the house they want to build. Last, and most important, they set a date to be married in Weilerbach. The only visible evidence of their change in circumstances is Chi-Lin who follows them everywhere, except when they ride the Vespa to shop at the Vogelweh Massa Mart. Anna still walks to the shops in Siegelbach for certain purchases, Chi-Lin on a leash.

Willi and Anna choose Weilerbach's Catholic Church for the wedding, having attended services in Weilerbach the past two years because no one there knew them. As a result of their new wealth, Willi made a sizable, anonymous donation to the church. They arrive in a taxi hired for the occasion. The civil ceremony has already been performed, and the service at the church is shortened by the priest because he does not really know any of these people (if he had known who the anonymous donor was, perhaps the service would have been more elaborate).

There are few guests at the wedding; Renata and Rudy bring their sons from Ludwigshafen. Willi's sister Ludwina and her husband drive down from Kassel. Willi discovers his sister was living 30 miles from him when he was in the displaced persons camp. (Money brings lost family out of the woodwork.) Klaus Boucher and Beate attend. Hans Berber, the Kaiserslautern chemist and friend from prisoner of war days, brings his family to share in the wedding. Unable to attend, Nina Tokma Wilson sends best wishes to the couple.

The Donesyvna Collection, as it is later called, sells for 2,200,000 DM. A picture of Anna and Willi appearing in the news attracts the interest of Reinhard Kreutz a former government official in Bonn. Kreutz telephones his former superior in the ministry, Herr Hauptman, and tells him about their "old friend" from Camp Florence. "The man has dumb luck," is Hauptman's crisp response and terminates the conversation.

* * *

There is a small, white house with dark brown trim in Eulenbis, on a street bordering the fields. Flowers fill the garden in spring, cascading over a stone retaining wall following the contour of the slope. Stones are carefully laid to allow ample soil for blue and white alyssum to grow. Inside the house, just past the entry, is an icon, framed in walnut, a small frame but the initials DD are visible. Willi rebuilt the frame using parts of the old frame, making it somewhat smaller. Anna and Willi touch the icon every morning, each murmuring a prayer of thanks; she makes the sign of the cross, then smiles as she starts her day, remembering her mother's words, "It will bring us good fortune." Willi looks at the image and risa and thinks, "how blessed can we be?"

Willi was working in his garden when we met. Noticing his strawberries were beginning to turn red and using my few words of imperfect German, I greeted him and said, "Das erdbeeren ist scheon". He walked over to the fence and said, "Ja, and they taste good too," using almost perfect English. I asked where he learned English and he responded, "I was POW in Arizona during the war." We had several visits over the fence in the following weeks. In one corner of the garden a miniature windmill spins in the April breeze, red blades flashing in the sunlight. Strawberry plants dominate that corner because of the sunlight, and southern exposure.

In another part of the garden, I noticed three hand-made crosses, each about two meters tall. They each look the same. When asked about them, Willi gave me a serious look over the top of his glasses and said: "I'm glad you ask," (I Peter 3:15 ...always be ready to give an answer to anyone who asks about the hope you possess.) he paused, "the crosses are my testimony. I have good fortune to live so long, have Christian parents, and faith in God. The first cross is mine, my Christ died for me before I was born in Lützen. The second is for you, friend. He died for you if only you believe Him. The third is for all the 'peoples', so they may know He died for them. Some ask me, 'why three,' I tell them 'alles' have a cross to bear." I never questioned his theology, liked his testimony and the way he chose to share it.

* * *

Vegetables and flowers mix with berry vines and apple trees in the garden at the top of the hill. To the east, a big C-5 transport aircraft approaching Ramstein Air Base seems to float noiselessly in the distance as it slowly descends below the tree tops. Tractors in the field behind the house make a little noise, but are a pleasant sound to Willi's ear. And, the smell of fresh turned soil is full of memories; the smell of barnyard manure farmers spread on their fields is not so pleasant, but he tends to ignore the slight whiff in the wind. Anna comes from the house, Chi Lin following close behind. With a small paring knife, she clips some greens for tiffin. Tiffin is their meal for the day. A bit of meat, some potatoes or "kasha," (you can take the girl out of Russia, but you can't take the Russian tastes out of the girl) carrots and green beans every day and something fresh from the garden, is Anna's typical menu. She gathers enough for their meal. Taking the hem of her apron and pulling it up to make a pocket she drops the greens inside with the knife. Willi stands at the fence looking at the field of rye growing next to their garden. Anna walks slowly over to stand beside him and look at the blades of rye, about six inches high, bending with the fresh breeze. "Are you happy?" she asks.

"*Ja*, more so than I've been in all my life. If only I were younger and could farm the fields, I would be happier." Looking down at Anna, her glasses slipping a little from the bridge of her nose, he nudges them back to the right position and puts his arm around the soft shoulders of his Russian lady. "Are you happy?" he asks. "*Ja*", she replies, "it is good to be alive, have you to share this place, the happiness, the miseries when they come. I hope God will let us stay here until he takes us both home!" Anna had found a man who would never leave her. In 1990, Willi revisited Lützen. East Germany had opened the border and family reunions are making news everywhere. He returned to Eulenbis and never left again.

In the hill top cemetery at Eulenbis a black marble marker gleams in the morning sunlight. The inscription reads:

ANNA UND WILLI
ZUSAMMEN FUR IMMER
(TOGETHER FOREVER)

Willi

Anya

Peter and Anya
in Samara (1914)

Anya and her schoolmates in
Manzhouli (1928)

Klara's Sister (1990)

Women Talk! (1979)

Harbin / Kulinas (1932)

Raya getting her commission as the first female dentist in the Air Force.

Seichi Sakamoto
aka Sydney Sako

Willi at home in Eulenbis!

Willi watering Klara's grave (1990)

Route of the Kulina Icon from Palekh, Russia to Eulenbis, W. Ger.

Epilogue

Anna and Wilhelm were living in a German village near Ramstein Air Base when we met in 1980. Anna would tell my wife stories of her childhood in Russia and young womanhood in China, stories only women confide with each other. Wilhelm, always loquacious, told me stories of pre-war and post-war Germany, not for Anna's ears. They were born into a turbulent time, Germanys' preparation for WWI and Russia's Bolshevik Revolution, surviving two World Wars.

Writing their life story, I took them copies in 1990; the year the border wall came down. Renting a bright red, German-made Ford, Willi and I drove to Lützen in East Germany and visited sights he remembered. We by chance met the brother of a girl he dated in Bothfeld back when he was a teenager; she had married and moved on in life. At the cemetery in Lützen, we asked a lady if she knew the location of his family graves. The lady pointed out the area to search, then asked, "Do you know you have a relative living here now?" Willi's nephew, thought to be killed on the Russian front, survived and returned to Lützen. The kindly lady got on her bicycle and, pedaling as fast as she could, led us to his apartment building where "Uncle Willi" got the surprise of his visit, more family. I couldn't tell who was more excited, the lady who led us there, Willi, or the nephew.

We visited Klara Keitel's grave site in Mannheim and I met her sister (see photo section), sharing an *erdbeer kuchen*. I met a young man named Harold Lachner during that last visit. In 1997, I received a letter from him telling me "Mr. Rudolph (Willi) died on 7 April 1997, after a stroke on 14 February 1997…I think you and Mr. Rudolph were good friends, that's why I took it as my duty to give you this information." Anna preceded him in death.

About his mom and dad, he told me "I wondered how my father could put up with my mother, they were very different, and now I know—he loved her.

Growing old is difficult, but with someone you love, it's easier. In all, I am satisfied with my life and thank God for it."

The life story of Willi and Anya was not enough to convince a publisher to print the book. Moving into the Army Residence Community (ARC) in 2017, I began re-writing their story as a mystery within a love story. Other real-life characters surfaced and made the story more involved and complex than first imagined. Instead of a true story it has become a novel based on several true stories, I'll mention a few.

Helene Smith (Elena Kochergna) lived in San Antonio after Verval passed away. She and Verval attended a church in Kirby, Texas, pastored by my friend Kenneth Brown. Verval retired at Fort Sam Houston and was buried at Fort Sam Houston National Cemetery in 1979. Helene invited us over for tea as Ken was retiring from the ministry in 1994, and presented him with a retirement gift, giving me a gift as well. She told me her life story, the story of Elena. During our last visit she mentioned moving to an Army retirement home near Kirby. She told me the children she cared for in China had asked her to come to England and live with them; they were her only "family". There are no records of Helene moving into the ARC, or if she moved to England. She passed away 30 July 1999, and is buried with Verval at Fort Sam Houston, grave site section 6-293.

From an address Anna gave me, I located Anna Tokmacheff (Nina Tokma Wilson) visiting her daughter Jenny McMurtray in Jackson, Mississippi. She (Anna T.) was a successful office manager for a banking firm and retired to a town house in Las Vegas, Nevada in 1989. On a Kentucky Derby Day in 1987, I was met at the Jackson Mississippi Airport by Jenny's husband, Henry (Mac) McMurtray, and spent the afternoon visiting with them, taking some notes. Years later they were living in Las Vegas and there I discovered another connection to Anna Kulchinia, Tamara Lessaro. Tamara knew Anna and Jenny in China, went to school with Jenny, called Anna's mother Tiotia Doosia, and remembered her as Evadakia Koolchihina (her spelling).

Seichi Sakamoto's stories of being a missionary in Japan, service in the Japanese Army, being a POW in Russia and finding his brother in Japan after the war, are all true. He was a survivor, married and had a family; after WWII he changed his name to Sydney Sako, worked at Lackland AFB in the language school before retiring. He met Anna and Willi vicariously in our conversations and provided significant input on Shanghai and Harbin in our visits. His son, Dr. Thomas Sako, is a dentist in San Antonio.

The female Russian dentist Anna recalled was perhaps Raya Rachlin. An Air Force Reserve Dentist I met at Randolph AFB in the 1980s asked about my retired life; I told him the story of Anna and her dentist in Shanghai. He saw a similarity between Raya, whom he knew, and the dentist in Shanghai. Raya attended Howard College Dental School in Washington, D.C., and was one of the first women commissioned in the Air Force as a dentist. According to the Reservist, Raya was born in Eastern Europe, perhaps Latvia, spoke Russian and German among other languages. Her parents moved to Germany in the 1920s, after WWI, and lived in Berlin. She went to dental school in Berlin and Vienna in 1935, left in 1938 to travel to Shanghai, via Japan, a route taken by many Jews. She was practicing dentistry in a Shanghai clinic in 1946, when hired to work for the U.S. occupation force. In Arlington National Cemetery Sect. 35, grave #4805, there is a marker with a Star of David on it:

Raya Rachlin, Nevada, Major, US Air Force, 25 December 1910-11 March 1965.

Anna's mother returned to Russia and lived on a commune near Kuibyshev until her death in 1962. She worked in a clinic at the commune most of her later years still using nursing skills learned in WW1. Nikolai, Anna's father, died of a stroke in 1950, while awaiting sentencing for an escape attempt, and was buried in the Khabarovsk Prison cemetery. Peter, Anna's brother, lived in Khabarovsk until retiring in 1981, and then moved to Kuibyshev to live on his pension and be near his mother's grave. Willi's first wife, beautiful but unfaithful Katarina, divorced Willi in an East German court in 1950 and married her Russian lover.

The young black soldier at Camp Florence, with self-ascribed names "Zoot Suit" and "Prisoner Third Class", came from a story Willi told me about his experiences there. He described the young man as humorous, philosophical, and prone to get into trouble. In a world full of turmoil, these people survived. This is the "Rest of the Story", as Paul Harvey would say. More could be told if only the *dead* could talk and the living could hear their stories!

Two old Aggies in San Antonio.

Ingram Content Group UK Ltd.
Milton Keynes UK
UKHW050202050623
422739UK00009B/177